Richard S. Ferguson

Moss Gathered by a Rolling Stone

Or Reminiscences of Travel

Richard S. Ferguson

Moss Gathered by a Rolling Stone
Or Reminiscences of Travel

ISBN/EAN: 9783337205447

Printed in Europe, USA, Canada, Australia, Japan

Cover: Foto ©Andreas Hilbeck / pixelio.de

More available books at **www.hansebooks.com**

MOSS GATHERED

BY

A ROLLING STONE;

OR,

REMINISCENCES OF TRAVEL.

———

PART 1.—EASTWARD HO [EGYPT & UP THE NILE].
PART II.—GUIDE BOOK TO THEBES AND ITS RUINS.
PART III.—ROUND THE WORLD.

———

BY

RICHARD S. FERGUSON, M.A.,

BARRISTER-AT-LAW,

*Author of " Cumberland and Westmorland M.P.'s from the Restoration
to the Reform Bill," and other Works.*

———

CARLISLE: C. THURNAM & SONS.
CAIRO AND ALEXANDRIA: DAVID ROBERTSON & CO.
—
1873.

PREFACE.

I wrote these letters on board ship to amuse myself. I, under the *nom-de-plume* of " A Roving Cumbrian," sent them to the *Carlisle Patriot* because the editor thought they would amuse other people. I now reprint them because I see a chance of selling them.

PART II.—" Leaves from a Theban Guide Book," is an attempt to supply, what is much wanted, a Guide Book to Thebes, cheaper and less learned than Murray.

R. S. F.

Carlisle, October 1873.

EASTWARD HO!

January, 1871.

Doomed to exile by a committee of learned physicians, who gave me no option as to the place of my banishment, but dismissing Italy and Spain as too liable to cold, Algeria as too unsettled, and Ceylon as too damp, dictated Egypt, I found myself on January 21st, 1871, careering down St. George Channel in the fast new steamer *Scotland*, 2,200 tons burden, bound from Liverpool to Calcutta *viâ* the Suez Canal. For the first day or two we were rather uncomfortable, the weather was raw and cold; the Bay of Biscay behaved as the Bay of Biscay should, and gave us many a pitch and roll. Dinner was difficult to get down one's mouth; for it would rather hop into one's lap, or jump on to the floor; while, spite of fiddles or wooden frames on the table, there was a perpetual crash of falling glass: yet to most this was but scant loss; few, for the first four or five days, could show up at meals, so that I and one or two tough customers had the long tables and all on them to ourselves. Other miseries were that the sea one midnight came on board, washed out the deck cabins, and then descended with hideous noise into the cuddy; that there was a leak in the stern from which dribbled over cuddy and cabin floors a perpetual and annoying stream of water, causing captain, carpenter, and engineer ceaseless labour day and night to discover and plug up the *fons origo mali ;* that, the greatest woe of all, the cook had a habit of retiring early to bed, first dousing his fire, and thus, until we learnt his habits, depriving us of hot grog at night. These public ills did not afflict me much; I was not sea-sick; I had a fine hunger and thirst upon me, and enjoyed my meals; I built an island in my cabin, and thus dodged the leak; I was only bored, for it was too cold for me on deck, and I was reduced, *pour passer le temps*, to take it out in bunk (nautical for bed) between meals. Things soon improved: by 10 p.m. on the 24th we made the light on Cape Finisterre, and thus passed out of the " weary

Bag o' Biscuits," as a nurse-maid on board was heard to mis-
cal the Bay of Biscay. Next evening we passed first the
Berlings light, and then that on the rock of Lisbon ; the weather
grew warmer, the sea smoother, the sun brighter, the ship drier,
and undreamt-of passengers crawled out from their bunks, and
began to develop jovial and social qualities up till now undis-
covered ; while, as we were running close to the Portuguese
coast, its scenery gave us, as yet strangers to each other, a
common subject of interest. The coast scenery was fine : high
cliffs of slate and red rock, with a lofty range of barren
mountain towering up behind them ; no sign of cultivation,
not a living thing to be seen save vast flocks of gulls and sea-
fowl, hovering about the cliffs, and in the distance looking like
clouds of midges. About noon on the 26th January we
doubled Cape St. Vincent: miles of brilliant-coloured cliff,
varying from red to black, stretched right and left far away,
glistening brightly under a blue and cloudless sky and burning
sun, while a lighthouse of dazzling white was perched on the
summit of the cape, beyond which was a lovely little bay with
some ruins, either of a castle, chapel, or hermitage ; above,
again, were a mass of white buildings, formerly a monastery,
but now a State prison. With its foreground of blue sea, and
frame of blue sky, the Cape, as we saw it, would have well
suited Mr. Hook as a subject for a picture. A large Italian
steamer passed close by us at this point, and we sighted several
ships bearing up for the Straits of Gibraltar. In the previous
night we had by the way run through and nearly over a whole
fleet of Portuguese fishing vessels, which would not get out of
our way, so we had to get out of theirs—a noisy process, by
no means conducive to quiet repose ; the babies too, (we had a
large supply on board) howled largely and loudly at night, and
their mothers and nurses being mostly ill, they did not get the
attention and whipping they required. Our skipper, an old
P. and O. Captain, was the great patron, attendant, and nurse
of these children, and seemed most proud of his small
friends ; in truth, he was a man most marvellously attentive to
his passengers and their comforts : his wife was on board,
accompanied by a little Maltese dog of great curliness of hair
and curiosity of mind, which latter nearly worked him bitter
woe. The lazarette hatch was open, and doggie needs must see :
the ship lurched, and doggie flew head over heels below on the
top of the steward, who was getting up jams and other stores.

Leaving the babies and the curly dog to themselves, let us get on. On the morning of Friday, 27th January, at 6 a.m., a lovely morning, we entered the Straits of Gibraltar, and we were all up early to enjoy the lovely view, and get (some at least) our first view of the famous rock, of the pillars of Hercules, and of the continent of Africa. Both coasts were studded with towers of Moorish architecture, the watch towers of old wars; while on the Spanish side the white buildings of Algeciras occupied a conspicuous place. Giving the Pearl Rock, afterwards so nearly fatal to the *Agincourt*, a wide berth, we entered the harbour, and were soon moored by a dingy coal hulk, once the famous *Java Indiaman*. Of it " I tell the tale as 'twas told to me " :—

THE LEGEND OF THE "JAVA INDIAMAN."

" Once upon a time, and a long time ago too, the mate of an *Indiaman* was walking on the sea shore in Java, when he espied a naked woman, and a white woman too, crouching under shelter of a bush. Walking up to her backwards, for he was a man of delicacy, he flung his boat cloak over her, and offered his services. The lady proved to be the daughter of the Dutch Governor of Java, whose servants had stole her clothes as she bathed. The mate married the lady, and for her dower the Governor built him a fine *Indiaman* of the old-fashioned stamp, then in vogue ; broad in the beam, ornate with carving over her lofty stern, and having, as figure head, a naked woman crouching under a bush. For years the *Java* sailed the seas ; she played her part in the famous action, when ten *Indiamen* (merchant ships), under Captain John Smith, beat off Admiral De Souffrien, and the French fleet. Even thirty years ago she was trading to Bombay and considered a crack craft. Now, poor old hulk, a century old or more, dismasted, dirty, and begrimed, she rots in Gibraltar Bay as a coal hulk ; her figure head disappeared a year or two ago, and the carving of the lofty stern is crumbling into bits. One can't help thinking the old heart of oak must feel her downfall ; better to have foundered in mid ocean, or to have blown up in action, or gone to bits on a lee-shore, than thus unhonoured to decay."

So soon as we were moored we were surrounded by bum-boats, manned by Gibraltese, or rock scorpions, as they are

called, a very handsome race of men, but whose room our
captain preferred rather than their company, greeting them with
threats of dropping a round shot into their boats : the innocent
looking cargoes of oranges, cigars, and vegetables conceal
bottles of potent spirit, highly tempting, but deleterious to Jack
Mariner and Jim Stoker.

Breakfast over we all rushed ashore, and I for one was
charmed with Gibraltar. The streets are narrow and uninteresting, but the mixtures of costumes and nationalities are
kaleidoscopic : English civilians in their orthodox garments,
English and Highland soldiers in scarlet, blue, white, and
tartan, nuns, Catholic priests in the most wonderful hats, who
seemed to have walked out of the pictures in Gil Blas, Don
Quixote, or the Academy ; Spaniards, dons and most veritable
hidalgoes in voluminous cloaks and saffron trousers, others in
pork-pie hats and tight jackets with scarlet scarves wound
round their waists ; their whiskers of jet black hair shaved
and trimmed to the most formal pork chop, and their hair done
up in chignons, but having, some of them, a look most ludi-
crously Irish. Amidst these European picturesques stalked
jet black negroes in enormous turbans, and bare legged, red
fezzed, and yellow-slippered Moors hugging round them their
great brown burnouses, for with my usual luck I had arrived
at Gibraltar on the coldest day known there for thirty years,
actually frosty, and a bitter cold wind from the snow-clad
Sierra de Nevada. By the aid of a friendly corporal of High-
landers, I found Major ——'s villa. He had gone off to
Spanish ground to hunt in the corkwood, but Mrs. —— was
at home, and very kindly and speedily made me feel at home
too. I saw the rock under the most favourable circumstances,
for she was good enough to order her pony carriage and to
lionize me wherever there was anything to be seen ; she drove
me to Europa Point, and *en route* I saw for the first time
oranges growing apple-like in the open air (fruit and blossom
all on the same tree at once), and cactuses in full bloom of
scarlet flowers. From Europa Point I was taken to the neutral
ground betwixt Spanish and English territory, across into
Spain, just to say I had been there, and there I saw the most
gorgeous *militaires* I ever came across, veritable General Boums.
After a most enjoyable day, I returned to the *Scotland*, no
pleasant task, as the sea was very rough, and we had over a
mile to sail.

About 8 at night we started, or rather attempted to start from Gibraltar, but no sooner did we move than crash went something, and we just moved, but we did no more. " Can't you give me another turn?" yelled the captain, frantic, from the bridge. " Not a quarter," replied the engineer, from the depths below. There was no help for it ; a too energetic first officer had got the anchor on board and it could not speedily be let go. We drifted into an old coal hulk, and we chawed the old rotten tub up amazingly, knocking her ladders and bulwarks into matches. So soon as we got our anchor out we swung clear, and the skipper of the hulk appeared on board demanding much coin. Our skipper said to him—"Why did you not raise your ladder, and put out fenders when you saw us coming ?" " Hadn't hands to do it; my owners only allow three." " Then we can't pay for your owner's mean-ness ;" and thus injured and insulted, he was, *apractos* of his object (or coin) hustled over the side. The damage took but an hour or two to repair, and after much labour in raising the anchor, for the too energetic chief officer had let go unneces-sarily countless fathoms of chain cable, we left Gibraltar Bay an hour before midnight. The day after leaving the rock we were running fast along the Spanish coast, having the wind in our favour, an unlucky thing for a large steamer we saw trying to make Gibraltar under sail only, her engines having probably broken down. The Sierra de Nevada was covered with snow, and a cold north wind blew off them forcing me below, whence I did not reappear until Algiers was in sight some four and twenty hours later. Algiers seemed a fine town, nestled under a Moorish castle, with towers and cupolas on the hill above, while its environs seemed to abound with villas, of which, indeed, as we coasted along, we saw several, and also some large villages. So severe was the winter, that the chain of Mount Atlas was covered with snow to the sea, the like of which no mariner on board had ever seen before. We saw also the Isle of Zambla, Cape Bon, and the Isle of Pantellaria, the Italian convict depôt.; and on the night between 31st January and 1st February, we saw Gozo and Valetta lights, the last land until we made the Egyptian coast. A singular circumstance occurred one night : the officer of the watch saw land and a light right ahead where no land should be seen for 1,000 miles; he immediately stopped the ship,· and called the captain, who made out the land to be a low, heavy bank of clouds, with a rising star just shining through it.

After leaving the rock the ship's bullock formed an object of great interest to all the idlers on board. This unhappy wretch was born, bred, and fattened in Portugal, conveyed per steamer from Lisbon to Gibraltar, and there purchased by us for 20 dollars, in good' condition, but the ingenious rock scorpions, who put him on board, ran him up about 14 feet high, and then dropped him on deck, where the poor brute laid unable from his bruises to rise, and as the ship was pitching bows under, he laid in some half foot of cold salt water, whereby he took rheumatism and shivering fits. The steward twisted his tail, pinched his nose, kicked his stomach, but all in vain : he did not reciprocate these kind attentions, and declined to stand. A committee of passengers then operated upon him, and by the stimulus of a bottle of gin, and the aid of a tackle and fall he was got up. It was all in vain ; to save his life he was killed, and for some days no one would touch beef at meals, though I believe his body was committed to the deep and to the stomachs of the Jacks, who have no inconvenient scruples.

After the lamented demise of the bullock, the crew gave us a litttle excitement. They refused to practise sending up the top-gallant-yards ; a nautical operation, which they did not do to the captain's liking. All hands were mustered ; the ship's articles read ; the ring-leader, a fine specimen of the " sea-lawyer," knocked down, put into irons, and lowered into the hold, there in darkness, and on bread and water to meditate on top-gallant-yards and how to strike and raise them. His comrades thereon went to work as quiet as mice, and plenty of work they had to do, as in addition to the top-gallant-yards game, they were practised at fire and boat quarters, during which latter games the steward mounts guard over the spirit room with loaded pistols, for in such emergencies the British Jack in the merchant service generally misbehaves until he sees he had better not, and then' he works bravely. A confounded shark did us out of another amusement ; he swallowed the patent log, a brass apparatus of the size and appearance of a roasting jack, and thus we could no longer know hourly our pace.

Early on the morning of Sunday, February 5th, word was passed that Damietta light was visible : a general rush on deck ensued to see a tall lighthouse and some palms growing apparently out of the sea, the land being so low that it was quite invisible. As we passed the Damietta mouth of the Nile, we could see the peculiar rig of the Nile boats, but never an inch of soil. The water here shoaled very fast down to $4\frac{1}{2}$ fathoms, and huge porpoises and bonitas played round us. As we sighted the ships at Port Said, we also discovered ahead of us, to our disgust, the *Agamemnon*, a Liverpool steamer that had started one day later than ourselves; our stay at Gibraltar, and one or two stoppages to cool bearings inevitable in a new steamer, accounted for our defeat.

LETTER II.

SUEZ AND THE SUEZ CANAL.

February, 1871.

Port Said is approached from the sea by a long narrow passage between two breakwaters, stretching far out from land, and made of huge blocks of concrete heaped rudely together, so that the sea washes through them. The channel between these is very narrow, and great care is required to take in so large a ship as the *Scotland*. This passage leads into a basin, where on our arrival lay several vessels, and in this basin we spent most of the day (a Sunday) lying alongside a steamer which was being coaled by gangs of Arabs. We were soon surrounded by bumboats, manned by as odd specimens of humanity as ever I saw, some offering to take us on shore, and others wishing to sell oranges, fish, fruit, sweetmeats, and photographs, which goods concealed a secret store of liquor for the Jacks. So soon as we could get pratique, a party of us got on shore and proceeded to explore Port Said, which would remind me of Silloth, with which it has not one feature in common save the sea, and great intentions of future greatness. Port Said is a poor place, mainly composed of small wooden houses, arranged in French style, grand boulevards and places, the chief being the Place Lesseps, remarkable for some stunted and withered trees rather smaller than their neighbours the gas-lamps, and for the Hotel Pagnon, a wooden hut patronized by the great Mr. Cook. But if the houses, hotels, and public buildings were not much, the inhabitants were; there they were, turbaned and tarbooshed men, veiled women, supercilious camels, and ill-tret donkeys, exactly as if they had walked out of Lane's "Egypt" and the "Arabian Nights." The main occupation of the inhabitants appeared to consist in sunning themselves in long recumbent rows in the streets, and the blacker a man was the more sun he seemed to absorb, and the more he seemed to like it. Port Said has the most villainous collection of inhabitants possible. The making of the canal collected together the scum of all France and Southern Europe, as well

as of the East, and sufficient still remains to make a walk after
dark down the chief boulevard a dangerous amusement, while
gambling rooms and still worse places abound.   There is no
fresh water in Port Said ; the town is supplied by pipes from
Ismailia, a distance of 50 miles ; the water is distributed by
men, who carry skins full of it on their backs.   There was
little to be seen in the town, except a very poor bazaar, where
a scabby monkey and an infinitesimal sucking pig were the
chief articles exposed for sale.   We, however, found some good
and cheap cigars, and also after much bargaining purchased a
lot of oranges, two dozen for a shilling, from a veiled lady, who
sat cross-legged on a table, and who had a brass pipe down her
nose to hold up her blue cotton veil.   An Arab imp agreed to
sell us a basket, and carry our purchases to the boat for 3d. ;
but the wily barbarian, on arrival at the boat, chucked in the
oranges and bolted with the basket, pursued fruitlessly by one
of my fellow-passengers.   Had the boy been civilized and
educated, he could not have cheated us out of 3d. more neatly.
Towards three or four o'clock in the afternoon all formalities
were completed, the pilot came on board, and we started
through the canal, preceding the *Agamemnon*, but most
unluckily preceded by a huge, lumbering, old-fashioned French
man-of-war, freighted for Cochin China with troops and priests.
For some way after leaving Port Said the canal passes through
the waters of Lake Menzaleh, from which it is separated by
low banks : westwards the lake extends a great distance, its
shallow waters, two or three feet deep only, teeming with fish,
on which feed countless swarms of ducks, geese, coots, ibises,
spoonbills, cranes, storks, paddy birds, and pelicans ; in fact,
the place is a very paradise for sportsmen, and it is now
becoming the fashion for English visitors to Egypt to visit
Menzaleh for shooting.   These birds and a camel or two quite
excited the children on board, and Master —— expressed his
opinion that this was the Zoological Gardens, and we believe
he considered the natives to be large and fine specimens of
monkeys.   Eastward the lake extended no distance, and beyond
it was the veritable desert, the Desert of Arabia, stretching
away to Sinai.   We had here the pleasure of seeing a mirage,
an apparently large expanse of water bordered with shrubs,
which, on approaching, resolved itself into arid desert and a few
stones.   At 6 o'clock we had to moor, all large traffic on the canal
being prohibited between 6 p.m. and 6 a.m.   After dinner a

few landed just to say we had put foot in the desert, but soon
returned, for a heavy dew was falling, and it was very dark;
later on a most glorious silvery full moon arose.

On the following day we started at 6 a.m.; a wind
blowing across the canal rendered the navigation difficult,
while the old French tub ahead was perpetually grounding:
we could not pass her, and so had to stop the engines, thus
losing steerage, and being generally blown ashore in consequence. At an awkward letter S curve we struck stem and
stern, and all hands, even cooks and passengers, had to bear a
hand at the capstan bars before our craft would budge. A
large dredger laid near, and from a cabin on it there emerged
three French ladies and a child dressed in the latest Parisian
style; they brought out chairs and put up their parasols, and
sat down to watch our struggles as if we were an entertainment;
possibly we were to all but ourselves! This S corner, which as
I recollect is near Serapeum, ought to be done away with; the
narrowness of the canal, however, is in some mariners' opinion
an advantage; when a ship grounds fore and aft she is now
easily pulled off, but were the canal broader, a vessel grounded
at the bow or stern would be swung by the stream of the canal
almost perpendicular to that stream and suffer much from
straining, and as well as being difficult to warp off. The pilot
service, by the way, is execrable; inefficient Neapolitans or
Maltese, who cannot make themselves understood in English,
and yet two-thirds of the vessels that use the canal are English.
The second one we had grounded us, and knocked bits off two
of our three screw blades; he was a helpless idiot and lunatic.
As vessels cannot pass one another in the canal, *gares* or passing
places are provided every seven miles, and communication is
had from one to the other by telegraph. At these *gares* there
are pretty little Frenchified villas erected, with gardens.

The travelling through the canal was pleasant. Early on
Monday we passéd Kantara, a place of a few huts, but
important as a station on the caravan route between Egypt and
Syria. As we proceeded, we had views of the desert right and
left, and saw many little bits of desert life, Bedouins, and camels.
On one place were à herd of thirty camels grazing apparently
on sand; verdure there was none; while further on we saw a
caravan of camels in single file journeying from Palestine to
Suez in the fashion and by the route used for countless generations past. At times we passed through high banks, formed

of the stuff dug out of the canal, while in the broader parts
numbers of enormous and strange dredgers and derricks, used
in the construction of the canal, were lying to rot.

On our second day we passed through Lake Ballah and
Lake Timsah, where were three or four steamers, all, as I
afterwards learnt, as well as the *Agamemnon*, commanded by
Maryport skippers. On Lake Timsah stands the town of
Ismailia, the central and principal town of the Isthmus. It has
been described as "one of the prettiest and most charming
spots imaginable; its trim houses, well-kept streets, and beautiful little gardens, form a characteristic picture of French taste
and neatness;" but this, I think, is bunkum, engendered by the
Khedive's champagne in the brain of some penny-a-liner
present at the opening of the canal. Of Ismailia it is also
said that it will become the sanatorium of Europe; one advantage it certainly has: it could easily be left for a more
amusing place—rail to Suez and rail to Cairo, rail to Alexandria
or steam launch to Port Said. The channel through Lakes
Ballah and Timsah is marked out by gas-lamps, regular
London street gas-lamps, rising from the water. We moored
for our second night in the canal soon after leaving Lake
Timsah. The following day we had most lovely desert views,
with the mountain ranges of Gebel Attaka, and Gebel Geneffe
in the back ground. We were also gratified by seeing the
desert assume that pink glow seen in all pictures of it: it is
always gratifying to see nature come up to art. Our route this
day lay through the Bitter Lakes, which, until lately, were
merely a sandy depression, but which are now by the art
of M. Lesseps, an inland sea of great depth, and as big as
Loch-Lomond. These lakes were no doubt formerly sea, and
probably the Red Sea once extended to this place: in Colonel
Leake's map of Egypt, published in 1802, and to this day the
most accurate map of Egypt, these depressions are marked
with the prophetic note that water communication between the
Red Sea and the Mediterranean might easily be restored by
means of these lakes: the colonel's prescience should be more
widely known and credited than it is. By four o'clock we
were within a mile of the end of the canal where, horrible to
relate, the disgusting French tub struck, and was pronounced
immoveable until next tide, thus causing us, the *Agamemnon*,
and another steamer, what amounted to a whole day's delay.
The coaling agent, a very intelligent Maltese, was, however,

kind enough to take myself and a friend to Suez in a very
pretty little steam launch, but not without some adventures *en
route.* First of all the stupid native who steered ran us foul
of the Frenchman's hawser, and nearly bereft us of our funnel.
In the second place a custom-house officer informed the Maltese
that a steamer had just arrived with news of disasters down
the Red Sea, and he felt obliged to go and make out all he
could about them, nor could he land us at the nearest point,
as it would have been unsafe to have walked across to the hotel
in the dark; thus we got a trip of some four miles or so down
the Red Sea to the *Breadalbane,* the vessel that brought the
news. Returning, we stopped at the coal barges, which were
lying in the Bay ready to coal the *Scotland* had she got out of
the canal that night. With a yell, up jumped, out of the
darkness, some sixty or seventy wild figures, and made a rush
for our boat, which would inevitably have been swamped but for
promptness in sheering off, and the blows with which we
received the intruders. These poor Arabs were to be pitied;
they had been brought there to coal the *Scotland,* and on her
non-arrival left to pass a cold Suez night without other protection than their burnouses and their coal baskets, which most of
them had converted into night-caps.

Owing to these delays we did not land at our hotel until
late at night, where we were waited on by Madras boys in
Oriental costume. We afterwards visited a *café,* where we
saw Italian sailors solemnly dancing mazurkas, two and two.
Some favoured individual had occasionally a round with the
lady of the establishment, but most danced *à la* Spurgeon.

The Peninsular and Oriental Hotel at Suez is in my opinion
one of the best in the East, clean and comfortable, quad-
rangular in shape, built round an open space which contains a
very charming garden, full of cactuses, cotton plants, and
other novelties, all beautifully green, as they are well supplied
with water. Suez itself is a miserable place, mainly built of
mud, and a very Sodom and Gomorrah of vice: nowhere in
the world can the most gross vice be more openly rampant.
During the making of the canal no European resident at Suez
dare venture out of his house after dark, while a huge gambling
hell, now burnt, was a centre of rowdyism: no stranger could
carry his winnings away from that place unless well armed
and accompanied by armed friends. After the works were
finished, Suez became safer, but still the environs abounded

with ruffians : shortly before my arrival an English hospital sergeant had been stabbed by Greeks : and the interpreter of Her Britannic Majesty's steamship *Jumna* having been run over by a locomotive and his legs cut off, was robbed by an Arab, who first seemed inclined to help him, but could not resist the jingle of money heard as he raised the bleeding wretch. Still the place amused me ; it was a novel sight to one who had never before seen the East, and the hotel was comfortable, so I stayed some four days. The inhabitants, too, were curious from the variety of their costumes and colours, and the promptitude with which they demanded "baksheesh," for what it was often hard to say ; possibly merely because they existed. The bazaars and streets were (poor as I soon learnt to consider them) perfect kaleidoscopes of curiosities, and I found ample enjoyment in lounging up and down them. I was much pleased to find the East and Easterns exactly as books describe them, plus much squalor, filth, and stink : it was also interesting to stumble at every corner over some illustration of sacred writ.

At Suez I made first the acquaintance of that wonderful animal, the Eastern donkey ; the Suez specimens were but poor, and it was misery to ride such illtreated animals. Without exception each Suez donkey has a huge bleeding raw established on each quarter, and by the insertion of a stick, armed with an iron spike, into these raws, he is induced to go at a tremendous pace. The Cairene donkey is a much superior animal, the very essence of aristocratic donkeydom, high in the shoulders, sometimes as big as a horse, curiously shaved and cropped into fancy patterns, ornate with an elaborately worked saddle cloth, with red and yellow leather, and with brass fixings, while his saddle bow rises into a huge hump, and is covered with Brussels carpet. Except for one purpose no Eastern would thank you for the best Brussels carpet ever wove ; he would consider it only fit to cover a donkey saddle with. £15 is the usual price for a moke in Cairo, and some fetch £70 or £80.

My first donkey ride at Suez was down to the docks, where we, that is I and a friend, hired a sailing boat to take us to the *Scotland*, which had got out of the canal and was in the gulf. A corporal of the Marines asked us to take him to the *Jumna*, which we gladly did ; but we had another passenger, a most gaudy Oriental, an Arab pilot, arrayed in silk and fine attire,

the only sign of European civilization about him being an
opera glass : round his head, shoulders, and waist, were rolled
beautiful silk handkerchiefs, all glittering with countless gold
threads woven into the warp, of a kind made either at Aden or
Damascus, and worth, as I afterwards learnt, some £4 or £5
apiece.   This noble swell got into our boat on the supposition
that we would be green enough to take him to some ship miles
out of our way : this we would not do, but having done our
business, brought the man of many handkerchiefs back to
where he started from some two hours before ; we then set the
boatman to demand a dollar from the gent for his passage,
which he paid with many scowls and curses.   Thus was "the
biter bit :" he trusted to our ignorance of Arabic to getting a
ride for nothing, which we would willingly have given on a
civil request, were it not adding four unneccessary miles to
our sail.

    The only excursion to be made from Suez is to the Wells of
Moses, Ayoun Mousa, or Ain Moosa, the spot according to tradi-
tion where the Israelites rested after the passage of the Red
Sea.   It is also the first stage of the caravan route from Suez
to Mount Sinai, and at it are some wild palm trees, and a small
garden irrigated by the brackish water of the springs and cultivated by a few fellahs from Suez.   I visited the wells in company with an American doctor travelling with his wife, a stout
woman of great pluck and curiosity, and with a poetess and
authoress, who was taking notes with a view to a book wherein
I horribly fear to figure.   This poetess or authoress was a
puzzler ; she quoted Scott, Byron, Milton, and other classics
by the yard, and occasionally went into ecstatic gushes over
the Arabs and the scenery ; she wore a man's shirt, collar, and
jacket, and a crinoline ; had on a wedding ring, talked of
her children (in New York), and was called Miss by her
friends ; from her personal appearance no man could reckon
up her age.   With this party I went to the Wells of Moses.
As a preliminary we hired a dragoman, a romantic-looking and
copper-coloured individual, who answered to the name of
Selim, and who was gaily appareled in a red tarboosh, a white
gown, and yellow slippers.   I know he had nothing more, for I
saw him turn a somersault off his donkey.   This gentleman hired
for us five donkeys, a supply of donkey boys, and a boat, into
which the donkeys, each with two raws on his quarters,
were *chucked ;* I use the word chucked with deliberation ; no

other word can describe the disregard to the donkey mind, feelings, and pride, shown in the embarkation. The donkeys, the donkey boys, the lunch, the crew, and ourselves, brought the craft's gunnel to the level of the water. The poetess quoted Scott and Byron ; I quaked with fear, for the slightest ripple would have sunk us, and there are sharks in the Red Sea, but whether they prefer white man, brown man, or donkey, was on this occasion undecided, and we got across in safety, mounted our mokes and started. The gay Selim careered ahead with the lunch basket balanced in front of him, but suddenly his donkey fell, and Selim performed that manœuvre to which I have before alluded as allowing me to inspect his wardrobe. The stout *Americaine* was very uneasy on her donkey; she tried first one donkey, and then the other, and finally requested me to ride ahead, while she took off her crinoline and mounted astride; for the rest of the day Selim cantered along with the crinoline around his neck, the oddest traveller that ever travelled the desert of Sinai. An hour's ride through country, which we could well see was fitly designated Arabia Petræa, brought us to the wells, some dirty pools of water, and dusty enclosures of palms, cotton trees, pomegranates, dates, onions, and radishes. Here we lunched ; the poetess rode on to the shores of the Red Sea. I, as an invalid, declined to accompany her, but I regretted my want of gallantry on seeing the lovely shells she brought back. On our return we met a Bedouin with a camel—a poor, starved, mangy, sore beast ; nothing would satisfy the American party but a ride on this beast, so each had one ; the poor brute, at this unexpected imposition, roared, sobbed, and cried, and the poetess asked me " if camels ever turned ugly !" I thought that nothing on earth or in heaven could make this brute uglier than nature and man combined had made him, but I found that " ugly" is the Yankee for vicious. I would not touch the beast, which should have been killed, and its owner whipt for cruelty. I saw on this trip an illustration of Eastern cruelty to animals. As we disembarked, I noticed four very black villains living in a hole, their sole belongings a kid, a fire of sticks, and a dead donkey prone on its side, and covered with ulcers from head to foot—dead, as I imagined it, it was a sickening sight. On our return from the wells we passed the place again, and, horrible to relate, the brute proved to be alive, and raised its head. I was perfectly sickened ; on inquiring, Selim said that the beast had laid there for three days to his knowledge, without food or drink, and under the broiling sun and cold nights of Suez. I wished to negotiate for its instant death, but Selim would not; he was afraid of the four villains, its owners.

The tide being out, we had to be carried to the boat; for the accomplishment of this, to the horror of the ladies, the mahogany-coloured boatmen calmly tucked their garments up under their armpits. The doctor's wife was so stiff with riding astride that she had to be lifted off her saddle. Plucky woman! I heard that she nearly killed herself by insisting on doing all the Pyramids, inside and outside. *En voyage* Suez-wards, we passed some curious Arab dhows or ships, used to convey pilgrims to Mecca, white-painted, and having high poops and gaudy-coloured sterns. From one an enormous jet-black Negro appeared, and saluted us in the most affable manner, which would have been more interesting had we known the tongue he spake in, and had he had even a postage-stamp by way of raiment.

By the way, the town of Suez during my visit was full of Turkish soldiers, and Turkish transports full of troops lay in the bay, much to the Khedive's disgust. A revolt had occurred in Arabia, and the Sultan, instead of calling upon his vassal, the Khedive, to put it down, had availed himself of the facilities of the canal, and sent his own troops, who had landed at Suez and encamped. To the Khedive this was a perfectly new and disgusting light thrown upon the canal, and he has since erected three forts to command its passage. The canal is small boon to him or his: a mere conduit pipe for traffic to the far East, it brings no commerce to Egypt, and it has brought his master's troops: this omens ill for the maintenance of the canal.

LETTER III.

GRAND CAIRO.

On Saturday, the 11th of February, 1872, I left Suez by rail for Cairo, and got into a carriage with a Colonel of R.A., late commanding in Ceylon, a Mr. M——, a young American returning home from China, and an old gent, a Mr. Y. J——, doing the grand tour of the world, with a view, as was conjectured, to a book, and known on board the Peninsular and Oriental boat *Mongolia*, as the "old lady," a *sobriquet* derived from his anxious and fussy habits. On comparison of notes, we found we had all been cheated over our railway tickets except the wily colonel, for the rascally railway clerks had done three of us out of more than the price of the ticket, and had done each of us out of a different sum. The journey was very hot, though the carriages were provided with double roofs, double windows, Venetians, and other contrivances for excluding the heat. For some way (to Zagazig, where we lunched well but expensively) the way was through the desert, but at that point we entered the rich scenery of the Delta, where were palms, dates, and grain crops growing with great luxuriance. At a station called Nefishe was a most curious museum of reptiles, horns, and birds; at Tel-el-Kebin there was a large camp of soldiers, whose commander, a most ornate personage, in full uniform, was riding about on a white ass. Fancy the Duke of Cambridge careering about Aldershot on a Jerusalem!

The distance between Suez and Cairo was only 150 miles; no one could foretell the probable hour of our arrival, but we did turn up at Cairo at 5 o'clock, having left Suez at 8. The American and I took a carriage to Shepherd's Hotel, and were all but upset at the start, and had to change for a machine with less restive steeds.

Shepherd's Hotel has a cosmopolitan reputation, but in my opinion, it wants a few improvements. The meals do not suit English appetites : coffee and bread and butter only are

3

given in the morning; for anything more you pay extra beyond your 16s. a day; breakfast is at 12-30, and is a regular dinner, at which wine is drunk, and concludes with a cup of coffee; while dinner is at 6-30, an enlarged edition of lunch. There is no smoking room attached to the hotel, except a very small room, where ladies have to sit, and gentlemen may and do smoke; wine is dear and bad. Yet, with all these faults, I would recommend Shepherd's; its company and its verandah make amends for all. At Shepherd's the traveller picks up and makes parties for excursions with the nicest people possible, or, if lazy, lounges the day on the verandah, and the whole East passes in review before him, while conjurors, snake charmers, and vendors of curiosities, are ever ready to amuse. One can scarce tire of watching the motley European and Eastern stream of picturesque humanity, of wonderful carriages, of horse, camel, donkey, and buffalo flesh, that ever flow through the Uzbekeeh, or Grand Place of Cairo. This place was formerly under water, but is now reclaimed, drained, and Frenchified, with Egyptian variations, such as a hole or two just sufficient to break a leg. It behoves to be cautious in crossing the Uzbekeeh by dark.

I arrived at Cairo on a Saturday; on the Sunday I went to the English Church, held in a room at the New Hotel, a vast but desolate building, formerly the property of a Company Limited, and then of the Khedive, who was said to meditate its conversion into a gambling house; as no clergyman could on this occasion be got, one of the English consular officers supplied his place.

After the midday breakfast Capt. R——, of Her Britannic Majesty's *Jumna*, asked me to go exploring with him, as he had a carriage and a dragoman in his employ, and wanted company for himself and work for them. The streets and bazaars of Cairo are very crowded, thus making a foot runner essential to every carriage—swells have two. These runners precede the carriage, shrieking out " O, camel! O, darkey! O, old man! get out of the way!" They are almost universally dressed in a white garment, with long flowing sleeves knotted together behind, leaving the dusky arms and legs bare. The runners to a swell wear a gorgeously-embroidered sleeveless waistcoat, of red or blue velvet, embroidered with gold or silver lace. Each runner holds perpendicularly in his hand a long stick, and their picturesque *tout ensemble* adds much to the novelty of Cairo street life. The carriages are mostly old English and French ones, drawn by two horses, and driven by natives; of course the swells have the best carriages that can be got. To see the horses and carriages of Cairo, the visitor should, any fine day between four and six drive down the Shoobra Road, the Rotten Row of Cairo, running under a magnificent avenue af acacias, and past some beautiful palaces and villas. The *elite* of Cairo are a motley lot: pets of the harem in the most Parisian of toilettes, Long-Acre broughams, and diaphanous veils; *rats d'opera* in open carriages : resident Greek and Italian swells in, to their minds, the real Parisian style ; Orientals placidly snoozing in their carriages, or bestriding a gorgeously caparisoned steed, or lordly donkey ; curious travellers from Shepherd's all agog to see the sights : and a frame work of beggars and Eastern rubbish fringing the side paths.

Our first day's ramble through Cairo was not up the Shoobra road, but through the bazaars and streets, and up to the Citadel, whose ancient walls, destroyed partly by intent and partly by accidental explosions of powder, are now replaced by modern bastions and curtains. Here stands, like a fairy dream, the Mosque of Mahommed Ali, built all of Oriental alabaster, and supported by countless pillars of the same. Critics say this mosque is not of pure Oriental character, and that its minarets are painfully too elongated, and out of all proportion. The mosque consists of a large arcaded court with a fountain in the centre, all of alabaster, leading to a magnificent building covered by a huge and lofty dome, and supported by countless pillars, some, it is said, being merely of painted wood, the rascally custodians having stole the valuable alabaster ones. The interior of the building is very fine ; unbroken by seats or partitions, it is covered with the finest prayer-carpets, while innumerable glass lamps hang some eight feet from the floor at the end of long silvered chains : the only light admitted is through windows of coloured glass, and the interior of the dome is covered with geometrical patterns in jewel-like mosaics. From the mosque one steps out upon the " Mameluke's last leap," from whence a delicious view can be got of the valley of the Nile, of Cairo, and its environs, and of the distant Pyramids. Close to this is Joseph's Well, the work of a Caliph Juseef or Joseph : it is a shaft 280 feet deep cut in the solid rock, and having a staircase winding round to its very

bottom, where is a cistern containing water; half way down
or up is another cistern, and a third at the top; the water
is raised from one cistern to another by an endless rope with
earthen jars fixed on it, and worked by mules.

From the Citadel we drove to see the ruins of Old Cairo,
or El Fostat, where we visited an old Coptic Church, marking
the site of a cave in which Joseph and Mary are said to have
been concealed. We saw here some very curious old paintings,
and some panel work inlaid with ivory figures of St. George
and the Dragon, the patron saint of the Copts as well as of
England. Thence we went to Boulac, the port of Cairo, and
made the acquaintance of that famous father of all rivers, the
Nile. At Boulac it is divided into two by the island of
Rhoda, which we visited to see the Nilometer. The Nilometer
is a slender pillar standing in a cistern in the gardens of Hassan
Pasha, and formerly supporting a dome now fallen into the
cistern. The gardens are now utterly neglected, but in their
prime they must have been beautiful, with long lines of vine-
clad trellises, and with paths, not of gravel, but of white
marble.

Of course, I did the Pyramids of Ghizeh: Captain R——,
the American, and myself, drove there in a carriage. The road
lay through Boulac, crossing the Nile by a bridge of boats,
and then proceeding for some 5 miles through an avenue of
acacias. The country we drove through was very rich, being
periodically inundated by the Nile. In some fields by the side
of the road the Khedive's stud was grazing, each horse tethered
separately, and a syce or groom living with them in a tent.
Some of these horses were Arabs of the purest blood, valued at
£1,000 apiece, and procured by much diplomacy from the
interior of Arabia, or from the wild nomadic tribes of Asia
Minor; many of these horses were white, but there were also
chestnuts and browns; some fawn-coloured and much-prized
buffaloes were similarly tethered out. Long strings of camels
and buffalo carts met us, bringing great bundles of sugar-cane
from the fields, where we saw the natives busy reaping it;
almost every native we met had a six-foot stalk of sugar-
cane in his hand, which he chewed as he walked. One
thing struck us much: the sheep, the goats, the dogs, and the
pigs much favour one another; at first sight it is difficult to
say to which of the four a particular animal may belong; the
sheep are generally brown and black, with large fat flat tails,

and some are painted fancifully with saffron stripes. In the rice fields, where were buffaloes yoked to the plough, we saw the white pink-eyed ibis, the sacred bird of the ancient Egyptians. We also saw myriads of pigeons, which lived in round mud pots, perched all over the common mud houses of the country, and making them look like embattled fortresses.

Long ere we arrived at the Pyramids, their mighty masses seemed to press upon us, the clearness of the atmosphere and their size, unscaled by any neighbouring object, deceiving one as to their distance. They stand on the edge of the desert, just where the *hagar* or cultivated ground ends. As we approached we could see the eagles, or Arabs, gathering together for the prey, and by our dragoman's advice we handed him all our money but a few sixpences, not from fear of robbery, but to avoid being talked out of it. We were received by the Shekh of the Pyramids, who, by the regulations of the place, gets a fee of one dollar per head from visitors, for which he finds a party to conduct the visitor to the top and inside the interior. Five men and a boy were assigned to convey me to the top of the Great Pyramid, the chief being a very loquacious and impudent fellow, who said he was a Hakim or doctor. The steps are quite breast high : an Arab held me by each hand, and a third shoved with his head in the rear, all singing in rude chant "That is very good—Hele-e-o-saurah"—with a prolonged howl. I insisted on resting very often, when the water bottle came into play, and the doctor rubbed my aching legs affectionately. I was hardly so enchanted with the view as many travellers are ; perhaps I was too winded ; my main idea was that I had fulfilled a dream of boyhood by getting to the top of the Great Pyramid. The Arabs then became very clamorous for "baksheesh," which I sternly denied them, until they rendered me safe on the ground : they then offered, for "baksheesh" of course, to run up to the top of the second Pyramid in no time, or to cut my honoured name in large letters on the top of the great one, all which I declined ; finding I was firm, they brought me down, to a chorus of "I satisfy you, you make me satisfied." If once one yields, and gives them "baksheesh" *en route*, they will get very troublesome, and the beggars in helping one up and down feel whether one has coin or not. At the bottom I presented them with sixpence each, at which they were highly disgusted and clamorous for more : again I was firm, and they desisted at last, and became highly civil, a sure sign I had satisfied them and given enough. My friend went inside the Pyramid, but I did not; I sat outside and conversed with my Arabs, the doctor having considerable command of English and French. My Arab friends then interrogated me; they asked if I was a captain, and how much the Queen paid me? how much land, and how many houses, cows, sheep, and camels, I had? I owned to none, but said my father had some land. They then inquired how many acres, and I owned to a million or two. They seemed to pity me much, as owning no other means of travelling but afoot; and inquiry as to my ways of getting a living followed. I tried to explain what a barrister was, but my friends had hazy ideas of law and justice; they jumped to the conclusion that I was by profession *a great thief*, and they respected me.

When my friends emerged, hot and dusty, we walked on to the Sphinx. At first she disappoints; is simply grotesque; but she grows upon one: her face, though hideously mutilated, is wonderfully calm and serene. Hard by are some tombs of granite and alabaster; the stones are of great size (I measured one of granite, 15ft. by 9ft. by 5ft), all perfectly jointed and worked smooth. One tomb, known as Campbell's, is a granite pit over 50 feet deep, having round it a trench 70 feet deep; and having a colossal image of black basalt flat at the bottom. Some energetic people insist on going up and into all the three Pyramids; but we didn't. We preferred at this period to discuss the excellent lunch M. Zech had provided us with from Shepherd's Hotel. This we did in a pavilion belonging to the Khedive. A tall Arab brought us coffee in little cups, and we much enjoyed our coffee and pipes and the drive homewards through Eastern scenes. We stopped at Boulac to see the museum there—a magnificent collection of Egyptian antiquities, worthy of close study for some days.

So pleased were we with our visit to these Pyramids, that we three agreed to go to the Pyramids of Sakkara, and the bull and ibis pits at that place. To do this we had to send donkeys on the night before, drive to Embabeh, and then rail to some station, whence we donkeyed. At this station a large party, all bound the same way, disembarked, a Scotch party and a Yankee party, with a very cute Yankee girl, who chaffed our Yankee silly, and kept us in roars of laughter by her odd way of expressing herself. She informed us that her donkey

" had as many paces in a dozen minutes as a tall sword." On being asked to stop because her saddle was askew, she said, " Guess I won't stop, I'll *wriggle* him *wright* awhiles." Our road was through a beautiful rich country, sugar-cane and melon fields. We passed the ruins of Memphis, once a town sixteen miles in circumference, but now only a few mounds, a few shapeless ruins and mummy pits, and a colossal statue turned back up in a pool of water. The village of Metrahenny stands on part of its site. A lake still remains, the ancient lake of the dead, and some of the Scotch party hoped to get a shot at ducks there, but could not get near enough ; they however shot a few brown hawks. At Sakkara we found that thousands of mummies, black common people, were being dug up in the most shameful manner, some say for manure, others that they afford fuel· for the railway from Cairo to Alexandria. These mummies (and after all a mummy is a human corpse) were crunched under our donkeys' feet, being everywhere strewn about, and we scrambled for relics from them.. The Yankee girl wanted a toe, or said so. I secured a head, and a hand with a ring on it; but whole bodies might have been had for the lifting. There was also a fine supply of Pyramids at Sakkara (there are over a hundred Pyramids in Egypt), but none so big or so famous as the Great Pyramids of Ghizeh. We fixed up for lunch at a small pavilion belonging to Mariette Bey, near the Serapeum, where are buried the sacred bulls, each in an enormous granite sarcophagus, occupying a subterranean chamber. The heat in these chambers being too great for me, I left exploration to others, and devoted myself to smoking the chibouk of peace and watching our donkeys fight until my comrades appeared to lunch, after duly honouring which, we took it easy homewards, buying, *en route*, a few antiquities from the Arabs.

By the way, in the morning, while waiting at the railway station, we saw a most amusing illustration of how discipline is preserved in the Egyptian army. A large number of troops, encamped close by, were out for company drill. The pivot man of one company did not halt when he should have done, so he was called to the front, and his ears were boxed by the irate captain, who then kicked the covering sergeant on that organ which we hope the sergeant will never show to the foe.

Of other excursions from Cairo I did not do many. Heliopolis I left to take care of itself, as I did the dancing dervishes.

I and another gentleman rode out on donkeys, under the charge of one Hassan, prince of the Cairo donkey boys, to see the Petrified Forest, situate six or seven miles off in the desert, of which we saw some characteristic views, and where we fell in with some wandering Bedouins pasturing their flocks on apparently nothing at all. The forest was curious, but hardly worth the ride. While inspecting it we let our donkeys loose, expecting them to stand, but they did not, and quietly sloped when our backs were turned. Hassan tore off into the desert, swearing the Bedouins had stolen them, while we, disgusted, started to walk back, thinking how horribly we should be chaffed at Shepherd's. After a long trudge we espied our donkeys in the hands of some dozen most villainous Arabs. Not knowing one word of Arabic, we walked up, seized the donkeys, and jumped on ; then arose a mighty clamour for " baksheesh." By good luck my pocket was full of small coin, sufficient to go round, and we got off : had we not had that small money I think we might have fared but ill. Hassan rejoined us as we got to the gates of Cairo, dead beat with running and in mortal fear (so he said) that we should be robbed ; indeed, night was falling, and shoals of ruffians were streaming out of Cairo to their usual abiding-place for the night, namely the tombs. Exploring about these said tombs is a very pleasant way of spending a day. Every Eastern city has around it a still vaster city—a city of the dead, where repose countless generations under tombs and in inclosures, which, in an Eastern climate, afford good shelter to scores of " dwellers in the tombs," homeless vagabonds, and ruffians of every degree. Six of us made up an exploring expedition, and started, four in a carriage, and two on donkeys. We first drove through the oldest part of Cairo to El Fostat, or old Cairo, where we revisited the old Coptic Church mentioned before, and then went to a Greek Convent, with a Greek Church on the top of it, up countless flights of stairs. We were there introduced to a Greek bishop, a most venerable looking ecclesiastic in black robes and a tall brimless hat, and with a beard of patriarchal snowness and length. We had a long conversation with him in mongrel Italian and Latin, and I highly amused him by reading him the first chapter of St. John's Gospel in Greek, as pronounced at Cambridge in the year of my little go. He was much gratified on being informed we were not followers of " Il Papa," the Pope, and gave us a long disquisition on the number of sacraments held by each Christian Church, enforcing his arguments by producing some very curious books on divinity, one of which had quaint illustrations of the various sacraments. The church contained some very odd pictures of the virgin and of some saints in the old hard outlined Italian style, with huge gold nimbuses around their heads. Old Cairo is a very Eastern place of the oldest type, and of most unimproved mud houses, latticed and projecting windows, enormous doors with huge wooden locks, and with each an aloe growing over the lintel. Just outside of old Cairo is the Mosque of Amer, a large square enclosure of colonnades enclosing an open court, in the centre of which stands an octagonal fountain : 230 pillars form the colonnades, being one row deep on the western side, three rows deep north and south, and six deep on the Mecca side, where is the preaching platform, and the niche which marks the direction of Mecca. On the stability of this mosque hangs, it is said, the Moslem power in Egypt ; near the door are two columns, between which no one but a true Mussulman can pass ; we, all six, failed, but two or three natives easily got through. The entrance to this mosque lies through a pottery, where native pots were being made and dried in the sun, for they are not baked. An old man waist-deep in a clay-hole, and all clay-besmirched asked " baksheesh," and got it, for his resemblance to " Punch's " picture of Dirty Father Thames welcoming the Corporation of London was irresistible.

From here we entered the silent city, the city of the tombs, which extends far and wide, amid great mounds of rubbish, round this part of Cairo. The common form of a Moslem tomb is an entablature of wood, mud, stone, or marble, or sometimes a coffer-like erection : from the foot rises a flat stone, on which is recorded the dead man's name and style, while from the head rises a pillar supporting his head-dress, turban or tarboosh, from whose shape the occupant's rank can easily be told : a gilt-tasseled tarboosh denotes the last home of a military officer, while a religious man or a servant can easily be told by the formal folds of the turban. Thousands and thousands of these tombs abound round Cairo ; those of the poor are unprotected, the rich stand within enclosures, while those of shekhs and dervishes have domes over them, and those of caliphs and sultans have mosques, or buildings rich with plate-glass windows, and gilt railings. South of the city we found

the tombs known as those of the Memlooks, the chief of which
has a dome surmounted by a weathercock shaped like a boat.
The sepulchre of Mohammed Ali and his family is close to
this, consisting of a long corridor and two domed chambers :
the tombs are of marble, fantastically carved, gilt, and painted,
and their covers are of the finest silks.   The tombs on this side
of the city are very curious, and offer interesting subjects for
the pencil of an artist ; they well repay a long ramble.   We
then journeyed through the town to the Mosque of Sultan
Hassan, the largest in Cairo, built of marble stolen from the
Pyramids, and now frightfully out of repair : it is a vast
hypæthral court, with a square recess on each side, covered by
a noble arch, that on the east being the largest, while behind it
is a domed chamber covering the tomb of Sultan Hassan.
Passing through the Bab e'Nusr Gate we found more tombs ;
one, that of a dervish, is simply a huge arch.   Here are the
tombs known as those of "the caliphs," each having a ruinous
mosque attached, built of alternate courses of red and white or
red and black stones ; the interiors are plain, hung with lamps
and ostrich eggs.   In one we were shown a stone with a mark
on it, said to be the footprint of Mahomet.

In all I stayed at Cairo nearly a fortnight and enjoyed it
much.   Time passed amusingly : a lounge on the verandah, a
stroll or ride up the bazaar, and up the large street called the
Moskee showed novelties enough to amuse any mind.   Once
or twice I joined an American party, and went round the
bazaars with them, an economical proceeding for me, for the
lady of the party was spending £200 or £300 in Cairene
curiosities, and thus I saw, without expense to myself, the
contents of the best shops in the place ; gold embroidered
burnouses and opera cloaks, table cloths, with the Sultan's seal
wrought round them, slippers bedecked with pearls, handkerchiefs from Aden and Damascus, gay with many colours,
muslins from India, silks from China, carpets and attar of roses
and preserved apricots from Persia, swords of Damascene
steel, amber necklaces from Constantinople, and jewellery from
Paris.   All these and more did I see, express an opinion on,
and bargain for over fragrant Latakia and coffee in choice
cups, while the American paid the whistle (and paid it
like a man).   By no means let any one suppose that an
Eastern bazaar is like a European one ; it is narrow, and roofed
from the sun by mats of reeds; the shops have neither signs

nor fronts, and make no display : each merchant sits cross-legged in a sort of cavern *sans* table or chairs ; you join him, accept his hospitality, and he produces the rarest goods from dingy holes and boxes ; he don't care whether you buy or not, and you must offer him about a third of what he asks.   Each trade has its own bazaar : braziers, saddle makers, each after their kind, congregate together, and in the little visited bazaars of such trades more Orientalism is to be seen than in the ones thronged by travellers and Europeans.   Travellers, almost invariably, are victimized by their dragoman who, of course, gets a percentage on their purchases, and has his favourite tradesmen, or they fall into the hands of Jew brokers, of whom the most famous, much patronized by Americans, is Far-Away-Moses of Constantinople and Cairo, a man as honest as an Eastern can be expected to be, and who will at his customers' option deal either European or Eastern fashion, that is, he will state at once the lowest price he can put the articles at, or will chaffer for them.   My humble purchases consisted of necessaries for going up the Nile, and were mostly bought under care of the well-known Mustapha Aga, and my servant Mahomet, who looked sharply after my interests, and introduced me to many black and blackish merchants of great wealth : I bought two common carpets, a buttaneeh or cover for my bed, two okes of tobacco, a gazelle skin for a tobacco pouch, and a stock of other necessaries for the journey up the Nile.   Returning to the subject of the bazaar, the crowds that swarm in them are a perfect panorama of gay costumes ; so thronged are they that a pedestrian can with difficulty save himself from a rude jostle from donkey, horse, or heavily-laden camel, while carriages and buffalo carts and trucks drive over his toes, for at first he probably does not understand the warning cries in Arabic, perpetually sounding all around him.   Itinerant vendors of sweetmeats, of sherbet, and of water, add to the row, through which grave Turks or Arabs stalk perfectly unmoved ; while veiled ladies on foot or donkeyback, dressed rarely in gay colours, but more frequently in sombre blue from head to foot, pique Western curiosity.

If the day went fast at Cairo, the nights at Shepherd's hung somewhat heavy for want of a proper place for people to meet in, while Cairo evening amusements are few, consisting of a *café* or two with German or Bohemian musicians, and an occasional masked ball commencing at the hour of midnight.

The opera, the French theatre, and a circus, of all of which the Khedive pays the expenses out of the taxes, afford something to do. I went to the opera on a grand night in honour of two English Dukes who were in Cairo at the same time that I was; a charming litttle house, with many of the boxes covered with lattice work to conceal the harems of local swells. The piece was a *grand ballet*, called " Brahma," the most magnificently mounted piece I ever saw, as it ought to be, for I was told it cost the Khedive £4,000 to mount, and £400 each night of its being played. The *corps de ballet* consisted of 100 Italian girls picked for their beauty, and maintained and paid most extravagantly. The chief *danseuse* was a first-rate *artiste*, no mere mechanical dancer, but one who danced all over and seemed to enjoy it. At least four hundred supernumeraries and a troop of horse were on the stage at once, while the scene changed rapidly from India to China, China to Japan, and Japan to I don't know where, but all, dresses and scenery, were perfect of their kind. During the *entr' acts* all the gentlemen adjourned to smoke in the hall. *A propos* of *ballet* I was in Cairo during the Carnival, and saw some shabby masqueraders buffooning about.

During my stay in Cairo I appeared in a new character. A Coptic lad, introduced to me by some friends, took me to see the Khedive's schools ; the one I visited had some 500 boys ; the professors received me with delight, stood coffee, made me inspect everything from drawings to dormitories, and finally I found myself much embarrassed by being made to examine some forty native boys in English. I made them write the following wise sentence on a blackboard : " London is a fine town ; I live in London," and then parse the words, which they did very fairly, and seemed highly proud of being called on to exhibit.

LETTER IV.

ON THE NILE.

I went up the Nile under circumstances somewhat unusual for an Englishman : I was banished to Egypt for the winter, Cairo was terribly expensive, and to do the Nile in ordinary fashion was a matter of £400 or £500, for dragomen have combined to raise expenses in a way that can only be done in a country where travellers are wholly at their mercy. I had too, rather an objection to living in a boat for three or four months, and determined to strike out a line of my own. By good luck, Mustapha Aga, the English Consular Agent at Luxor, was in Cairo, and to him I applied; he at once offered to contract for my conveyance to Luxor and my return back when I wished, for the sum of £40, to board and lodge me for £10 a month, and for £3 extra to provide me with a servant who spoke English. Mustapha, whom I learnt to both respect and like, is an Arab of pure blood, a descendent of the prophet, with a venerable white beard and with a greater capability for tobacco than any human being I ever saw. He has been in English employ some forty years, has travelled everywhere, from Persia to the Cape of Good Hope, from Calcutta to London, and is one of the most wonderful linguists I ever met; he speaks Arabic (his native tongue), Turkish, Persian, Hindostanee, French, Italian, and English; the latter two perfectly, and all learned by ear, for he can neither read nor write. The servant he got me, Mahomet by name, was a very black man with a broken nose, sharp as a needle, and a great dandy in his appearance: his turban was a gay-coloured Damascus scarf, wound round a red fez, while his dress was a Zouave jacket and pantaloons of light slate blue with another gay scarf round his waist: red slippers and bare legs completed him, and both at Shepherd's and up the Nile my servant was vastly admired for his smartness. He had travelled from Stamboul to Khartoum; his English was not much, but he made the most of what he had. While at Cairo, prior to starting, Mustapha often drove me about the bazaars shopping, with Mahomet in attendance, and I used to wonder what Lincoln's Inn would say to me careering about in a carriage and pair with Mustapha and two black chums of his, Mahomet on the box with the driver, and a white-robed flying-sleeved runner in front. One very black gentleman to whom I was thus introduced was a personage—son of the Shekh of Khartoum. He had been sent by his father to see the world at Cairo with 200 camels for pocket money, which, when turned into cash would give him about £1,200 to spend. He was very anxious Mustapha and I should visit him at Khartoum, promised an escort of horses and camels to meet us at Korosko, where the land journey of twenty-five days through the desert begins, and talked of lion and elephant hunting on the White Nile : alas, alas, I was no Baker, or Speke, and had to decline.

My unusual proceedings excited a little comment ; indeed the noble fraternity of dragomen were vastly irate that I should escape them and do the Nile reasonably, for were many to follow my example it would be death to their trade : I afterwards found my fame, as "Mustapha's Englishman," had got even to Constantinople. One Englishman, travelling in great magnificence with wife, son, and daughter (it took thirty-two camels and two horses to convey the four across the desert of Sinai), interested himself greatly in my doings. He drew me so gloomy a picture of the miseries that would befall me as almost to make me repent my bargain : invalid as I was, he really scared me. He was, however, the occasion of much kindness being shown me. An American gentleman heard these well-meant endeavours and said nought; next morning he called upon me, said he had overheard these remarks (they were made at dinner), and pitied me; that in consequence he had been to Dr. ——, the head of the American mission in Cairo, a man who knew Mustapha well, and who had stayed with him ; and that he had got from that authority an utterly different account of what I might anticipate. This information was a great relief to me, and a piece of real kindness on the part of the American.

When the time came for starting, Mustapha appeared somewhat loath to leave the pleasures and flesh-pots of Cairo, and I had to stir him up considerably. We embarked on the afternoon of February 23rd, and at once hoisted the British ensign and set sail. Now, thought I, "we're off :" alas, we went no further than the bridge of boats across the Nile, which is open only for boat traffic once in the twenty-four hours : there we lay for the night, and a rare scramble we had to get through in the morning, so great was the rush of boats. We made little progress the next two days, though the wind was always favourable ; and at the end of this time we were only at Old Cairo. Each day indeed I rode or drove back to Cairo to inquire (but fruitlessly) after letters. I utilized the time in buying one or two forgotten necessaries, a looking-glass and an enormous jar or *ballasee* to serve as a filter. The crew made Mustapha and myself subscribe for musical instruments, to wit, a drum of earth, like a drain-pipe, and a tambour. We got also a sackful of copper coin wherewith to buy milk, eggs, &c., on the road, for the *fellaheen* never have coin to give change with.

We made our real start on the night of the 25th, and the following night I was well aware I had left civilization, for I was awoke by hyenas howling around us at night. I must confess I felt pretty miserable : the non-arrival of letters was a bitter disappointment ; the unfiltered Nile water disagreed with me ; I was alone with ten black men ; in fact, I felt thoroughly hipped, and more than half inclined to take the rail which runs by the Nile to Minieh, and go back. Thus meditating in my bunk, early on the 28th of February, I felt a mighty crash, and a huge dahabeeh, flying the British ensign, ran into ours. Before I was dressed a dragoman appeared with two cards, bearing the names of two gentlemen from my own county ; he was followed by one of them, whom I had last seen in Cumberland in pursuit of the wily fox. I and Mustapha breakfasted with them, and their cheeriness and good fellowship thoroughly restored me. We sailed in company all the morning, but their big boat soon left us behind, with an agreement to meet at Luxor.

The first place of any importance at which we stopped was Minieh, a large town encircled in date groves, and 170 miles from Cairo. We moored just off a large building, either the local Bey's palace or a sugar factory, where the river bank was most unpleasantly foul. Mustapha and I went off to call on the Bey, who was not at home, and then to the bazaar to buy bread, milk, and provisions, and also that Mustapha might get his head shaved. Hundreds of excited *fellaheen* were rushing wildly about the bazaar, shrieking and howling madly, each

armed with an enormous hoe or adze, men pressed to clean out
the canals which irrigate the country. Mustapha chose to be
afraid I might come to mischief among these men, and insisted
I should go back to the boat under escort of two sailors. There
I spent the afternoon a little stupidly, taking occasional prome-
nades on shore, and inspecting the action of the *shadoof*, or
ordinary machine used for raising water from the Nile. This
machine is common up to the first cataract, above which the
sakia or wooden wheel, worked by buffaloes, supersedes it.
The *shadoof* is simply a long pole, balanced midway on a pivot,
and weighted at one end with a pear-shaped lump of Nile mud;
from the other hangs a leathern bucket; and the machine is
worked by a dark brown-skinned *fellah*, naked save a breech-
clout and orange-coloured cap. *Shadoofs* are always erected
in pairs, side by side, and where the bank is high three or four
pair, one above the other, are employed. The creaking of
these machines is hardly ever out of the Nile *voyageur's* ears,
and they add greatly to the picturesqueness of the scenery.

A large dahabeeh under the American flag was berthed
close by, and as I knew they could have no newspapers I sent
mine in, and so made the acquaintance of an American party,
a brother and two sisters, Cairo bound, and who had had no
European news for three months. I spent some time in their
boat smoking and doing coffee. Two large dahabeehs came in
later—one that of Lord B—— and the other of Colonel
P—— S——, to whom I had a letter of introduction, directed
vaguely " Egypt." I presented this ere the colonel was up,
misled by the early rising of the natives. The colonel returned
my call, and insisted on my carrying off an armful of novels
and some valuable books on Egyptian antiquities, which afterwards were very useful to me. Mustapha returned from the
bazaar somewhat late, in company with two highly-armed
individuals, whom he styled Bashi-Bazouks: whatever they
were, the three did pipes and talk until the small hours.
According to the custom of the river, our sailors were entitled
to a sheep at Minieh, but we gave them about eight shillings
instead; they bought some intoxicating mixture of hemp with
it, and smoked themselves stupid, for which Mustapha whacked
them all round with a stick. We left Minieh next day about
10-30 p.m., under a blaze of musketry: Mustapha had
purchased from some Cairene tradesmen, for £35, six of the
most dilapidated fowling-pieces I ever saw; they had originally

cost, I should say, some 20s. apiece at Birmingham, and had for years been let out on hire to travellers; locks, barrels, and stocks were equally rotten, but Mustapha would never understand why I invariably declined the loan of one of his guns. The blaze of musketry was due to the Arab propensity for making a row on all occasions, and was by way of salute to the Bey of Minieh. We invariably fired a salute whenever excuse could be got, and I invariably retreated as far as possible from the operators, generally Mahomet and a sailor or two.

Our next stopping place was a village or town named Shekh Timay, where we moored for the night. When breakfast-hour came Mustapha had disappeared, so I fed alone. A messenger presently came for me, and I was carried off to the house of the Bey of Shekh Timay, in the courtyard of which I found Mustapha and several native gentlemen seated on divans, smoking and drinking coffee. I joined the party, and found I was expected to breakfast. An adjournment was soon made inside, into a large 'whitewashed room, along two sides of which a divan or raised seat ran, covered with cushions and cloths. The windows had no glass, but bars across them, and a curtain hung over them, tied up in a knot. In the wall were one or two niches holding brass candlesticks and water bottles, while one or two cupboards had rudely-daubed, rather than painted, doors. Some beautiful Turkish carpets lay on the floor and divans. As it was some high Arabic festival, all the local aristocracy were continually coming in to pay their respects to the Bey. The meal commenced by the appearance of a servant with ewer and basin and napkins, and another with a brass tray on his head containing cakes of bread, some honey, and a dish of rice. All present washed their hands, tucked up their sleeves, and fell to with fingers, I among the rest; but I found poached eggs a puzzling dish to devour in that manner, with no instrument but a bit of bread. Some eight dishes followed, all good; and then hand-washing, pipes, and coffee. The whole party escorted us out of the town when we left, the Bey walking arm-in-arm with me: the parting was tremendous, such bowing and salaaming. The Bey, a friend, and his servant and gun, came with us in the boat as far as Roda, our next stopping place, the terminus at present of the Upper Egyptian Railway. Letters are carried on from here by foot runners, but the telegraph is continued as far as Khartoum.

4

At Roda we stayed two nights and a day for want of wind. We paid our respects to the local aristocracy, a very mighty Bey, dressed in European fashion, black surtout with pink cuffs and collar covered with gold lace. He presided over one of the Khedive's sugar manufactories, a huge white building, from which emanated a sickening smell of syrup. This syrup the Bey wished me to taste, but I declined; it acted on poor Mustapha as a fine emetic. The machinery is English, and hundreds of men are employed in the factory, all working nearly naked. I saw an unbroken string of camels, head to tail, nearly three miles long, driven by the wildest imaginable sons of the desert, enter the factory yard at one gate, deposit their burdens of sugar cane, and stalk out at another. In the bazaar I found a great prize—some tins of sardines for sale, and seized them as a substitute for butter; the native butter is nasty, and jam I had forgotten to bring. Our other purchases were bread, figs, coffee, and an enormous Nile fish, some 20lbs. weight, but eating very poor; it cost under eighteenpence.

I began by now to like old Mustapha, and found him good and intelligent company. What astonished me most was his power of smoking; he only desisted for meals, coffee, and prayers, for full five times a day did he go through the posturing and genuflections prescribed to strict Mussulmen by their creed, and that no matter what the place or company might be. The moment he awoke in the morning a lighted chibouk was thrust into his mouth, and that or a cigar never left his lips the whole day long; he retired for the night with pipe in mouth, and should he by chance awake during the night he smoked.

We sailed from Roda in company with a small dahabeeh, commanded by a funny little man, four years prisoner in Russia during the war. He entertained Mustapha with wonderful accounts of Russia; the best being that he prayed to his God, who thereon taught him the whole Russian language in one night. This successful linguist was some sort of small official on an inspection cruise; his cook had bolted, and so we fed him, for which he paid by yarns of Russian life, incomprehensible to me, but delightful to Mustapha, who ever an anon would utter "waugh" by way of approval and astonishment. The wind was feeble; we made but 15 miles between 11 a.m. and 5 p.m., and then moored for the night at some nameless village, which I and the Russian prisoner explored, partly for reasons of curiosity, partly of commissariat ; we purchased fifteen eggs for about twopence, and a cock and hen for fourteenpence ; the cock's spurs were worth all the money, for they were enormous. Mooring at small villages is rather stupid at nights ; there is nothing to do, and it is dark too early to permit a stroll : on the other hand I could tub matutinally in the open air, and have a morning walk under charge of a sable mariner to get milk or eggs ere the wind came. The north wind, as a rule, blows during the day and lulls at night, and by it our movements and progression were governed. The sailors enjoy their evenings highly ; they sit in a circle on the forecastle and tell stories, each man provided with six feet of sugar cane to chew, while one hookah (a cocoa nut and two canes) is handed round the party ; one fellow bangs the drain-pipe drum, and another the tambour, and a third sings a romantic sounding ditty with a perpetual chorus, each man rolling his head and eyes sentimentally to and fro, while the charms of some dusky Nile beauty are chanted out. They were a merry and civil lot, our crew : first and chief was the Reis (Captain or Pilot), Reis Daree, a Nile mariner of great skill, craft, and gravity, a grave and civil man, whom I much respected ; then came four A B's, the first a gigantic Berber, a black Arab from the cataracts ; then two editions of the same, Berbers also, but younger and more boyish ; the fourth an Arab of browner hue, a man who besought my advice as a physician, because "his belly had swelled," producing it for inspection : it had been bad for four months, and so far as I could judge, he was suffering from a severe rupture ; the poor wretch said he was taking daily doses of castor oil to cure himself, but on producing his bottle, it turned out to be rancid cod liver oil out of an old hair oil bottle. I, of course, could do nothing for him. These four worked the boat, towed it by a rope when the wind was foul, and were for ever singing and laughing ; their civility was wonderful, I could hardly stir without one of them jumping up, to give me an arm. Attendant on them, cook boy and what not, was a brown sprite, or Arab boy named Ryab, for ever grinning and in mischief, a most veritable pickle. The delight of these four and of Ryab was to greet me with "good morning," the sole English they knew, and to point out to me aught they fancied would be new or strange to me. Abdul-Azim came next, a retainer of Mustapha, a sour depressed man, who acted as cabin steward,

and whom I loathed for his servile air, and contrast to the
others. Mahomet, my man and cook, made up our party,
occasionally augmented by strays to whom we gave a lift. The
boat itself was one of the smaller sized dahabeehs, some forty
feet long : the afterpart was occupied by the cabins, of which
there were two : each occupying the whole width of the boat :
the foreward one was living and meal room in name, but we
generally lived and mealed *sub Jove*, and in it Mustapha slept,
a simple process ; he doffed his boots, rolled himself up in a
blanket, and lighted a pipe : passing through this cabin, a
passage, having right and left a bath and store-room, led to my
cabin in the stern, some eight feet long, with a seat on each
side : on one of these I made my humble and hard bed, while
the other covered, as was the floor, with prayer carpets, was
generally useful and ornamental. My cabin was well lit ; two
windows in the stern and three at either side, all with
Venetians to exclude the sun. Right and left to the entrance
to the foreward cabin were cupboards, one of which was the
larder, the other held an enormous filtering jar. The deck
foreward was lounging-place, smoking-place, and prayer-place
for Mustapha, but our favourite haunt was on the cabin roof,
where stood the ready and watchful Reis, tiller in hand. The
main mast, some 30 feet long, was far foreward, almost in the
bows, supporting across its head a yard longer than itself.
About the mast the sailors lived, and Ryab cooked their humble
victuals at a fire burning in an earthern pot, banked up with
mud. Foreward of the mast was a cooking place also built up
of mud ; here Mahomet reigned supreme, cooked and kept up
an everlasting supply of coffee and pipe lights. In the stern
was a small mizzenmast; the boat was painted green, relieved
with white, and with the British flag floating in the breeze
was no mean object to view.

After Roda our next great stage was Siout, or Osiout, the
capital of Upper Egypt, and the point where the caravans from
Darfur strike the Nile. Between these places we passed under
the lofty cliffs of Gebel Aboofaydee, feared by Nile mariners
for their sudden gusts and winds, and the favourite haunts of
crocodiles. The approach to Siout, or rather to its port, for
Siout is not on the river, is very winding and the boat had to
be trecked a great deal, hardish work for the crew, but amusing
to me, as I always jumped ashore with them for a walk. We
made Siout about 3 p.m. on Sunday, March 5th ; there are

some fine buildings at the port, a palace of the Pasha's among others, and several of the Khedive's steamers were lying here. Mustapha, the Reis and I set out on donkeys for Siout, distant some mile or more, and connected with the Nile by a raised dyke or causeway and a canal; the situation is very charming and the country rich and fertile. The local authority here was a Pasha, a much bigger man than any I had yet come across. Mustapha went to pay his respects to him, while I roamed about; presently a cavass came for me, and carried me to the great man, a fine portly Turk: he was holding high divan, secretaries in attendance, people coming and going in business, and bringing documents for his approval and signature; the room was whitewashed and furnished with hangings and curtains of black relieved with geometrical patterns on white. I was made to sit on his right hand, given a first rate cigar out of his own cigar case, and coffee in a cup of the usual small size with a silver gilt egg cup thing for saucer. Siout is a most thoroughly Oriental town; myself and the Pasha's London phæton drawn by two handsome chestnuts, and driven by a jet black driver in turban and white dress were the only products of Western civilization visible. With the bazaar I was delighted; it is the best in Egypt out of Cairo, wide and spacious and well shielded from the sun by matting. Mustapha had lots of things to buy here; but buying in the East is rather tedious, first you bargain for the price of the article and then you have a discussion as to the value of your money and a probable adjournment to a money-changer, and another bargain to make with him. This place is the seat of the well-known red and black pottery manufactories. I bought a few specimens, including some of the famous pipe bowls, and also some pretty and useful fly flaps.

Next morning the Pasha sent us a present of bread, and an order for our being towed by a steamer that was going up. So dilatory was the steamer that we set off without waiting, and, having a fine wind, outsailed it completely, carrying on both day and night. About 2 a.m. I was awoke by a noise, and went out. Mustapha was smoking in his blankets; he told me, "The Reis afraid; Gebel Shekh Heredee, big mountain, go puff." The mountain at this place is close to the river, and boats have to go cautiously for fear of sudden squalls, to which the place is liable. The cliffs were very fine,

the moon just full, and of a silvery brightness: a most beautiful
scene, but too cold to look at long; and so to bed again.

In the morning early we stopped at some village for milk
and eggs; I went with one of the sailors and found the village
—a collection of dogs and roofless screens of sugar canes,
miscalled houses. While the women got the milk I squatted
under a screen of cane and smoked with the head men,
delighting them highly with my proficiency in Arabic. The
children who crowded round were horrid sights, eyes sore and
swarms of flies walking over them; all had their heads shaved,
bar a tuft on the crown. The chief had a fine lad about two
years old shaven like the rest: in one ear he had a wonderful
ear-ring of silver, a large circle with a red and blue bead
thereon, and a rudely-cut model of a horse's head between
them. On returning to the boat, I found Mustapha shooting
doves, and also the owner of a sheep, for which he had given
16s. It was exactly like a brown shaggy retriever dog, and
had a hoarse voice like a bark. The Arabs killed him for us,
saying over him, "In the name of God : God is great ; God
give thee patience to endure the affliction he hath allotted
thee." This pious and beautiful performance in no way consoled or comforted the sheep, who struggled violently on
feeling the knife. The Reis objected to the purchase of this
sheep; he and his merry men wanted money, not mutton ;
remembering their "hasheeh" debauch at Minieh, Mustapha
declined, and walloped the Reis with a ropesend for his
impudence.

After passing Souhag, noticeable for a handsome white
house in a garden of acacias and palms, we made up for the
night at Mensheeh. Effecting thence an early start, the wind
failed, and we came to a stop at a village called Lahaiwa. To
improve the shining hours Mustapha and I set off to buy
"antiquities" from the Arabs ; so the whole village—grey-
bearded shekh, and bangled, necklaced, and braceleted women,
with swarms of children, shorn as to their heads and fly-eaten
as to their eyes, soon gathered around us : one imp, scarce able
to walk, lightly clad in a scull-cap and a brass ankle-bangle,
was specially moved by our appearance, and made hideous
noises. After an hour or two jabbering and smoking, we got
"twenty-three antiquities" for about 3s. 6d. or 3s. 8d.—scarabæi,
seals, idols, hawks—a bargain with which Mustapha was highly
charmed, for he said we could sell them to European travellers

for £3 or £4. We divided our treasures into two lots of eleven each, and tossed for choice and for the odd one, which I won and gave up to Mustapha. Eastern-like, he chizzled a little : he made me pay more than half the money, and he secured the better half of the spoils. This so pleased the old gentleman that he gave me some of his lot, and in 24 hours I had become owner of the whole lot by gift, except one, which I afterwards got in the same manner. It is a very odd trait in an Eastern's character, that in money matters he must do some one : he would do his father, mother, or brother ; it is not cheating, because each Eastern expects it, and is on guard. But the same man will be most hospitable and generous in other matters. For instance, Mustapha, after doing me delibe-rately out of twopence in dividing the expenses, yet gave me all the proceeds of our bargain. Again, he carefully excluded from the contract for my board certain luxuries, and yet he provided them and others for me gratis, even to cigars and tobacco. Not a soul else dared cheat me ; Mustapha saw to that ; and if I was purchasing in the bazaars, he would spend an hour in chaffering to save me a halfpenny ; in fact, to bargain, chaffer, and beat down seems a rich treat to an Eastern ; on no account will he forego it.

How was our next stopping-place ; the river winds greatly here, and Mustapha had an idea of riding across to Luxor. We landed at Hôw, a mass of ruins, where I picked up a curious coin, but no horses could be had. The Shekh pre-sented us with an enormous bundle of sugar canes, six or eight feet long, and each cane two inches in diameter. I contrived to eat a foot, but some of the crew chewed up their own length in no time ; it is horribly sweet.

Just past Hôw was a saint to be seen, one Santon Selim. I followed my crew, and found seated in the hollow of a bank a vast and monstrous black man, naked as ever he was born, weather-beaten by the storms of the few centuries the na-tives believe him to have sat there, into hideous yellow sores, while the thick thatch of hair or wool on his head is bleached the colour of straw. He answered exactly the description given in some mediæval writer of "a fat foul saint," but was jovial and jocose withal. He is ever surrounded by a circle of admirers, with whom he smokes and jokes, while he gets from every native that passes the tribute of a copper or two to keep him in food, tobacco, and firing ; shelter he has none, day and night he sits in his hollow ; prayers he never says, and his only claim to holiness is apparently his squalor and dirt.   The natives, however, believe that he has another body, which, clad in brightest green, is ever worshipping at Mecca before the prophet's tomb, while the unclad body squats in the hollow near How, and enjoys itself,—of that there is no doubt, he looked thoroughly happy.   From How, where we were on a Thursday, we went on rapidly, and arrived at Luxor on Saturday following at 11 a.m.   There we disembarked under a salute from guns, pistols, and cannons.

So ended my dahabeeh voyage.   For an invalid I can re-commend nothing better,—the balmy air, the utter laziness, are health-restoring, while, as the traveller floats along, a panorama of new and Eastern scenes is ever unrolled before him, serving to dissipate all *ennui* and divert his thoughts : the change from Western life is thorough, and thus beneficial in the highest degree to the jaded and wearied mind.   There is a splendour in the cloudless sky, an elasticity and warmth in the air to which the Western is wholly unaccustomed.   The scenery through which he glides is of a striking and varied character. At every turn he will see villages of mud huts, embowered in groves of palm, swarming with pigeons, and noisy with dogs ; white-domed tombs of saints and shekhs lurking 'neath the shelter of tall palms ; sandy shoals, alive with flocks of ducks and geese, and gay with the plumage of the flamingo and the ibis, and with strings of pelicans and cranes ; Nile boats of every kind, varying from luxurious dahabeehs, conveying some English traveller, or enormous barges, with 300 or 400 labourers for the Khedive's works, to dingy cangias and cobbled ferry boats, so laden as to require an extra gunwale of Nile mud and sticks ; great rafts of pottery ware, hugh ballasees, going to Cairo for sale ; busy *cafés*, nestling in the shade of far-spreading sycamores, with motley groups of customers ; creaking shadoofs, and sakias, or water wheels with slow pacing buffaloes ; fields of sugar cane, tobacco, wheat, or lentils ; and in the background, beyond the emerald strip of fertile valley, the yellowish rosy-hued hills of the desert.

Nor will the animal life which swarms upon the river banks fail, from its abundance, its rarity, and its newness, to attract the traveller's gaze.   Fox-red dogs and countless pigeons swarm round the villages, turreted and embattled with jars, wherein the latter multiply and replenish the air ; hostile to the pigeons sweep by brown bright hawks and kestrels, while bare-necked vultures, and kites, and hooded crows prowl for more disgusting food ; water fowl of many sorts swarm for the shoals ; flamingoes and cranes range themselves in military line, and the pink-eyed white ibis, sacred in the eyes of the old Egyptians, is interesting from that very fact ; herons, pelicans, spoonbills, and paddy birds, march about in grotesque, but lively processions ; crested hoopoes, and feather-crowned sparrows flit rapidly about, while sandpipers and plovers run about the shallows. Strings of camels pace along the banks, or are slowly ferried across ; buffaloes lounge lazily in the water, or plod slowly along the banks. Natives of all sorts swarm ; brown and poor fellaheen trudge along ; wealthy swells bestride donkeys, or more rarely, velvet and lace-bedizened horses. On the Nile one has only to live to be amused.

Then a stroll ashore with gun, if so minded, under the groves of palms, dates, and acacias ; all will delight, from the emerald-coloured lizards that dart about the broiling banks to the erect and stately-figured women, who come down, jars on head, to the Nile for water, and their quaint pot-bellied shaven-headed children. May I again re-visit Egypt, and again feast my eyes on all those wondrous sights !

LETTER V.

LUXOR.

Four small towns or villages now occupy the site of hundred-gated Thebes, namely, Luxor and Karnak on the eastern, and Goorna and Medinet-Haboo on the western bank of the Nile.

Parallel to the river Nile and about 150 yards from it runs the grand colonnade of the temple of Luxor, fourteen enormous granite pillars in double row; under these pillars stand two native houses, one that of Shekh Yuseef, made famous by the admiration of Lady Duff Gordon, and the other that of my landlord, Mustapha Agha, Consul or Consular Agent at Luxor for the kingdoms of Great Britain, Russia, and Belgium, and formerly for the United States of America. The house was approached by a flight of steep steps, and entered through a great timber door, fastened, on the rare occasions of its being shut, by a huge wooden lock, whose key was some eighteen inches long, but, which lock could easily be opened by the simple process of putting a hand round the staple. This led into the chief room of the house, having divans or sitting places built up all round; here the great business of the place went on; right and left of it were two other rooms, one dark, having no window and used chiefly for midday siestas; the other the reception room for all European and American travellers, and for natives of distinction; this was also my sitting room, and a charming one it was, with a divan down one side, and a table down the other under a window which gave me a peep into the chief room, and enabled me to take quiet mental photographs of Eastern oddities, who little suspected that a "giaour" was noting them down. The external window to this room was a door looking to the Nile; the room was papered in English fashion and ornamented by large mirrors. From the end of the chief room an open-air staircase led to a space on the roof having walls and window apertures, but neither roof nor window glass:

this roofless space was Mustapha's open-air or fine-weather bedroom, where he slept *sub Jove* on a vast palm-stick bedstead, with his faithful attendant Abgeed at his feet. From this space three detached groups of two rooms each were entered; one group was locked up, a second formed Mustapha's bedroom and private apartments, and the third were mine.

My "diggins" consisted of two whitewashed and plaster-floored rooms, new whitewashed and plaster-floored on my advent. The first one was a fine large room with windows on three sides, but precious few panes of glass; the deficiencies being supplied with linen, which was cooler. A palm-stick bedstead, two Arab carpets, a chair, and a few odds and ends were all my furniture, and in that lovely climate more than necessary; indeed my room looked precious like a barn, but that was its beauty. An innocent English lady traveller one day asked me why Mustapha did not make his house comfortable; paper and carpet the rooms and glaze the windows. He did not do so, as I replied, for the simple reason that to do so would be to make his house uninhabitable; the carpets would gather the desert dust, and after twelve hours of khamseen wind be full of sand; no paste ever invented would in Theban climate make paper adhere to Theban walls; it would from the dryness, peel off in great flakes, as it did in Mustapha's one papered room, cracking from the parched walls with pistol-like reports; carpets and wall paper, curtains and hangings, would all, in Luxor, be choice lurking and breeding places for scorpions and lizards, and even for poisonous snakes; as for chairs, tables, and the like, unless made of iron, the dry Egyptian heat would twist, and warp, and crack them into all sorts of shapes in no time; an Egyptian must sit on a divan, or on the ground, nature forbids him chairs. Thus it is that in Egypt, and countries of similar climate, nature itself makes a bare and barren, almost unfurnished house, the most convenient residence, and the one that can best be kept clean and sweet. Of course my lady friend could not be convinced that at Luxor Mustapha's house (the sort of house all swell natives have) was not infinitely more luxurious and comfortable than any English house planted down there could be.

To return to my rooms; my second room was not of much use; intended for my tub room, it was untubbed in by me for two reasons: *imprimis*, there was no tub in all Luxor; *secondo*, a daily swim in the Nile was better by far than any tub that ever was hooped. These rooms formed my den; from the larger room I had the most lovely view over the Nile, extending from Medinet-Haboo to El Goornah. I could see the ruins of Western Thebes, with the ever-grand Colossi of the Plains solemnly silent in their midst; behind them the pink and purple glowing Libyan hills, o'er which the sun set gloriously in such a flood of rich colours as can only be seen in the desert. This was the view from the front of Mustapha's house, and often did I enjoy it from seats and carpets placed on the sand under the shadow of the great grand columns. Indeed, under the shade of these great grand columns did we live much of the day and night; there in the open air did Mustapha and the Governor of Luxor administer justice and transact municipal business: there was much chatter parliament got through, and many chibouks and cups of coffee discussèd : there did we frequently dine *al fresco* in the dark after the sun had set, and smoke and gossip in the moonlight or starlight until well nigh the small hours. Nor were we singular in our habits; all the open space in front of the houses right down to the Nile would, after dark, be full of jabbering laughing groups of natives, who seemed all alive in contrast to their habits during the heat of the day.

Some half-mile away from this place Mustapha owned another house, a new one, yet unfurnished, but which had a large garden to it. It was a nice resort for an afternoon's lounge, there to lie in the shade under the trellised vines and the scent of the lemon plants, smoking until drowsily lulled to sleep by the creaking of the *sakias* and *shadoofs* employed to irrigate the garden, while Said the head groom, and old Hassan the head gardener, would gather me bunches of roses, marigolds, and fragrant lemon leaves. The whole of this garden was cut up by little water-courses, which were constantly kept full by *shadoofs* and *sakias*, at which relays of labourers worked all day. The greater part of the space was devoted to vines, which were trained up mud pillars, and over horizontal frame works of palm sticks, under which was the most delicious shade. One corner was full of English vegetables, grown from seeds given to my landlord, but which were all running to waste from ignorance, and neglect. The only fruit ripe during my stay was a poor white cherry. Mustapha's farm lay all round this garden, some magnificent crops of barley being just over the mud wall. A camel, and a buffalo or two were generally tied up outside the garden, and in a corner of it two horses were tethered; one a dark brown stallion, which I generally rode, the other, a young chestnut mare, bred by Mustapha himself, a beautiful animal, but almost unbroke. Southwards of Mustapha's dwelling house extends the ruins of the great court of the temple of Luxor, now used as a Government depôt for receipt of taxes in kind. Frequently would I be awoke at first sunrise by the groans of the camels, who were being loaded there. The house used by Lady Duff Gordon is perched up aloft on the end of this place, and beyond it is the tomb of some saint, and a back-water of the Nile with the massy remains of an old Roman wharf.

Northwards are, among a congeries of mud huts, the ruined approaches of the temple, over which the one solitary obelisk rears its lofty head, pining for its brother, now in Paris. In here is the mosque, with the tomb of some Mahomedan saint, one Yuseef Aboo Hadad and his three sons, in a building behind it. On Friday the mosque would be crammed, green banners over the doors, and rows of worshippers, unable to find room within, genuflecting outside. They all stood up, sat down, turned their heads right and left like soldiers at drill; the oddest sight was, when they bowed until their fore-heads touched the ground, while their red, white, and green turbans made the mosque look like a tulip bed agitated by the wind. Between the mud houses and the river were the houses of Teodoros the Prussian Consul, and of one Ali Murad; beyond was a sandy plain, which was the market-place of Luxor, and a narrow lane leading thereto was its mean and shabby bazaar. Across this market-place, on what was once the site of a Coptic Church, are the graves of four Englishmen and one or two other Europeans who have died in Luxor. These tombs were in a miserable state, and during my stay I had them repaired and put in order as well as I could. I also succeeded in identifying the tombs, and marking them, and put a plan and register of them in Mustapha's book of visitors, and an expression of my hope that future travellers would give a look to the place, dreary and shadeless enough, and thus stimulate the natives to keep it in repair.

About Luxor the hills on either side of the river fall back to a considerable distance from it, thus giving a wide extent of cul-tivated ground, all which is under water during the inundations.

In this tract are raised most wonderful crops of barley, beans, wheat, sugar cane, tobacco, lentils, &c., with an occasional orchard or enclosure of dates or palms, where camels may be seen grazing with foals at foot, the oddest and most ungainly animals imaginable, and gifted with voices like those of peacocks. The tobacco plant is curious, much resembling a tall lettuce run to seed, and having a whitish blue blossom at top. Water melons and cucumbers grow like mad in the mud at the river side, as the water falls during the summer season. I much enjoyed a walk or ride through the country: strange and grotesque humanities would pop up from unexpected places; perhaps a savage woman with woolly hair twisted into ringlets, silver rings in her ears and a gold one in her nose, or wild looking Nubians. One boy I captured for examination had the brass part of an old Eley's cartridge stuck through his ear for ornament. The roads are mere tracks, and all the carrying is done by donkeys, buffaloes, and camels—horses being never used except for riding. The beasts too that I came across in the fields were wonderful; goat-like sheep, dog-like goats, besides the mangy and supercilious buffaloes, and quaint camels already mentioned.

DRAMATIS PERSONÆ.

Of these, old Mustapha was of course the chief; a very strict Mahomedan, who traced his descent from the Prophet himself. He told me that at the time of the Mahomedan conquest of Egypt three Arab brothers came to Egypt and settled, one at Luxor, a second at Karnak, and a third at some other point on the Nile. From the Luxor one Mustapha is descended, and is head of the Luxor and Karnak descendants of the two brothers who settled there. He was a strict follower of his religion, and very regular in his devotions; at the same time he was a man of liberality in religion, and did not look on me as an irredeemable heathen, though he did tell me that he and all good Mahomedans considered all Christians to be idolators, an opinion he salved over by saying, "Christian religion very good for you, Mahomedan religion very good for me; both pray the same God." He presented the site on which the present Coptic Church of Luxor stands, and he also provides a room in his house for English service, whenever a congregation and clergyman can be found. He was, during my visit, almost induced by two Italian Roman Catholic Missionaries to give them a site; but as there were no Catholics in the place, and not likely to be any, he did not.

To me Mustapha was wonderful kind, and after my interests he looked sharply. To all he was open-handed and generous, except with money; that no Eastern will part with unless forced. He kept free house for all who choosed to feed; me he furnished with many luxuries not included in, or even excluded, from our board, and was specially angry at my bringing tobacco. "What for you buy tobacco? Abgeed got plenty in my magazine: tell him." The old gentleman was wont to take almost ludicrous care of me. When I went for my daily bath in the Nile, he would send his son and a huge one-eyed fellow, named Hassanein, to swim about me; while Abdul Azim was in attendance with Mustapha's English boat. " You take care," would be the old boy's speech when he saw me going Nilewards about bathing hour, and then he would send Hassanein and Abdul Azim after me, rather to my boredom; but, indeed, Europeans are considered to require much help, and my native servant always insisted on helping me up stairs to bed as if I was eighty.

I have said before, that though Mustapha could neither read nor write, yet he could speak Arabic, Turkish, Persian, Hindostanee, French, Italian, and English; the latter two almost perfectly. He had travelled everywhere,—from London to Calcutta, from Cape Town to Persia. His dress was an odd mixture of English and Arabic; he was generally clad in long dark stockings, knickerbockers, black vest, or else a red one— embroidered with gold. Over these he put on a long white linen dressing gown that reached to his heels, and over that again a black surtout; and in his best attire he looked a very gentlemanly old boy. Spite of his travels and his shrewdness, he was a devout believer in dervishes, and such rascals, and also in magic, though a little afraid of being laughed at by Europeans for this. Like all natives, Mustapha had a horror of the French, and of Napoleon. When I read him the news of the capture of the Archbishop of Paris by the Communists, his comment was at once, " Very glad, hope they kill him; bad man, he and Napoleon have one great intrigue to make the Mussulman Christian. I pray de God all the French go to the debbil." This is what the poor Archbishop earned by attending at the opening of the Suez Canal. Mustapha is a great admirer of

ivory, about which the Reis was very mysterious, refusing to let
me see them, and mooring well out of my reach.

Other leading inhabitants of Luxor were Teodoros, the
Prussian Consul, Ali Murad the American, and Snodi the
Austrian, none of whom spoke English, but Teodoros had a son
who did, and with whom I used to go and have an occasional
pipe, and a glass of some curious *liqueur*.

There is in Luxor an American gentleman who has resided
there for fifteen years, and devoted himself to the study of
hieroglyphics with considerable success.   He collects and sells
antiquities and relics from the tombs and temples, and is generally supposed to be the fabricator of all the false antiquities and
relics in Egypt, but this is not true.   As he refuses to pay
black-mail to the dragomen and the guides, they spread these
reports.   He showed me a select· collection of relics among
which were most beautiful things, some being scarabæi carved
in emerald.   Travellers can rely on· his selling only genuine
articles.

There were one or two other public characters in the place
worthy of mention; a very nasty boy, a snake-charmer who
used to bring me live scorpions, but I noticed he disjointed
their tails first ; he was anxious to eat them for a consideration,
but I declined, purchased the brutes for three-half-pence a
piece, and plunged them into a bottle of whiskey to keep as
curiosities.   Then there was an idiot or two, considered holy
by the natives, but rather alarming to strangers : one Abdera-
soul, a very humble fellah, who lived in an old tomb, and was
the owner of a wonderful gun, was a very decent, honest man,
never bothered for baksheesh.   He was very anxious I should
go with him to shoot hyenas, but this meant sleeping out all
night, which I was afraid to risk, and the chance of an hyena
was very doubtful.   He is a good man to take as a guide on
sporting expeditions, and a handful of gunpowder will put him
in the seventh heaven.

LUXOR   HABITS, HORSES,   ETC.

I spent my time at Luxor in a very *dolce far niente* manner ;
the house used to rise at some very early hour, so early that I
never could succeed in finding it out, but I believe that Mustapha got up somewhere about four o'clock.   I made an appearance between six and eight, and breakfast depended upon my

appearance. After it Mahomet or Abgeed brought me a lighted chibouk and coffee *à la* Arab, or without milk or sugar, a refreshment that appeared about hourly during the day.

My next proceeding would be my Arabic lesson; this generally came off on the steps, outside the house, when I would sit and count my fingers, and repeat my sentences and words to Achmet and Yuseef amid an admiring circle of natives, who took intense interest in the proceedings. Then I would move inside and give Achmet an hour or so of English, make him read to me, and also dictate to him in English. My great difficulty was to find, in my limited library, a suitable book of big enough type for his weak eyes. The Bible he would not look at, possibly afraid it might damage his strict Mahomedanism.

The rest of the day I would walk or ride about, followed by Yuseef; possibly go some excursion with passing travellers or with Mustapha. Visitors from the travellers' dahabeehs would call and have a pipe and a talk, and thus the day would go without, as a rule, my doing anything very energetic. So soon as the sun began to go down, about six o'clock, I had a glorious plunge in the Nile, jumping from a boat into deep water, and never touching bottom at all during my swim. Almost always I was accompanied by the retinue I have before mentioned, as sent by Mustapha to look after my safety, though now and then I would give some of them the slip. At this time, dusk, the whole bank of the Nile would be alive; all the women in the place came down for water, each erect as a dart, and bearing on her head an enormous jar; when filled, her companions lift this up to her head again, and away the woman goes, balancing with ease, on her head, a weight that many men would not like to lift. All the donkeys, horses, camels, and buffaloes in the place are, at this time, brought out to water, and in many cases for a swim, which they seemed highly to enjoy. One beast of a buffalo gave me a rare fright. I was swimming away in the dusk, when a huge animal came against me; for a moment I fancied it was a crocodile, and that I was an eaten man, but it was a buffalo, as much afraid of me as I of the supposed crocodile. The donkeys and buffaloes were generally under charge of an innumerable mob of children, who raced the donkeys about, and made a frolic of the whole matter, careering round me and shouting, "Good night; I spike English, baksheesh," to which my answer was the Arab chaff, "mish, mish;" (when the

apricots blossom, *i. e.* never, for they never blossom in Egyyt).
The horses were generally treated to a rattling good gallop.
One man, the owner of a white stallion, was very fond of a display; he would pelt down on me full gallop, stopping the horse
in full speed as its head came over mine; or he would go full
bang at a wall and stop as he touched it. I always found these
evening scenes full of life, amusement, and interest. When
this hubbub subsided it was time for dinner, generally indoors,
but sometimes *al fresco* by lantern light. Frequently Mustapha
and I dined with travelling parties in their boats, or they dined
with us, or came up for a smoke and talk. Thus and by reading (books were plenty, for each traveller I met changed with
me, and many gave me books seeing I was alone), did I kill my
sojourn at Luxor. More special events I have jotted down
separately, and the great sights, the ruins (in whose examination I of course spent much time), I have described apart.

My great want was a gun: I could have had quail ducks
and pigeons for ever, but I had no gun, and my regard for my
valuable person would not allow me to let off any weapon out of my
host's crazy armoury. I might too have got many strange and
beautiful birds, and a jackal or two. I saw two large fellows in
broad day at Karnak; very like foxes but bigger, and duskier,
not so red coloured, and with beautiful brushes. My chief
slaughter of beasts was confined to a curious sort of lizard, a
disgusting white transparent beast, harmless, though the natives
say the contrary. These lizards have five toes on each foot,
and a sucker on each toe, and are thus able head downwards to
run about a ceiling with as much ease as a fly. They chirp
like a bird. Even dead the natives would not handle them,
but I had no such fears, and came to no harm in consequence.
My great exploit was the massacre of flies; they are the real
pests of Egypt, and swarm everywhere, infesting the unwashed
faces of children to a loathsome extent. They were in my bedroom by hundreds of thousands. One Sunday morning I awoke
and found every square inch of my room covered with dead
flies: the like had happened nowhere else, and neither I nor
any one has ever been able to account for it. The natives admired me greatly, "curious fellow that Englishman; he kill all
the fly," and put it down as magic, and me as a magician.

One luxury I enjoyed at Luxor, that was horses: Mustapha
had eight or nine, these horses stand out unclothed day and night,
tethered to a rope fastened to pegs, and stretched out along

the ground; to this both fore legs and one hind one are fastened tight. In very hot weather a shelter of palm branches is put over them supported on four palm sticks. Most of the horses about this part of Egypt are Arabs of the Howara breed with good necks and shoulders; poor trotters, but rare good walkers, and gallopers for short distances; the favourite native pace is an amble; few of them can jump so much as a broomstick. They are mostly unshod in Upper Egypt; indeed, the nearest smith to Luxor capable of shoeing was at Keneh, 60 miles away. The apple of Mustapha's eye was a chesnut mare bred by himself. Arab-like, one of Mustapha's most valued possessions were his horse fixings, for which he had paid a large sum. The saddle and saddle cloth were of blue velvet with housings and holsters to match, all covered with gilt metal, while the head-piece and bridle were hung with countless gilt tassels. Bridle and whip are all in one, that is, at the end of reins is a long strip ending in a ball and loops for a lash. The saddle is peaked very high before and behind. The stirrups are murderous weapons, great shovel-shaped things, with sharp corners used for spurs; very awkward to manage, and dangerous, as one might injure a horse with them; most horses are more or less blemished by their use. I had a lesson or two in "horse play" as practised by the natives, but was much bothered particularly when on the before-mentioned white stallion (who was wicked) by my awkward stirrups; with English stirrups and whip I should have had little difficulty. Each player is armed with a long palm stick or "jereed," and they carry on a sort of tilting match, careering one round the other in very small circles. Another great point is to gallop rapidly round a very small circle, then reverse the other way, and do the figure of 8: or two riders will gallop round and round in a circle keeping the points of their jereeds touching on the ground in the centre of the circle.

EASTERN EXPERIENCES.

DEJEUNER, NOT A FOURCHETTE.

During my stay at Luxor I several times dined Arab-fashion both at Mustapha's house, and at other places. One description will serve for nearly all, and I will select a dinner Mustapha gave to some passing travellers. Including myself, my own county furnished three guests; America gave one, in the person of a young banker of the great house of Astor; Westminster Abbey furnished a canon of most gorgeous appearance, and Rome sent us her English chaplain; Shekh Yuseef and Mustapha made up the number to eight, and we agreed that as a gastronomical jury we were a well selected lot, qualified to give an author-itative opinion on any dish that came before us; we got our appetites in condition, sharpened our teeth, and prepared for the fray.

The first stage of an Eastern dinner is that each guest has given him a napkin, sometimes gorgeously embroidered, to use during dinner: a couple of servants then appear, one with a basin with a false bottom, perforated with holes, and with a piece of scented soap, the other with a jug of water, which he pours over each guest's hands, a very necessary preliminary to a dinner to be eaten with fingers. Meanwhile other servants bring in a stool, which they place on the floor, and then balance on it a large circular copper tray; this is the dinner table, and round it the guests squat on carpets and cushions: plates, knives, and forks are there never a one; only a cake of bread, a napkin, and a spoon to each guest. A bowl of soup is placed in the centre of the tray, and into it each man dips his spoon; the soup Mustapha gave us was pronounced by the jury to be equal to any that ever came under its notice; then followed fruit and boiled fowls, and next a whole roast sheep; these we tore to pieces with our fingers, as we did a huge roast turkey

stuffed with rice and vegetables, which was most excellent:
then succeeded (only one dish at a time and all eaten with
fingers) roast chickens, a dish of chicken liver, (Heliogabalus
himself could have had nothing better), a dish of kabobs à la
Turk, stewed kidneys, a sort of Irish stew, tomatoes, and little
balls of seasoned rice wrapped up in tender vine leaves. For
sweets we had boiled rice, a species of blanc-mange, mish-
mish, or preserved Damascus apricots, and a dish of rice boiled
in milk, Persian-fashion, which we all agreed to be simply
divine. All this dinner was cooked by an old Nubian woman,
a slave named Mabouba, nearly eighty years old, and for thirty-
five years in Mustapha's ownership; she cooked it all at a sort
of oven built of mud, with a charcoal fire. For drink, by a
relaxation of the usual Arab rule, we had claret, and each man
his own glass: Arab swells would have stuck to water, and all
drank out of one glass, or rather bottle. Then we washed our
hands again, and lounged about the divans, while dancing girls
performed ingracefully for our benefit, dusky charmers with
silver bangles on wrists and ankles, bells on their waists, castanets on their fingers, blue tatooes on their chins, and the most
indifferent of private characters: the jury considered that those
charmers who weren't as ugly as sin were uglier. The musicians
were a drummer on a sort of drain pipe, a tambour player, and
a violin player; the violin player was a very celebrated man,
and his performance (that is how he did it, for what he did
was "pigs under a grate") was extraordinary; his instrument
was a bent stick with two horse-hair strings, midway on which
was a cocoa-nut shell, covered with parchment on one side, and
perforated with holes on the other, to form a sounding board.
During this performance we smoked and drank coffee; perpetually little cups of unsweetened and unmilked mocha were
handed round, while long yards of silk and gold covered pipes,
with mouthpieces of amber big as eggs, were ever being put to
our lips, all ready alit, by attentive servants.

This is the common form of a native dinner, but of course
there are trifling variations. The very first day of my arrival
at Luxor, Mustapha Agha and I dined with one Ali Murad, a
native gentleman of the place, the Brazilian Consular agent
there, and Mustapha's supercessor in his American Consular
agency. This was a dinner to afford a French Duchess and her
daughter an opportunity of dining Arab-fashion. The dinner
took place at the usual time, just after dark, or about six

o'clock, at Ali's house, in a whitewashed room with broken
windows, much resembling a stable loft, and lighted by a
mixture of stable lanterns and oil lamps, but carpeted with
beautiful Turkey or Persian rugs. The Duchess, a *passée*
affected Frenchwoman, arrived shortly after Mustapha and
myself. Her daughter was with her, and also an English-
woman, either companion or lady's maid. Another guest
was one Ali Bey, an enormously tall Arab, the Bey or
Lord-Lieutenant of Keneh, having Luxor under his rule : a
French Baron, cousin of the Duchess, and our host, completed the party. The dinner table was as usual a large
circular tray placed on a stool, and we all, some eight in
number, squatted on cushions on the floor, and ate with
our fingers out of the dishes. At this the Duchess and the
Frenchman were quite *au fait*. She took pieces from the
natives' fingers and swallowed them, and gushed with delight
and conversation all the while. The daughter did not get on
so well, as she could hardly eat for laughing ; and, indeed,
Madame la Duchesse, with the leg bone of a sheep in her hand,
and gnawing it, was a sight for gods and men : the companion
was rather too grand for such a manner of feeding, but the Baron
was a fine performer. After our dinner at Ali's, we all, preceded by the Duchess, moved to another room, where we
found four native ladies in gay attire, much bangles and necklaces. The Duchess rushed forward and shook hands with
them all in her very best manner : I, in my then innocence,
thought our host must be a very advanced Mussulman indeed,
and that these ladies were his four wives, and I followed her
grace's example, but soon discovered that they were anything
but the characters one would expect a Duchess to associate
with. Pipes and coffee appeared immediately, and until long
past midnight did we drink coffee and smoke. The Duchess
smoked seven of these pipes, and as many cigars, which she
produced out of an ivory cigar case ; her companion smoked ;
the dancing girls danced until they wellnigh dropt ; their
music (the usual pigs under a grate) was unceasing ; thicker
and thicker grew the atmosphere, until among us we brewed
a very neat little pandemonium in mimic.

The night following this, Mustapha had the Duchess to
dinner, and also Lord and Lady D——. I am afraid Lady
D—— was rather unprepared for and surprised at the finger
business ; she was also surprised at the Duchess, who in her

turn was rather suppressed by Lady D.'s presence, but who consoled herself by telling the gentlemen very *French* stories. One story she told is worth record : she listened to the singing of her boat's crew, picked up words and tune, and then, thinking to gratify them, performed for their benefit : they *were* gratified, demanded an *encore*, and her grace recommenced. At this moment appeared the dragoman, horrified, and with reason ; her grace was singing the most indecent song in the whole Arabic language. Mademoiselle de —— does not smoke : the Duchess, enjoying a long pipe, said to Lady D——, " so very odd ; I smoke, all my sons smoke ; I can't get my daughter to smoke."

AN EMBARRASSING REPUTATION.

The art of medicine is not much advanced among the natives. The barber is generally the local surgeon, and he bleeds his patients to death. Charms and magic are greatly relied upon. . I saw one unhappy lad suffering from severe bleeding at the nose ; a holy man held his head, and holy man and fainting patient were hard at work reciting the Koran when I appeared. Being a hakem or physician of great repute among the natives, I was called in, and prescribed cold water and the door key down the patient's back. I was, on one occasion, introduced to a very holy and saintly physician, a pilgrim from Bagdad, an old man, beautifully dressed in pure white, and carrying a long staff and a white fan in his hands. He was rather offended at my curiosity about him, and particularly at my touching his fan ; however, he condescended to prescribe for me, and proposed to bleed me at intervals of six inches down my left side, and rub me with lemon juice. As may be imagined, I did not follow the Bagdad practitioner's advice, but I asked him for a charm such as I had seen him give Mustapha's son. He would not give me one, for he said I was a scoffer and the son of a dog, or language to that effect. Mustapha had a much better prescription for me, " Live like Arab man,—plenty breakfast, plenty lunch, plenty dinner, plenty beans, plenty meat, plenty water, and plenty horse," not, however, meaning me to eat or drink the horse. He also strongly advocated the " Luxor doctor," as the natives call the seat under a certain couple of the columns of Luxor, and if fine air is a doctor, that seat deserves its reputation, a reputation it has enjoyed (*on dit*) from the days of Remeses the Great. Mustapha told me the Coptic bishop had all this in a book.

My troubles as a hakem arose from having a small medicine chest, and from having given a sailor a piece of diachylon plaster, which he immediately applied to the mainmast of his ship, and in due course his finger healed. I first became aware of my reputation by meeting in the fields three vast and extensive black gentlemen, who surrounded me, and I at first rather fancied, meant to rob me. After wondrous kotoings, one of them presented me with a few yards of sugar cane (as fee), and then produced a knife, his head, and a large tumour thereon, and signified by signs that I was to apply the knife to the tumour. I fled like the wind, leaving the three black individuals with their mouths wide open. On another occasion a whole deputation arrived to ask me to go and doctor a child that was choking. I flatly refused, fancying I should do more harm than good. I was made to go ; but, luckily, on arrival, I found the wretch had gone to sleep ; and so, looking as wise as possible, I said I would not disturb him. Another time one Snodi, a man of local consequence, wanted me to go and prevent some mother or aunt of his, an old woman of eighty years and odd, from dying. I, by the way of evasion, told him she had lived long enough ; but he stuck to it that caster oil would lengthen her life (an Arab will confidently take castor oil for a broken leg). As I did not believe him, I declined to waste castor oil on the old lady, and sent her a rhubarb pill. I never heard the result ; I presume the old lady lived. I frequently gave rhubarb pills instead of castor oil, which I really could not spare, but one man I nearly "castor oiled" to death. He came for a dose, and I sent him one, which produced the most terrible effects ; this convinced him that it was the right medicine for him, and he applied next day for another and got it, as I did not recognize him. Dose No. 2 almost sent him to his grave, and he appeared a third day for a third dose. Then I found him out, and was horrified ; far from being a black man, he was, from much castor oil, rapidly turning pale. One man having ague made things doubly sure. First, he went to his priest, a Copt ; the priest wrote him out a neat charm in Cufftee on his (the patient's) left ankle, and gave him three charms on paper ; these he was to burn and inhale the smoke, and yet the greedy beggar wanted quinine from me and got it too.

An European is sure to be taken for a doctor in Egypt : it seems hard to refuse, particularly when he may be able to help in small cases, and yet he will find himself drawn into very awkward positions. A plaster for a cut, or a bread poultice for a gathered hand (a common thing with the Nile sailors) was within my knowledge, but because such was, I was expected to be *au fait* with all medical skill, and thought a churl if I hung back. My great success was in scorpion bites : my first patient was a strong woman, and a dose of ammonia put her right, but my second was a child, and I was afraid it would go hard with him. I was taken into a native hut, where about a dozen women were crowding, and howling round the lad, and anxious I should use the knife ; of course I refused, but administered brandy and ammonia, and then boldly said the child would do well, a prediction I hazarded on faith of the loudness of his yells. Next morning he was all right, and a grateful deputation of father, mother, and infant appeared to kiss my hand.

During the course of my stay a genuine English doctor appeared, a very nice fellow ; he spent a day in doctoring the village, and left their medicines, made up in old whisky bottles, with me. It is not safe to trust a native with medicine : give him medicine for a week, and he will bolt it all at once. I had some trouble to keep some of the patients to their prescriptions, which did them good.

MARKET DAY IN THE EAST.

A favourite lounge of mine was the Luxor market on Tuesday, the weekly market day ; it is held on an open place, just past the bazaar ; there gather weekly 2,000 wild Arab males and females, with, perhaps, half as many donkeys ; they sell wool, cotton, linen, palm mats and sticks, tobacco, camels, goats, donkeys, and buffaloes. I amused myself once by bidding for a camel, and found I could have a small white one for £6, and a brown fellow, big as a house, for £8. The various dealers sit in rows according to their trades ; money-changers in one row ; cobblers in another, cobbling like mad, and with lots of red shoes for sale ; eggs and poultry in one place ; pigeons in another ; sugar canes in a third ; while sham jewellery, Manchester cottons, fleeces (black and brown, never white), each have their ordained place. I generally spent a few coppers in odd trifles, skullcaps, brass earrings, or palm sticks ; sometimes I helped Abgeed to buy sheep, pigeons, melons, or cucumbers for the house, and then comforted myself with Arabic beer or coffee at the *cafés*. My chief business of importance at these bazaars was to get money, English or Arab, changed ; no easy job. I used to go down a long row of money-changers, and see who would bid highest for my sovereigns. This weekly bazaar or market is distinct from, but adjacent to, the ordinary bazaar, a narrow lane of mud-built caverns, in one of which a weaver used to interest me by weaving deftly at a loom about the size of a cigar box. There was only a *café*, and a store kept by two Greeks, that could at all pretend to be called shops. Now and then I would drop into the *café* and have a pipe and some coffee, and occasionally fall in with some amusing scenes. On one occasion I traded my pocket handkerchief with a native for his, embroidered by his wife or wives with flowers. So poor was the bazaar that ink could not be purchased in it. My stock ran short, and I found I should have to send thirty miles for more. Yuseef, however, was equal to the occasion. I gave him a sixpence and an empty whisky bottle, and in half-a-day he returned, black from top to toe, with some he had made ; it smelled and looked odd, but it marked.

CHICKEN HATCHING EXTRAORDINARY.

One market day I invested the large sum of three piastres (threepence), in the purchase of brass jewellery. This intensely amused Mustapha, for though curious to me, such things were mere naught to him. He kept going off into a sort of chuckle to himself over my proceedings. However, it seemed to remind him of other sights ordinary to him, but curious to me, for as we were, the same afternoon, going to his garden, he said, "I show you something very handsome," and dived behind a screen of sugar canes, and through a sort of dog hole in a mud wall. Much wondering, I followed, and found myself in a lofty apartment steaming with artificial heat. Right and left were raised platforms, perhaps 6ft. by 18ft., perfectly covered with eggs in every state of hatching ; in some the bird was chipping the egg, in others it was rather more advanced, while in many cases the chicks were just out and crawling over the eggs. The space between the platforms, divided into compartments, was covered so close with newly-hatched chicks that we had to brush them away to find foot-room. There must have been thousands of both eggs and chicks. The attendants of course set upon us for baksheesh ; a copper or two satisfied them, and in their gratitude they in-sisted on my taking away a half-hatched chick, much to my embarrassment. The process was completed in my pocket, and I was heartily glad to find a native to take the beast, and give it a chance for life. Another establishment of the same sort was under the same roof. Mustapha was the ground landlord of both, and received an annual rent of 500 or 800 fowls, I for-get which. The establishment does not produce its own eggs; it hatches those of its customers gratis, returning so many chickens for so many eggs, the balance being the manufacturers' profit. This mode of artificially hatching eggs is of great antiquity in Egypt, and mentioned by many ancient authors.

A FLARE-UP IN A COURT OF JUSTICE.

Many were the interesting scenes I here witnessed under the grand columns which stood in front of Mustapha's house. Sometimes an old native, earnest and graphic, even pantomimic in relating some tale of woe ; sometimes a dervish or a traveller from afar, amusing his hearers by accounts of foreign countries ; sometimes a stately Bey, Effendi, or Shekh on ceremonious visit bent ; now a conjuror or snake charmer, or perhaps some work-man for orders. Once I saw a sad, but too frequent scene: twenty people sent to prison by Mustapha and the Governor, because one of the family had deserted from his regiment at Cairo. There was terrible weeping and wailing, but the orders from Cairo were imperative. On one great occasion a trial was held here—some sailors belonging to an English party had been fighting with the country people, and had in turn been well thrashed and robbed by the market police. Mustapha was chief judge ; his puisne judges were two native swells and myself; we sat on chairs under the columns and drank coffee and smoked pipes ; around sat the whole town on their hams like monkeys. An old Copt, in a tremendous black turban, also on his hams, took down the evidence with a reed and an inkhorn, and for this purpose each witness squatted on his

hams cheek-by-jowl with the Copt. ' The witnesses witnessed
and gesticulated ; the chief and his puisnes looked wise ; and
the town grunted " waughs" of emotion at intervals. The
barber or surgeon spoke to the wounds, when suddenly one
witness called one of the puisne judges a liar, whereon the
learned puisne knocked him head over heels minus a tooth or
two. Instantly the whole court was in a hubbub; this puisne, who
now writes, was up the steps, chibouk and all, in half a crack.
The chief had his pipe put out and broken ; the Copt and his
papers were rolled over, and a free fight seemed imminent. At
length the tumult was allayed; Chief Justice Mustapha fined
his learned brother about ten shillings, and adjourned the
Court until next day. The defendants were completely enveloped in chains and led off, while the wounded complainants
had to remain with their sores undoctored for another day, that
being the law ; the evidence must not be tampered with until
the trial is over. Next morning the defendants caught it.
Mustapha had them *corbagged ;* they were laid on the ground
and flogged by two men with corbags or whips of hippopotamus
hide. None of the witnesses were sworn on the trial. It
appears the custom is to swear them only on particular points,
thus on this trial it came out that the complainants had been
beaten and robbed ; of that there was no doubt. The question
then arose, of how much ? and each complainant, four in all,
said he had been robbed of an English pound—a most unlikely
story. The Koran was then produced, and they were told to
swear to the pound : each man declined. Mustapha thereon
ordered the defendants to be flogged, and to pay each complainant ten shillings in recompense of wounds and losses.
The *fracas* came under Mustapha's jurisdiction, as English
Consul, because the sailors were in English employ.

    While out riding one day I saw an example of rough-and-
ready justice which highly amused me. Mustapha, the Governor
of Luxor, and myself had crossed the river and were going to
the telegraph office : our road lay across a broad lagoon, and
then up a very steep bank, some sixteen or twenty feet high,
leading into a tobacco field, and being almost perpendicular.
The proprietor of the tobacco field had, we found on this
occasion, cut the only path into steps, and armed the edge of
each step with a row of sharp thorns, thus making the place
awkward for any horse, but a poser for an Arab, who can't
jump a broomstick. We had great difficulty in getting up,

but on arrival we found the proprietor working in his field. He was caught, made to lay down, and was well thrashed by Mustapha and the Governor, who promised him ditto ditto if the road was not made easy by our return. When we did return the improvements had all vanished, and our descent was unimpeded, but the proprietor took good care to be well away. All Egypt is ruled by the stick. Mustapha used to welt any one with anything handy. Mahomet was thrashed with a chair for not having my breakfast ready; while on another occasion Mahomet and Abgeed were beaten black and blue for playing pitch and toss, when they thought Mustapha was asleep. The old boy, however, came downstairs with a yard of pipe in his mouth; soon as he spied them, off came the head of the pipe, and he applied the stem to the two gamblers in a way that made them jump. Once my servant took it into his head to wash my room floor with my sponge; for this he got stick, which made him so energetic, that when set to wash my clothes, he washed them all, clean as well as dirty, indiscriminately.

DOWN AMONG THE DEAD MEN.

Living as I did among the Arabs without European companions except stray glimpses of passing travellers, I acquired a considerable knowledge of native manners, made many friends, from humble fellahs to mighty Beys and Pashas, and was taken to many sights not usually seen by white men. Among other sights that I was introduced to were the excavations being made by order of the Khedive in the tombs at Thebes. For some reason great mystery is preserved about these excavations; and, save myself, no white man was encouraged to visit the scene, but as they were conducted under the supervision of my host, Mustapha himself, subject to occasional supervision from the Bey of Keneh, I was made free of them, and indeed, as owner of Wilkinson's " Ancient Egyptians," was regarded as a high authority on mummies.

The site of ancient Thebes is divided by the Nile into two portions, of which the western extends to the hills of the Libyan deserts; these hills are one vast necropolis full of tombs opened and unopened. No systematic search has ever yet been made throughout this vast burying ground, and quantities of tombs must yet remain to be examined. Except, however, in certain localities, in the Valley of the Tombs of the Kings (Biban-el-Molook), the western Valley, and the Valley of the Tombs of the Queens (Bel-Hareem), it is not probable that anything of great importance would be revealed : in the places we have mentioned it is almost certain that such would be the case, but the search should be systematic, directed and closely watched by Europeans, for the natives look only for treasure, and with that in view, break and destroy much that is of interest to the antiquarian and the historian. The tombs in these places are those of royalty; the tombs known as those of Assaseef are peculiar to the priesthood, those of Quornet Muranee, of the hills of Shekh Abd-el-Koorneh, and of Drah Aboo Nega, are those of private persons. On my first visit to the excavations I saw but little; in a house said to be the property of the British Government, I found the Bey of Keneh, and his two secretaries engaged in arranging a variety of relics just found; these included a very fine papyrus illustrated with coloured pictures, being a sort of calendar and manual of ancient Egyptian religious rites (this I state on the authority of an eminent Egyptologist to whom I afterwards described the papyrus), a wooden model of a greyhound, quantities of blue beads, and some score of blue earthenware images of mummies. The Bey, having got his secretaries out of the way, directed my attention to the scenery, and then quietly stuffed a handful of the images into my coat pocket, he and Mustapha looking all the while most innocent. Had it not been for the secretaries I might have got the papyrus; I might just as well have had it: it was carelessly chucked into a basket with the images, Arab-fashion, and, when I next saw it, it was pulverized to bits. A day or two later Mustapha and I again set off to the excavations, they were high up on the side of a steep hill; half way up was a native village, in whose houses we stabled our donkeys, and then scrambled up on foot. The scene was a cavern high up in the hill, from the back of which a shaft ran some 80 feet perpendicularly into the rock; over this a rude triangular derrick was erected, and by its aid some forty brown men, all naked (save a breech cloth and skull cap) were hauling up baskets of dust, which equally naked boys carried off and searched for odds and ends, finding beads, bits of mummy case, and occasionally more valuable prizes. Niched up in crevices of the rock Mustapha and I would spend from seven in the morning till three in the afternoon, watching the workers; nor did the time hang heavily: for miles up and down we commanded a view of the valley of the Nile; a fire of bits of mummy case and even of mummy kept us in coffee and pipe lights, and the native women brought us from the village, lunch of milk, rice, fowls, eggs, hot pancakes and good things, while a book, rifle practice, a gallop on the Shekh's horse, or an exploration into the native houses would furnish an agreeable divertisement; on one occasion the Shekh's ladies, three jolly black wenches, with very large grins, and very white teeth, made me prisoner, and put me through a regular catechism as to my belongings, showed me their stock of bangles, some of silver, some of hair, and others of glass, and only released me on payment of a piastre apiece. We generally staid at the works until three 'o'clock, because by then the sun got sufficiently behind the western hills to give us a shady ride Nilewards.

At last, one day it was announced that mummies had been found : Mustapha and the Governor of Luxor immediately stripped and were lowered down ; I petitioned hard to be allowed to follow, but in vain: Mustapha was afraid of the risk, and so was the Shekh, a very marine looking old gent with an iron walking-stick. The find consisted of four mummies; one was soon hoisted up, a large painted case all over figures of gods, and men, and animals : it is something to have seen a gentleman disinterred, who was entombed at least 3000 years ago ; little did he suppose a fellow from England (unheard of country) would hold an inquest over him in A.D. 1871. So perfectly preservative is the climate of Egypt, that we even found the very rope by which, over 3000 years ago, the gentleman had been lowered to his rest, and I now have a coil of it, dried almost into powder; handfuls of beads with the string still in them were found with him, and no doubt, according to ancient custom, he had been buried with a large net work of them over his breast. Because of my often importunities, and asseverations of my agility, the Shekh consented to let me down ; I stripped to breeches and shirt, put on a pair of native slippers and a cap, was inserted into a loop at the end of a rope, and lowered, old Mustapha's honest black face actually looking pale with anxiety : "You hold tight : my heart afraid," said he. Down I went : I did not feel afraid ; yet I was pleased when, after descending some 80 feet, Ali Makmoud, the Governor of Luxor, caught me by the feet ; bobbing through the air at the end of a string is, to me, an unusual method of travel. There, at the bottom, were Ali, myself, and two labourers, and a confused heap of mummies ; I felt like a ghoul ; mummies and mummy cases in a museum are very well, but in their tombs they are simply corpses and coffins, and not always the prettiest of corpses and coffins. We sent to ground two or three tolerably perfect mummies, one a large black one of a black lady, probably a Rose of Sharon, and several smashed-up ones : this raised such showers of sand, that to avoid suffocation I got into the bight of the rope again, and ascended, but after my ascent there was found a tablet with an inscription on it in those characters in which hieroglyphics slide into Cufftee, thus showing the mummies to be comparatively modern, say only 3,200 years old. From the bottom of the pit a passage was found to lead horizontally into the rock for a long way. At the end of this would doubtless be a sarcophagus, and a personage of some distinction. Before the passage was cleared, new discoveries were made elsewhere; Arab-like, off rushed the explorers, abandoning the passage, and I lost the chance of going down to posterity with Belzoni and with Bruce, for Mustapha had determined in case of a find to call the tomb by my name.

The new scene of excavation was a hole in a plain not far from the Remesium; a chimney-like orifice, about thirty feet deep, was dug; down this one proceeded spreadeagle-fashion, bare hands and feet stuck against the opposite sides: where the width was too great for me to straddle across a naked Arab preceded, and I stood on his head or back, as most convenient, à la Astley. Here we found a few articles, sandals, ointment sticks, and beads of no great value, and a beautiful tablet of stone, with figures of Osiris and Anubis, and hieroglyphic inscriptions on it; it was broken, and the remainder could not, in all probability, be far off, but I could not induce the natives to search for it. Had it all been found, it would have been a prize, for it evidently represented one of the most interesting scenes of Egyptian mythology, the judgment of the dead, and the weighing of their good actions against a feather. Lower than this we broke into a large tomb, and determined not to rifle it of its contents except in the presence of the Bey of Keneh, the Ali Bey, whom I have before mentioned. Ali Bey was an enormously tall Arab, of purest blood, descended from the Prophet, but endued with a most insatiable and indiscriminate appetite for alcohol, when he could get it. Not knowing one sort of wine from another, or from beer, he would drink in happy mixture, champagne, claret, sherry, beer, and spirits, with the result of getting shockingly tight, and in that condition would smile sweetly on me, and repeat "lal taxsieedee" (good evening), which phrase grew to be his universal nickname. Lal taxsieedee was engaged, when we summoned him, and did not appear for some three weeks. When, at last he arrived, he arrived in state, "with his tail on," as a Highland chieftain of old, and in high feather, at having shot a crocodile thirty feet long.

We formed an imposing procession en route to the tombs: first two runners with guns and scarlet ammunition belts and pouches; then two pipebearers, jet black Nubians, each with three blue gashes scored in either cheek for ornament. The

Bey followed, and out of all the quadrupeds submitted to his
choice he had selected the smallest donkey, so that his long
legs touched the ground on either side. His fool ran by him, a
Nubian boy, aged eight, with but one eye, and an inquisitive-
ness and precocious nastiness far beyond his years. He was
grotesquely attired, and had a talent for squeaking, yelling,
and dancing, that vastly amused the Bey.   Mustapha,
the Governor of Luxor, and Shekh Yuseef followed on
donkeys. I came next on a bay Howara stallion belonging to
Mustapha, with saddle and housings of blue velvet, covered
with silver ; the chief of the local telegraphs rode with me on
a mare blotched with odd white patches, but of great pedigree,
as the documents round her neck proved ; her foal trotted
behind. The rear was brought up by a large number of native
swells, officials, secretaries to the Bey, syces, pipe-bearers,·
donkey boys, water girls, and tag-rag.
    The ride was a very pleasant one. We crossed the Nile
before mounting our steeds, and then rode over a sandy plain,
through a shallow lagoon, and up a steep bank into a tobacco
field ; then we made for the Colossi of the Plains, but deviated
south of them ere we reached them, passed a pleasant farm-
looking house, and through the wheat fields up to the Remesium,
and then over a sandy plain full of holes, made by mummy
hunters, to our own hole.
    Into this the Governor of Luxor, myself, and two fellahs
were lowered. We broke the side of the tomb open, and
hauled out the spoils. The first thing we found was a case
containing the mummy of a baby, with skull as thin as paper ;
then three large cases containing mummies, another baby, and
an enormous case. With these we found some red jars holding
what were once preserved dates, a wooden pillow hollowed out
for the neck, and a large circular covered basket, about two feet
in diameter, made of fine reeds, in a red and yellow pattern,
and in perfect preservation. On being opened, this proved to
be an ancient Egyptian lady's dressing case. In it we found
her slippers, or rather sandals, with a peg for her toes to hold
on by, her comb, a metal mirror, an alabaster pot of green-
coloured ointment half used, the little sticks used for putting it
on with, two or three small baskets, and some small jars of red
clay with alabaster stoppers, containing what must have been
cosmetics.   Below these things lay what at first puzzled us,
but which we found out to be my lady's false hair : strings and

strings of shining black ringlets twisted up close and tight, the thickness of a little finger, just as represented in the paintings in the tombs, and just as Nubian women now wear their wool.

We then turned our attention to the mummies got out of the tomb, which all proved to be so broken and damaged as to be unworthy of a place in the Khedive's museum at Boulac; they were at once broken up by the Bey's orders, and a search made for jewellery; none, however, was found. We made out the owner of the dressing-case. A plain-looking mummy on being opened discovered a much-dilapidated but highly-decorated inner case. On blowing the sand off the case, the inmate's portrait came out most startlingly life-like, as fresh as when painted. A round-faced, low-browed, light brown-coloured girl, with large black eyes, was represented, wearing the very ringlets we had found; and her eyebrows, eyelashes, and below her eyes were painted the very colour of the green ointment in her dressing-case. So fragile was the whole affair that it broke in the handling. Her bones were bleached white as ivory, her teeth beautiful; as her wisdom teeth were still in the bone, she was evidently young. A ring was found on her finger, a small stone set in silver. I am sorry to add, that a kick from an Arab sent the poor girl's remains flying. Her bones are now dispersed about the hill, or burnt for fuel. One mummy out of this lot was a perfect one, and was preserved to go to Boulac. The vault must have been the burying-place of a wealthy family; apparently we disinterred father, wife, and daughter, two infant children, and the unopened mummy. From the first tomb we searched, we had got four mummies; these were next overhauled; one reserved for Boulac, and the rest kicked to pieces. I could do nothing to prevent this desecration, though I much regretted it; it is ghoul-like. Throughout Egypt the remains of the old inhabitants are treated with a want of respect that is horrible; it is said that they are used for fuel on the Egyptian railways, but this I doubt; but they have been shipped to England to be ground down for manure. Apart from any commercial use being made of them, they are dug up by myriads in the search for relics or treasure, and just scattered heedlessly about. The Arabs do not even seem to recognize that these dry bones were once human; nor do, to my thinking, European and American travellers. I saw one young lady rejoicing in the possession of a *mummy's* toe, and another proud of a *mummy's* hand;

yet neither of them would care to carry about a bit of a *corpse.*

This ended my *excavations* for dead men, but on other oc- casions I searched largely among the tombs around Thebes, opened by previous travellers, many of them standing show- places for tourists.

My first visit of this sort was in company with a friend from my own county, and was to Biban-el-Molook, the Gate or Gates of the Kings, and was made in due tourist-form, attended by my friend's dragoman Paulo, by a guide on a donkey *sans* bridle or saddle, by several donkey boys in shirts and caps only, by a man and a boy or two with relics to sell, and by three little girls with water pitchers on head, little wretches bedizened with brass and lead jewellery, rings, necklaces, and earrings, who trotted merrily the whole day on chance of a copper coin or two, and who at all halting-places devoted them- selves to a game somewhat like that known at Eton as " Nux." On this occasion we went and came the same route, through a valley of cliffs and rocks of vast height and barrenness,—" a fi scene," writes Lord Lindsey, " for the funeral processions o mighty Pharoahs; fit, indeed, for the last home of the extinc dynasties of a vanished nation." On subsequent occasions I pre ferred reaching the tombs by crossing the hills for the sake of th lovely view thus obtained, not only of the valley of the Nile but of the Western Desert, with the track across it, leading t the Great Oasis, some dreary three days distant. The road ove the hills is steep, and at places one must dismount. I wen without guides, but with two boys, who, however, were s afraid of hyenas and jackals as to insist on the addition of man with a preposterous native gun that probably would hav declined to go off.

When Sir Gardner Wilkinson wrote his books, he foun open and numbered twenty-two royal tombs in Biban-el Molook. Since his time, one or two more have been found but none of importance. Of these tombs only about twelve ar now open; the sand has filled up the others, or they are merel tunnels in the rock, unworthy of a visit. I, however, visite every one, much to the disgust of my boys, who only knew th ones generally visited by travellers, and did not like my dis covery of their ignorance of the others. I also hunted u all the private and other tombs mentioned by Wilkinson : som are now sadly dilapidated, and the most curious, and therefor most visited, are spoilt by the smoke of the torches used to light them. Some of the private tombs are used as dwellings, and occasionally I found whole families living among mouldering mummies.

In the chapters of this little work devoted to guide book, I have given some little account of these tombs, to which I refer my readers.

EASTERN RELIGIOUS MEN AND CEREMONIES.

Nothing strikes the visitor to the East so much as the Mussulman at his devotions : in the bazaars, in the streets, in railway stations, on the decks of steamers, in the hours of business, and in the intervals for amusement, he sees the Mussulman spread his carpet, his blue cotton wrapper, his own or some one else's coat, and go through the posturing and genuflections prescribed by the Koran. At all hours and in all places the Mussulman may, too, be.seen telling his beads, and conning over them to himself the ninety-nine names of God. Acute observers say that in Turkey at least this is mere ritual; that the old proselytizing spirit of Mahomedanism is dead, and that this strict attention to ritual covers either indifference, routine, or worse.

The visitor to the East should get a peep at a mosque during service on Friday, when the sacred banners are displayed, and the worshippers fall into long ranged lines like soldiers, whose drill their simultaneous posturings and genuflections much resemble, while their many-coloured turbans remind the spectator of a tulip bed shaken by the wind. In the famous mosque of San Sophia at Constantinople, once a Christian church, the *mehrab* or niche denoting the position of Mecca does not coincide with the east end of the church, and the lines of worshippers consequently run diagonally across the building, having to a spectator in the gallery a most singular effect. Such peeps, however, at Mahomedanism as this will little astonish the visitor ; he will know that every religion must have its own ritual and ways of worship. It is intended rather, in this letter, to draw his attention to religious developments, which have no parallel at present in England, and at first of hermits and saints.

The visitor to Egypt will probably be boarded, as he sails up the Nile, by a few of these gentry, who swim off stark-naked and unceremoniously climb on his boat. Should the invader be a Mussulman, the sailors will probably kiss and caress him, and donate him plentifully with coppers; should he, however, be a Christian (a Copt), they are more likely to duck him, or beat him ; but to such treatment he is used, and he will claim the traveller's alms and pity by loudly vociferating in Arabic " I am a Christian." These religious devotees will be met with wandering up and down the villages, beating a drum to let people know they are hungry, and that they expect the best the poor fellaheen have to give away. Some of these rascals condescend to work a little, and one I met with was serving as sailor on board an English dahabeeh ; he was the best trencherman and the worst man at the end of a rope among the whole crew. Others of these saints are hakems, or doctors. I fell in with a magnificent specimen of this class at Luxor, in the medical practitioner from Bagdad, who wanted to bleed me from top to toe. When this holy hakem journeyed, all the population of each village he passed through turned out to escort him to the next. The great saint of Egypt is that " fat fowle naked saint," whom I saw at How, by name Santon Selim.

There are in the East many communities of these holy men : of the Greek, Roman, and Coptic convents I know but little, but I may mention that their inmates are often as ignorant as the fellaheen around them : the communities of Mussulmen saints are formed into colleges of *dervishes*, of which there are eighteen or twenty in Egypt, but whose chief quarters are at Constantinople, where are to be found in perfection the *dancing and howling dervishes*. The dancing dervishes have their abode in the Pera quarter of Constantinople, not far from Misseri's hotel. Their mosque or church is a fine building, not unlike in its interior arrangements to an English circus, save that the arena is floored with the finest woods, highly polished. A small portion of the galleries is appropriated to infidel spectators, who come from motives of curiosity, while the remainder is filled with Musselmen, who come from the same motives that actuate Christians in going to church. The service commenced with the entry of the dervishes, nearly thirty in number, headed by a very fine and handsome old man.* Each dervish wore a tall drab conical

* This chief dervish died in 1872, at the supposed age of 108. The " son of the grave," for such was in Turkish his name, is said to have

felt hat, and a long cloak of brown or blue, except the old man, who had one of green. I was much struck with the appearance of the dervishes ; I had expected to see a set of coarse fanatics ; but I saw a set of men whose features bespoke education and intelligence, and who reminded me of the fellows of a College at Cambridge or Oxford. They seated themselves in a circle around the arena; the windows of the building towards Mecca were thrown open, and a service commenced, in which all the Mussulmen present joined. Travellers have, I think, much misled people at home about the dancing; from their accounts one would suppose the whole religious service done by these dervishes is to twirl : the twirling is in reality merely an occasional interlude in a long service, a sort of anthem ; and to the devout Mussulman has some such mystical meaning as the position of the priest at the altar has to an English High Churchman. After much prayer, all the dervishes, except the chief (the one in green), arose, and marched slowly around the arena to music, bowing as they passed the chief, and finally flinging off their cloaks, began to twirl round rapidly. The under dress was a long white surtout coat, with immense skirts reaching to the heels, and bound at the waist by a girdle. Each dervish extended his arms at right angles to his body, and twirled round with the greatest solemnity on his heels, until his skirts flew out straight. The curious thing was that they never got in one another's way, but just spun steadily round and round like a top, with the greatest gravity, and with an utter absence of any excitement. Every now and then they stopped, and one of them would read a chapter from the Koran ; then they would resume : finally they all sat down in the attitude of prayer, and were cloaked up by an attendant, but the service went on, praying, reading, and singing for an hour more. The order is a very wealthy one, and owns much property in and about Constantinople, and the chief has a fine house on the Bosphorus. The

---

been born in his mother's grave after she was buried as dead. Thirty years ago he himself was buried as dead, but rose from the grave, having been only in a trance. There are dancing dervishes in Cairo, but I did not visit them, though they can easily be seen ; and I saw barking dervishes in Upper Egypt.

In this letter I have brought together several " sights " only connected by the bond of being, to me, religious eccentricities, and thus it jumps from Egypt to Turkey, and back again.

dervish is caught young, and apprenticed by his parents to the profession.

The howling dervishes are to be found across the Bosphorus in Scutari, in the middle of that wonderful burial-ground and cypress forest where sleeps the horse of Sultan Mahmoud under a marble canopy, supported by six pillars. Their Church is a shabby little place, possessing the usual fittings of a mosque, and also a crazy wooden gallery, into which infidels are allowed to go, having first doffed their shoes, or boots. The principal dervishes were seated up and down the mosque ; at its lower end, opposite Mecca, was a row of some twenty, standing shoulder to shoulder like soldiers, and continually augmented by comers-in. These dervishes wore no distinctive dress. As the service went on this row swung itself violently to and fro, sometimes backwards and forwards, and at other times right and left, shrieking out with a howl or bark that seemed to tear their very entrails, the name of God, " Yo illah, yo illah." This went on for upwards of an hour, the howls increasing in intensity until they were perfectly fearful,—a display of genuine fanaticism. I could understand, and almost feared the per-formers running a-muck at the infidel lookers-on. The physical exertion was tremendous ; the howlers ran with perspiration, their heads rolled masterless on their shoulders, and the whole room seethed with steam from them. When they stopped many were, from exhaustion, unable to stand ; one in particular, an enormous and muscular negro, reeled as if he was drunk. The chief dervish seemed to go perfectly mad with excitement. As a finale, there were brought to him sick men and children to be cured. He filled his mouth with lemonade, and spat into his patients' mouths ; they were then laid flat before him, and he danced up and down them madly. This concluded the enter-tainment; I don't know whether any of the patients recovered. These howling dervishes are highly esteemed by the natives. Apparently laymen come in and join in the chorus, for I noticed an officer in uniform and a soldier fall in and howl, and one or two performers were Turks of young Turkey, and wore European costume.

In the Coptic Church I took much interest : but of its distinctive tenets I learnt little : the officials spoke only Arabic, and were generally very ignorant. I fancy they are Gnostic in their origin, Koptos on the Nile having been the seat of the Gnostics, and amid its ruins Gnostic gems are to this day found. It was afterwards the head-quarters of the Coptic Church.

My first visit to a Coptic Church was at Luxor on Palm Sunday : the Church was a plain mud edifice of five aisles : across the lower end ran a mud wall some six feet high, pierced with holes and separating the women from the men. The upper part of the church was curtained off, except the centre aisle, where stood a mud altar in a circular apse behind a screen of wood inlaid with ivory : in front of this was another similar screen forming the choir, within which was the bishop's throne, a high wooden chair covered with a rug : here sat the swells, and I was installed next the bishop on an old rush-bottomed chair, which he had brought for my accommodation. The bishop was a portly one-eyed man of 40 or 50, clad in black robes ; he had in his hands a small crucifix of ebony and ivory, and a similar one, but smaller, was attached to his episcopal ring ; he held also an episcopal staff or crozier of ebony, some four or five feet long, with which he thumped the congregation on the head when they did not behave, and they never did behave ; at last he sent for a huge palm stick, and used that to keep his flock in order. The officiating priest was dressed in a white surplice with gold and scarlet crosses embroidered on the back and front, and he wore also a pallium, similarly decorated. The choristers were in white dresses that would have been decidedly better for washing. The place swarmed with children, who ran about, and made what noise they pleased ; every one talked : many smoked : ever and anon the bishop, the priests, and the congregation had a friendly wrangle as to what was the next portion of the service   be proceeded with. As it was Palm Sunday every one present was weaving little mats of palm leaves : the sacramental bread consisted of cakes with an inscription in Cufftee thereon : these cakes were distributed to the worshippers, who inserted them in the mats, which were very neat contrivances, and took them to preserve as charms for their houses until next year. Two were given me, and I afterwards had the honour of breaking and eating one with the bishop. When the sacramental service was over, a large bowl of water was set in the centre of the Church : in it was placed a brass candlestick and a lighted dip ; round this every one put a goolleh (native bottle) of water, and the bishop blessed the lot, and besprinkled us all from the big bowl with a switch, first tucking his episcopal garments carefully out of the way between his legs. During the ceremony one old Copt amused me much; he was so anxious to have plenty of holy water that he kept filling up his bottle from those of his neighbours : this was seen, and a squabble ensued, which the bishop allayed by hitting out freely with his crozier. When all was over the bishop asked me to smoke a pipe and drink some coffee with him in his palace, a room over the Church. I found him very pleasant, but he only understood Arabic.

The Coptic Easter ceremonies are curious : they kill the paschal lamb, and they have "Pache eggs" as in Carlisle, and the north of England. On Easter Sunday they pay ceremonious visits on one another, and on Easter Monday all the Egyptians, both Copts and Mussulmen, go into their gardens and smell onions. I didn't. On Easter eve I went to the midnight service at the Coptic Church. When I arrived, about an hour before midnight, the Church was full of natives sitting on the floor, and moaning out a service ; the Church was almost in total darkness, lit only by a few tallow candles. Presently the bishop entered, and, after shaking hands with me, began the special service, but he first went inside the altar rails to robe. His full dress was white, with gold embroidery of crosses down the front, and a gilt mitre ; over all, including the mitre, he put a cloak and hood of scarlet and gold with a tassel at the top, so that, when he turned his back on the people to celebrate, he looked like a huge, animated bedroom candle extinguisher of gay pattern. I could not follow the service, but there was much singing, chanting, ringing of bells, and incense-swinging, all done in a free and easy way ; if the reader stuck over a word—no unfrequent occurrence— one of the congregation corrected him ; even the bishop tripped now and then, and was prompted or set right by a very old and cantankerous Copt, who ever and anon opened his mind freely to the officials about the performance. The lessons were read by chorister boys, who had their ears boxed with the lesson book if they made mistakes. Shortly before twelve o'clock the bishop and officials all retired within the altar rails and shut the doors, which reached up to the ceiling (to represent our Saviour in the tomb), while the congregation began to wail horribly : at midnight the bishop kicked the doors, which opened, and a procession came out. This procession consisted of two men bearing red flags, one ringing a pair of silver bells, another beating a pair of cymbals, a third with a censer, and several with tallow dips, while the bishop carried three of these dips in one candlestick to signify the Trinity; the priest followed him, bearing a curious old red and yellow print of the resurrection, which the crowd rushed at, and kissed, while the choristers and congregation sang an Arab Easter hymn. The moment the procession left the altar rails, a Copt sitting next me said, " Jesus Christ be risen, all the Copt very glad;" a scene ensued of which I have never seen the like; every fellow in the congregation pulled out a *pistol or a gun*, and *began to fire* like mad, by way of showing his joy, while a tall fellow in white climbed up on high, and lit up a magnesium torch. The scene would have made a fine picture; the dark Church, so dimly lit that the flashes of the firearms showed like tongues of flame; the silver moonlight struggling through the small windows at the top of the Church walls, and the glare of the torch over the procession, whose tawdriness was thus completely converted into the imposing,—all would have given a painter's genius fine scope for his art, while the Eastern costumes, and the excitement of the congregation, added to the strangeness of the spectacle. This lasted for some twenty minutes; then the procession returned to the altar rails. Here a hitch occurred; the performer on the cymbals, a priest or elder, insisted on giving a solo, to which the authorities objected : another priest or elder snatched the instruments out of his hand, whereon he showed fight, and was only quieted by the application of a stick to his head by a bigger priest or elder. After this the ordinary service went on, but I came away.

My Mussulman host, when I told him next day, by no means approved of the firing in Church. " Church to pray the God in, not shoot, shoot like debbil."

By the way, when a new Coptic patriarch is elected, he persistently declines the honour; his deacons finally make him prisoner, put him in chains, and conduct him to his official residence, as if he was a felon. This is a curious gloss on *Nolo episcopari.*

LETTER IX.

AN EASTERN WEDDING.

Some time in April 1871 the Bey of Erment, in Upper Egypt, gave a grand *fantasia* in honour of the marriage of his eldest son to a slave girl presented to him by H. H. the Khedive of Egypt. I was honoured with an invitation.

For long before the time fixed for the festivities, the barbers' shops and the bazaars of Upper Egypt were filled with rumours of the expected glories of the *fantasia*. The cooks that were coming from Skandereeah (Alexandria), the musicians from Cairo, the luxuries from Stamboul, the dancing girls from Esne, Keneh, and Luxor, were all discussed and magnified by a thousand tongues, until expectation was worked up to its highest pitch. As the day drew near the whole country seemed to be alive ; troops of fellaheen from all quarters, each headed by a shekh, trudged along the banks of the Nile, while the river itself bore the more aristocratic visitors, among whom were a company of thirty dancing girls, forming the cargo of a dahabeeh or travelling boat. On the day itself all the great men of Luxor started early in the morning, some by boat, others by road ; and to the latter and smaller party I and my host, Mustapha Agha, joined ourselves.

The first thing we had to do was to get our cattle and ourselves across the Nile, and as we had to transport my horse, and nearly twenty donkeys and mules, this was a work of some time. Their embarkation was easy, but the disembarkation was otherwise, and was chiefly effected by pitching the animals bodily into the water, in which they generally disappeared for a second or two before swimming ashore. Our cavalcade was rather an imposing one, when fully mustered ; the occasion was a full-dress one, and so each native swell was accompanied by as many attendants as possible. Five was deemed the fitting retinue for my humble self; a *syce* (or groom) ran in front of my horse, carrying the picket-ropes; my servant, Mahomet, rode behind me on a donkey, as my *chiboubaski*, or pipe-bearer, which important instrument, a cherry stick, some four or five feet long, was carefully swaddled up in a muslin bag. Yuseef Hassan, on another donkey, carried other of my belongings, and each of these lazy beggars insisted on an attendant on foot to drive their steeds. Our road laid across the sandy plain opposite to Luxor, then through large wheat stubbles, after which we came into a very rich country, devoted to the cultivation of sugar cane. The last three miles of our ride was through an avenue of mimosas, whose shade was most acceptable, the heat even at 9 a.m. being tremendous. *En route* we passed through some villages, where we halted for a drink of water, or of native beer, a concoction made from barley, looking like water gruel, tasting sharp like cider, and befitting only to the "*dura ilia messorum*" or *fellahorum*.

As we neared Erment there fell upon our ears that indescribable sound, always made by large crowds of any nation. Rounding the corner of one of the magnificent Erment sugar factories, we came upon upwards of 200 Arab horsemen engaged in the national sport of *jereed* playing, while beyond were a vast multitude of natives of every hue engaged in various sports, or chaffering in the market-place for camels, buffaloes, sheep, melons, cucumbers, sugar cane, cotton cloths, and other commodities. We rode to the bazaar (closed for the day) and there dismounting and leaving our steeds, went on foot to the Bey's palace, a building by no means so grand as its name, its rooms being merely whitewashed chambers, with mud divans round the sides, and a little drapery over the windows; but the lovely look out over the Nile atoned for all other deficiencies. Our host, a fat, smiling, and sickly-looking Turk, was seated outside his palace, in company with the Medeers (Lord Lieutenants) of Keneh and Esne, and with Beys, Nazirs, Makmouds, and other dignitaries and officials innumerable, who were all employed watching a sack race, which was got up by an individual, in semi-Eastern dress, whose nationality for long puzzled me; he turned out to be a renegade Frenchman; "I am of no nation, but of the world, cosmopolitan," he told me. If cosmopolitanism consists in adopting the vices of other countries than one's own, Frenchmen generally succeed therein, and this particular citizen of the world proved good his claims to that title, by having one wife besieged in Paris, and others confined in his harem in Egypt. This I was told by a Mussulman friend in tones of great disgust; your true

Mussulman has little respect for the so-called Christian who does not stand by and act up to the precepts of his religion.

So soon as the sack race was over we were conducted by the Bey into his palace, and served with coffee. I was desired to make myself free of the place, and told I might wander unrestrained up and down. I joined myself to some of the younger men, and set out to see the humours of the fair. Chief among these was the *jereed* playing, for which was collected, as I have said, over 200 horsemen ; and though the Arab steed is not quite the noble animal that poets, romancers, and travellers have made him out, yet among the lot were some of great beauty and value. Most of them were of the Howara breed, which is famed for stoutness, and of which the predominant colour is bay ; these horses can go a tremendous bat for about a hundred yards, and are trained to turn round on a fourpenny-bit, or else to stop dead whilst at full gallop; for this purpose they are ridden in tremendously severe bits. As a rule, the housings and accoutrements were gorgeous,—saddle, saddle cloth, bridle, holsters, &c., of blue, green, or red velvet, or of fine black cloth, hung with countless gold or silver tassels, and trimmed extensively with lace of the same metal ; but one or two horses had no saddles or accoutrements at all beyond a rope halter. All almost had their pedigree tied under their throats in a little parchment bag, together with some charm to avert the evil eye ; some were fired in patterns, which told the initiated their breed and pedigree ; thus one chestnut stallion had three rings fired round each fore arm, and a system of dots marked in between them. Nearly all the horses I saw had their flanks scored by the too free use of the Arab stirrup, a thing with a bottom like, and as big as, a fire shovel, whose sharp corners are used as spurs, and terrible ones they make. The *jereeds* are long palm sticks from 10 to 14 feet long, and with these a sort of combat or tournament is waged to the shrill sound of wild Arab music. Two competitors take up their stand, perhaps 100 yards apart, and, as the music plays slowly, they make their steeds prance a slow march ; suddenly the music becomes quick, each competitor then gallops down on the other at full speed, and the two fly round one after the other, turning in the smallest circles and figures of eight possible, and fencing and menacing each other with the *jereeds*. A favourite test of skill is to place one end of the *jereed* on the ground and, holding the other end in the hand, to gallop full speed round and round the circle thus

defined ; sometimes two horsemen would tear up full spin from
opposite extremities of the course, plant the ends of their *jereeds*
together in the ground, and circle round thus.   It is terrible
work for the horses ; the sharp gallops, the sudden pullings up
on the haunches, all done under the African sun, and going on
from morning to night, are most exhausting work, only varied
by an occasional procession through the fair of all the horsemen, headed by a band of music.   The best performer was one
Said, a groom of my host Mustapha Agha, a singular neat and
active man, mounted on a bay stallion, gorgeous in blue and
gold housings ; this bay and the tattooed chestnut were the
finest horses there.   Leaving the *jereed* playing, though so
graceful and spirited was it that I oft returned, let me notice
some of the other amusements provided for the assembled
crowds.

Of these amusements there were plenty ; besides such
familiar to England, as sack racing and pole climbing, more
African ones abound.   Troops of mummers and buffoons, in
every variety of dress and undress, paraded and performed
up and down ; Nubian and Berber sailors, excited by the
fumes of hasheesh, sang the songs and cut the capers of
their native countries ; filthy baboons were being put through
filthier tricks ; a Nubian maiden, with gold rings through her
nose and through the tops and bottoms of her ears, danced
Nubian dances ; countless guns and muskets were being
discharged for sake of the row they made ; but chief and
most popular of all the amusements were the troupes of
Ghawazee or dancing girls, brilliant in red and yellow dresses,
and bedizened with their sham jewellery.   Several troupes
were performing up and down the fair ; the best, that from
Luxor, composed of the six ugliest women in the world, had
secured a position under the windows of the palace, where sat
a select circle of officials whose plaudits the girls strove to
gain ; their efforts were aided by the antics and capers of a
gigantic black lunatic from Luxor, who brandished an enormous
scimitar of such curliness that its scabbard was slit down the
back to allow it to enter ; his efforts were aided by those of the
household fool of the Bey of Keneh, the one-eyed Nubian idiot
mentioned in a previous letter.

About midday a grand procession was formed.   First came
all the mummers, and buffoons, and dancing-girls, all dancing,
as they went, to their music, which also formed part of the

pageant; then followed dancers with drawn swords, and things like the old English fire cressets done up in scarlet cloth, ushering a string of country waggons and wains, drawn by buffaloes, and decorated with gay hangings; in one waggon was a drinking shop; in others, various trades were carried on—a tailor stitched, a dyer dyed, and even a baker baked and distributed hot bread around; finally a large boat was drawn along full of sailors, smoking themselves drunk on hasheesh (a decoction of hemp) and singing the songs of the Nile, After the boat came men bearing palm leaves with scarlet flowers tied to them, and great frames of palm leaves interspersed with scarlet flowers and berries; next a portly and dignified man, the barber of Erment, whose apprentices carried high over their heads their master's sign-board, all lapped in scarlet and yellow cloth, and having the barber's mirror suspended in front. A magnificently caparisoned horse followed the sign, bearing the Bey of Erment's youngest son, a lovely and sleepy-looking child of about two years, evidently of a Georgian mother, and dressed, exactly like a man, in the Government official uniform; he had little black trousers, with gold stripe, white vest, and black surtout coat covered with gold lace, while his scarlet tarboosh or fez was covered with strings of gold coins. This manly urchin was held on his horse, and a gaily-coloured umbrella was supported over him. The hero of the procession rode next, another son of the Bey, whose circumcision was being thus celebrated; he was dressed in similar fashion, and was preceded by censer and incense-bearers, and officials, who besprinkled the crowd with perfumes, while at his side walked attendants with huge fans of black ostrich feathers, such as would make any lady's mouth water. The procession was closed by all the respectable children in the place, riding two on one horse, and clad in new dresses, a sort of bedgown, of striped chintz; all these children had their finger nails stained with henna, a deep orange colour.

When this festive pageant had passed away, I was summoned to the breakfast, which was simply one of the best cooked dinners I ever sat down to, either in London or Paris. There were two duplicate dinners, nine sitting down at each table, or rather circular copper tray. As I took my place with eight black or blackish gentlemen, my servant, Mahomet, whispered in my ear " Eat much, very good cook, Skandereah (Alexandria) man." Mahomet's advice was good; the twenty dishes which succeeded one another in rapid succession were excellent, though for my life I could not make out what some of them were. Of course, we all used our fingers, bar a spoon, which was allowed us for the soup and the sweets ; plates there were none ; each dish came to table in the red earthenware pot it had been cooked in, and into that pot each guest dipped his fingers. This was far from being the first Arab meal I had partaken of, and I was quite *au fait* at feeling about for the tender bits in a turkey's breast, or a joint of mutton ; the great secret, I had found, was to be the first man at table to dip my fingers into every dish ; by so doing, I earned the credit of being a " good Arab," and I anticipated my friends, who would have handed me tit-bits with their fingers, which, though religiously washed before every meal, yet during its course visit their masters' lips too frequently and too closely to make their well-meaning attentions quite acceptable. After this meal, coffee and pipes, of course, followed, and I spent the afternoon much as I did the morning, in watching from the window the ever-varying kaleidoscope of Eastern manners and Eastern costumes that was presented to my amusement.

About five o'clock the cosmopolitan came in search of me,—" De handsome girl be come," and carried me off to see the famous Zenab and her troupe of Ghawazee, but before they began to perform, a Nubian slave appeared to me, and bowing low, said, " fodder," by way of announcing dinner ; he was followed closely by the Bey, who paid me the high compliment of personally conducting me to the dinner-table, and of placing me at the highest table, where our napkins were embroidered with gold, brought, as Mahomet told me, from Stamboul (Constantinople) for the occasion. The guests had now increased to over a hundred, and we sat down by twelves to copper trays, on each of which a complete dinner was served, similar to the earlier meal, but more substantial, including a roast sheep for each party of twelve. Fingers were again the vehicles of communication between the meat and the mouth, but we were allowed the European innovation of wine. Five hundred more guests of lower degree were feasted out of doors, so that the Bey entertained right royally. During dinner the Khedive's firman was read, by which he presented the bride, and we drank his health, and that of the Bey. The cosmopolitan and a friend of his, Mustapha Bey, came out great on this occasion. They insisted that every man should make his national noise all at once ; so I cheered, the Frenchmen (there were one or two present) cried " *Vive*," and Arab, Turk, Nubian, and Berber, each after his own kind, while the cosmopolitan proved his claim to that title by making all the several noises.

Dinner over, we adjourned to the large room, round which a divan ran for three sides; here we assembled, had pipes and coffee, and made ourselves comfortable to see the dancing. On the vacant side sat on the floor Zenab and her eight maidens, a gorgeous mass of Oriental but dusky beauty, and of brilliant colouring, well thrown out by the sombre dresses of the musicians, who sat behind them. The chief musician played a wondrous fiddle, whose sounding board was half a cocoa nut with parchment stretched over it; he was ably assisted by a gentleman who officiated on the usual earthenware drum, much like a large drain pipe in appearance, while a lady player banged about a tambour in tremendous style.

Up to this time I had been much disappointed in the magnificence of the dresses of the Ghawazee,—realization had fallen short of the anticipation : now it surpassed what I had been induced to expect. Each of the nine performers wore a dress of crimson, cherry, red, magenta, light blue, or some such brilliant-coloured silk, embroidered most elaborately with gold and silver flowers. The dresses were made like short French walking dresses, but with loose sleeves; most voluminous trousers of like material covered the ankles. Three rose to the dignity of stockings, and French boots covering rather large feet; the other six wore the common red slippers of the country, and danced barefoot. Gay handkerchiefs covered their heads, and their hair, mostly false, was done up in large ringlets and loaded with gold chains. From chin to waist was one mass of chains of gold coins, with waistbelts, bracelets, and bangles to match; hanging round their hips were strings of silver rattles and bells, being, with silver castanets, the insignia of their tribe; the great art of their dancing is by a wriggling undulation of the body to set all their bells and rattles going. Each lady had also an opera cloak of the latest European fashion.

The position these girls fill is curious; they answer somewhat to the old Greek *heteiræ*. Zenab herself, famed through all Egypt for her beauty and dancing, is one of the very few educated women in the country. She is said to be the only native woman who ever went ten yards to look at any of the monuments of Egypt's departed greatness, and her house at

Keneh is said to be full of European luxuries and refinements.
As to her beauty, that is matter of taste : dressed in English
fashion she would pass as an English woman in any ball room,
and be set down as a brunette beauty, but *passée*. A most
amusing squabble took place for the honour of having her to
sit alongside of on the divan.   Mustapha Agha got her, and
defended his prize most lustily with his pipe stick.   Another
Zenab, a very plump, comely, but dusky beauty, was brought
by the Bey, introduced to me, and put to sit beside me.   The
being (I cannot call her fair) smoked a full-flavoured cigar with
great avidity, but soon left me for some one whose Arabic was
more fluent.   Flirtation with a blackish woman who smokes is
difficult, when you have no common language to go upon.

Soon four of the troupe took the floor, and dancing commenced ;   the four performers being every now and then
relieved.   The dancing was more graceful than any I had seen
in Egypt.   At first slow and quiet, as the music grew more
weird and eldritch-like, so the dancing grew more furious,
until at last the girls flew round the room in wild bounds ; the
dusky complexions of performers and spectators, the Eastern
costumes, the atmosphere heavy with tobacco smoke and with
perfumes, the strange and screeching music, and the excited
demeanour of the girls, all combined to give the *tout ensemble*
a picturesqueness, a *diablerie* that was at once novel and
charming ; and yet an English lady might have sat through it
all, as indeed did the Princess of Wales, who saw Zenab and
her company perform.   Meanwhile, the spectators smoked,
drank coffee or cold water, gossiped, and played practical
jokes, such as tipping an old gentleman's turban off, or empty-
ing pipe ashes down his back ; ringleaders in the fun were the
cosmopolitan and Mustapha Bey.   To me, a stranger, nothing
but civility and kindness was shown ; a better or more attentive
host than the Bey of Erment cannot live.   A Bey (by the
way) is the second rank in the kingdom, coming immediately
after a Pasha, or Bashaw, as the natives call it.

The *profanum vulgus* outside were by no means neglected.
The whole place was lit up by innumerable coloured lamps,
and the sports of the day were continued far into the night,
and varied by torchlight processions.

About ten or eleven o'clock our party, having refused many
invitations to go with Mustapha Bey to Esne, started Luxorwards in a large covered boat ; the contrast between the noise

of Erment and the silence of the Nile under a lovely silver moon being most refreshing,—a silence that was only made more silent by the occasional barking of some village cur or wandering jackal, or the howl of a prowling hyena. The Southern Cross just culminating on the horizon added to the beauty of the scene, and reminded me of how far, far away, under the cold North star, were all my friends and belongings. Romance soon gave way to sleep; tired nature asserted itself, and snores predominated.

P.S.—I have written an account of a wedding and forgot the bride and the ceremony. I never saw either; she and it were somewhere in the recesses of the harem, far from rude male eyes. I asked to have the bridegroom pointed out to me; and was told I should know him by his having one eye and light trousers; one eye and light trousers were so fashionable that I failed to recognize him.

CAIROWARDS WITH A PASHA.

Towards the end of April the heat at Luxor grew oppressive; the *khamseen*, or hot south wind, heavily laden with desert dust, would blow the whole day, and life was only supportable in the very early dawn and after dusk, which commenced about six o'clock. In this weather one could only lounge, half dressed, the life-long day in a darkened room, waiting until the growing shadow indicated the time for a dip in the Nile, the preliminary to our *al fresco* feast of lanterns, or dinner after dark in the open air, at which attendants held lights for us to see the several roads to our respective mouths. All the town, buried in sleep throughout the day, now awoke up, and everywhere could be heard, though not seen, chattering groups of natives smoking, coffee drinking, and enjoying the cool of the evening.

But the heat was getting too much for me; a thermometer at 108 deg. in the shade, and 140 deg. in the sun, is oppressive, and I warned Mustapha, spite his " You leave us very dull," that I must be off, and that he, according to his contract, must find me conveyance to Cairo. An opportunity soon came; His Excellency General Salee Pasha, prefect of the police and governor of Cairo, arrived at Luxor, travelling in great state with a full suite. He readily assented to Mustapha's request for my passage Cairowards on his steamer, and I was introduced to him at a dinner (*à la* Arab) given by Mustapha to the Pasha and suite. Salee Pasha was a very fine, dignified looking gentleman, close shaved, bar his moustache, and clad in a long yellow or golden-coloured garment reaching to his heels, over which he wore a long white linen surtout. He had with him one Shekh Ali, a wealthy native, one of the finest-looking and best-dressed men I have seen in Egypt, enormous white turban, and flowing violet, lavender, and yellow robes of the olden fashion, without innovation. A doctor was also *en suite*, an Arab, who spoke a little French and had seen

Paris; and two military officers, aide-de-camps, gorgeous in full uniform, but slovenly when not on duty. Then he had also a band, five sentimental and ugly looking youths, who, dressed in fine attire, played on romantic looking instruments, and by favour of my servant drank up my last bottle of whisky. Add to these, several Nubian slaves, black as jet, clad in the newest and brightest of chintz, and ranging in age from a tall and solemn abomination of thirty to some cheeky lads of thirteen or fourteen. Bar the Pasha, all these travelled on board one of the Khedive's iron steamers; he dwelt in a dahabeeh, which the steamer towed, and with him was Mrs. Pasha No. 2, for whose health he was voyaging, her child, and attendants.

The day after Mustapha's dinner I went with the Pasha and a party to Karnak, where we pic-niced, and I acted as guide: in the afternoon the Pasha left for Erment, promising to return for me in two or three days. Meanwhile I made preparations for my departure, and was, on it becoming known, much bothered by claimants for baksheesh, in distributing which I was not over lavish, as I was short of money until I got to Cairo, and could only borrow £2 or £3 from Mustapha; however, I gave everyone what Mustapha advised, but one or two were discontented, and displeased because all were not put on a level.

The Pasha returned on the 30th of April, and that evening I embarked, Mustapha taking a most affectionate farewell of me, and Shekh Yuseef falling on my neck, and embracing me. Next morning early we made our start. We lived in great magnificence, and not a little dirt, until I made Mahomet clean out my cabin. We had a large supply of Persian carpets, china, and silver plate on board, but never a knife or fork beyond our fingers; the cooking was good, but Turkish, not Arabic in fashion, and consequently highly sauced and spiced: breakfast was only a little fruit and sweet biscuits, at no time in particular; lunch at 10-30, and dinner at 7, but I speedily sent my servant to cater for me, and to get me a more substantial breakfast; indeed, I was soon left to choose my own hours. I should not forget to mention that the tall and solemn Nubian abomination had charge of a box of prime cigars, but when I asked for one, he invariably lit it, and had first suck. I can't say I much enjoyed the voyage: the heat told on an iron steamer boat most awfully; mealing with fingers is very

well now and then, but not nice for a continuance; another
unlucky circumstance was, that no one on board spoke English
but my servant, and his English was but small, while both the
doctor's French and mine were at variance, a fact which led to
mistakes and misapprehensions; besides, too, I found it very
dull with no one to speak to, and with few books to read,
Life on the steamboat was in this wise :—We journeyed in
the early morning; for the afternoon and night we staid at
some town where the Pasha visited ceremoniously the local
swells, and afterwards held a divan or levée for them on the
steamer in the evening.   Here much ceremony was observed,
and etiquette was rather a bore, as we all had to rise when his
Excellency did, but this hardship was much assuaged by
smoke, coffee, and music, all of which the Pasha's suite supplied in excellence and abundance.

Our first stoppage after leaving Luxor was at Keneh, a
town some mile and a half distant from the river.   I went off
on donkey back to survey it, and *en route* nearly suffered a fate
similar to that of Absolem, for my donkey darted under the
branches of a low-growing tree, and left me clinging thereto
with might and main.   Keneh is famed for the manufacture of
earthen pots, and of preserved dates; in both I invested a
trifle, and also in some tea, and in the very worst brandy I ever
imagined.   My rascal Mahomet, being entrusted by me with a
pound to change, spent it, and brought me back two bottles of
champagne and one of beer, as the proceeds, thus leaving me
without money enough to carry me on.

The third of May we spent in a most agreeable manner;
the Nile had fallen greatly, and whole acres, under water when
I went up, were, on my return, dry and growing water melons.
Thus it fell out that, spite of two *reises*, one at the helm, the
other at the prow with a long pole, we grounded at 10-30 a.m.,
and stuck fast until after dark that day.   The dahabeeh floated
alongside, and Mrs. Pasha took the opportunity of exhibiting
herself at the window to my gaze as I sat on the steamer's
deck.   Her husband was out of the cabin in a moment with
a polite recommendation to me not to sit in the sun.   I was not
sitting in the sun, but I took the hint, and slued my chair
round.   It is never worth while to dispute with Pashas
tinctured with jealousy.

Siout was our next great stoppage.   We tarried here from
early on a Thursday to the morning of Saturday, to my hideous

disgust, as I was very seedy owing to the heat. The Pasha was much distressed at this, and was good enough to flog his cook, because he forgot to get me milk for my tea. There being a very high Pasha at Siout, my Pasha put himself in full dress, black surtout and pants, and blue velvet vest with glass buttons, a costume far from so dignified as his usual one ; his slaves were also crammed into European liveries (black) and boots,—poor devils ! Here, as at Keneh, and afterwards at Minieh, his Excellency invested largely in the local manufacture ; at Keneh he loaded the steamer with a hundred of earthen jars ; at Siout he indulged largely in red and black pottery, and at Minieh (our next stage) he possessed himself of piles of boxes of sweetmeats.

From Minieh there is rail to Cairo, and I determined, if possible, to go by it, and cut the steamer, as the heat was so awful ; but I had no money, a fact of which the Pasha was made aware by Mahomet, who by way of atoning for his misdeeds in champagne, gave me a Nubian spear, and an odd-looking specimen of Siout red pottery. The Pasha pressed me much to stay, and to go as his guest to some sulphur baths for a week ; but I declined, and so on Sunday, 8th May, I was called about 5 a.m., and found the Pasha ready up and dressed to say good-bye. He lent me five Napoleons, and I was rowed ashore bag and baggage to Minieh, and marched in grand procession,—myself, Mahomet, and a sailor to each article of my traps, to the railway station. There I found a large number of natives waiting for the train, which came from Rhoda at no particular time, and no one seemed surprised at having to sit there from 6 a.m. to past 8, an interval which I employed in breakfasting, for coffee, bread, hard-boiled eggs, and cold fowls were easily got, and my portmanteaus formed chair and table. At last we got off ; at every station the train stopped an indefinite time, mainly regulated by the number of pipes and coffee the officials of the train wished to discuss in company with the officials of the station. The passengers invariably on arriving at a station precipitated themselves on it, and were by no means easy to collect and get in again. Of refreshments, however, there were plenty at each station to employ the passengers, for all the inhabitants of the place appeared with something edible or drinkable for sale. Thus progress was slow, the dust was great, and the heat was terrible.

Thus journeying we arrived at our destination at 10 p.m.

Bradshaw (continental edition) says 4 p.m., but it was 10 p.m., intensely dark, and the terminus was nowhere ; somewhere four or five miles from Cairo ; no station, no carriages, no donkeys,— I was helpless, resigned myself to fate and to Mahomet. He came out a trump ; he seized the only lantern in the place, and banged the only official on the head with it until he found my luggage. Then we scrambled through a wood yard, and got to a boat, by which we crossed the Nile and arrived at the mooring place of the dahabeehs. Here Mahomet proposed I should sleep ; but leaving him and the luggage, I found a donkey and rode up to Shepherd's, where I arrived about midnight, and which place I left shortly for Alexandria, in company with Mahomet and my luggage.

ALEXANDRIA: VOYAGE TO CONSTANTINOPLE.

I cannot say that I was much charmed with Alexandria; it is more European—Italian—than Eastern, and its inhabitants are a most motley lot, almost every nation under the sun being represented, and well represented, among them. The remains of old Alexandria are, mainly, mere shapeless masses of masonry, and the only two relics worth a visit are Pompey's Pillar and Cleopatra's Needle, those old friends of one's childhood, now much hacked curiosities, but some seventy years ago, in the times of Mussulman arrogance, rarely to be got near by Europeans. In company with a large party of Indian officers and officials, I drove round the suburbs of Alexandria, and did the sights. The Pillar stands on a lofty hill, and to my mind is likely soon to come down, unless its foundations are speedily repaired. Cleopatra's Needles—there are two—are to be found in a stonemason's yard close to the Ramleh railway station: one still stands, but the other is prostrate and buried in sand. Beyond these and the Mediterranean I found little to see or admire in Alexandria. One small adventure I had. On a Sunday afternoon I was taking a stroll, and came to some fortifications by the sea. The sentry saluted (taking me, no doubt, for one of the Khedive's American generals), and I passed on, and smoked in peace o'er the blue Mediterranean. After some time I heard a shout of "Usbar;" out came the guard; a huge sergeant collared me, and I was made captive in no very pleasant manner, with a black man's knuckles in my neck. The sergeant and the guard jabbered Arabic, and I emitted the pure Saxon, and brandished my umbrella. I informed the sergeant that "Civis Romanus sum and particular brother to the English Consul;" but he did not understand me. No go: I was dragged off, an outraged British subject. When we got to the sentry, he explained how I had got on the fortifications, and I was released. The sentry was called to "attention" and to "shoulder arms" in front of his box. The sergeant then fell on him and banged him about the head in the most terrific style.

My great piece of luck at Alexandria was the being invited to the ceremonies attendant on the laying the foundation stones of a new dock. The English Consul at Cairo, Mr. George Stanley, a Cumberland man, was kind enough to procure me an invitation. Early on the day of the ceremony, a cavass with an enormous scimitar at his hip was ushered into my bedroom by Mahomet, and presented me the Khedive's commands in French for my attendance at the laying of the stone and at the ball in the evening. Accordingly, I arrayed myself in the costume prescribed for the Queen's breakfasts at Buckingham Palace, that is, light bags and a dress coat with a due proportion of under clothing, and proceeded on a donkey to the scene of action. Arrived there, Mahomet without hesitation cantered his moke down the ranks of white tuniced soldiers that kept the roads, and was incontinently knocked off, but on production of my invite I was spared that fate and allowed to pass to a tent full of the *elite* of Alexandria, all dressed in gala attire, and fringed by rows of the Khedive's generals in gold tasselled red fezzes and gold epauletted tunics of blue. Opposite to this tent were gay pavilions for the Khedive and for the *Corps Diplomatique*, who appeared in every variety of full dress uniform, among them the Persian Consul was most conspicuous: he was a very big, broad-chested man in a black fez, a dark tunic with scarlet breast, on which he displayed the Persian order of the Rising Sun, a piece of enamel work as big as a dessert plate ; round this he had twelve other orders. I fancy he was appointed to his office on account of the size of his chest ; no smaller man could have wore the Rising Sun, though he might have used it for a target in a broadsword combat. The Khedive appeared about 9-30, and the stone was laid in the usual manner. After this the Grand Mufti, a most venerable and dignified old man, with long snowy white beard, and long bright green robes, gave an address, and asked a blessing ; he was followed by the Greek Patriarch or Archbishop, an equally dignified, but younger man, in robes of scarlet and gold ; he was attended by several black robed priests, who, as well as the Bishop, wore tall cylindrical hats, with long black veils flowing behind and down their backs ; each had a jewelled or silver cross suspended from his neck. After the speaking was done, ices, sweetmeats, and champagne, were freely dispensed, and in a neighbouring tent a grand breakfast was set out.

In the evening the state ball came off in Palace No. 3, at which 1800 people were present. I joined a party and went; the approaches were lined by rows of soldiers bearing lighted torches. A grand staircase led up to galleries, one of which entered into a long ante-room running across the palace; from the centre of one of the long sides of this ante-room the guests passed into the ball room, lit by numbers of glass chandeliers, and having right and left large and well furnished lounging rooms. Returning to the ante-room, a wide passage from one end, well provided with chairs, sofas, and settees, led to card and smoking rooms. Here were provided cigars and cigarettes in bounteous profusion, and gambling was carried on for high stakes. At the end of this passage was a large room with a grand buffet, 10 feet high, down one side, all covered with sweetmeats, which it was the correct thing to pocket. These sweetmeats were works of high art; palaces and temples, pyramids and pagodas, fish, and fowl, and meat were all imitated in variously coloured sugars and candies, while of bonbons, comfits, and small delicacies there was endless profusion. At smaller buffets in this room every imaginable drink, from beer to champagne, was procurable in pailfuls. Corresponding suites of rooms, entered from the other end of the ante-room, were the supper rooms; in the room corresponding to the room of the sweetmeat buffet, the supper was set out on long tables, while in the smaller rooms tables were laid for four, six, or eight; only make up your party, and choose your table, and a complete supper at once appeared. Leaving the ante-room, and crossing the galleries over the grand staircase, the guests found a suite of rooms over the garden, and in front of these a great display of fireworks came off. Everything was beautifully done, even to the printing of the supper *menus;* servants in state liveries of gold and scarlet attended the guests' behests, and *gens d'armes* in blue and silver were posted all up the staircase and at the principal doors.

Of course there were no Eastern ladies present: all were Italian, Greek, and of other European nationalities: I was disappointed in both their looks and dresses. The men made up: several were in Eastern costumes, but save myself and my compatriots, almost every man wore ribbons and decorations; some had as many as fourteen or fifteen glittering on their

breasts at once. "Who can all these be? great warriors, great
diplomats and saviours of their countries at least" said I
to myself; at last one wearing fourteen ribbons came across
me, his face I seemed to know : I discovered he was the
agent of the Austrian Lloyd's from whom I had that morning
bought a passage ticket to Constantinople ; every Continental
power, who uses that line, gives the officials a ribbon or so, and
thus my friend's chest had blossomed like a parti-coloured
peony or a tulip bed.

The day following this ball, the 16th May, I embarked for
Constantinople in the Austrian Lloyd's steamship *Vesta*, a ship
whose passenger accommodation exceeds any I have ever seen.
The feeding was first rate, but foreign ; breakfast, tea coffee
and rolls only, from 6 to 8 ; lunch at 10, dinner at 5, and tea·
at 8. At lunch and dinner we were supplied with Sxezard,
a Hungarian wine ; at both these meals numbers of appetizers,
such as anchovies, sardines, caviare, radishes, Bologna sausage,
&c., were abundantly supplied. The bread, made on board,
was excellent.

Our deck passengers were a wonderful lot ; bar the poop,
the whole ship was covered with them, who all day long did
nothing but eat, sleep, play cards, and catch vermin. They
were a picturesque lot, Greeks, Italians, Jews, Levantines,
Arabs, Turks, and Negroes, each arrayed after his kind,
and accompanied by a curious selection of luggage, composed
of carpets and rugs, of rainbow hues. Many were Polish and
Russian Jews, returning from pilgrimage to Jerusalem, and
wore sheep skin coats woolly side in, and sheep skin caps like
busbies. We had also a friar of orders brown, with a rope
round his waist, a monkey, a parrot, several pet rabbits ; and two
Sisters of Mercy. The female deck passengers, white, brown,
and black, had one of the quarter deck alleys to themselves, and
there they built tents with rugs : each one, strange to say,
carried as a conspicuous part of her luggage, a——de chambre.
In the saloon we had an odd passenger ; a curly-headed Negress
nurse, dressed in European fashion, with her wool in a *chignon*
and net, and three bright blue marks tattooed on each cheek ;
her charge was a small Italian boy.

Our course from Alexandria was through the Greek Archipelago, the sea bright blue, and calm as glass, while lovely
islands were everywhere ; the sort of places on which to read
Byron to some fair Zoe, filling up one's leisure hours with a

little piracy. These islands are mostly uninhabited; among them we passed Patmos, the scene of St. John's exile; and Samos, now as in the days of. Horace, famed for wine.

At Scio, the ancient Chios, birthplace of Chian wine, we stopped; the loveliest place I ever saw; a land-locked bay, a town of white and light blue houses, with trees, and wind-mills, and green fields and vineyards down to the water's edge; *cafés* full of people, ladies playing *cróquet*, a background of mountain, and a foreground of blue, blue sea, bearing boats of the queerest description, manned by the most picturesque of ruffians in Greek costumes, long baggy red caps, baggy breeches, and loose jackets. Our captain gave me leave to go ashore, but I could find no Greek interpreter, and had to give it up. The boatmen by the way brought lemons, preserves in glass tumblers, and flasks of oil for sale.

We got into Smyrna Bay early on the 19th May, and staid there until the afternoon of the next day. No English vessels were in the bay, but several foreign merchantmen, and two Austrian men-of-war, one a huge iron-clad with a fine band on board. I hired a guide, a Jew, and under his care went a ride to the ruins of the Castle of Smyrna, on an eminence over the town. From here the view looked like that of a Scotch lake, the bay is so deep and land-locked, but the woods are of cypress and not of larch; the town below looked like a collection of Swiss wooden houses, all with red roofs and never a chimney. Like all eastern towns, Smyrna is com-pletely surrounded by burial grounds, and every dead Mussul-man has a cypress planted over him. The streets of Smyrna are very narrow, their width being regulated by the usual Eastern rule, sufficient for two loaded camels to pass.; I should have enjoyed the bazaars, but for my guide, who would walk me into shops, so I went on board, having, however, bought a good Persian carpet, though at first the dealers would only produce very common affairs.

We started on a Saturday afternoon, stopped at Mitelene late that night, and at Tenedos early in the morning, and shortly afterwards saw the supposed site of ancient Troy. Soon we entered the Straits of the Dardanelles, between the castles of Europe and Asia, scarce a mile apart, and passed the famous castles and batteries of the Dardanelles, where, and at Gallipoli, we stopped, and our deck passengers invested in baked sheep heads. Early next day we arrived at Constantinople, and ere

CONSTANTINOPLE.

Misseri's hotel is an hotel of great reputation. Misseri himself was Lord Lindsay's dragoman on his voyage up the Nile, and afterwards invested his savings in this hotel. Strange tales are told of the despotic rule with which, in Crimean days, he domineered over his guests; but those palmy days for him have fled, and Cook's tickets and competition have reduced him to the habits of an almost ordinary landlord. The hotel is situated in Pera, the European quarter of Constantinople, originally a Genoese settlement on a site granted to that republic in their palmy days; it is situate on a lofty hill, at the foot of which is Galata, the trading portion of what Westerns include in the term Constantinople. Galata is on an arm of the Bosphorus, called the Golden Horn; crossing this by a bridge of boats, one enters Stamboul or Istamboul, where are the remains of the original city of Byzantium. Across the Bosphorus, in Asia, is Scutari and its vast burial grounds and cypress forests. The streets in Pera and Galata are narrow and hilly; in the former suburb they are cut into steps in many places, hence carriages are rare, and the mode of progression is by sedan chairs and by horses, numbers of which—stout little cobby stallions with European saddles—are constantly being led up and down for hire by a smart syce. But the real way of going about Constantinople is by water; thousands of caiques ply for hire on the Bosphorus and Golden Horn. These caiques are curious-shaped boats, cocked up behind and before, easily upset, and generally highly ornate with carving and decorations. The oars are balanced by enormous swellings on their handles in-board of the craft; the passengers lie on cushions on the bottom of the boat. Certainly, to travel about in one of these caiques is most enjoyable, for seen from the water, Constantinople looses all its meanness, and becomes worthy of its site,—the finest in the world. I never spent a day during my stay without being some hours on the water.

My first day was spent in a general view of the sights ; I roamed about Stamboul with a guide, noting the wild figures that crossed me at every corner,—Kurds, Persians, Armenians, Circassians, and other Asiatics, differing widely from the Africans I had so long been accustomed to.   The Turkish women vary widely from the Egyptian ; in Egypt it is rare to see a woman in anything but the most sombre hues, black or blue from head to foot ; but the Turkish women plunge into the most brilliant of colours.   A pork-pie hat of straw, turned up with red or blue velvet, is the favourite head-gear ; and their head--hat and all---is enveloped in rolls of tarlateen, leaving the eyes alone uncovered, but so diaphanous is the tarlateen that the features, hair, and complexions can easily be made out.   The rest of a Turkish lady is rolled up in a huge bundle of red, blue, yellow, or any brilliant-coloured silk.   The waists of these gay bundles are apparently their thickest parts, and their ankles and feet, of prodigious size, are thrust into yellow slippers, while the Egyptian lady prefers red; some sport French boots, which make their ankles vaster than ever in appearance ; their gait is an ungainly waddle.   Their complexions are of a transparent, unhealthy whiteness, suggestive of bismuth powder, and their eyes are large.   It may surprise people to hear that there is a regular manufactory of beauty situate at Tophanieh, near the Turkish Arsenal.   Circassians and Georgians on first importation are sallow, dirty, half-starved, skinny wretches, with little pretence to good looks.   By various cunning old women, veritable Madame Rachels, the new importations are washed, Turkish-bathed, pampered up and fed to fatness, and having youth and good constitution, in six months they speedily ripen into high-priced lights of the harem.

I went to the famous mosque of St. Sophia, formerly a Christian Church, but until very recent days inaccessible to Christians.   For a dollar a most villainous Turk allowed me to ascend into the galleries, which in themselves are spacious enough for whole churches.   All the emblems of our religion have been whitewashed, but over a portion of the altar can still be traced the figure of our Saviour.   The preacher had a wooden sword carried in front of him, to signify that the Turks won and hold Stamboul by the sword.   Inside and outside the edifice is going uncared-for to ruin ; the villain who showed me round coolly knocked a lump out of one of the mosaics, and offered it to me to take away as a curiosity. The domed roof is of vast height, and the marble pillars that support it are said to have come from Ephesus. From the mosque I wandered to the hippodrome, and saw there the obelisk, and the column of bronze serpents said to have been smashed by the puissant arm of Sultan Mahmoud. Near here I saw the hall of a thousand pillars, a subterranean place now used by silk spinners, and also the burnt column, a tall pillar charred and blackened by frequent conflagrations, and only held together by iron hoops.

On the Tuesday I went to see the dancing dervishes of Pera; and, to complete the thing, on the Thursday I visited the howling dervishes of Scutari, but these gentlemen's exploits I have before given to the world in an earlier one of these letters.

A thing which no visitor to Constantinople should omit to do is to go down the Bosphorus by steamer to Buyuckterry, near the Black Sea. It is a most lovely excursion; each side of the Bosphorus is covered with palaces of the most magnificent description, standing close to the water's edge, and with flights of marble steps leading down to it. Several belong to the Sultan, for each Sultan builds in his lifetime two new palaces: opposite that of Dolmabatche lay some twelve huge ironclads: no naval monarch could have a finer situation for his palace than this, in the midst of most lovely scenery, and with his fleet moored at his front door. Other of these palaces belong to various Pashas, and to the ambassadors of great powers: those of the English and Russian ambassadors are at Therapia. All along the banks are vast gardens and woods, and at the time of my visit the scene was enlivened by great masses of flowers in bloom.

I found the bazaars of Stamboul a pleasant, but expensive resort. It is impossible to go and not spend money; the bazaars are such labyrinths of little passages, and it is so hard to know which is passage and which shop, that, ere one knows, one is some fellow's guest, and, pipe in mouth, coffee or lemonade at hand, is viewing his stores, which he does not want you to buy at all, only to inspect for pastime. It's no use trying to escape: every dodge is used to allure one in. Once in, curiosities and curiosities are produced, and one must be more than human, or else penniless, not to buy. Each trade here has its own bazaar: one has nothing but piles of red and yellow slippers; another fezzes, and so on. I found the bazaars not usually frequented by travellers very interesting, and there one escaped importunity; thus the drug, colour, and turners' bazaars pleased me much; the dexterity of the turners was wonderful, each working their toes much more than their hands.

The same day that I saw the howling dervishes at Scutari, I visited the English cemetery at that place. No less than 8000 of our gallant soldiers sleep there on an eminence over-looking the Sea of Marmora. There are few monuments, and the soft Marmora marble is weathering fast, so that what there are are rapidly growing illegible. Some of the monuments are to officers, some to private soldiers, rude erections, often the work of comrades, or of a wife, who could afford but little. On one I noticed simply the inscription " A Russian Officer." It is a sad place, but an Englishman cannot visit it without pride.

Not far from the English cemetery is the vast Turkish burial ground of Scutari, extending for miles : there are said to be there more than twenty times as many graves as there are living inhabitants in Constantinople. Every Turk dying in European Pera, or Stamboul, is, if possible, brought over to be buried in Asiatic Scutari, for as the Turks know themselves to be in-truders in Europe, and expect to be driven back sooner or later to Asia, their birthplace, they choose that the Giaour shall not defile their last resting places. More civilized than we they never bury twice in the same grave ; each Turk lies alone, a marble pillar at his head and feet and a cypress tree planted over him : thus all Scutari is one enormous cypress forest waving over thousands of marble monuments. On the pillar over the head is carved the departed's head-dress, turban or tarboosh, and by its fashion those expert on Eastern head-gear can tell the owner's station in life, and even guess at when he lived. Another form of monument is a tall thin slip of marble on which is written an inscription in green and gold running obliquely across the stone. Many are the varieties to be found in Scutari : some grandees have houses with huge glass sides erected over their family tombs, while the charger of Sultan Mahmoud sleeps under a marble canopy upheld by six pillars.

Friday, the Turkish Sabbath, is a great day at Constanti-nople for sight-seers. First I went off to the Asiatic side to see the Sultan go to the mosque in state, The ground was kept by a regiment of soldiers, slovenly but stalwart men, with dirty and worn rifles : huge negro pioneers marched at their head, and the colour was escorted by similar warriors ; the ancient, who bore it, was hugely bearded, while every other officer in the regiment was closely shaved. In the band, two negroes carried long poles, with bells and scarlet horse tails on the ends. The colonel was a lad of fourteen, the Sultan's son ; and his major was fat enough for Jack Falstaff. Picquets of Circassian cavalry, fine soldier-like men, were stationed about in their national dress, black lambskin caps, and long blue tunics. Prior to the Sultan's appearance, all sorts of equipages and paraphernalia for him passed ; led horses, carriages with French grooms and coachmen in hussar uniforms, broughams, omnibuses and four, containing wives and concubines, sumpter mules, with several changes of apparel, and with luncheons, and all manner of refreshment, packed in boxes; so that the Sultan, after saying his prayers, could at once have any pleasure he pleased. So far were these Monte-Christo-like preparations carried that the royal yacht was lying close by with steam up, and the state caique was manned in readiness; wherever the Sultan goes there follow him complete preparations for any caprice he may imagine. His horses were a mixed lot, some fine, others decidedly poor, and the broughams were very shabby. His ladies were gorgeously dressed in the latest French fashions, with diaphanous veils. I was looking about through an opera-glass, and so incurred the ire of the police, for it is a high crime to look at the Sultan or his wives too narrowly. At last the small commander of the soldiers and his fat major came running to their places : the line presented, and the band struck up. Then appeared the Sultan on a white horse, resplendent with gold lace, preceded by his generals, eunuchs, and chief officers, on horseback, and followed by the Albanian and Montenegrian guards on foot. These were splendid fellows of ferocious aspect, the Albanian in white, and the Montenegrian in scarlet dress and petticoats; each of them having his chest covered with highly-ornamented cartouche cases, each having also a whole armoury of weapons—pistols, swords, and daggers, swaddled around his stomach with costly shawls, and each man moving with that peculiar swagger and sway the Turks consider so martial.

When the Sultan had passed, I went back to my caique, and set off for the other Friday sight, the European sweet-waters. I sailed up the Golden Horn, past the arsenal, where many old wooden men-of-war are rotting, up to where the Golden Horn ends in a long winding canal, meandering through green fields, past a beautiful little wooden kiosk (or small palace) up to a big palace, in whose gardens the salt water is met by the sweet or fresh water from Belgrade. For two miles or more the whole canal was crowded with caiques, bearing holiday parties, and its banks were covered with groups of gaily-dressed Turkish women and their children, pic-nicing, gossiping, and eating sweetmeats, while the men sat apart and smoked ; bands of musicians, both on shore and in boats, abounded. I landed and roamed about for a long time. Many had come by land, some on horseback, others in carriages, varying from well-appointed broughams and waggonettes with velvet and gold curtains, to queer gilt arabas and painted carts drawn by oxen. I saw a singular scene ; a riding horse broke loose, ran at a horse that was drawing a brougham, seized him by the neck and worried and shook him as a dog does a rat, then turning round, he kicked him slap over on to his back, smashing shafts and harness all to bits. Many of the Turkish women were attended by hideous eunuchs ; Greek, Italian, and Levantine women were also there in crowds ; they do not veil except for caprice, convenience, or intrigue. All down the banks of the Golden Horn were similar parties to watch the returning boats, and music and song everywhere abounded.

At Misseri's hotel I met some nice people, whom I had seen before in Egypt, and I found many who had heard of me as Mustapha's Englishman. Misseri charges high, 20 francs per diem, and only gives breakfast and dinner for that. Breakfast is a moveable feast from 8-30 to 12, at which one is entitled to four hot dishes ; dinner is at 7-30, with dessert and coffee. His potatoes, strawberries, and cherries were beautiful ; and the fish at Constantinople is excellent,—sturgeon plentiful and good.

On Sunday, May 28th, I left Constantinople in a long four-masted steamer, the *Iberian*, 405 feet long. We had a lovely voyage to Smyrna, where we lay from the 29th of May to the 3rd of June, and where I had bad asthma, and fell into the hands of a little Irish doctor, a relic stranded there by the Crimean war, so that I was not much on shore at first, and gave up the idea of a trip to Ephesus. On recovering I enjoyed the bazaars much ; the ship's chandler sent one of his men with me, to ward off the interpreters and other rogues, who badger one so in most bazaars.

The skipper of our ship was a jovial man; let me occupy his room, and lent me no end of novels. The early part of our voyage from Smyrna was lovely, sailing along the main coast of Greece; on passing Cape St. Angelo we saw the hermit who lives on the very point thereof. Malta we just sighted. We coasted the African coast from Cape Bon, saw Zembla Island, Turtle Rock, the Fratelli Rocks, and went between Galita and Galena Islands by a passage just about a mile wide.

On Wednesday, 7th, a stoker threw himself overboard about midnight; he was never seen again, though the vessel stopped and a boat was sent to look for him. Owing to coals being bad we steamed very slow, and the captain wished to get more at Gibraltar, but as we arrived there after dark we did not. We arrived at Liverpool on Friday, June 16, 1871.

PART II.

LEAVES FROM A THEBAN GUIDE BOOK.

10

THEBES.

HISTORICAL.

The famous city of Thebes, called by Homer Hectatompylos, or "hundred-gated," in allusion to the numerous propylœa of its temples, stood on both sides of the river Nile, comprising on the eastern side the modern towns or villages of Luxor and Karnak, and on the western side a large extent of country stretching from beyond the temple of Old Koorneh on the north to beyond the temple of Medeenet Haboo on the south. The Arabs, however, have a legend that the Nile did not flow through the city of Thebes, but that it ran close under the eastern hills, from which it is now distant nearly 8 miles. Recent investigations, made by one of the English Consul-Generals in Egypt, rather confirm this view, for he found what he considered an old channel of the Nile close under the hills. The thing is neither impossible nor improbable, but is mentioned by no contemporary historian. The Arabs also assert that the grand avenue from the front of Karnak was continued on dry land to the temple of El Koorneh.

Ancient Thebes was the capital of the district known as the Thebaid, or Upper Egypt, one of the districts or "worlds" into which Egypt was from the very earliest times divided, Memphis being the capital of all Lower Egypt until it was subdivided, when Heliopolis was raised to that dignity for the new district. Both Thebes and Memphis were unwalled towns. Each of the two districts, Upper and Lower Egypt, had its own peculiar crown, and at his coronation each monarch who ruled both districts was invested with both crowns, a ceremony frequently to be found depicted on Egyptian tombs and temples. The crown of Upper Egypt is in shape like a modern wine bottle ; that of Lower Egypt (prior to its division) is a low cap, from the back of which a tall peak towers into the air, while a scroll, not unlike the upper half of the letter S, inclines forward from the junction of the peak and cap. The two are frequently combined into one by inserting the bottle into the cap ; examples of all these three crowns are to be found in the ruins and tombs of Thebes.

Thebes was the chief seat of the worship of the god Amun, ˚Amun-re, or Jupiter Ammon : under the symbol of the god Amun the ancient Egyptians represented "the divine mind in operation"; they gave him a human form, because man was the intellectual animal. From its connection with Amun, Thebes received the name of Magna Diospolis : its name in ancient Egyptian, and in Coptic was Tape (the capital): the letters "b" and "p" are to Egyptian ears but little dissimilar, as any one learns who tries to teach a native English ; and thus Tape grew into Tabe, Thaba, and through the Greek into Thebes. Although Amun was the chief deity worshipped at Thebes, yet other deities were honoured there, and Athor, whose emblem is a cow or heifer, was held in peculiar honour in the western portion of the city, and hence this was known as the Pathyritic suburb, and afterwards Pathyris.

The monuments of Thebes are generally supposed to have been destroyed by the Persians after their conquest of Egypt, and during their stay in that country, B.C. 525—B.C. 332.* A comparison of the ruins shows that this, at least to the extent generally supposed, is not probable ; they suffered most at the end of the three years siege which the city stood against Ptolemy Lathyrus, from whom it revolted between B.C. 117, and B.C. 107; the conqueror, exasperated by its long resistance, determined to destroy all that gave it dignity and importance, and in this he succeeded but too well. In addition to the havoc then made, other causes co-operated to work the downfall of Thebes : its

---

* The following dates in Egyptian history, taken from Zumpt's "Annales Veterum Regnorum," may be useful :—

1st. Pharaonic period, from an uncertain period to B.C. 656.
2nd. Pharaonic period, from the consolidation of Psammetichus of all Egypt, under one crown, to its conquest in B.C. 525, by the Persians under Cambyses.
3rd. Persian period, from B.C. 525 to invasion by Alexander in B.C. 332.
4th. Greek (Alexandrian and Ptolemaic) period, B.C. 332 to death of Cleopatria in B.C. 30.
5th. Roman period, from B.C. 30 to Arab conquest in A.D. 640.
6th. The present, or Mahommedan dynasty.

Several great waves of conquest have thus passed over Egypt. The Christian religion was once widely prevalent in it, the ancient Egyptians (supposed to be now represented by the Copts) having embraced it.

site placed it aloof from the commerce of Egypt, and thus it
decayed down to a mere collection of villages, becoming, until
the Arab invasion of Egypt, the great head-quarters of the
Coptic Christians, who plastered their mud churches and villages over its ruins, and in iconoclastic fury destroyed, wherever
they could, the faces of the figures their predecessors had
carved.   When the Arabs overran Egypt the Christians fled,
and settled at Esne.   A few remained, and they and Arabs
now form the inhabitants of what once was Thebes, identi-
fied by some antiquarians with the No of Scripture (see
Jeremiah, c. 46, v. 25 : Ezek. c. 30, v. 14, 15, and 16 ; Nahum,
c. 3, v. 8).

Nothing more almost is known of Thebes.   Lord Lindsay,
from whom we shall quote frequently, writes :—" Nothing can
be more unaccountable than the cloud of utter oblivion that
hung over Thebes until the middle of the seventeenth century.
No Frank traveller, certainly, had penetrated beyond Cairo ;
but that the Arab writers, who are generally apt to exaggerate
in their descriptions of architectural remains, should take no
notice of ruins like those of Thebes, is most extraordinary, yet
not more so than that Herodotus should pass them over so
completely.   Abd'altatif gives us no assistance ; he was not in
the upper country, and his valuable work on Egypt is merely
an account of what he himself had seen, extracted from a larger
compilation.   Edrisi, Ebn al Ouardi, and Bakoui are quite
silent.   Abidfeda, who finished his work in 1321, after be-
stowing just praise on the antiquities of Oshmunein Ensina,
and Memphis, pronounces a grave eulogium on the pottery of
Luxor.   Ebn Batuto, who ascended the Nile in 1325, mentions El Aksa (Luxor) as one of the stages of his journey, but
says nothing (at least in the abridgement, which is all we
possess of his work) of its ruins.   How Leo Africanus could
have omitted all mention of them is most surprising ; he must
have passed and repassed them by night, for he expressly states
that he sailed up the river as high as Essouan.   But did he
hear nothing of Luxor and Carnac ?   Were there no tales
current of those vast halls, that genii might walk under with
unbended brow ; of those awful statues, that, side by side, look
down on the Nile like the tutelar guardians of Egypt—works
worthy of the Preadamites ; were there no tales of mystery, no
talismans concealed there for Al Ouardi or Bakoui to record ?
One would almost fancy they believed that merely naming

them would wake Memnon and his brother from their charmed
slumber, let loose the sphinxes, and bring them down a mighty
army to revenge the wrongs of Egypt on her oppressors' heads.
Neither Carnac nor Luxor are to be found in D'Herbelet's
precious 'Bibliothèque Orientale,' published in 1697, and he
suggests that Cous in the upper Thebaid may possibly be the
ancient Thebes.   In short, the first notice I have been able to
find of them occurs in the brief narrative, dated 1668, of
Father Protais, a worthy Capuchin missionary, who, after
describing Luxor and Carnac with the simplicity and accuracy
of Buckhardt, does not appear to have been aware he had
trodden on the dust of Thebes."

MODERN THEBES, INCLUDING LUXOR.

The traveller, on arrival at what was Thebes, generally
moors his boat off the modern town of Luxor, which derives
its name (El-Uxor, the palaces) from the ruins it stands among.
It is a market town, having a weekly market on Tuesday, and
a bazaar in which nothing can be got that an European or
American will want to buy, except possibly sardines and brandy
and Arab tobacco, which smokes very well in a chibouk, particularly if mixed with a little latakaia.   For a bottle of ink
or for the commonest medicine the traveller must send to Esneh
or Keneh.   Luxor has a mosque, behind which is the tomb of
Abu-l-Hajjaj, a Mahommedan saint, and his three sons ; in his
honour an annual fair or festival is held.   It has also a Coptic
Church built recently on a site given by Mustapha Agha, the
English Consular agent, himself a rigid Mussulman.   There is
a Coptic Bishop at Luxor ; should a traveller be in Luxor on
any great festival of the Church, he should not omit to be
present at a Coptic service,—the volleys of musketry fired inside
the Church will rather astonish him, should he attend the midnight service on Easter eve.   In a burial-ground occupying the
site of an old Coptic Church, beyond the market-place, lie the
mortal remains of five Englishmen, who came for their health
and died at Luxor.   A Frenchman and a German are buried
beside them.   An occasional visit from travellers would be
beneficial, as they might give a well-timed word, now and then,
which would stir the natives up to protect and keep the place
clean and in repair.   The names of the persons buried there
are to be found in the visitors' book kept by Mustapha Agha.

One curiosity, a curiosity in ancient as well as in modern times, the traveller should visit at Luxor,—that is the system of hatching eggs by artificial heat. There is a very fine establishment, or rather two establishments in one building, not far behind the house of Mustapha Agha, to whom a ground rent of 500 fowls is paid.

The famous constellation of the Southern Cross is also visible at Luxor ; it is above the horizon for only a short period every night: travellers from northern climes should make a point of seeing it, when on the meridian,—that is when the Cross is perpendicular. It is easily known ; four stars of the first magnitude mark the four extremities of a Latin cross, and it must be looked for near the horizon. It is not visible from the banks of the Nile, but can be seen from the balconies of the houses in the town.

Guides, horses, and donkeys can easily be procured for all the sights of Thebes. In case of difficulty the traveller should consult the Consular representative of his nation.

Travellers should have their letters addressed to the Consular agent of their nation, and should send their letters from Luxor by him to an agent, care of their Consulate in Cairo, to re-post for Europe or America. The post from Luxor leaves daily by foot-runners to Roda, where it is transferred to the rail. No man can say when a letter will get to Cairo from Luxor, or *vice versa*,—any time between six and twelve days ; they do, however, get, and with safety, with much more safety than if entrusted to travellers. There is a telegraph station opposite to Luxor ; only messages in Arabic can be telegraphed. The line is not continuous to Cairo, but there are four breaks, at each of which the message is repeated, and English and American names transformed : altogether we do not recommend its employment, unless a traveller has plenty of money and can wait a week or two for a reply.

Persons who wish to stay at Luxor, either for amusement or for antiquarian research, or to benefit by " the Luxor doctor," as the natives call a seat between the pillars of the great colonnade, to which they ascribe healing powers, can easily get a room from one of the Consular agents. The writer (who came for his health and derived great benefit from his stay) can confidently recommend anyone who wishes to stay at Luxor, to apply to Mustapha Agha. That gentleman, who speaks English, Italian, and French, as well as several Eastern languages, will board and lodge a traveller for £10 a month, and also contract to bring him to Luxor, and send him back, providing him with an English speaking servant, for £50, to include provisions *en route*. The writer did this, living with Mustapha and having meals with him in English fashion, and can speak in the highest terms of his treatment. Of course he did not live in that luxury that travellers on dahabeehs do, but then it only cost him for a two months stay at Luxor, and the journey up and down, £70; to have taken a dahabeeh and lived in it for that time would have been £250. Anyone who wishes to do this should give Mustapha ample notice beforehand, and should stipulate for an upper front room in Mustapha's house under the colonnade, or for rooms in Mustapha's new house, situated just behind the town, with a garden in front, and beautiful views from its windows. He should take with him a couple of small carpets, a Turkish blanket, and a pillow for his bed. Should he object to sleep on a divan, or palmstick bed (which is very comfortable), he might take an iron bedstead; cotton sheets Mustapha provides. The writer took his own towels; that is not necessary, but is convenient. Mustapha does not provide wine or spirits; a person going to stay with him should take his own, and some tea; but if Mustapha has tea, he will give it and anything else he has; if not, his lodger must provide it, or go without. The writer took some potted meats and soups to supply deficiencies of cooking, but they were never necessary: pots of preserves, &c., &c., will be useful, as butter is not to be had. Of course pens, ink, paper, matches, &c., &c., should be taken. Of all stores, a person intending to follow the writer's advice should take rather more than he wants. He will be dealing with Easterns, who will ask for his luxuries without hesitation, at the same time giving him access to theirs: on the whole he will benefit by this. An European or American sojourner at Luxor is sure to be requested to do medical wonders. The writer inadvertently commenced by giving out diachylon plaster, forthwith the whole place beset him to cure every malady Egyptian man or woman or child is subject to.

The traveller or sojourner at Luxor can get plenty of shooting; quails are numerous towards the end of the harvesting season; his Consul will find him a man to guide him to their haunts. Crocodiles can be got in a lake near Dendera, but an introduction to the Mudeer of Keneh is necessary.

Hyenas and jackals are abundant, but not easy to get at. The sportsman, who wishes to shoot such, must bait for them with a dead donkey or bullock, and hide near ; let him beware that he has not the success of an English lord, who bagged a donkey at Karnak instead of an hyena. Geese are to be found early in the morning in the lake west of the Nile. Cranes, ibises, hawks, hoopoes, pigeons, &c., are also procurable.

Dancing girls can also be seen at Luxor ; the Consular agents, men of position and wealth in their own country, not unfrequently invite the traveller to a dinner, *à la* Arab, and a *fantasia* of native dancing and music, which is worth seeing, and ladies generally attend ; they must be prepared to sit on the floor for dinner and eat with their fingers, and they will probably be astonished to see their host tear a joint or fowl in pieces with his fingers and give each guest a piece. The Arab cooking is both good and clean, and many judges consider to surpass the French.

With regard to the curiosities which are offered to the traveller at Luxor, a regular manufactory of them exists there ; scarabœi and seals are made from a soap stone and hardened. In default of any other expert, the traveller had better consult his Consul, and he may thus get genuine antiquities. No advice can be given as to price, it varies with the demand, the supposed rank and wealth of the traveller, the nearness of his departure, the price given by his immediate predecessors, and the honesty or rascality of his dragoman. Gold and silver articles had better be weighed, and paid for at market price of bullion, with a percentage added for the work, say £5 per cent. The gold antique coins sold by the guides should be got for about a napoleon or a sovereign each, and the silver ones at the rate of about eight for £1 ; but of course if many travellers are in the place, or expected, they cannot be got at these quotations. As to scarabœi and seals, no advice can be given ; some are dear at two or three shillings, others cheap at as many pounds ; the Arabs do not know the difference, which depends on the work, material, size, and 'preservation, but mainly on the hieroglyphics on their under surface. The modern ones should be got very cheap, two or three piastres apiece, or at the most, for very superior ones, two shillings. For many purposes the confessedly modern scarabœi and seals will suit the traveller as well as the more expensive and doubtful ancient ones. There is an American gentleman (whom I have mentioned before) resident at Luxor, who has made a study of Egyptian antiquities, and whose knowledge and probity can be relied on : I say probity, because guides and dragomen, and a few travellers misled by such, put him down as a wholesale manufacturer of antiques. My residence at Luxor enables me to contradict that statement with confidence.

THE RUINS OF THEBES.

Before entering into a detailed account of the various ruined temples at Thebes, we will endeavour to give a stranger a correct idea of the positions of the chief monuments of ancient art, which it is incumbent on him to see : we will afterwards advise him upon the order in which he should take them, and the time he should devote thereto.

Suppose, then, our traveller to be in his dahabeeh moored off Luxor, or on the river bank at that place.

He will easily indentify the temple of Luxor, running from the conspicuous obelisk backwards to the creek at the end of the village. Half an hour's ride northwards on the same bank, the eastern one, of the river are the ruins of Karnak, which he will have passed *en route* to Luxor. From the one obelisk of Luxor (there once were two) ran the principal street of Eastern Thebes, passing through avenues of sphinxes under magnificent gateways or pylons, and hitting the ruins of Karnak about midway in their present length, and forming the southern approach to the great temple of Amunse at Karnak. From this street another deviated Nilewards through a pylon and temple to reach the front of the temple of Karnak ; the communication between Luxor and Karnak was thus by a bifurcated or Y-shaped road.

Turning to the opposite or western side of the river, the traveller will easily pick out the Colossi of the Plains ; from these two figures a street ran, carried over the Nile by a ferry, to Luxor. Any native will point out to the traveller the situation of the temple-palace of El Koorneh, the most northerly of the ruins of Western Thebes, and opposite the ruins of Karnak ; both these ruins fronted the Nile, and were connected by a street passing through avenues of sphinxes, and crossing the river by a ferry. Southwards, some little way from the temple of El Koorneh, are the ruins of the Remesium, or Memnonium, as the traveller will more generally hear it called. In the rising ground, behind an imaginary line joining the Remesium and the Colossi of the Plains, are mounds marking the site of demolished temples; one mound is called Kom el Hettan or mound of sandstone; another is conspicuous for the remains of crude bricks. These appear, all to have been connected with one another, with the Memnonium, and with the Colossi by streets : indeed it seems probable that the Colossi marked the cross roads, or perhaps a great square, whence a grand road led to Luxor. South of the Colossi again the traveller will see the ruins of Medeenet Haboo, its palace and temples all clustered together. Beyond that is a plain, which was once a lake, Birket Haboo, and beyond it again a small temple of the Emperor Adrian, which few care to visit. The two temples of Dayr el Medeeneh and Dayr el Bahree lie backwards from the river, niched into the hills; Dayr el Medeeneh being in a valley which lies between Medeenet Haboo and the Memnonium, and behind the Colossi, while Dayr el Bahree is immediately below the cliffs of the Libyan mountains. Immediately below the temple of Dayr el Bahree, and behind the Remesium, are the tombs of the Assassef; Biban el Molook (the gates of the kings), where most of the royal tombs are situate, is in a valley behind Dayr el Bahree, whose entrance is just past the temple of Old Koorneh. The hill above the temple of Old Koorneh, and between the entrance to Biban el Molook and Dayr el Bahree, is Drah Aboo Negga, where are situated the oldest tombs. The tombs of the Queens are in a valley behind Medeenet Haboo : between this valley and the valley of Dayr el Bahree are the hills of Koornet Murraee, and Shekh Abd el Koorneh, both honeycombed with tombs.

THE RUINS OF THEBES.—EASTERN SIDE.

1.—LUXOR.

The temple of Luxor in point of age consists of two portions, the more modern portion erected by Remeses II. (Remeses the Great, who reigned from B.C. 1311 to B.C. 1245) forming the entrance to the portion erected by Amunoph III, who reigned from B.C. 1403 to B.C. 1367. The most modern portion of this temple has thus an antiquity of over 3100 years, while the remainder is about a century older.

Let the traveller, who wishes to obtain a correct idea of the temple of Luxor, proceed to the easily found spot, where the

now solitary obelisk rears its head over the mud hovels of the
town, and he will find himself opposite to the entrance, from
which a street or dromos of sphinxes, one of the main streets
of the ancient Thebes, led to Karnak.   The entrance was between two obelisks, one of which is familiar to every visitor to
Paris, having been taken there many years ago; the other that
remains is partly buried in the sand, but on the unburied portion the hieroglyphics are so perfect and so deeply cut that an
Arab has ascended to the summit by the foothold they give.
Behind the sites of the obelisks are two sitting statues of
Remeses II, and a third, almost buried, is at the western end
of the propylœa; symmetry would suggest that a fourth figure
should be at the eastern end, and Lord Lindsay mentions four
in his "Letters from Egypt," but he seems to be mistaken.
On the propylœa behind the statues are some spirited battle
scenes.

Passing in between the propylœa the traveller comes upon
the modern mosque, and a congeries of mud hovels which conceal the columns of the great court, a parallelogram of nearly
two hundred feet in length by something less in breadth; this
is surrounded by a double row of columns; the enthusiastic
in Egyptology can see each of these columns by going into the
houses that surround them; he will, however, find little to
repay his curiosity, or worth the baksheesh he must give to
the ladies of the houses.   The street, if modern Luxor can be
said to have such a thing, passes out of the great court by the
ruined propylon of Amunoph.   Thus far we have dealt with the
erections of Remeses II, we now come to the earlier portion of
the temple.

The propylon of Amunoph leads into the great colonnade
of fourteen columns, of whose original height some fifteen feet
is now buried in sand.   The name of Amunoph III, the
founder, can easily be found; it is contained in two cartouches.
The principal element in one of them is the seated figure of a
god, holding the *tau* emblem, known to the guides as the "key
of the Nile;" a circle is over the figure's head, and an arc of a
circle below.   It will be found on a large scale on the third
pillar (counting from the south) of the eastern row, the pillar
immediately on the right of a person coming out of the window
of the inner room of Mustapha Agha's house.   The names of
Horus (an owl is the principal figure in one cartouche, and a
beetle in the other, see fifth column from south of eastern row)

and of Sethi (see first column of western row), both successors of Amunoph are also to be found. The natives of Luxor have a belief in healing powers attaching to these columns ; the person wishing to benefit must come and sit under them daily for an hour before sundown, and he will then speedily be cured of all sickness. To these columns, too, the natives say that Remeses II strung up three martyrs who refused to worship him as God : the three tombs of these martyrs have been shown to the writer, one in the centre, and one at each extremity of Luxor, but they are evidently many centuries posterior to the time of Remeses the Great. The colonnade leads into a second court about 150 feet square with twelve columns on either side, and on the northern end ; on the southern end is a portico of thirty-two columns. Behind this portico comes a number of small chambers, of which the centre one forms a vestibule to a hall of four columns, which again is the vestibule to the detached sanctuary. The sanctuary was, as an inscription on it tells us, rebuilt in Ptolemaic days. Behind the sanctuary are several more chambers, one of which (recognizable by its semi-circular niche or apse) has been used as a Roman Court of Law, and has the remains of Roman frescoes. Over this portion of the ruins is perched the house once occupied by the late Lady Duff Gordon. Behind the ruins of the temple are the remains of an old Roman quay, from which an excellent header may be taken into the creek below.

The traveller who stands between the rows of columns of the great colonnade will notice that the propylon of Remeses the Great is not " square" with the central axis of the colonnade. This was done purposely ; the position of the Nile, and the wish to connect the temple of Luxor with that of Karnak by a street, caused a slight inclination eastward to be given to the Remesean additions.

2.—KARNAK.

Under the general name of Karnak, or Carnac, is popularly included, besides the ruins of the great temple known by that name, several other buildings, which all stood in the sacred enclosure, and were surrounded by a wall or mound, whose ruins may yet be seen, in a vast heap of earth, enclosing a large space of ground. The description of the ruins of these buildings given by the usual authorities is a little perplexing, owing to its being unaccompanied by a map, and owing to its having been written by one who was so thoroughly acquainted with his subject as to have forgotten the difficulties of conception a stranger to the *locus in quo* would have to undergo.

From the propylœa and obelisks of the temple of Luxor, an avenue, guarded by sphinxes facing each other, and still traceable in the slack of the ground, extends northwards to the great temple of Amun at Karnak, meeting it at right angles just east of the great court of the temple of Karnak, which extends from west to east. The traveller, however, does not usually follow this avenue in going from Luxor to Karnak : he deviates Nilewards, along the western branch of the Y-shaped street mentioned in our general description of Thebes, in order to visit a detached temple, said by Lord Lindsay to be dedicated to Isis, and in order to reach the western front of the grand temple of Karnak.

Following this route from Luxor, he comes upon an avenue of Crio-sphinxes, or Ram-headed sphinxes, leading up to the pylon of Ptolemy Euergetes, who, with Bernice, at once his wife and his sister, and with Philadelphus and Arsinoe his parents, are represented in the sculptures here. The figure in a Greek costume within the doorway, usually pointed out by the guides, is that of Ptolemy, and is noticeable on account of the costume. This pylon is about 2100 years old ; it opens on another avenue of sphinxes, which conduct the traveller up to the propylœa of the temple of Isis, founded by Remeses III, and having, therefore, an antiquity of just over 3000 years. It has, however, been largely indebted to subsequent monarchs for additions and enrichments. The propylœa and the court of columns behind it are the work of a Pharaoh, Amunse-Pehor, who flourishêd about 1016 B.C., and therefore about twenty or thirty years before the era of Solomon. Behind this court is a court of eight columns, behind which again is the *debris* of the sanctuary and of some side chambers. This portion of the temple was begun by Remeses III, and completed by the fourth and eighth monarchs of that name, all three of whose reigns are included in the period before B.C. 1219 and 1161 ; it is, therefore, about 3000 years old, and coeval with the downfall of Troy, which happened circa B.C. 1184. In the easternmost of the chambers, round the sanctuary, are most beautifully-cut figures and hieroglyphics representing the investment of monarchs with the symbols of their rank by the gods. The chief of these symbols is that called by the guides the "Key of the Nile"; it really is the sacred *tau* symbol, a symbol in the shape of the Greek letter *tau* with an oval on the top. It is the sign of life, and denotes that the monarchs of Egypt had the power of life and death over their subjects.

Leaving this temple, the traveller then proceeds to the western entrance of the great temple of Karnak, and finds himself in front of the western propylon or gate of entrance. This was erected by Remeses the Great, more than 3100 years ago: he has often been confounded with Sesostris, and hence some have stated this entrance to be the work of a monarch of that name. Lord Lindsay ascended this propylon. He writes of it:—"The avenue of sphinxes, through which the god returned, in solemn procession, to his shrine at Karnak, after his annual visit to the Libyan (western) suburb, ascends to it from the river, the same avenue traversed age after age by the conqueror, the poet, the historian, the lawgiver, the philosopher,—Sesostris, Cambyses, Homer, Herodotus, Thales, Anaxagoras, Solon, Pythagoras, Plato,—and now the melancholy song of an Arab boy was the only sound that broke the silence; but that poor boy was the representative of an older, and a nobler race than the Pharaohs. Long did we gaze on the scene around and below us,—utter, awful desolation! Truly, indeed, has No been 'rent asunder'! The towers of the second or eastern propylon are mere heaps of stones ' poured down'—as prophecy and modern travellers describe the foundations of Samaria—into the court on one side, and the great hall on the other,—giant columns have been swept away like reeds before the mighty avalanche, and one hardly misses them. And that hall! who could describe it? Its dimensions, 170 feet by 329, the height of the central avenue of columns 66 feet, exclusive of their pedestals—the total number of columns that supported its roof, 134. These particulars may give you some idea of its extent, but of its grandeur and beauty none. Every column is sculptured, and all have been richly painted. The exterior walls, too, are a sculptured history of the wars of Osirei (Sethi I) and Remeses."

Our quotation has been a little anticipatory. Let us return to the western entrance, and notice the granite Colossi that still stand in front of it, and the French and Italian inscriptions within it. The holes through the propylœa were for the purpose of fastening the flagstaff that usually stood in front of propylœa. Passing through, the traveller comes into a large court with an avenue of columns down the centre, six on either side, and a covered way all round it. One alone of these columns is now standing : in the year 1739, or thereabouts, Perry found two standing, and the rest lying on the ground "like a pile of millstones thrown down." These columns apparently supported no roof, but probably carried ornamental figures. In the south-west corner of this hall is a small but model temple of Remeses III, which has been incorporated into the main temple ; in the north-west corner are some chambers erected by Sethi II. At the eastern end of the first hall is a ruinous propylon with a small vestibule before the gate, which goes into the great hall of assembly built by Sethi I, about 3200 years ago.

The roof of this magnificent hall was supported by a forest of columns, 134 in number, which, in their decadence, stamp Karnak to this day as the first architectural remain in the world. Twelve central pillars, six in either row, rising to a height of over 60 feet (without plinth or abacus being considered) form a central nave, while 122 pillars, some 20 feet shorter, ranged in seven rows on either side of this gigantic nave, form an appropriate series of side aisles to it, the centremost of which had by means of a clerestory, portions of whose delicate perpendicular tracery yet remain, their roof on a level with that of the central nave. The colours with which these columns were originally painted are still to be seen in sheltered places, weathered slightly, but still comparatively fresh. Leaving this hall by a gateway between propylœa erected by Amunoph III, more than 3200 years ago, the traveller passes into a small hall, where stood two obelisks. When erected, these obelisks, one of which is now on the ground, were in front of the then main entrance to the temple of Karnak, which then extended no further than this. The avenue of sphinxes we have spoken of as running from the temple of Luxor to the temple of Karnak, forming the eastern branch and main limb of the Y, meets that latter building here, and the traveller looking southwards from the smaller obelisks (so called to distinguish them from larger ones, at which we shall presently arrive), will see the propylœa through which this avenue led from Luxor to the then front of the temple of Karnak. The temple of Karnak was built from east to west ; each successive builder built on a larger scale than did his predecessor, and each in succession considered he had reached finality. This is proved by each successive propylon being bored for the support of flagstaffs, ornaments which stood at the front and not in the middle of an ancient Egyptian temple.

Returning to these obelisks—the smaller obelisks to distinguish them from the others of larger size—they were both standing at the time of Pococke's visit in 1737, but one had fallen or been upset before Perry's visit to Asia in 1739 or 1740. These two smaller obelisks were erected by Thothmes III, and are thus about 3300 years old. Passing on we come to two larger obelisks, one of which has been overthrown and broken by the use of wedges, while the other still towers to a height of nearly 100 feet. These were surrounded by a peristyle of figures. The obelisk that still stands is said by Lord Lindsay to have been erected, 3400 years ago, by the Princess Amense to the memory of Thothmes I, and yet the hieroglyphics on it are as sharp as if cut yesterday. From these larger obelisks the traveller passes betwen two ruined propylœa and a vestibule, and comes to two small granite pillars, ornamented with the lotus stalk and blossom, which introduces him to the sanctuary of red granite, rebuilt by Philip Aridœus, brother to Alexander the Great, about 2200 years ago, in lieu of the original one built by Pharaoh Osirtasen I, nigh 3900 years ago, and destroyed by the Persians. The sanctuary is surrounded by small chambers, and on its roof the colours still remain.

Beyond it are the remains of some of the polygonal columns erected by Osirtasen, the oldest remains in all Thebes, coeval probably with Abraham. Osirtasen, who began to reign B.C. 2020, probably was the Pharaoh who took Sarai from Abraham. If, therefore, chronology can be trusted, these pillars were erected about 350 years after Noah's flood, and possibly before Noah died. Beyond these columns are two pedestals of red granite which once supported obelisks; these would be the porphyry obelisks seen by Père Sicard in 1714, and which had disappeared before Pococke's visit in 1737. Père Protais, a Capuchin missionary, who visited Thebes in 1670, describes these two as of jasper. Another old traveller, Norden, describes them as of granite, fine as porphyry, covered with painted hieroglyphics, and apparently destined to support images on their summits.

Proceeding still eastward the traveller will come to a columnar building executed by Thothmes III, beyond which is an unfinished pylon bearing the name of Nectanebo, closing the eastern appendages to the great temple of Karnak. The traveller looking eastward towards this propylon will see another propylon of Ptolemaic date towards the N.E.; this stands in front of a confused heap of ruins, which once was a temple of Amunoph III, and decorated with an avenue of sphinxes and two granite obelisks, bringing up the number of obelisks at Karnak to eight; add to these the two Luxor ones, and we have the ten obelisks which Père Protais saw at Thebes in 1670.

We have hitherto said nothing of the historical sculptures, and for convenience of description have left them until now, though guides generally and advisedly point them out *en passant*. They run round the exterior of the great hall of columns, and represent mainly the victories of Sethi I and of his son Remeses II or the Great. The *debris* that has accumulated round these walls, the ravages of damp, and in places the peeling off of the surface of the stones, interfere sadly with the reading of the story these figures tell. The conquests of Sethi I are depicted on the northern exterior of the hall of columns, and here will be seen every incident of a successful campaign in an enemy's country, concluding with the triumphant return of the victorious monarch to a large city situate on the Nile, which he crosses by a bridge. The invaded country appears to be an Asiatic one. The conquests of Remeses I are on the southern exterior, and are over the same people, supposed to be the Canaanites. On the same wall, at the eastern end, and just close to the small temple of Remeses III, will be found the captives taken by Sheskonk I (the Shishak of Scripture : see 1 Kings, 14c.) when he spoiled Jerusalem. King Rehoboam is also depicted with the inscription in hieroglyphics, "Jehouda Melek," king of the Jews. Mr. Ramsey, the fellow traveller of Lord Lindsay, writes of the battle-pieces at Karnak :—"There is extreme spirit and boldness in the execution, and the story is told most distinctly and plainly. Though modern artists might have more correct ideas of perspective and true proportion, yet I doubt if any of them, following those rules, could so clearly represent in the same space the subjects contained in these. The liberty used by the sculptor of giving you ground plans, or elevations, or both, as it suits his purpose, is undoubtedly contrary to all just rules of drawing; but one's eye soon accustoms itself and ceases to be offended, while the story is told with much greater facility and correctness."

A scramble to the top of the walls, on whose exterior the sculptures are, will show that, especially on the south, stairs and chambers were formed in the thickness of the walls, and such no doubt the priests found highly useful.

Before we mentioned the sculptures we had conducted the traveller to the eastern end of the temple of Karnak, and pointed out to him the Ptolemaic propylon of the temple of Amunoph III on his left hand to the N.E. This he will hardly care to visit, but bending sharp round to his right hand, and following the exterior of the temple of Karnak, he will seek the avenue of sphinxes from Luxor to Karnak, of which we have already pointed him out one extremity at the obelisk of Luxor, and the other in the Karnak hall of the small obelisks, being the eastern branch and main limb of the Y. Before reaching the avenue he will pass a small lake of water, originally sweet, but now, from want of drawing off, impregnated with natron from the soil; this lake (the S.E. or eastern one of Murray) is embanked with masonry, and has a few ruins on its bank about 2200 years old. The avenue itself was crossed, near the great temple of Karnak, by four propylons, of which one, that nearest the great temple and connected with it by walls, was pulled down in very modern times—since Lord Lindsay's visit in 1837; three still stand in part: two roofless, one with the lintel still remaining. These four propylons are the work of the first, second, and third Pharaohs of the name of Thothmes, and of Amunoph III, and have therefore an antiquity of between 3200 and 3300 years. Magnificent colossi flank these gateways, and they were apparently connected by areas or avenues of sculptured figures. Of two of these colossi, now headless, but who were not so at Père Protais's visit in 1670, Mr. Ramsey writes thus—" On the last propylon towards Luxor are the torsos of two lovely statues, perhaps 25 or 30 feet high; they are much mutilated and have no heads, but what remains of their sculpture and contour is beautifully graceful, and yet in the Egyptian style, arms close to the sides, and left foot advanced. The priests seem to have employed real master geniuses, but to have confined them to certain fixed forms, at least in the human figure; for where they are freed from these shackles as in the phonetic hieroglyphics, nothing can surpass the execution of the drawing, as well as the finishing.

Hundreds of sphinxes, statues, and figures of all sorts, are lying about the grand approach. One sphinx in particular made a great impression on me. They say all sphinxes are male, but the features of a really sweet pretty girl could not be mistaken; and though her nose, part of her mouth, and chin were gone, yet one hardly missed them, what remained was so pretty and elegant. One pitied the poor thing being tacked to such an uncouth body as that of a sphinx, and obliged to sit down in line with a hundred uninteresting fellows for ever, as it were fascinated down by the wand of some ancient magician . . . . . We re-visited the crowds of sphinxes and broken statues on the grand southern approach (the avenue from Luxor to the middle of the temple of Karnak.) There is a great deal that is uncouth and unskilful, the effect of which is only to be estimated by their situation as parts of a grand whole, and the constrained stiffness of which must be explained and excused by the despotic influence of form and custom in religious matters, studiously inculcated and preserved by the priests; but there are among them forms of eternal beauty, such as remain henceforth part and parcel of one's mind—pure and clear as truth—no mystery, no mere symbol of mystical priestcraft, but a bright embodying of the soul of genius, which speaks from mind to mind at the interval of three thousand years."

Continuing Luxorwards the avenue leads to the ruins of a small temple, or else of three or four ruined small propylons close together, and connected by areas surrounded by figures. Near this is the western lake, where are sculptures and ruins of various dates.

The traveller who has followed our description will understand that the ruins of Karnak were enclosed within a wall: that from the entrance of the temple of Luxor an avenue or street of sphinxes (that by which he has returned) led northwards to what was at the time of the making of this avenue the front of the temple of Karnak: that when the temple at Karnak was extended Nilewards, the road from Luxor to the new front of the temple of Karnak of course deviated Nilewards: that on this new road (that by which our traveller went to Karnak) the propylon of Ptolemy Euergetes and the "ibis temple" of Remeses III was erected. Other remains there are in plenty within the circuit of the walls of Karnak: few care thoroughly to explore them; those who would do so must consult other books, even the great Murray himself is not for them a sufficient *vade mecum.* Besides Egyptian remains, those of crude brick Roman buildings are in several places to be seen.

THE RUINS OF THEBES—WESTERN SIDE.

1.—THE TEMPLE OF OLD KOORNEH.

This temple is remarkable for the irregular distances at which the columns in front of it are placed, and for the deviation its ruins exhibit from the usual plan of an Egyptian temple : it was, however, a palace as much as a temple, and this combination of two buildings into one may account for the deviation alluded to. It was once approached by two avenues of sphinxes, passing under two pylons, and apparently forming part of a street, which, crossing the river by a ferry, led through another avenue of sphinxes up to the temple of Karnak. In front of the temple-palace stood a colonnade of ten columns, placed at irregular distances, with three doorways, placed also at irregular distances, in the wall behind. The central doorway opens into a court, surrounded by small chambers, three on either side, and five at the end opposite the door, one of which leads into a room supported by four square pillars ; beyond this was the sanctuary, and chambers now in ruins, and too dilapidated to be clearly distinguishable. The roof of the great court is supported by six pillars ; westward of the chambers adjoining to the central hall are the remains of a hall whose roof is supported by the pillars, and also some more remains ; eastward is a large unroofed or hypœthral court, with an erection of some sort in its centre. The position of this hypœthral court is unusual in being at one side of the temple, and not, as is common, in front. This temple palace was erected by Sethi I, and the first three monarchs of the name of Remeses ; in age it varies, therefore, from 3080 to 3180 years. Most of these monarchs are represented in the sculpture of the hall of two columns on the west side.

2.—THE REMESIUM (GENERALLY MISNAMED THE MEMNONIUM).

This noble ruin has obtained the name of the Memnonium in the same way that one of the Colossi of the Plains has become familiar to every one under the name of Memmon, Mi-Ammon, beloved of Ammon, a title of honour applied to the

Egyptian kings having been confounded with the Memmon of Homer.   The Remesium, to give it its correct name, was founded by Remeses II, son of Osirei or Sethi I, hence called Se-Osirei and confounded with Sesostris ; he flourished about 3150 years ago.   The huge pyramidical propylon which forms the front of the Remesium is much dilapidated, and even now huge blocks seem tottering to their fall.   A climb up to the doorway, or, better still, to the top of one of the towers, affords a lovely view, and at the same time will give a clearer idea of the plan of this temple than can be got by any amount of explanation.

This doorway opens into an area that once had a double row of columns on either side, of which but scant vestiges remain.   From hence a flight of steps led into a court, while on the left of a person ascending the stairs was once the most stupendous colossal statue in the world, a granite statue of Remeses II seated on his throne in an attitude expressive of repose after his distant victories.   This now lies on its face " prone as great Dragon fell," the upper half split into two or three vast fragments, the lower shivered to atoms.   The figure measures twenty-two feet across the shoulders, about four feet more than either of the Colossi of the Plains, and must, when unbroken, have weighed nearly 900 tons.   How or when its destruction was wrought is not known.   Sir Gardner Wilkinson, in the pages of Murray's Guide, seems inclined to think that it must have been done in more modern times than generally supposed, and that gunpowder was the agent employed.   This seems very probable.   From the time of its downfall until the middle of the 17th century, when Père Protais visited it, Thebes sank into utter oblivion.   No European traveller saw it ; Herodotus does not mention it, and the Arab writers pass over it in silence.   Thus we have little to guide us as to the stages of its decadence.   We do know, however, that great destruction has been wrought at Karnak since the visit of Père Protais : and although we would not venture to say that the statute of Remeses II was uninjured in the seventeenth century, yet it well might have been so until long after the invention of gunpowder.

Leaving the shivered relics of this enormous statute, and passing up the steps by its side, the traveller enters into a court, whose sides are formed by double rows of circular columns, while at either end are square pillars with each a figure of

Osiris holding the scourge and crook, the emblems of authority, in front, thus forming north and south corridors. Three flights of steps lead up into the northern corridor: opposite each flight is a door into the grand hall, the centre door having right and left of it statues of Remeses II. On each side of the central door are pedestals, which once supported statues : two more statues stood within the grand hall, between the first and second columns of the central avenue. The roof of the grand hall is supported by forty-eight columns, of which twelve, some thirty feet high, are ranged as a central avenue, while the remainder form the side aisles. Remains of the blue, with which the ceiling was once coloured, may still be seen ; apparently the decoration was a blue ground studded with stars. The family of Remeses II, twenty-three sons and three daughters, are depicted on the walls of this hall, while the dedicatory inscription is on one of the architraves. This hall opens into a smaller chamber, most interesting as the repository of the books of Thoth,—the earliest library on record ! The ceiling is astronomical, and its records have been of great use in helping to unravel Egyptian chronology. On the north wall of this library Remeses the Great is represented, seated under the Tree of Life, which overshadows him, while Amun and Thoth write his name on the leaves. The small chambers round the library are mostly destroyed.

The sculptures on the towers of the entrance propylon, in the second court and in the great hall, represent battle-pieces, which Lord Lindsay says must remind every one of Homer. He continues, " The sculptures, however, Homeric as they are, remind me as much and more of the glowing war-imagery of the Prophets. Lend the eyes, the ears of your imagination, and you have the rattling of the wheels, and of the prancing horses, and of the jumping chariots ; the shield of the mighty man is made red, the valiant men are dyed scarlet, the chariots rage in the streets—they jostle one against another in the broadways ; the horseman lifteth up the flame of the sword, and the lightning of the spear, and there is a multitude of the slain, and a great number of carcases, and there is no end of their corpses—they stumble upon their corpses."

As one might well expect to find within the circuit of ancient Thebes, there are many remains in the vicinity of the Remesium. The stone-cased water tank of that temple is not far from the east of the outer court, and around are edifices

vaulted in crude brick, once used for habitation by the ancient
Christians. The vestiges of temple-palaces of Amunoph III,
with some much mutilated Colossi and figures are also hard by.
A street, or dromos in ancient Thebes, appears to have extended
from the Remesium to these two temple-palaces, and from the
one at Kom el Hettan to the Colossi of the Plains.

3.—THE COLOSSI OF THE PLAINS.

One of these two enormous statues is familiar to every
one as—

" Memnon's statue, which at sunrise played."

Most persons will, perhaps, feel that they have lost one of the
pleasantest illusions of their childhood, when they learn that
this designation is a misnomer, though one respectable from its
antiquity. Shama and Tama, as the Arabs call these gigantic
images, represent Amunoph III, by whom they were erected
some 3200 years ago, or, possibly, Amunoph and his queen.
The misnomer of Memnon is a corruption of Mi-Ammon,
beloved of Amun, a title confounded by the Greeks with the
Memnon of Homer, and applied by them to all Pharaohs
indiscriminately. That these statues were erected by Amunoph
III, and that one of them (that to the spectator's right) is the
vocal Memnon of the Greeks is abundantly proved by the
inscription on it. Among these inscriptions is one which
records a visit of the Emperor Hadrian and his wife Sabina,
with the names of all her ladies, and attests that the " unseen
melody" saluted the imperial pair thrice the morning they
were there.

The statues marked the termination of an avenue of much
smaller ones, which led to the temple and palace of Amunoph
III, now levelled to the ground ; two or three Colossi, which
once ornamented this grand approach, lie across it on their faces,
half buried under the soil accumulated by successive inundations. The total height of each of the two celebrated Colossi is
about 60 feet. The upper part of the vocal one has been destroyed, whether by an earthquake in 27 B.C., or by Cambyses, or
by some one else, is uncertain ; it has been restored. In its lap is
a stone which rings when struck with a metallic sound ; there
is also a cavity large enough to conceal a man from spectators
below ; these two facts probably explain the diurnal miracle of

old.   The guides, who clamber up to ring the sonorous stone,
generally present the traveller with what they say is a bit of
it : its grain will prove it is not, but let the traveller feign
belief; the large grained specimen will do to show in Europe
or America, and the real sonorous stone will be undiminished ;
otherwise, it would soon all go.

It is supposed the avenue, of which these statues form part
was the royal dromos or street of Thebes, which stretched from
the temple of Amunoph III, on the western side of the river, to
that of Luxor, erected by the same monarch on the eastern side,
crossing the river by a ferry.   The Arabs have a legend that
by following the prolongation of this dromos westwards for two
days, a traveller would come to the tomb of the founder of
Medeenet Haboo, who is buried with vast treasure around him.
Search has often been made for it, but magic arts confound the
seeker, and lead him astray.   A compass in the writer's possession was supposed to be of sufficient potency to withstand such
black arts, and he was asked to guide a party of explorers.

4.—DAYR EL MEDEENEH.

The small, but lovely temple of Dayr el Medeeneh should
on no account be overlooked by the sightseer at Thebes, for
among the sculptures is one of the most interesting scenes to
be found depicted on Egyptian monuments.   Its erection was
commenced by Ptolemy Philopater about 2090 years ago, and
finished by Ptolemy Euergetes II about 100 years later.   It is
situated beneath a mass of frowning rock, which threatens in
appearance to fall and crush it, and is surrounded by a dilapidated wall of crude brick with which the stone gateway in
front is incorporated.   The piece of sculpture to which we have
alluded is in the western chambers next the sanctuary.   It is
a representation of the Judgment Scene.   Ptolemy Philopater,
in a submissive attitude, is ushered into Amenti between two
figures of Truth or Justice, whose emblem, the ostrich feather,
he holds in his hand.   Osiris, the great judge of the dead, is
seated on his throne, holding in his hands the scourge and flail,
and ready to deliver the dread judgment.   Before him are the
four genii of Amenti on a lotus flower.   A figure of Hippocrates,
seated on the crook of Osiris, between the scales and the entrance
of the divine abode, is intended to show that the deceased on
admission to that pure state must be born again and commence

a new life, cleansed from all the impurities of an earthly career. Horus and Anubis weigh his good actions against an ostrich feather in a balance, on the top of which sits a cynocephalus, the emblem of the god Thoth. Thoth himself, the god of letters, stands ready with a scroll on which to inscribe the result and present it to the judge. That hideous animal, who guards the approach to the mansion of Osiris, and is called "the devourer of the wicked," a prototype of the Greek Cerberus, is near, ready to seize the deceased in case of an adverse judgment. Above in two lines sit the forty-two assessors, by whom Osiris was supposed to be assisted in his duties. The ostrich feather, against which the deceased's good works are weighed, is, as we have said, the symbol of Truth ; it is not used as some writers have fancied, from any poetical idea of the little good a man can accomplish.

Close to the door to the chamber where is this sculpture, was a staircase to the roof, lit by a very peculiar window. The stones, which compose the walls of this temple were joined by wooden cramps, of which vestiges may still be found. This temple owes its name of Dayr el Medeeneh (the convent of the city) to the fact of its having been used by the early Christians, who mustered strong at Thebes, as an abode.

5.—DAYR EL BAHREE.

A temple, which owes its name of Dayr el Bahree (the convent of the north) to the fact that it was utilized by the early Christians, stands at the very foot of the western mountains, which tower majestically over it. Artistic advantage was taken of this situation to form a series of terraces with covered corridors, once ornamented by two obelisks in front. These terraces, one above the other, were approached by a long avenue of sphinxes 1600 feet in length, with a pylon at the further end, rising finally to the scarp of the first terrace, through an enclosure in front of the temple, by an inclined plane of stonework, ending in a granite pylon. Behind, again, is an area and another granite pylon, giving access to chambers cut in the rock, and roofed with masonry so as to appear vaulted. These roofs, spite their appearance, are not vaulted, but are formed by squared stones projecting each layer beyond that below it until the topmost meet ; the ceiling has then been rounded off afterwards. This temple was erected by Amense or Amun-nou-het, about 3300 years ago. She was the princess who erected the obelisk at Karnak to the memory of her father, Thothmes I. Thothmes II and Thothmes III, who reigned with her, have, however, erased her name and inserted their own. Enough still remains, or did until late years, to make certain that the credit of founding this temple is due to her. Great portions of the sculptures once here have in late years been destroyed, or taken away to ornament various European museums. The Arabs long had a belief that there was a tunnel through from this temple to the Tombs of the Kings. Sir Gardner Wilkinson searched fruitlessly for this, but found it not.

6.—MEDEENET HABOO.

Medeenet Haboo, pronounced Medina Tabu, *i.e.*, the city of Thebes, comprises the ruins of more than one building, though all were connected together. The first building at which the traveller arrives is the small temple of Medeenet Haboo; the guides generally pass by this, and take the traveller first to the palace of Remeses III and return afterwards to the back of the small temple: the traveller should, however, not do this: let him see the small temple first, and enter it at the front; he will thus get a much more correct idea of the building than by doing it backwards.

When Thebes fell into decay, Medeenet Haboo became subsequently an early Christian village, and mud houses, now in ruins, swarm all over the older temples and the grounds attached thereto. As the traveller approaches (we suppose he is coming from the Colossi of the Plains), he will see on his right hand, close to the small temple, the remains of a stone wall, once embattled; this surrounded the *temenos* or sacred ground, common to both temples; within it some green rushes point out where was once the tank usual in such places: hard by are some broken stones and statues. In the *temenos* was also a subterranean passage leading to a tank of water; this is now blocked up with dust.

7.—THE SMALL TEMPLE.

The small temple of Medeenet Haboo has in front of it an open court-yard, with entrances at either side, and in front two columns, all that now are perfect out of eight, stand on either side of the doorway, right and left of which is a screen

formed by building walls half way up the columns we have
mentioned.   Behind this is a propylon which leads into a
small court, with a second propylon at its north end.   This
court was formed by a row of four columns on either side,
connected by screens which rose half way up them.   Thus far
we have only seen only mere additions of yesterday to the
original temple.   The outer court, columns, screen, and propylon are the work of the Ptolemies and the Cæsars, barely a
century older than the era from which we at present compute.
Ptolemy Lathyrus, the Emperors Titus and Antoninus Pius, and
several of the Roman proconsuls contributed to the erection of
this portion of the building.   The inner court and propylon
are the work of an Ethiopian Pharaoh, Tirhaka by name, the
rival of Sennacherib, who flourished above 1450 years ago :
Pharaoh Nectanebo, and Ptolemy Lathyrus have in many places
effaced the name of the Ethiopian and substituted their own.
The propylon of Tirhaka is succeeded by a vestibule, and then
comes the sanctuary, right and left and front of which are corridors of pillars, while behind is a congeries of small chambers.
Thus, the original kernel of the temple is coeval with the great
obelisks at Karnak, and is the work of the first three monarchs
of the name of Thothmes, and of Amun-nou-het or Amense,
daughter of the first : it has thus an antiquity of nearly 3400
years.   Other monarchs have restored or altered the buildings
from time to time, and their cartouches are found thereon.

When the traveller has concluded his examination of the
small temple, he should return to its front, and thence to the
palace of Remeses III, which is connected with the small
temple by a wall.

8.—THE PALACE AT MEDEENET HABOO.

The ascent to this between two pavilions—porters' lodges,
probably—built in advance of the lofty towers.   These towers
enclose a parallelogram, at whose end is a gateway with rooms
above, the whole being not unlike the entrance to a Norman
donjon keep ; one almost expects to see a moat and portcullis.
The resemblance is increased by the walls having been embattled, and by the projecting balconies supported by grotesque
figures, once painted almost as if they bore coats of arms.   The
sculptures represent Remeses III, and various prisoners and
chiefs, whom he has subdued.   The rooms of the palace are
all destroyed except one, a charming room, over the gateway,

with a most lovely view towards the Nile, to facilitate the enjoyment of which a stone seat runs under the window : on no account should the traveller omit to climb up to this lovely boudoir, from which the mighty Pharaoh, or the lovely ladies of his court, must often have gazed on military triumphs and sacred pageants streaming between the lofty towers and beneath the gateway, as they passed to the glorious temple behind.   While in this room the traveller can note the holes in which the window shutters once turned, and the colours which still decorate the sills and lintels, while high round an upper room, whose floor has collapsed, he will see Remeses III attended by his harem ; the monarch is seated, and in one place a girl offers him flowers, or fans the flies away ; a third endures his caresses, while in another corner he is represented as about to play draughts with a favourite lady.   Remeses III, who built this temple, flourished about 3000 years ago.   From this palace the traveller proceeds through the gateway to the

9.—GREAT TEMPLE OF MEDEENET HABOO.

This is connected with the palace by an avenue and by curtain walls leading to an enormous propylon, on which are representations of the founder Remeses III in the act of slaying prisoners as offerings to the gods.   Behind this is an hypœthral (unroofed) court, remarkable for its magnificent disregard of symmetry.   On one side is a row of eight huge circular columns ; these are balanced on the other side by seven square pillars, with figures of Remeses III in front, accompanied by a son and daughter at his knees.   The propylon, which terminates this court, has a hieroglyphic inscription of great length east of the doorway, and a representation of Remeses offering prisoners to Amunse on the west.

The great court is one of the most magnificent among Egyptian remains ; it is surrounded by a huge covered corridor, supported east and west by ten huge circular pillars, and north and south by sixteen Osiride pillars ; on the north the corridor is double, that is, behind the Osiride pillars is a row of circular columns.   The feeble columns that lie about the centre are no part of the original temple, but were erected by the Christians, who turned this area into a church, pulling down one pillar at the east to make way for their circular apse, smashing the figures of Osiris, and using the architraves for

building materials. The ceiling of the corridor has been beautifully painted a blue and gold diaper, which, as well as the
colouring of the columns, is still fresh. The usual routine of
travellers is to lunch on some stones in the south-west corner of
this area. Near these, on the south wall, is a representation of
Remeses in his war chariot charging the enemy, this tableau is
continued on the west wall; the king, victorious, is seated in
his war chariot, while the arms and hands of the dead and
other trophies are piled around him. On the south wall is
depicted the king's triumphal return: on the north he offers
sacrifices to the gods, attended by his children in procession;
the east wall represents his coronation.

The next area contains halls and chambers, whose walls
were only about half the height of the walls of the area. The
traveller first comes into a court supported by twenty-four
massive columns arranged in six rows, those of the two centre
rows being bigger than the other. On either side of this hall
are chambers. The hall opens into a vestibule supported by
eight columns, opening again into another similar one. Side
chambers are taken off each of these vestibules. Behind these
vestibules are the ruins of the sanctuary and small chambers.
The traveller can easily from here ascend to the roof of the
corridored area, and note the precautions taken to prevent the
soaking through of rain, by strips of stones being let in over
the junctures of the roofing stones, and by carrying it off by
gurgoyles of lions' heads. He will also find various flights
of stairs made in the thickness of the walls. The sculptures
on the east exterior wall should be examined. They tell the
full history of a successful invasion conducted by Remeses III.
The story begins at the north-east extremity of the east wall
with his reviewing his troops, attended by a trumpeter and by
a tame lion; it then continues with his march, the formation
for the attack, a victory, after which the hands and tongues of
the dead are brought to the king, a distribution of rewards,
and the mustering of the implements of war taken by him;
after this victory the march is resumed, and another victorious
action follows, in which the Egyptians are assisted by allies:
the king still proceeding on his route is attacked by lions, of
which he slays two or three: the enemy take refuge in ships,
but are defeated: the collection of trophies, hands, &c., is
again depicted, followed by the distribution of rewards, and the
king's triumphal return home to offer presents to the gods.

The rest of the eastern wall represents the assaults and sieges of various towns. The western wall is covered with hieroglyphics. Mr. Ramsey, who was with Lord Lindsay, writes of these sculptures, "It is difficult to analyze one's feelings with regard to these drawings; except in the hieroglyphical representations of animals, which are perfect, nothing is critically correct; you infer that the drawing of everything is most faulty, yet the soul and fire, the animation and expression in the figures are most wonderful! A lion wounded, for example, strikes you as the most admirably expressive living thing ever drawn; but look again, and though the idea of a lion in agony and rage has been most forcibly represented to your mind, yet there is not a single line of the lion critically correct.

10.—OTHER RUINS NEAR MEDEENET HABOO.

A small Ptolemic temple, consisting of an outer court and three chambers, and dedicated to Thoth, is some 220 yards south-west of the palace of Remeses. The hieroglyphics here are historically valuable. The plain beyond it was once a lake of importance in funeral pageants, and called Birket Haboo. Beyond it some way is a small Roman temple, built by the Emperors Adrian and Antoninus Pius. There are two pylons, an isolated sanctuary, and some small chambers.

THE TOMBS.

A requisite preliminary to a visit to the Tombs is to be provided with lights. While quite agreeing with Sir G. Wilkinson's remarks in the pages of Murray on the impropriety of using torches, indeed some tombs are now almost completely defaced by smoke, yet we think that candles alone do not enable the traveller to see much. In default of magnesium torches, some torches that do not smoke may easily be made. Take a quantity of old rags (a flannel shirt will do to tear up), and soak them in salad oil; then make them up into thickish rings, about two and a half or three inches across, the hole in centre being an inch and a-half or so. To use these, take a long palm stick and thrust about six or eight inches of its length through one of the country cakes of bread; this makes a holder for the ring of rags. These torches, if well made, give a beautiful light, and make no smoke: a Maltese dragoman showed the writer how to make them.

The whole extent of the hills on the western side of Thebes is one great necropolis, full of tombs opened and unopened. No systematic search has ever yet been made throughout these vast burying grounds, and quantities of tombs must yet remain to be examined. Except, however, in certain localities, such as the Valley of the Tombs of the Kings, the Western Valley, and the Valley of the Tombs of the Queens, it is not probable that anything of very great antiquarian importance would be revealed; in the places we have excepted, it is almost certain that such would be the case, but the search should be systematic, and directed and closely watched by Europeans, for the natives look only for treasure, and with that in view break and destroy much that is of interest to the antiquarian and historian. The tombs divide themselves into various lots or sets, known as the Tombs of the Kings, situated in Biban el Molook, and in the contiguous Western Valley, the Tombs of the Queens, known as Bel Hareem, the Tombs of Koornet Murraee, of Shekh Abd el Koorneh, of Drah Aboo Negga, and of the Assaseef.

1.—THE TOMBS OF THE KINGS

Are situate in a valley, called Biban el Molook (the Gates of the Kings,) which opens near the temple of Old Koorneh, and winds round behind the cliffs, which overhang Dayr el Bahree. The traveller should go or return by the path over these cliffs : not only will he acquire a clearer idea of the localities, but he will be able to feast his eyes on a lovely panorama of Nile and desert scenery : the inland track which he will notice high on the hills leads to the Great Oasis. The valley is desolation itself, long and winding, shut in by lofty rocks ; not a trace of vegetation, "fit scene," writes Lord Lindsay, "for the funeral processions of mighty Pharaohs,—fit, indeed, for the last home of the extinct dynasties of a vanished nation." At the time when Sir Gardner Wilkinson made his survey of Thebes, and numbered the tombs, twenty-one were opened or known ; two or three have since been discovered, but ones of no great importance or curiosity. The author from whom we have just quoted says of the tombs, "They are temples rather than tombs, broad passages and gorgeous chambers opening one into another, till you find yourself in the lofty hall of the sarcophagus terminating each. Some of them run 300 or 400 feet into the heart of the mountain, a gradual slope figuring the descent into Amenti, the Egyptian Hades, or the world unseen. The most beautiful are those of the Pharaohs, who reigned from Remeses I, grandfather of Sesostris, to Remeses V in whose reign Troy was taken B.C. 1184, inclusive. A regular series of portraits of the Pharaohs might be taken from these tombs ; the likenesses are always exactly preserved."

Of the twenty-one numbered tombs, No. 3 (Remeses III), No. 4 (Remeses VIII), No. 5, No. 7, No. 10 (Amunmeses), No. 12, No. 13, No. 16 (Remeses I), No. 18 (Remeses X), No. 19 (a Remeses), No. 20, and No. 21, and the unnumbered tombs, are either now closed, or are mere tunnels in the rocks, and unworthy of a visit. No. 10 is generally used as a place of shelter for the donkeys and donkeyboys. Tombs No. 1 and 2 (those of Remeses IX and IV) are very elegant tombs of somewhat similar design. No. 1 runs about 130 feet into the rock, terminating in a hall, where is a sarcophagus of limestone with granite lid. No. 2 is about 100 feet larger, terminating also in a hall, round which are recesses, where slept the bodies probably of the Pharaoh's chief officers. The sarcophagus, an enormous mass of granite, is still *in situ,* but broken at the side. The passages in both these tombs are covered with painted hieroglyphics, but in places much defaced.

No. 6, the tomb of Remeses VII, presents a somewhat precipitous descent through passages, whose walls are painted with figures and hieroglyphics, to a hall, distant about 250 feet from the entrance, on the wall of which is a painting of the child Harpocrates seated in a winged globe; this is an emblem of the idea common to the Egyptians and other philosophers, that to die was only to assume a new form—that nothing was annihilated—and that dissolution was merely the forerunner of reproduction. This tomb contains two halls; there are also side niches, where probably reposed the Pharaoh's chief baker, butler, &c.

The sides of No. 8, that of King Pthahmen, are covered with a profusion of hieroglyphics; on one side is a group representing the king and the god Re. It terminates, so far as is open, in a vestibule and hall, and has also large side chambers.

No. 9 is one of great celebrity, and obtained the name of the tomb of Memnon in a manner similar to that in which the vocal Colossus was misnamed. It belonged to Remeses V, and runs into the heart of the mountain for a distance of about 350 feet to a perpendicular depth of about 25 feet below the level of its entrance. " The roof of the passage leading to the principal chamber is most richly painted, red and black, in the style of the Etruscan vases. The ceiling of the chamber of the sarcophagus is quite beautiful, and delightfully mystical, describing the procession of the Sun through the hours of the day and night—emblematical of the life of the terrestial luminary—Phayre the Sun, a Pharaoh of Egypt. The symbolical paintings are enclosed by the double body of Nith, the goddess of the firmament, prolonged like the folds of a serpent round the ceiling and through the middle of it, separating the day from the night. In the east, Nith becomes the mother of the Sun, an infant, who is carefully placed in the bark, in which he descends the celestial river with a large *cortege* of deities. Each hour of the day is marked by a globe —of the night by a star. They begin sounding at the seventh hour, and a pilot comes to steer them through the remaining hours of light, the river growing shallower and shallower, till,

at the twelfth the scene changes, and, veering round in the
great western lake into which the river empties itself, they
commence their return eastward through the hours of the
night, towed by ropes up a branch of the celestial river, which
terminates, like the main stream, in the western lake.   The
Sun is attended only by the pilot and one other deity during
this nocturnal voyage.   .   .   .   Tablets of hieroglyphics are
interspersed with the symbolical paintings, describing the
celestial influences of each hour on the several parts of the
human body.   In a recess at the end of the hall, Tethys, the
wife of Oceanius, stretches out her arms to receive the descend-
ink bark of the Sun."—*Lord Lindsay*.   The ceiling which his
lordship describes is vaulted ; underneath it lies a broken sarcophagus ; the ceilings of the other halls in this tomb are also
painted with astronomical subjects.   The sides of the passages
and walls are also painted with symbolical subjects, indicative
of the descent into Amenti, and of the mysteries of the
Egyptian religion.   Grotesque animals, birds with human heads
and legs, serpents of every description, some with vultures'
wings, swarm among the paintings.

No. 11, that of Remeses III, known as Bruce's or the
Harpers' Tomb, so called because Bruce the traveller, copied and
published the harps delineated in it, is peculiarly interesting on
account of its side-chambers.   This tomb is more than 400
feet in length ; its direction is not quite straight, and its end
is about 30 feet below the level of its entrance.   The ten-side
chambers in the first and second passages are illustrative of the
manners and domestic life of the ancient Egyptians.   In one is
depicted the mysteries of Egyptian cookery ; on another you
see the boats used by them on the Nile : a third is a painted
armoury : in a fourth is every description of Egyptian furniture, arm chairs, ottomans, sofas with head and leg rests, bed
steps and the like ; a fifth gives the whole process of reaping
and sowing, and shows the inundation of the Nile ; two show
various emblems and forms of Osiris and other deities : an
eighth is illustrated with various productions of Egypt, birds,
fruits, and herbs ; the ninth contains rudders and sacred emblems, while the last contains two blind harpers and their instruments, of most elegant construction ; one of the performers
seems to be damping the strings, just like a modern performer.
These side-chambers appear to have been the burial places of
the monarch's great officers, each having painted round him the

emblems of his office. The sarcophagus has been removed: beyond its hall are places for bodies: the paintings on the sides of the passages refer to the descent to Amenti. "The Deity of Nef, Nu, or Num, and representative of the Spirit of God" that moved on the face of the waters, is here frequently depicted in his sacred boat, while over him the asp, emblem of royalty and goodness, spreads itself as a canopy. In the first hall is a procession of variously attired and coloured people, representing the four quarters of the world.

Nos. 14 and 15 (those of Pthahseptah and Sethi or Osirei II) are unfinished tombs, each containing a broken sarcophagus; they do not contain much to interest. All the tombs we have described were open in the time of the Ptolemies, and were then, 2000 years ago, visited by the curious as remarkable works of great antiquity; this is proved by Greek inscriptions found in them.

The most famous and magnificent of all the tombs is that numbered 17, and called, from the name of its discoverer, for it was not opened until recent years, Belzoni's tomb. The suspicions of the peasants directed Belzoni where to search. After clearing away the *debris* of the mountain and the masonry that blocked up the door, the discoverer broke into the tomb. Two steep staircases and two passages led the discoverer into a chamber about 12 feet by 14 feet, where was a deep pit. The sides of the staircases, passages, and all around the chamber were covered with sculptures and hieroglyphics painted on stucco. In the first passage the hieroglyphics relate to the occupant of the tomb Sethi, father of Remeses II. On the sides of the second staircase are long processions of different genii, and in the following passages are the sacred boats of Nef, Nu, or Num, with the emblematic asp, the whole painting referring to the descent of Amenti. In the chamber are representations of the king making offerings to the deities. Induced thereto by certain indications, Belzoni conceived that this pit and its chamber were mere blinds; filling up the former, he tested the walls of the latter with an extemporized battering ram, and burst through into a hall supported by four pillars, opening by a door into a second hall supported by two pillars. The paintings on the pillars of the first hall represent the king's reception after death by various deities; on the end wall is his introduction by Horus to Osiris and Athor. On the walls is, as in the last tomb, a procession of people, typical of the four quarters of the world. The drawings of the next hall are peculiarly interesting; they are unfinished, and we can see the manner in which they were drawn. An inferior artist, pupil, or apprentice, first drew the outlines in a red pigment, with a bold and decided sweep; then came the master spirit and corrected the deficiencies with black. To him followed the sculptor. That they are unfinished is curious; the care taken in painting the walls of the chamber over the pit shows that want of time could not have been the reason. From the corner of this hall a staircase descends still deeper, conducting by passages and an anti-chamber into the grand vaulted hall of six pillars, where stood, 320 feet from the entrance, and 90 feet below the level of the ground, a sarcophagus of alabaster, beautifully covered with richly gilt hieroglyphics. This sarcophagus is now in the little known but curious and wonderful museum of Sir John Soane in Lincoln's-Inn-Fields, London.* There are chambers right and left of this hall. The sculptures in the passages leading to this hall refer to the ceremonies performed in honour of the Pharaoh, who was interred in the alabaster sarcophagus; those in the side chambers represent various mysteries and ceremonies, while the decorations in the hall of the sarcophagus represent a series of mummies in their cases, and other subjects. The spoilers have, however, been at work in this tomb, but while pillars and figures have been mutilated and carried off, it is still wonderful and brilliant. From behind the place, where once stood the sarcophagus, an inclined plane with stairs on either hand descends mysteriously to unknown depths in the bowels of the earth; this gloomy passage was once concealed by a false floor and wall. The decorations of Belzoni's tomb are rich in snakes; some winged, with three or four human heads and legs; others with heads at each extremity, crowned and mitred, the body curving downwards, supported by four human legs, two looking each way. The binding and conquest of the snake, frequently seen in these tombs, represent the subjugation of the great serpent Apophis by the gods, their victory over sin.

From our description our readers will have learnt that the

---

* Copies of the sculptures on this sarcophagus, most beautifully drawn by Mr. Joseph Bonomi, the keeper of the Museum, and described by Dr. Sharpe, were published by Longmans in 1864.

chief tombs to be visited are No. 17 (Belzoni's), No. 11 (Bruce's),
and No. 9. Then follow in order of merit No. 6, 2, 1, 8, 15,
and 14. The tombs of the Western Valley, four in number,
are hardly worthy of a visit, except for those who are interested
in the study of hieroglyphics; one, that of Amunoph III, is of
large extent, and another has a broken sarcophagus in it.

2.—THE TOMBS OF THE QUEENS.

Much the same may be said of the tombs of the Queens,
situate in a valley behind Medeeneh Haboo and of the tombs
in the valley of Dayr el Medeeneh.

3.—THE PRIVATE TOMBS.

We now come to a totally different class of tombs from
that with which we have hitherto been dealing. In the royal
tombs, excavations of vast extent are brilliantly decorated with
mysterious scenes illustrative of ancient mythology: in the
private tombs, mainly those of priests and royal scribes, we are
introduced to the history of manners and daily life among the
old Egyptians. Lord Lindsay writes of these, "Every light
and shadow of human life is portrayed in them, from the
laughter of the feast to the tears of the funeral—ointments
poured on the head at one, dust heaped on it at the other. You
see on one side the arrival of the guest in his chariot, white
horses, and a train of running footmen, betokening his consequence; the other guests already assembled and seated, the
men apart from the women, wait for their dinner, and beguile
the intervening moments with smelling the lotus flower and
listening to the music of the dancing-girls. The master of the
house and his wife, richly dressed, and lazily seated side by
side, preside at the entertainment. But the *tableaux* would be
incomplete without side views of the shambles and the kitchen,
and a beggar at the gate, receiving a bull's head and a draught
of water from one of the menials. Facing this on the opposite wall, the mourning women, with wailing cries and
dishevelled hair, precede the coffin that bears the hospitable
Egyptian to his long home; the wife or the sister walks
beside it, silent in her sorrow; a scribe takes account of
the dead man's riches, his cattle, his horses, his household
chattels;—death, and then the judgment; the deceased is
ushered into Amenti; Horus and Aroeris weigh his merits

against the ostrich feather, the symbol of truth. Thoth, the god of letters, presents a scroll, the record of his thoughts, words, and works, to the judge Osiris, into whose presence he is at length admitted on the favourable result of the scrutiny. And amidst all these varied scenes, as if to show how narrowly joy may be partitioned off from sorrow, how the merry-hearted and the broken-hearted may unconsciously pillow within an inch of each other, and how the world jogs on in daily routine, indifferent to the feelings of either,--the occupations of every-day life are pictured in their minutest details around you— scenes of industry, scenes of frolic, parties pledging each other's healths, young folk dancing to the music of the harp, husband-men in the fields, artificers of every trade at their work (many of them with tools precisely like those now in use), carpenters, smiths, glass blowers, shoemakers, wheelwrights, statuaries, idol-makers."

The private tombs are mostly to be found on the hills of Quornet or Koornet Murraee, and Shekh Abd el Koorneh, so called from a Mussulman saint who has a tomb on the top. On this latter hill Sir Gardner Wilkinson surveyed and num-bered nearly forty tombs, of which many have since been closed or destroyed, and new ones opened. The numbering, too, is lost. To describe each tomb would be impossible; it is best to let the guide, who is here an indispensable necessity, take the lead; he will be able to point out the scenes. Such, however, is the destruction wrought in these tombs, that a traveller visiting them after the tombs of the Kings will pro-probably feel disappointed. There is nothing to see in the tombs of Drah Aboo Negga, mere pits in the rock, unsculptured and unpainted: the writer explored one: after being let down by a rope 80 feet into the one, a passage running for about 100 feet horizontally was discovered, and some dilapidated mummies: and nothing else of the slightest interest.

Lord Lindsay's description is a combination of tombs, 5, 16, and 17. No. 14 is remarkable for the introduction in its paintings of a drove of pigs. No. 35, known as the "most curious tomb," is much blackened and defaced. It consists of two chambers: the inner of which is a long passage cut into the rock, the roof rising higher as it recedes, thus (on principles of perspective, well known to theatrical scene painters) giving to a spectator at the entrance the idea of much greater length than really is the case. In the outer chamber are depicted all the nations of the earth bringing tribute to Thothmes III. The characteristics of each people are strongly marked, and the differences of dress are well portrayed. The various tribes are very distinctly made out. On the walls of the inner chamber are to be found joiners, carpenters (using glue), rope makers, sculptors, brick makers (supposed erroneously to be Jews), and other artificers. On the opposite wall are some curious social subjects and a picture of an Egyptian garden, singularly illustrative of the Egyptian style of drawing. Among the numerous tombs in Koornet Murraee, two are worthy of notice. In one is a much dilapidated drawing of a chase in the Theban desert, all the animals common to that locality being depicted; in the other the Queen of Ethiopia and her subjects are represented as bringing tribute to Amun Toonh, one of the stranger Pharaohs. Any one curious in Egyptian art, and art design, could collect from the walls and ceilings of these tombs most beautiful patterns for wall decoration, geometrical, floral, and animal.

4.—THE TOMBS OF THE ASSASEEF.

These and certain tombs behind the Remesium form a third class of Theban tombs, differing in magnitude from the private tombs, and in plan from those of the Kings. Some, those behind the Remesium, have rows of pillars in front of their entrance. The largest of these tombs is that of the priest Petamunap; it is the largest tomb in all Thebes, and we may add the dreariest, dirtiest, most uninteresting and foul smelling of them all, inhabited by hundreds of bats, who fly in the traveller's face, startled by his lights. This tomb consists of an acre and a quarter of excavations, in places two or three stories deep, and its sides are covered with hieroglyphiced sculptures, unpainted and hardly to be seen in the dark and gloom. Let the traveller here beware of his footsteps; there are many pits, and accidents have happened even to the Arabs. Its date is said to be the seventh century, B.C.

HOW TO SEE THE RUINS OF THEBES.

As to the time requisite to be given to the ruins and tombs of Thebes, we can only say the longer the better : travellers are, however, often pressed for time, and we therefore furnish diurnals for the usual period allowed by the steamboats, omitting such places as may best be overlooked.

STAY OF THREE DAYS AT THEBES.

(*A-day*). *Biban el Molook.*—Start early in the morning, and go to the Valley of the Tombs of the Kings, Biban el Molook, by the path over the mountains, past the temple of Dayr el Bahree, which may be taken *en route*. Travellers should go or return to the Tombs of the Kings by this magnificent route, which is practicable for donkeys, with the exception of a few yards here and there, where it is necessary to dismount. The views are lovely. The track seen going inland is the road to the Great Oasis, three weary days away. After having inspected as many of the Tombs of the Kings as pleases him, the traveller may go to the western valley if he likes, and see those. He should return from Biban el Molook by the valley, and lunch may conveniently be taken in the temple of Old Koorneh, where shelter can be got from the midday sun. The traveller can return after lunch by the Remesium and the Colossi of the Plains.

N.B.—The excursion to the Tombs of the Kings may be shortened by the traveller in a dahabeeh having his boat moored just opposite Old Koorneh, thus saving some four miles of riding, which is of importance to ladies.

(*B-day*).—Go to the Memnonium and Dayr el Bahree (if not visited the day before) ; thence to the hill of Shekh Abd el Koorneh, and see tomb 35, and as many more of the private tombs as pleases ; thence to Dayr el Medeenet, and afterwards to Medeenet Haboo, and lunch there. Home by the Colossi.

(*C-day*). *Luxor and Karnak,*

As to the order in which these diurnals should be done, Luxor and Karnak should certainly be reserved until after a visit to the ruins of western Thebes. If a traveller stays in his boat at Luxor the whole three days, he should take the sights as we have put them (*A*, *B*, and *C*). Should he resolve to drop down in his boat to opposite El Koorneh, as we have suggested, he should take the days in following order:— *B, C, A*. On his second day (*C*) he should ride from Luxor to Karnak, while his boat drops down the river to pick him up there: he will miss a good deal if he goes in his boat. He may, if he pleases, omit Dayr el Bahree.

These diurnals omit a great deal of the tombs; but the fact is, most people will be content with six of the Tombs of the Kings, and No. 35; an additional day might be given to the Tombs other than those of the Kings and those in the western valley. The diurnals are arranged for travellers by the steamboats, who have only three days allowed at Thebes, or for travellers by dahabeeh who go no further: other travellers can arrange for themselves, but each diurnal contains the sights which lie most conveniently together.

Of course the question of time is one for each to decide. A day might well be spent at Medeenet Haboo only, and several at Karnak. Some may cram the whole things into two days. For those who have only two days, and do not wish to undergo much fatigue, we recommend *B* and *C* days, omitting Dayr el Bahree.

For those who wish a fourth day, we give them one of tombs:—

(*D-day*). Begin with Tombs of the Queens, then those of Koornet Murraee, Abd el Koorneh, and the Assaseef, lunching and resting during the heat in some convenient one. A precise itinerary cannot be given; these tombs are unnumbered, and a guide being essential, it is better to trust his advice.

As for guides, one is unnecessary for Luxor and Karnak, but convenient; on the other side he is essential, particularly in the tombs, where are sometimes dangerous pitfalls.

LIST OF THINGS USEFUL TO BE TAKEN
UP THE NILE.

The lists given in Guide Books comprise a long list of things for fitting-up and provisioning a dahabeeh : those lists are now obsolete and unnecessary. The dahabeeh system is well understood now, and the dragoman will see to the fitting-up and provisioning a dahabeeh. The traveller need not take fireworks unless he pleases, though some dragomen say it is necessary ; a little coarse powder is useful for firing salutes.

The following list is compiled from what the writer took for a stay in a house at Thebes, and is suited for such as do the like. A few articles (marked with an asterisk) are personal comforts and necessities that all should take, however they go.

Two carpets (Segadee), cost about 19s. each at Cairo.

A Turkish blanket, cost about 15s. at Cairo.

A railway rug and Scotch plaid were also useful.

Sheets, mattress, and pillow, were provided the writer by Mustapha Agha, but it would be advisable to take such as are used for a bunk on board ship ; a pillow should be taken.

Towels, rough and smooth, two or three.

Mats, to put on floor, can be got in markets at Luxor.

Soap, brown Windsor or fancy.

Soap, common, for washing clothes.

A graduated medicine glass.

A folding chair : cost tremendous in Cairo, and is useful on ship coming out from England.

An air cushion, also very useful on ship, as well as in Egypt.

* White umbrella, lined with green or blue } Both indispensable.
* Blue spectacles

Sun helmet. These can be got very good in the hotel at Suez. A white cloth folded, and put on the head under the hat, is a very good protection against the sun ; it should hang down over the nape of neck. A puggaree is also good.

A fez or tarboosh is most useful, as it need never be taken off the head, and so can be worn in native houses, which are generally draughty. A European should, however, beware of going into the sun with a tarboosh alone.

Mosquito net ; got at Cairo. The writer did not take one, and never wanted it, but many people found them useful.

Flea powder, ditto.

* Ammonia, bottle of, for insect or scorpion stings,

Eau de Cologne.

* Hair oil, or something of that sort; much wanted in so dry a
    climate.

Pocket corkscrew.

Tobacco ⎫ Got best at Cairo. The local tobacco sold at Luxor
Chibouk ⎬ smokes well in a chibouk, particularly when mixed
Mouthpiece ⎭ with a little Latakia.

Pipe bowls; got best at Siout.

A brass plate to rest the pipe bowl on, and a wire cover to it will be
    useful. The traveller unaccustomed to a chibouk 4ft. long will
    probably much damage his carpets by upsetting the ashes; Cairo.

Magnesium torches for the tombs; England.

An India-rubber folding tub; England.

A small leather purse, for gold and silver.

* A bag for copper money.

Matches.

Guns, pistols, England. A revolver is a useful plaything, if the
    traveller does not load it. He can exhibit it to Beys and swells,
    and the exhibition will do instead of conversation. A traveller
    might easily sell, at high prices, his English guns and pistols
    when done with them to the wealthy natives. They will give
    £20 to £30 for a second English breech-loading gun; but the
    vendor should have ammunition to sell them also. A cheap
    English gun, or revolver, and some ammunition may be useful to
    give away.

* Ink, paper, envelopes, blotting paper, pens, pencils, india-rubber,
    wafers, &c.

* Housewife, with black and white thread, tapes, needles, pins,
    buttons, bodkin, and scissors.

Some string and a packing needle may be useful.

Some nails, and hammer.

A saddle and bridle from England may be brought; the writer would
    recommend as better a pair of English stirrups and leathers,
    and a pair of English spurs,—to buckle on, not fit into a boot
    heel.

Telescope or opera glass, or both; England

* A fly flap; Cairo.

A canteen to hold knife, fork, &c., would be useful for lunching out
    among ruins; England.

A pocket flask; England.

A pocket drinking cup very useful, but best of all is a patent pocket
    filter; England.

A wine glass or two will be useful; a native establishment does not
    rise beyond tumblers.

A few visiting and blank cards, and luggage labels.

A pocket almanac.

Thermometer, aneroid barometer, measuring tape, instruments for
    observations, chronometer, compass, *ad lib.*

Paper collars; England or Cairo.

A canvas bag for dirty clothes; useful also on board steamboat
    coming out.

Light flannel suits, or linen, best for wear. Traveller should wear
    flannel underclothing,—it absorbs the perspiration; England.

Keith Johnstone's map of Egypt.

A national flag for his boat. English travellers are, as a rule, most ignorant of what is their own flag. With certain exceptions, the only flag English travellers have a right to hoist is a red flag, with a jack in the upper corner next the flag staff. The white and blue flags are appropriated to the Royal Navy and Royal Naval Reserve, and certain yacht clubs.

A private flag may also be useful as a distinguishing mark.

Books. A sojourner at Luxor had better take plenty : Lane's Modern Egyptians, Lord Lindsay's Letters, and Sir J. G. Wilkinson's Manners and Customs of Ancient Egyptians, will be very useful. He should take a lot of the Tauchnitz editions (procurable at David Robertson & Co.'s, Cairo). A deal is done among Nile travellers in the way of swopping novels and papers.

Newspapers. The best to order is the *Pall Mall Budget*, thin paper edition, issued on Fridays just in time for the mail, and the *London Illustrated*, on thin paper, &c.

Letters and newspapers should be addressed care of British Post-master, or Consulate, Cairo, and Messrs. David Robertson & Co., instructed to forward them on to the traveller's Consul at Luxor. Letters from Luxor should be sent, per the Consul, to the same firm to repost to Europe or America.

Money. A traveller should arrange to take what he wants up the river in English or French gold. Circular notes, bank notes, &c., are only to be cashed up the Nile at about £40 per cent. dis-count. The sovereign is worth rather more than 5 dollars, but the traveller will only get 5 for it ; the napoleon 4 dollars. The French 5-franc pieces count as a dollar. The shilling is about 12½ copper piastres. English shillings and rupees, Turkish shillings, and an Austrian coin (worth about sixpence) are current ; but the traveller should change as little gold as he can, and insist on silver change that he knows the value of. He should never be without copper money for baksheesh, &c., or else he will pay a deal more than he ought. By arrangement with Messrs. David Robertson & Co. a traveller can, in case of need, procure gold to a small amount from Mustapha Agha at Luxor.

On no account should a traveller pay or baksheesh a native beyond what is absolutely necessary : every traveller who does so is a criminal, and defrauds those who come after him, for he permanently raises prices. A native who once gets two shillings for a one-shilling job, permanently raises his price to two shillings, until another traveller gives him three, when he raises it again. Travellers now are expected to pay in Cairo about six times as much for a donkey-ride as a native pays. I had a boy as attendant, who was satisfied with a few piastres a-day, until an Englishman gave him half a sovereign for an afternoon's work : the lad at once grumbled because I would not pay at that rate.

Every traveller, who goes up the Nile, abandons all medical assistance. He should therefore take certain medical comforts with him—diachylon plaster, spermaceti ointment, and lint, some cooling astringent wash for his eyes, some rhubarb pills, castor oil, and such other things as his medical adviser may recommend.

Printed at the Offices of C. Thurnam & Sons, Carlisle.

PART III.

—

ROUND THE WORLD.

LETTER I.

LONDON TO MELBOURNE;

OR,

THE VOYAGE OF THE "AGAMEMNON."

The *Agamemnon* left Gravesend at 2-30 p.m. on Tuesday November the 7th, 1871, and anchored that evening off the Chapman Beacon, as the wind was contrary. Next day the wind still continued foul, and the capstan proved to be out of order, so we did not move ; but at daylight on Thursday morning we made our start, and stood off for that day and the next towards the French coast, and, on the other tack, back to Beachey Head, passing the masts of a shipwrecked vessel on the Goodwins, and also a large iron ship that had evidently been in collision with another and sustained much damage. Next day (Saturday) we had a favourable wind, and were soon off the Start Point, where we put down our pilot, and whence we took what is called in nautical language our " departure," dipping the Start Light at 7-30 p.m. on Saturday Nov. 11, the last we saw of Old England after some delightful views of the Devonshire coast in the neighbourhood of Torquay, Torbay, and Dartmouth.

Once off, for sailors don't reckon a ship to have begun her passage until the last of the land has been seen, we had some roughish weather and foul winds, which considerably thinned the attendance at meals. One night the spanker sail was carried away amid tremendous noise, and next morning we had a strong gale in our teeth, so that we had to shorten sail, taking in the mainsail and reefing topsails; the vessel laid over considerably, and took in, to a landsman's ideas, much water over the forecastle. During this rough weather a lurch of the ship one night, while the writer was undressing, sent him against the cabin bulkhead, a badly fastened door, which gave, and he appeared in the next cabin, to the astonishment of its inmates, "under bare poles," as seamen say, that is, in nothing but a shirt, and not much of that. This adverse weather drove us off our course, and was succeeded by calms and light winds, during which 've made but little progress; indeed, we had light winds and baffling calms all down to the line, to which our passage was very slow; once or twice we had a good day and did a good run, having all stun'sails set, but it was followed invariably by a calm, the N.E. trades being very light.

On Thursday, 23rd November, we sighted the Madeiras, namely, Porto Santo, distant far away on the starboard quarter, the Desertas on the starboard bow (distant 15 to 20 miles), and Madeira behind them (distant say 35 miles). Of the Desertas we had a most lovely view—two very elevated rocky islands of apparently volcanic formation and of very irregular outline—reminding one much of the hills over Loch Scavaig, and the Cuchullin in Skye, and others in the Isle of Arran. With a good glass we could see most lovely cliffs of beautiful colours in the Desertas. Of Madeira we did not see so much, as it was behind, but we could make out the entrance to Funchal Roads.

The following day (24th November) we sailed along in sight of the islands of Palma and Ferro (two of the Canaries). The former is a very high and rugged island, over 7,000 feet high. The ship rolled a good bit here, and sundry careless fellows on the main deck, leaving their ports open, got a sea in and their bedding well soaked. About this latitude we passed a small vessel (the *Glen Esk*, of Leith, from Belfast Lough to Buenos Ayres) so close as to be able to talk to her crew, though we had rather to elevate our voices.

Being soon after this becalmed, we got so hard up for amusement that, on a report being raised that the cow had put her head out, there was a rush of all the passengers to look. The cow lived in the long boat, which was on skids midships; in confinement with the cow were some half-dozen sheep, of which, at starting, we had about eighty on board, and also a large stock of pigs. Of geese, ducks, turkeys, guinea fowls, and cocks and hens we had whole flocks, whose fights and struggles at feeding time were a constant source of amusement. On one occasion sundry of these fowls got loose; some "with high ambitions fraught" proceeded to ascend the rigging, but others of non-aquatic habits, yet rendered gloomy and morose by sea sickness, precipitated themselves into the sea. We did not stop to pick them up, and I know not what monster of the sea or air devoured them. It may be noted that when these fowls did get their sea-legs, their sea-legs were uncommonly tough.

A day or two afterwards (27th November) we were again dead-becalmed, and two boats were manned by the passengers and lowered. We had an enjoyable row for a mile or two, and were much struck with the majestic appearance of the ship as she rose and fell with the swell, all her light duck set, and great stun'sails like wings on either side. She looked like an old-fashioned man-of-war frigate, for which, indeed, she was built, only the Peruvian Government, who ordered her, would not pay for her. All these calms and baffling winds were attributed by the sailors to the facts that some cruel fellow had flung a poodle overboard to drown, and that a passenger had shot a Mother Carey's chicken. During this weather we enjoyed most beautiful moonlight nights, and the water was so clear that we could see right under the vessel's keel; it was curious to think that between that and bottom was over 2,000 fathoms (or 12,000 feet) of water. In the evenings the sea was beautifully phosphorescent, huge masses of light being flung right and left by the ship's bows, and left in her wake. By fishing with a bucket we ascertained this was due to the presence in great abundance of the medusa splendens, a jelly fish about the size of a finger, and which affords food to the whales. As we were at this time in the tropics, we had to give up pork and butter at meals on account of the heat, and substitute potted meats for one, and jam for the other. The heat, though great in the tropics, was not oppressive; we had, however, awnings spread, and wind-sails put up. On the 1st of December we sighted San Antonio, one of the Cape De Verd Islands, a very lofty, rugged island, along whose coast we sailed all day. It is inhabited, but we saw no signs of inhabitants or cultivation; nothing but extraordinary wild and desert hills tumbled about in wild confusion. We sighted also the Isle of St. Vincent, a mere volcanic cinder in the ocean, at which the African coast steamers coal.

On the 4th and 5th December we went through four or five squalls, such as are common in the tropics. " Stand by the royal haliards" was the word, and royals, jibs, and stun'sails all came fluttering down; the rain fell in perfect torrents, like sheets of water deluged over the ship; the weight of water on the awnings, and their consequent contraction, bent great iron stanchions, as thick as a man's wrist. These squalls could be seen approaching : a long line of foam on the water hurrying towards us, and a mass of cloud behind ; what with the whistling of the wind, and the pace the ship flew during them, the scene was exciting. One squall, occurring at night, was very fine ; the ship flew through the water, throwing up huge sheets of phosphorescent light, and leaving in her wake a vast track of liquid fire. From the forecastle her appearance was majestic, the masts bending and the sails all bellying out, while sheet lightning vividly added to the terrors of the scene. As from the sublime to the ridiculous is but a step, it should be here recorded that the preliminary step to encountering these tropical squalls was for everyone (all ranks, including passengers) to put on his oilskins, take off his boots and socks, and pull up his bags.

On the 7th December we sighted St. Paul's Island, not the one of *Megæra* fame, but another of that name, called also by the name of San Pedro. Many of us climbed to the mizen crosstrees to view it, and were pursued by the middies, and on capture fined a bottle of champagne as our footing, all but one bold passenger, who, hotly chased, slid down a backstay, and escaped. The St. Paul's Island much resembles the *Megæra* one, and is a volcanic rock, whitened with the dung of thousands of sea fowls, and having a crater in the middle. It is inhabited by sharks and groupers (a sort of fish), in addition to the birds, and rarely has human foot ever been set thereon. It is very low, and looks in the distance like a ship under full sail.

We crossed the line the same evening, crossing much west of the usual course taken by ships ; to this we were forced by the great equatorial current, which drifted us far west, while the winds being light we could not head against it. Thus we were carried to within 250 miles of the American coast, near Cape St. Roche, and were forced to make a very disadvantageous tack for fear of being jammed north of that Cape, and also to clear the dangerous reef of the Rocas. We were afterwards within 150 miles of Pernambuco, but we never sighted land after San Pedro, though we later on passed very near Gough's Isle, and also the Croziers.

About the 10th December we got the S.E. trades in south longitude 4 degrees, a little more or less.

On the 16th December we passed the sun, and at midday

it was vertical over the main truck; the heat was hardly so great as further north, for though the sun was hotter, yet the wind was colder, and we had much damp, and complaints of rheumatism were very rife. Squalls of rain with fog succeeded. In one of these fogs a large barque came suddenly out of the fog, steering direct for us. She passed close under our stern, but could not be signalled, owing to the fog. She appeared to be a foreigner. An hour later the fog lifted, and showed us a large ship under full sail, bearing down on us, only a mile or two astern. The fog shut her out soon; our skipper spread more duck, and hauled his wind, so as to put the *Agamemnon* on her best point of sailing, and we never more saw this sea child of the mist.

Christmas Day was cold and miserable, but fined up in the evening. The Christmas puddings were all spoilt, as the cook boy neglected his work, and let them soak for twelve hours in cold salt water. After Christmas we got into intense cold, and the ship's officers began the most ominous preparations for rough weather, which generally is expected "down south," and of which they told us the most appalling tales, until everyone caught the infection, tried to tell the most horrible yarns he could, and "down south" became a cant bye-word for everything dreadful and disgusting.

On December 30th the cold was very great, but the wind grand, and the ship did 314 knots that day, and 306 the next, or 366 and 357 miles respectively, about as fast as ship or steamer ever went; she did it very quietly, and quite dry, without fuss; carrying all sail, bar the spanker and studding-sails. The sight from the crosstrees was very grand as she rushed along, at times doing 17 miles an hour—tremendous pace for so huge a mass.

We passed the longitude of the Cape of Good Hope on the last day of the year, about 600 miles south of it. After this the cold and fog got worse, and many of the invalids (we had seventeen in the cuddy, travelling in search of health) suffered severely. About the 6th January we got anxious as to our position, having quite lost the sun, and the Crozier Islands being near, and how near being unknown, while at times we could hardly see ahead at all; consequently we put a little northing into our course to be safe. On the 8th we got the sun, and it speaks well for our captain's skill in navigation that, after five days of dead reckoning, the ship was only 13 miles out of the place he reckoned her at: during the five days she had run over 1,000 miles.

From this time to the 20th we had fine following winds dead aft, and the vessel in consequence rolling heavily, and plunging her dolphin striker and figure head into the huge and magnificent seas that heaved and fell around. One evening she rolled her boats into the water; and also rolled away the framework and gratings over the principal cuddy skylight, smashing it severely, one passenger getting a heavy fall at the same time; shortly afterwards a sea came on the poop and knocked five passengers in a lump into the meat safe. During this rolling sleeping at night was difficult; "rocked in the cradle of the deep" is all very well in poetry, but in practice it is bad for the shins and skins, when one's bunk is constantly vibrating to and fro. Meals too are not satisfactory when the dishes travel from side to side of the table, and one has to hold one's liquor tight, or take it externally. Off Cape Leeuwin, the south-west corner of Australia, which we passed some 600 miles to our north, we had some hard squalls, and finally, when expecting almost hourly to make Cape Otway, were to our intense chagrin becalmed just out of sight of land, or baffled by foul winds. At last, on January 26th, we made the land about 12-45 p.m., a well wooded hummocky land, looking vastly like a huge whin covert, from which it would be difficult to make a fox break, while a long streak of heather broom indicated the ravages of a recent bush fire. About 6 p.m. we passed the light on Cape Otway, and we signalled our number for telegraph to Melbourne, while a flight of black swans passing near the ship kept us well in mind of our proximity to a land where nature in all its aspects presents the reverse of what it does in Old England. This was the first land we had seen for fifty days, since dipping St. Paul's Island, while a sail we this day sighted on the horizon was the only one we had viewed for thirty-seven days, so solitary is the vast expanse of ocean. Gliding gently by moonlight along the coast we made the Heads in the early morning, picked up our pilot, and from him learnt three important pieces of news—(1) The Prince of Wales's illness; (2) The wreck of the clipper ship *Sussex* just outside the Heads; (3) And that the famous *Thermopylæ* had left the Lizard Point six days after us, and had got in four days before us. In fact, she had overtaken us at the Cape, and gone away from us then. She is a much smaller ship than the *Agamemnon*, but spreads much more canvas, and about the fastest ship in the world.

From the Heads to Sandridge Pier is but a few hours, and we were landed and ashore in Melbourne.

Of the *Agamemnon* itself, the fine craft which bore us so far, and of the skill and courtesy of her officers, one cannot speak too highly. Whenever she did get a favourable wind (a rather rare occurrence during the early part of the voyage), she certainly made the most of it, logging in south latitude an average of 204 knots, or 238 miles a day for thirty-five consecutive days, besides doing the big runs we have already mentioned. She was a very dry ship, and though she did roll a good deal at times, yet it was slowly and majestically, and not with jerks.

Of the wonders of the deep we hardly saw so many as we expected, and our captures amounted to very few. A few whales were seen blowing in the distance occasionally, or a stray grampus; south of the line we were frequently accompanied by shoals of porpoises of a curious kind; they were piebald, black and white, from four feet to six feet long, with a broad horizontal tail. These fellows could swim faster than the ship at full speed, and would rush alongside of her, leaping out of the water as they went, two or three at a time, and cross her bows; sometimes three or four would rub their backs against her cut-water at once, and she would have to shove them aside like pigs. Attempts were made to harpoon them from the dolphin striker, but with little success. Of sharks we only saw one, and he rose at an empty bottle, but did not bite; as pilot fish were seen near our rudder, it is probable some carnivorous gentleman was cruising along under shelter of the ship's bottom. An enormous "thresher" fish, the mortal foe of whales, whom it flogs to death, took a look at us one morning, and reared its vast bulk some 20 feet out of water before it sounded. Of albicore and bonita we caught none, but in fishing for them we hooked no less a monster than a flour cask, which had been pitched overboard, and fouling the fishing lines carried them all away, a loss not easily to be replaced on board ship. We were very unfortunate in this way, and lost a great quantity of hooks and lines by various accidents.

Down south the ship was followed by numbers of sea birds, of which the most magnificent were the albatrosses,

who measure from 10 feet to 16 feet across the wing ; they
sweep along with most majestic flight, watching with piercing
eye for any garbage that goes overboard.   They are believed
by sailors to be the ghosts of old sea captains, and an enthusiastic quarter-master went so far as to recognize in one white-
headed albatross " old Barney Martin," who was lost in the
London.   We fished for these birds (excuse the bull) with line
and bait, and captured five albatrosses ; others were hooked,
but escaped, carrying off the hooks, while one was released by
a brother who flew against the line and broke it with his wing.
We last saw the two sitting on the water together side by side,
the one endeavouring to vomit up the hook : the other looking
anxiously on, which made many accredit him with very fine
feelings, imagining him to be in waiting as a doctor, or
sympathizing friend, or a sorrowing spouse, whereas the more
probable truth was that he was an expectant executor, waiting
his comrade's demise with a view to gobbling him up, and so
becoming his tomb and monument.   The albatrosses we caught
were fine birds, though by no means very large specimens,
none of them exceeding 10 feet 10 inches in expanse of wing.
In addition to their coat of feathers, they are also protected by
a thick covering of fine down.   Their weight was from 21lbs.
to 25lbs.   We also caught by hook and line some birds, called
by the sailors " mollyhawks," which were even handsomer
birds than the albatrosses, though measuring only 3 feet
from beak to tail, and 7 feet 3 inches across the wing : they
were wonderful masses of down and feathers, and their necks
and breasts were white as driven snow.   Albatrosses and
mollyhawks were speedily dissected, and their wing bones
made into pipe stems, and their webbed feet into tobacco
pouches.   One or two small birds of the Cape pigeon variety
were caught by hanging threads over the stern, in which they
got their wings entangled.   The great difficulty, we found,
was to ascertain the names of the strange birds that followed
us — mollyhawks, mutton birds, bos'uns, boobies, stinkpots,
Cape hens, Cape cocks, Cape pigeons, &c., to *infinitum ;* but
no two sailors ever gave the same bird the same name.   The
first thing to be done on catching one of the larger sea fowl is
to tie up his prodigious bill, which is a most formidable
weapon, capable of taking off a finger or two with great
facility, and the next is to kill him, which we effected with a
dose of prussic acid, prescribed and administered by the ship's

doctor, *secundum artem*, or else by strangulation. We also shot a good many, but rarely got their bodies ; still we knew we were doing the tribe a good turn, for they speedily devoured a sick or wounded specimen. Near the line we saw shoals of flying fish, sixty or seventy at a time in the air ; they are about the size of a herring, and their flight is much more bird-like than one would expect.

Once we saw a perfect double lunar rainbow, like semi-circles of silver light, of which the principal ring was slightly blue tinged on the inside, and orange without. We also saw several prismatic halos round the moon of large size, and a fine double one round the sun. The zodiacal light we were not lucky enough to see.

Astronomy afforded much amusement. Jupiter's satellites were easily seen through a glass, and the appearance of the Southern Cross, the Magellanic clouds, and the Coalsacks, were watched for with great interest, while the various changes of colour from red to green, and back again, presented every minute by the star Canopus, gave rise to much speculation. Alas for the romance of our childhood, most of us voted the Southern Cross a take in ; it is not a very brilliant constellation, but "down south" they have not many, and so they make the most of what they have. In the tropics the rose-coloured glow of the sunsets and the lovely moonlight nights were great sources of pleasure.

The killing and slaying of sea birds, and the observation of natural phenomena, by no means filled up all our vacant time ; various were the devices we resorted to for that end. One may here remark that people who have never been a long voyage, or whose experience is confined solely to that most pleasant of all things, a coasting trip round the Mediterranean, and through the Grecian Archipelago, have usually very erroneous ideas of a long sea voyage. They imagine a perpetual panorama of foreign coast scenery, of novel sights in the sea and land, and of strange and weird vessels. They will be speedily disillusioned by a voyage to Australia ; most ships never see the land from leaving England's shore until they sight the Australian coast at Cape Otway. Vessels are but few and far between ; from leaving the Start Point, on November 11th, up to December 20th, we saw barely a dozen, some mere specks in the horizon, while of four or five alone we were able by signalling with flags to ascertain the name. From that date to

Cape Otway we saw never a one, nothing but a dreary waste
of sea and sky.   Another class of persons, alike doomed to be
disappointed, are those who intend to study hard at sea, and
bring with them libraries of abstruse books.   Strong minded
must be the being who can manage to work at sea ; idleness
reigns on board ship, and the very atmosphere is fatal to study.
Mr. Anthony Trollope is, indeed, said to have written a novel
on his passage to Australia, but he must be an exception, and
I should have been sorry to have been his fellow-passenger.
How all of them will figure in his new production!   What,
then, do people do at sea ?   Eating, I am sorry to say for the
credit of poor humanity, becomes of vast importance ; breakfast
at 9, lunch at 12-30, dinner at 4, tea at 6-30, and grog
at 8, become objects of prominent importance to persons
who on shore are little given to watch eagerly for such ;
tobacco is an immense resource, while an invariable and never-
failing one is to bother the skipper and his officers with
questions, morning, noon, and night, about the course, the
sails, the weather, the this, that, or other, why he does so
and so, and why he does not do something else.   Great was
the good nature of all on board the *Agamemnon* in replying to
our landlubberly questions, and in teaching us the difference
between the flying jib and the spanker, a tack and a sheet,
and a haliard and a chain cable.   If now and then a little fun
was poked at querists, much must be excused a nautical man
who is asked and expected to prophesy the weather for periods
of time to come varying from twenty-four hours to as many
days, and to be a complete guide-book to every land that
ever a ship sailed to or past.

Bets of beer on the ship's run, posted daily at noon, were
an unfailing amusement ; every possible game of cards had its
turn both by day and night.   Drafts, chess, cribbage, and the
like, found many admirers.   A little singing was occasionally
got up, and a French *militaire* (who went heart and soul into
every scheme for amusement) came out strong in *La Grande
Duchesse* and *La Belle Hélène*, giving us on one occasion
General Boum to the life in full costume.

For the rest, we all became boys again, aye, and girls
too, and took to childish sports and gambols spiced with a
soupçon (perhaps more than a *soupçon*) of the full-grown
vice of betting.   We played deck quoits with grommits of
rope till we made ourselves universal nuisances ; we tried

cricket, and knocked three or four balls of rope yarn overboard daily; we did football, we basted the bear, we slung the monkey, we shot with pistols at a mark, we ran, we jumped, we chalked lines on the deck with our feet suspended in a bowline; and, most extraordinary of all, we had a chewing race for a bottle of gin. A rope was suspended athwart the poop, with long ends of thread suspended from it; each competitor took the end in his lips, and, at the signal of start, proceeded to chew it up, his hands being tied behind his back. Then we made kites of gigantic size, strange shapes, and wonderful colours, and flew them with great success, generally leaving them in the sea. Once a fit seized us all to make windmills. Soon the whole poop was decorated with bizarre creations spinning round, some with full suits of paper sails, top gallants, royals, and all; others had merely wooden blades, like screw propellers. Once, and oftener, we were reduced to Hop Scotch. Over all these gambols a committee of amusement presided, and in some mysterious ways raised funds for a champagne drink on the Saturday before Christmas, the captain kindly standing a very handsome supper. That evening the steerage passengers celebrated it by a free fight, and the skipper had to threaten them with handcuffs.

Occasionally our amusements approached the intellectual: we tried a penny reading, and failed; we talked of acting, and didn't, having no ladies to act, nor to dance either, so we didn't dance. We supported a weekly newspaper, in MSS., edited by a steerage passenger, and supposed to contain more bulls, misspellings, and bad grammar, than any production in the world. We finished our voyage by subscribing to print this paper, and confidently gave the money to the editor, who got handsomely drunk thereon, and did *not* print the paper.

Occasionally our amusements deviated in the opposite direction: we practically joked, that is some of us did; sawed a deck chair or two in bits; pitched a water can overboard; or made night hideous with strange sounds, as when the four heaviest of the cuddy passengers danced on the poop deck a grand "pas de quatre fantasque et diabolique," and intoxicated, in the small hours of the morning, by way of greeting the New Year. Oddly enough, this performance was not much admired by those who slept the New Year in, and was not encored by special request.

The crew and the steerage passengers afforded us some

fun, and treated us to an open-air Ethiopian concert or two, while we also had the usual nautical performances on the occasions of "drowning the dead horse," and "crossing the line." Most people have heard of the last of these ceremonies, but the former will be to many a novelty. It appears that the Jacks receive on entering the ship a month's pay in advance, and until their pay again begins to run, they say they are working the "dead horse." The termination of thus working the "dead horse" is an era of great rejoicing in the forecastle, and our Jacks celebrated it. Sometime about three bells in the first dog-watch, when it was dusk, the sailors hauled aft on a grating a model of a horse, artistically made out of an old beer barrel and some rolls of canvas, with two glass bottles for eyes. His jockey, on arriving in front of the break of the poop, where the officers and passengers were assembled, proceeded to chant his steed's praises, and to offer him for sale by auction. No bidders coming forward, but rather a rapid fire of depreciatory remarks, the horse was declared dead, and, with his rider, ran rapidly up to the lee mainyard-arm, and thence dropped (*sans* his rider) into the sea, amid a fire of blue lights, after which grog was served out, and the Jacks betook themselves to mirthful song and jocund dance.

The other ceremony has been often described, but some may like to hear it again. We will be brief. One evening, as we neared the line, Neptune's secretary came on board, and delivered an intimation of his master's intended visit, and departed astern in a chariot of fire, otherwise an old tub well tarred and set in a blaze. A day or so later his godship himself came on board, and was received with due ceremony, the mainyard being laid aback, and other nautical rites gone through. He wore a crown and gorgeous robes, while his godlike limbs were bare and ruddled red. In one hand he brandished a trident decorated tastefully with red herrings, while with the other he brought to bear upon us a stupendous opera glass craftily made of empty whisky bottles lashed together with rope yarn. He was accompanied by his wife, who wore a straw hat, and a striped gown, and was closely shaved for the occasion; she carried in her arms an oakum babe of tender age. The chariot of this noble pair was drawn by three horses or sailors on all-fours, who, as the weather was warm (thermometer up to 80 degrees or so), were clad in oil-skins supplemented by the somewhat putrid hides of muttons eaten at an early period of the voyage. A doctor with a variety of bottles, a dentist, a barber with strop and razor of portentous size, an assistant with lather of the nastiest description in a biscuit tin, another with the barber's pole, several policemen, and certain drummers, or beaters of old preserved meat-cases, were in attendance. Neptune paid his respects to the captain, and then a general move to the forecastle took place, where several unfortunate sailors and miserable boys were dosed, dentisted, shaved, shampooed, soused, and ducked, to everyone's satisfaction but their own, until at last the victims' spirits rising, the tables were turned, and the god and goddess themselves, and all their motley suite, were well drenched with salt water, which flew about in every direction, a well-directed fire being kept up from the foretop, where a supply had previously been accumulated. This ceremony has, however, in modern days been shorn of much of its nastiness and extent. The Jack's holiday on the occasion is but the evening, and not the whole day, while they are made to confine their delicate attentions to one another, and dare not touch passengers, or extort fines from those unwilling to be shaved.

We have already said that we numbered among our passengers some seventeen invalids, all travelling in search of health. The Australian voyage is now becoming a favourite nostrum with doctors for certain complaints, and so this sketch may be interesting to many. Although we went through great extremes of heat and cold (extremes particularly of cold, which people rarely anticipate on such a voyage, yet are certain to have) all our invalids got stronger and heavier. Persons intending such a voyage should, before starting, ascertain from an expert what clothes and comforts they should take; of course, they cannot expect all the comforts of the land, but they can, by forethought, do much for themselves. In the choice of a ship they can do no better than take the *Agamemnon*, and embark under Captain Marsden, R.N.R.; but they must apply early, as the ship of so popular a commander soon fills up.

LETTER II.

VICTORIA.

So soon as we got on shore from our ship, the *Agamemnon*, we chartered one of the common conveyances of the country called a buggy, a rattle-trap sort of machine on two wheels, holding two in front beside the driver, and three behind ; it has a leather hood over it, and is of American parentage. We speedily trotted up to Melbourne, and established ourselves in comfortable quarters at Menzie's Hotel, and then sallied forth for a stroll. Melbourne appeared very dull, for, as it was a Saturday afternoon, all the shops were shut. We noticed one reminiscence of home in the fact that Carlisle ales were in several places advertised for sale, and we felt proud and pleased. On the Sunday we hired a buggy and had a drive round the suburbs, which pleased us much. Melbourne is surrounded by quantities of handsome, well-built villas, of various architectural styles,—Italian, English, and Indian,—standing in their own grounds No person, who can afford it, lives in Melbourne, except the doctors, and they are all to be found in one place—the Treasury end of Collins Street. The roads around Melbourne are beautifully wide, with generally broad strips of turf on the sides.

Monday we occupied in moving our luggage from the ship, satisfying the custom officials thereon, and in hunting for lodgings. Lodgings, in the English sense of the word, are not to be got in the Australian Colonies ; boarding houses are the only things, and all the inmates feed together and have one sitting room, a fashion to my taste especially disagreeable. Being, however, a party of four, we did not so much object, and got in a place in Fitzroy, a Melbourne quarter not far from the Parliament House, the Treasury, and the top of Collins Street. We had but one other lodger, a quiet enough man. Our first dinner was rather ludicrous, for the landlady, according to Australian custom, herself presided ; we had, however, previously stipulated for a licence for tobacco at all hours and places, and we found that a good smoke, altogether, shortly before dinner choked her off, and in future we dined unpresided over. Another objectionable feature in these boarding houses is, that they wont give dinner on Sundays except at one o'clock — take that or go without. The ladies, who condescend for dirty dross to do the household work, will not have their Sundays interfered with. The marchioness who waited at our house was very peremptory on this point. She insisted also on three evenings out a week, and was not to be sent messages; so, if we wanted a buggy, or any trifle, our landlady had to go herself. Servants are the great difficulty in the colony; they demand high wages and great privileges : even at the best houses they will only just put the dinner on the table and then retire; the guests must hand the dishes round themselves. Men servants are not to be had except at awful wages : a groom gets £80, and a gardener from that to £120. One friend of mine, with groom and gardener, and a moderate establishment of maids, spent £600 per annum in wages. Endless are the comic stories told of the colonial maids and their pretensions and impertinences, and the slavery in which they keep their so-called mistresses. I heard of a lady who resided out of Melbourne, who engaged a Betsalinda, and paid her buggy down. On arrival, Miss B. began by inquiring if the "Washing was done at home, for she could not abide washing?" the lady promised to put it out; "Had they many gentlemen to dinner, she could not abide strangers?" it was arranged that she should not appear on such occasions; thus answered, she went to bed, but next morning she showed in a red and yellow bonnet, thanked the lady "for the night's lodging and the buggy ride, but didn't mean to stay; didn't like the place." Another informed her mistress that she had "had a present of a horse and saddle, and wished to leave before the races," and gently asked for the loan of the astonished lady's habit in which to figure on the race course.

The inhabitants of Melbourne are very proud of their city. I confess I can hardly rise to the height of admiration they expect; probably all accustomed to European cities would agree with me, it wants the mellowness of age, and the dignity of old historical associations. The real point of admiration is that so fine a city, so many fine buildings, should have taken under forty years to build. Its main streets are of magnificent width, with huge water-courses down each side. When the plan of Melbourne was originally laid out, it was intended that a back access should be had to every house by means of a back lane. Space having now grown valuable, this project has worked badly ; · the back lanes have come in for building, and form squalid alleys alternating with magnificent streets. The town is wholly unsewered,—cesspools, and a few surreptitious drains into the Yarra-Yarra, are its only sanitary conveniences. Thus it happens that Melbourne occasionally smells, and is subject to typhoid fever, while the broad water-courses in the streets,—actually requiring and having bridges over them to enable people to cross,—are fast becoming open drains. It possesses some fine public buildings, such as its Town Hall, Post-office, and Treasury, of high artistic architectural merit. Its Parliament Houses are built, but unfronted until the battle of the styles shall be decided. Its Banks are magnificent buildings, each, as one is proudly told, an exact copy of the Thingimbobiolenzi Palace at Florence, or the Vatican at Rome. The two institutions of which Melbourne should be proudest, and from which any city, European or American, might take wrinkles, are its Public Library and its University Museum. The former is free to every one, is most extensively used, and not abused ; while the latter is in every way admirable. One special point is that every bone in every skeleton there exhibited has a number on it, while on the walls can be found the scientific name corresponding to that number. The numbers throughout each skeleton are everywhere the same : thus No. X is always the femur, No. Y the scapula. The help this system is to the students of osteology is evident. Another feature is the arrangement of the stuffed beasts, not in long dusty rows, but in groups beautifully set up and enclosed in large glass cases, with scenery and belongings appropriate to them.

Collins Street is the principal street of Melbourne, a fine, long, broad street. The inhabitants talk a good deal of the " block," and " doing the block" is their equivalent for a " stroll down Pall Mall.", The "block" is a quadrangle formed by four streets, of which a portion of Collins Street is one. From four to six, on fine afternoons, the beauty and fashion of Melbourne is supposed to be " doing the block."

A noticeable feature in the streets is the number of

conveniences for hitching up horses to, necessary in a country where every one rides, and a riding horse may be bought at public auction for so low a sum as a pound. The colonial saddle is to English eyes clumsy, having enormous projections in front of the knees to protect them in riding through the bush. Confirmed buck-jumpers are sometimes ridden with a stick affixed across the saddle. The fancier of horse flesh will be disappointed with the Australian horse; he is an ewe-necked, hard-mouthed, buck-jumping brute. The fact is the breed has run wild ; up the country wild horses swarm, and are awful nuisances. Utterly useless and valueless brutes, not only do they destroy the grass, but they tice away valuable horses, and corrupt the morals of valuable mares ; consequently they are shot as vermin, and I was told of one sheep-run on which 2,000 horses had been shot in one year, a man being permanently employed to do it. Wild cattle and wild sheep are a similar nuisance. Valuable stallions, bulls, and rams are now being imported from England to keep up the standard of all these. It seems odd that in a climate where all these animals are highly prolific, their tendency, particularly when wild, should be to deterioration. Pigs, rats, rabbits, and sparrows are also importations to Australia, and have taken kindly to the place. At Colac 16 guns in a day shot 2,000 rabbits on one estate, whose owner has in vain spent £5,000 in one year to extirpate Master Bunny. No one considers a rabbit worth bringing home. Sparrows were imported lately by the Victorian Acclimatization Society, as a pleasant reminiscence of home ; they have bred so fast as to be already a curse to the place.

Returning to the streets of Melbourne, a " new chum," or fresh arrival, is at once struck by a difference from what he left at home. The place has a great dash of Americanism in its appearance and manners ; the latter are free and easy ; go into a shop to buy a hat, and the shopman will probably take your hat off your head and clap it on his own by way of ascertaining your size. Sun helmets and summer coats abound. Rough-looking diggers and squatters are to be seen in plenty. Bars are everywhere, and people are fond of "shouting" or standing drink ; in these bars placards state " all drinks a shilling, sixpence, or threepence," according to the style of the bar ; and one may hear frequent offers to " shout all round."

Chinese swarm in Melbourne, where they have a quarter, Little Burke Street, to themselves. They are very industrious and successful in market-gardening, fishing, and peddling, and make a good living where others would starve. Some of them are wealthy merchants. They have their own tea houses, stores, gambling houses, and joss houses or temples. One of these joss houses, near St. Kilda, is a fine building, decorated inside with a wonderful assortment of paper lanterns, tinsel, and other gorgeous rubbish.

Paddy's market is another Melbourne curiosity; a market and a fair place much crowded on Saturday night. Fruit is cheap there, pines 3d. a piece; grapes sometimes 3d. a pound, but up country I have got them for 2d. a pound, and fine grapes too.

One good feature in Melbourne is the ease and cheapness of locomotion. Besides omnibuses after the American fashion, buggies start at appointed intervals for all the suburbs, and so soon as a new chum knows the lines he can go any way for 3d. or 6d.

The river of Melbourne is the Yarra-Yarra, a narrow, deep, muddy, and sluggish stream, but having places of peculiar beauty on its manifold windings, where grow the finest specimens of weeping willow I have ever beheld. We enjoyed several rows on it, taking up some lunch with us.

All round Melbourne are situated charming suburban towns, where live the chief people of Melbourne—Hawthorn, St. Hilda, Brighton, Elsternwick, and many more, all well worth seeing; prettily situated, with much of the country about them in its original state of gum forest. Thanks to the kindness of an old college friend, I enjoyed some pleasant rides around Melbourne on an animal that did not buck-jump, and that had a mouth. Brighton is a pleasant place on the sea, on Hobson Bay, and at Bolton Hall (called after a place in Cumberland) I met with great hospitality, and enjoyed real fun; colonial men of business, when away from the mill, make holiday in real earnest.

Beyond Brighton is Mordialloc, some fourteen miles from Melbourne, and a favourite place for pic-nics. After clearing the Melbourne suburbs the road lies through country that has been little disturbed since the original settlement of the country; and kangaroos, opossums, and snakes abound. The hotel at Mordialloc is pleasantly situated, not far from the shores of

Hobson Bay. The landlord is a great character, master of the Melbourne hounds, which are kennelled hard by, a dog and a bitch pack about whose performances the master will yarn for ever. They hunt anything, dingoes (which are a large red wild dog), kangaroos, and deer; some savage specimens of the first were at the time of my visit tethered up for consumption when the season commenced in June. A very fine bitch dingo had the morning of my visit been killed by a snake, which abound here. There are about fifty-four sorts of snakes in the colony, and forty-nine of them are known to be poisonous, while the other five are supposed to be so. Of these hounds I heard a good yarn. A half-bred dingo used to give them fine sport. He was often hunted, and usually ran for a certain bar, where he bolted into a hole under the counter, and the whole field stopping to "shout," he escaped. One day a new landlord came, who knew not his best friend, and when poor dingo came panting in, kicked him into the jaws of the pack, who broke him up in two cracks.

Beyond Mordialloc again is Snapper's Point, near the entrance to Hobson Bay (the inland sea, almost on which Melbourne stands, some 40 miles from mouth to Melbourne). Snapper's Point is the fashionable Melbourne watering-place, and a great place for kangaroo hunting. Thither I and a friend determined to go, but we had to give it up, as no accommodation whatever could be got, so crowded was the place owing to its being the season there, and to an impending election for the neighbouring district.

In another direction from Melbourne, on the Sydney road, lies Pentridge Stockage, the great criminal depôt. An ex-mayor of Melbourne kindly drove myself and a friend out to see it. It covers a large acreage, nearly all walled in; its walls are patrolled on the top by warders with loaded muskets; its buildings are arranged like the most approved English prisons. In its first beginning it consisted of a few moveable iron houses; then a permanent building was erected, in which the prisoners all slept in tiers in open wooden racks like wine bins. This Pandemonium, for such it was, is now a wool store, and the convicts all have separate cells. One ghastly sight we saw there; a gang of prisoners under sentence of solitary confinement came filing in before us from exercise, each man with a linen mask over his face with eyeholes in it. The long lines of white masked men had a most peculiar effect. We saw too the out-door gangs come in to dinner; many were heavily ironed, and the clank of their chains jarred unpleasantly on one's ear; not that I wished them unchained; far from it, the ruffians richly deserved all they got. A notorious bushranger, one Powell, was pointed out to us. This fellow had for years baffled all attempts of the Sydney police to catch him, but was laid by the heels by the Victorian force. He would alone enter some lonely station, and make the ladies play to and dance with him. Occasionally he would "stick up a bush coach," make the passengers strip and dance before him in buff. He escaped the gallows, as he was never known to have actually shed blood.

An account of my stay in Melbourne would be incomplete without acknowledgment of the hospitality I received there, both from an old college friend, and from others who were total strangers to me before I arrived in the colony. I was made free of the Melbourne Club, an establishment on the scale of a London Club, which extends the most liberal hospitality to all travellers, and where many right pleasant fellows are to be met with. One difference there is from a London Club, all dine together, instead of each at a separate table; an arrangement which takes well in Melbourne, as, different from a London Club, the members all know each other. At those dinners much fun went on. On one occasion, a discussion arising as to the merits of colonial wine, a gentleman present put us to the test. He ordered first a bottle of the best colonial wine, and then, when it was drunk, a bottle of the best European claret, some on which the club, and with reason, prides itself. Opinions were then collected; most abused the colonial wine and praised the claret. Then our entertainer owned to having done us; he had given us two bottles of the same wine, of the European claret. I escaped being taken in, for I suspected his game; there was, however a difference; the second bottle was better than the first, but this arose from its having been longer in a warm room. I believe the Australian wines will in time rival the Continental, but experience is yet to be gained, and the wine growers have not the capital requisite; they are obliged to sell at once, and the wine is thus rarely kept long enough. They have not yet discovered the art of making a vineyard always produce, as in France and on the Rhine, the same quality of wine in successive years; until this is done the brands cannot be relied upon. I have tasted a very

fine Burgundy grown near Adelaide, which I have seen old
judges take for French wine ; some of the Reissling wine is a
very fine hock, and very cheap. The Australians are very fond
of hoaxing "new chums" about wine, and getting them to
condemn the best French and German wines as colonial rot.
They are rather apt to carry this to other matters, if a new
chum gives himself airs and talks of writing a book. They
did it to Sir Charles Dilke, and with great success ; and during
my visit they were doing it to Anthony Trollope, whose airs of
patronizing the colony were intensely amusing, as he at the
Melbourne Club instructed his colonial grandmother how to
suck eggs.

People who come out to Australia must make up their
minds to find it much changed from what it was during the
gold rushes. Fortunes are not made in a week ; diggers no
longer order rum, and tell the landlord to charge it as champagne ; nor do they now-a-days wash their feet in the latter
liquor. Ballarat hotels do not take £1,500 over the counter
in one day in champagne nobblers ; these stories (matters of
fact) are of the past. New chums must work, avoid drink,
and they will do. The colony is a paradise for the working
man ; half a sheep costs from 1s. 6d. to 2s. 6d. ; wages are
high, and he is independent to an extent he would not dream
of at home. For the upper classes it is not so advantageous ;
house rent and servants are so high that they counterbalance
cheap food ; and I was told by persons well qualified to speak,
that an income of a £1,000 a-year elsewhere is in Melbourne
equivalent to only £840. Many working men have their plot
of ground and a house ; their daughters become too grand for
service, call themselves ladies, though wholly uneducated,
perhaps pretend to a little millinery, and sponge on their
parents till they find some one to marry them, or till they
go to the bad. The curse of Australia is its youthful population, or "larrikins." They are wholly uneducated, and for
rowdiness and independence beat anything Europe can produce, either the London street boy or Parisian gamin. The
cheapness of food makes them independent, and Melbourne
police reports, or a walk on Sunday evening down Burke Street,
reveal a hideous amount of juvenile depravity. The legislature
are getting alarmed at this ; flogging was recently proposed as
a remedy for the disgraceful assaults constantly committed on
inoffensive Chinamen by gangs of young boys. Dining at

Elsternwick, near Melbourne, the ladies of the house told me that, on the previous Sunday evening, service at Church was interrupted by a gang of larrikins, who opened the church door, put an opossum in, and hunted him up the aisle. No one dared interfere with them and their hunt.

Another Australian danger is that of growing corruption in its legislature, and in its civil service, *more Americano ;* to both of these Australia is awakening up and directing its legislature. The Chinese are another puzzle; they are industrious, frugal, and careful, have many good qualities, but they bring no women with them, and their morals are nasty. Yet they have votes, or soon will have them under universal suffrage. The labour question, or importation of Polynesian labourers, is another puzzle; it is simply downright slavery of the worst form, and with it the Imperial Government must soon interfere.

From Melbourne I made a very pleasant excursion up the interior, by way of seeing the country. My first stage was the new flourishing town of Castlemaine, reached by railway. These new colonial towns have a Silloth-like appearance; they are intended for great things, have wonderfully wide streets, and some fine buildings alternating with the very reverse. Just outside the town of Castlemaine is a hill, where stands a fine column in commemoration of Burke the Australian explorer. From this point a fine view of the country is obtained; it is well wooded, but has great scars and gashes made all over the surface by mining operations. Ten minutes is sufficient to see all the objects of interest in Castlemaine, so I hired a buggy and requested to be driven to the most interesting place in the neighbourhood. The driver turned out to be a very cute fellow, and selected Campbell's beck as his point. The route was a very picturesque and interesting one ; gold mining was everywhere in progress,—Chinamen were washing the takings, and Jehu was full of anecdotes of the early gold days, and the fortunes then made. We drove through a Chinese camp, a miserable collection of wooden shanties, and turned into a red and blue gum bush, where the whole ground was honeycombed with shafts. We found a very civil miner, who explained to us the stamping machinery, and would have taken us underground, but we declined that, for one hole underground is much like another, and I've been down a copper mine. The stamping machinery, and the mode of extracting the gold by quicksilver, was very interesting.

These mines deface a country sadly ; all the wood disappears for fuel ; the whole country is dug into holes, pits, and shafts ; the streams are befouled by washing operations, and deposit whole acres of white refuse, utterly useless, and on which nothing will grow. To this picture add the incessant din of countless batteries of stampers at work, and some idea may be got of a gold country. One redeeming feature it has over an English mining district,—it is unsmoked, the sky is as bright, the woods and foliage that remain as green as in the days ere Captain Cook was. On the drive we purchased beautiful grapes at 2d. the pound, and were told that other fruit and vegetables were equally cheap.

From Castlemaine I went on by rail to Sandhurst, another great gold place similar to Castlemaine ; thence I went on, also by rail, to Echuca on the Murray River, which separates Victoria from New South Wales. Once past Sandhurst, I was in a country of new interest ; I was in a pastoral instead of a mining country ; in it mutton superseded gold ; and stations superseded steam engines : while preserved meats, and not shares, were the subject of speculation. From Sandhurst to Echuca, some 70 miles or more, if I recollect rightly, the railway runs through the primeval forest ; now a long barrenish pasture, and now the original gum forest loved of the 'possum. This was what I came to see, and I was quite satisfied. Here and there was a clearing, with a station and its outhouse, but most of the way gum forest with occasionally open country. The fences, where they occurred, were just trunks of fallen trees piled one over another to a sufficient height. A gum forest is not a beautiful object ; it is a weird, night-mare sort of forest ; the gums twist their trunks into fantastic demon-like shapes ; they shed their bark, and not their leaves, and thus acquire a bleached and ragged look, while their leaves perversely turn their edges to the sun, and so throw no shade at all. A gum forest would be a fit haunt for Herne the hunter, and Lord Lytton did well to choose one as the place for an incantation scene in "A Strange Story." Echuca itself is a straggling town, and the terminus of the railway, which merely runs to Echuca because some day it hopes to run further, cross the Murray into New South Wales, and get to Sydney, now reached from Echuca by six or eight days of bush coaching across the Deniliquin Plains, past the famous Wagga Wagga. There is at Echuca a pleasant hotel, much frequented by squatters, and there I enjoyed myself much, for the squatters, the aristocrats of the colony, are gentlemanly, squire-like fellows, and from their conversation I learnt much that was curious about wool and mutton. The Murray at Echuca is a narrow river with high banks; at the time of my visit it was low water season, and the steamboats could not run, but in the rainy season they run from Echuca down to Adelaide, a thousand miles and more. One or two tailwheeled steamers, fearfully and wonderfully made, were moored near Echuca; from some mechanics I heard extraordinary stories of the so-called steamers running on the Murray; sudden deaths would be the better name. Any old rotten thing that can work at all is considered good enough, and its safety valve is screwed down *in toto*. At one time a favourite speculation with carpenters was for a party to come up the Murray, encamp on its banks, where fit timber was plentiful, build and launch a lot of barges, float them down to Adelaide laden with wool on the squatters' accounts, and there discharge cargo, sell the barges, and off again for another spec.

From Echuca I returned by rail to Castlemaine. Large ditches fringe the track, in which first-rate water-melons grow wild. They re-sow themselves, and are travelling all over that part of the colony, for each feaster on a melon expectorates the seeds, which forthwith grow. A friendly engine driver put a melon as big as my head into my carriage.

At Castlemaine I slept in an hotel called the Cumberland Arms, and situate, I believe, in the Victorian county of Cumberland. Next morning I started by bush coach for Ballarat. Cobb's American coaches are the mode of conveyance in the colony,—huge red machines of wood, iron, and leather, a cross between a stage coach and a waggon, and drawn by four or five horses. The one I went by was provided with picks and shovels, in order that the passengers might dig a road for it if necessary. To my intense disgust, there were at starting few passengers, and on no account would the authorities allow anyone outside until the inside was full; it was dangerous in the bush, would upset the coach, and, unhappily, I was crammed inside with one man, seven women, and four nasty babies. At the first stage more women and more babies appeared, and so I got outside on the driving seat by the coachee, a character who had twenty years ago been body-coachman in London to Lady ——, and to the Duke of

Northumberland. The first stage of eleven miles was over a track such as in England timber waggons use. The next two stages, some twenty miles or more, were over nothing so good ; the coach just went through the bush anywhere it could, up and down hill, and over obstacles that nothing but a Cobb's coach could do ; no English machine would have stood the jerks, and jolts, and strains. Occasionally we stopped, while coachee meditated, not which road, but which direction we should take next. Once he had a grand consultation with a stock rider ; a fence was being erected across his usual line, and the point was whether on its completion the coach should leave a station, known as " the old German's," on its right, cross a creek, and hit another some three miles east or west ; or whether, leaving " the old German's " on the left, it could descend a formidable hill known to be in that direction, and whether there were any fences there. A fence in the bush is a poser,—trunks of trees piled six feet high, or else an erection of rails, the least of which is as big as a railway sleeper. In the bush we left newspapers at all sorts of little wooden shanties and houses ; we passed one or two large stations, or sheep farms ; we saw some huge tilted bush waggons, drawn by twenty-four oxen apiece, lumbering slowly on ; we met stock riders in red shirts and with huge whips, while green parrots, cockatoos, and colonial magpies—which are not magpies at all, but large black and white birds—flew about. Our next stages were over goodish roads, improving to very good near Ballarat. The descent from the hills to that place is through lovely country, affording a wide and far view, but much obscured just then by bush fires, which, raging over great areas at once, completely filled the atmosphere with murky smoke.

Ballarat is a very fine Australian town ; very fine streets, very fine buildings, especially banks, and very fine institutions, but not very interesting. Chinatown, where the Chinese live, is one of the Ballarat lions, but I was disappointed in it : little celestial, two tawdry joss houses, and a lot of ricketty wooden shanties and huts.

From Ballarat I returned by rail to Melbourne.

LETTER III.

NEW SOUTH WALES.

April, 1872.

Of all the disagreeable times I ever spent at sea the most disagreeable by far was *en voyage* from Melbourne to Sydney in the screw steamer *Alexandra*, a craft with a well-earned reputation for rolling. We left Melbourne on Monday, March 18th, and arrived at Sydney on the Wednesday, during the whole of which time we had a heavy cross sea, and the *Alexandra* rolled from side to side in a most maddening manner. I was not sick, but I was simply knocked about from side to side until I was weary. We did not see much on the voyage : one or two heads were pointed out to us, a coast of bush land, and Botany Bay, conspicuous by a tall water-works chimney. Night fell as we reached Port Jackson Heads, and we could see nothing of the lovely harbour.

Sydney immediately strikes a traveller coming from Victoria as being much more English-like than any town in that colony. Its streets are but of moderate width, they do not cross one another at right angles, and they are, occasionally, even crooked. It possesses many fine buildings, banks of course being prominent, and it has plunged wildly into architectural magnificence in its Town Hall and its Cathedral, but, alas! uncounting of the cost. The latter has been for some years at a stand, with half-built walls, for want of funds; and the former has just come to a similar pass. The glory of Sydney is its harbour, probably the finest in the world, bar Rio Janeiro. The harbour is an inland arm of the sea, most bewilderingly intricate in its convolutions, creeks, and bays, studded with islands, and surrounded by lovely scenery. To follow round the coast line of all its convolutions, creeks, and bays, is a circuit of more than 300 miles. In it all the navies of the world might ride safely at anchor in all winds. The visitor to Sydney should go to two points from which to get a view of this beautiful harbour—one the Observatory and Signal Hill, the other Lady Macquarie's Chair, so called after the lady of a former governor, and situate at the water's edge in the domain or park of Sydney.

Owing to the kindness of some gentlemen at Sydney, my travelling friend and myself were taken round the harbour of Port Jackson in a small steam launch, and we thus thoroughly explored its various beauties; in one bay we landed on a half-tide rock, and there and then had a worry of delicious oysters, with which the rock was completely covered. The entrance to the harbour of Port Jackson is very fine; two rocky, surf-beaten heads guard the entrance, which is safe and easy, the only danger in the whole harbour being a rock awash, called the Sow and Pigs, not far within the Heads, and marked by a light. Outside, the coast is lofty, both north and south, bar a chasm, called the False Gap, close to the Heads. A fine emigrant ship, the *Dunbar*, once went into this place at night, taking it for the Heads; in the morning the beach was covered with wreck and corpses, and but one survivor was there to tell the tale. Two lighthouses are now erected to prevent similar mistakes.

I was unable to make many excursions about Sydney, for out of ten days' stay there I passed most of my time in bed in the doctor's hands. I managed an occasional run up and down the harbour, and one glorious drive to Botany Bay by the South Head. The road lay through a moor-like country, covered with a profusion of strange and lovely plants and shrubs, which at home would be hothouse rarities, but about Botany Bay are mere weeds; time after time did we stop our hansom to examine or pluck some new gem of beauty, our curiosity being a little damped by our driver's caution about the snakes, sure on so hot and sultry a day to be basking in the warmth. Cockatooes, parrots, and other gay-coloured birds, and enormous butterflies,. everywhere flit about the scene, to which the deep blue Pacific Ocean formed a fitting background. At Botany Bay we found an hotel and a garden with many tropical plants in it, bananas and the like; strolling down to the shore our emotion can be better imagined than described, as we stood on that strand to which ungrateful England has cruelly sent so many patriots to pine in hard-worked and miserable exile.

We left Sydney on the night of the 3rd of April, by the *Maitland* steamer, to join our ship, the *Francis Thorpe*, for San Francisco, at Newcastle, New South Wales. The chief

justice and acting governor of New South Wales (*vice* Belmore
going home) Sir Alfred Stephens, aides-de-camp, and all the
colonial swells, were our fellow passengers. The journey is a
short one; starting at eleven at night, it terminates at six a.m.,
for which time I had the honour of sleeping in a bunk verti-
cally under that occupied by a Prime Minister—the Premier
of New South Wales—while secretaries of state snored all
round.

Newcastle is a beastly place, at the mouth of Hunter's
River, and exists by the coal trade. We left it on the 5th
of April, in the *Francis Thorpe*, for San Francisco.

THE ISLANDS.

The traveller at Melbourne or Sydney will probably hear
much of certain places vaguely designated as "The Islands";
and the stories he will hear will convince him that romance
has not yet entirely left the world, and that some of the old
buccaneering spirit is still alive. By "The Islands" are
meant the various coral and other islands which cover so
much of the Pacific, and which, as adding to its dangers,
are avoided as much as possible by the traders from
Australia to America, but which are much frequented by
whalers and island traders, generally swift and piratical-
looking three-masted schooners. Pitcairn, one of the most
easterly of these islands, is still famous as the refuge of
the descendants of the mutineers of the *Bounty*, a race,
if travellers are to be believed, of singular simplicity and
purity. Easter Island, another of these, is a puzzle to the
Anthropological Society, from some wonderful carved images
that exist there of gigantic stature. Among these islands
there is a curious population to be found; originally on many
of them the natives were friendly to white men, and escaped
convicts from Australia and runaway sailors often settled
among them, attracted by the climate and the prospect of a
dolce far niente life. In some places the islanders have got
a thin varnish of Christianity, together with more than a
varnish of European and American vices. Honolulu has even
advanced beyond this, and risen to the dignity of a theatre,
in which Charles Matthews has actually played " Patter *v.*
Clatter" to a fashionable audience of Honolulese.

The group, known as the Feejees, presents at this moment

perhaps the most curious stage. There are on it many English settlers, who grow cotton (as there are on others of these islands), and who have formed a Chamber of Commerce, and there is also an hotel called the Criterion. There is, too, a black king —King Cakombau I.—who has a white ministry, headed by one Burt, formerly mayor of Melbourne, and by a chief justice, formerly an attorney in London. Between the ministry and the Chamber of Commerce there is war, for the king and his ministers have instituted a system of taxation, a civilised blessing the planters by no means calculated on finding in Feejee. One way and another the ministry raise a revenue of a few thousands a year. Occasionally the native tax-collectors are done, as by one Yankee, who paid his dues with the labels off Coleman's mustard tins, which he represented to be dollar notes. The income thus raised is expended in salaries. Any man, who makes himself obnoxious, gets a post and a salary to quiet him ; the last who did this was at once appointed brigade-major to the Feejee army of seven poor whites and nine blacks. The government is carried on with great vigour, though opposed by the planters. A vessel that, a month or two ago, attempted to escape paying its dues, was chased by the Feejee navy and made to shell out. Recently a difficulty had arisen with the planters : a planter and a native chief had some disagreement as to the ownership of certain cocoa trees ; the chief ascended one of the trees, and from that airy elevation disclosed his—what civilised people sit upon—to the planter, who thereon spoilt the chief's capabilities for sitting by shooting him in that very place, whereon the chief died ; the planter adjourned to the Criterion and liquored up. But King Cakombau and Premier Burt resolved that the planter should be brought to trial, and the army—brigade-major, seven poor whites, and nine blacks— marched on the Criterion Hotel to seize him. He had, however, taken to himself many other planters with six-shooters, and defied the army, including the brigade-major, whereon the ministry resigned, or threatened to resign, and there was a general mess, still unsettled up to my latest advices. Had they caught him, he would have been tried in due form, for the ex-attorney C. J. has promulgated a most elaborate code, worthy to rank with that of the late Napoleon, and administers it energetically. He recently laid hold of a ship-master, who had been ill-treating two natives, tried him, vindicated his own jurisdiction in a most able judgment, and fined the peccant skipper heavily. Quite right too, for horrible villanies are now being perpetrated among the islands on the unhappy natives. All the formal ceremonies of government are observed in Feejee rigorously; consular and diplomatic authorities are received under fire of many guns; a German man-of-war, was there recently, and was duly saluted; the officers were received on shore by a guard of honour of the whole army, and entertained by King Cakombau I. at a state ball given at the Criterion Hotel, whereat Premier Burt took off his coat in order to dance with more vigour. Altogether, the Feejee Government is a very promising one, but the British will probably have to interfere, as the planters own neither it, nor any law, and some protection is due to the natives, who, throughout the islands, are now much ill-used. The whalers, who come about them, are not a very scrupulous lot of men, and a new trade has recently sprung up,—a trade in men to supply labour to Queensland. Of course, the labourers are supposed to come of their own accord; how far that is likely the following will show. A scoundrel moored his ship off one of the islands, flew the South Sea Mission Flag, dressed a man up in white, and imitated a religious service. The natives, deceived by this, flocked on board, were at once made prisoners and carried off. The result was the murder of Bishop Patteson, and also of white men in several other places, and a consequent bombardment by a British man-of-war, thus made necessary for the safety of whalers and shipwrecked seamen. This Polynesian labour traffic must be put down somehow, before it gets too far ahead. The natives are now making reprisals, and ships becalmed in the islands are not unlikely to be rushed and captured. Whalers recently coming into Sydney have tales to tell of men murdered in attempting to communicate with the natives, and have seen stranded ships, of whose crews' fate they dare not land to inquire. One American saw very recently a white woman and child, evidently prisoners, on an island where was a wreck, and could do nothing by way of rescue.

Connected in some way or other with this is the story of a schooner I saw in Newcastle. Her Majesty's ship *Basilick* found a water-logged schooner at sea with fourteen blacks on board, dead or nearly so. No explanation could be got from these men, not a word, except "Solomon," whence it was supposed they came from an island of that name. They were utterly ignorant of how to sail the schooner, from which every mark that could possibly identify her had been with care erased, thus showing she was up to no good ;—she was evidently not of British build. What has become of the white crew ? have not the blacks murdered them, and why ? Nothing to throw light on these points had been found up to the time I write (*i.e.* April, 1872), except that by scraping the vessel's stern her name was discovered to have once been the *Peri*, of where cannot be told.

Another terrible tragedy anent these islands occurred just before I was in Sydney. A brig set sail from Sydney with a party of eighty adventurers drawn from all ranks in Society : all ranks have their scamps, and the colonies are their haunt and home. They were bound for New Guinea, a country little known ; what they were to do there has never been explained, but probably no good. They started without even the most ordinary instruments of navigation, got far out of their way, and struck on the Great Barrier Reef. The captain seized the first boat and deserted. He and his •crew were murdered by the Australian natives on that coast, a very savage and treacherous race. Of the rest some were drowned, others landed and were murdered ; in all more than half the expedition lost their lives ; those that were saved sufferred terrible hardships, and that was the end of the New Guinea expedition. The account of it, as given in the Sydney papers, reads like the wreck of the *Medusa*, and will probably become an equally famous tale of suffering by sea.

The little I have written is sufficient to show that some light should be turned upon the doings of unscrupulous and cruel men in the Pacific, and on the British the duty will for many reasons probably devolve.

N.B.—This paper was in print August, 1872, before the agitation in the English papers on these kidnapping practices prevalent in the South Seas, and I am glad to see that English and Colonial opinion is gradually forcing the authorities to interfere. I strongly think we should annex the Feejees. Both Americans and French are quietly establishing themselves among the islands, and acquiring strong harbours. Russians and Germans were said to be searching for similar positions, all which menace our Australian possessions, and tend to exclude us from the Pacific carrying trade, a great object with the Americans ; hence their anxiety about the San Juan arbitration.

LETTER IV.

THE VOYAGE OF THE "FRANCIS THORPE."

July, 1872.

We sailed from Newcastle, N.S.W., early on a Friday morning (5th April, 1872), a day considered by sailors an unlucky one for the commencement of a voyage, but though it was the commencement of my voyage to San Francisco in the ship, yet her voyage was reckoned to have commenced when she left Liverpool, and the omen was thus supposed to be averted.

Whether owing to this or not I cannot say, but we were favoured with a month's bad weather and foul winds. Early on the Sunday after we sailed, a heavy squall and "southerly buster" struck us, accompanied by tremendous sheet and forked lightning. My fellow-traveller aroused me out of bunk about 2 a.m. to see the sight, which was magnificent, but calculated to make one nervous. The ship was plunging along under close-reefed topsails and a foresail : the night was dark as Erebus itself: one could not see one's own hand, but almost momentarily every rope in the ship would be vividly lit up by blue lurid lightning. The weather moderated towards morning, but for days afterwards we had a heavy cross sea, which, rising in huge pyramidal masses, would pitch heavily on to our main deck, deluging it from end to end, and occasionally even wash the poop. All round us the horizon was overcast with masses of cloud heavily charged with electricity, which after sunset showed itself in constant sheet lightning, and in great balls of fire, which seemed to run round the horizon and burst: from sunset to sunrise for nights this beautiful but somewhat terrible sight (the more terrible as we were in an iron ship coal-laden) lasted, sure precursor of something worse to come. With occasional periods of quiet, the worse did come, and we found we were under the influence of a typhoon or cyclone, or rotatory storm, whose centre travels in a straight line, while the whole thing spins round, producing the most rapid and dangerous shifts of wind with occasional lulls. Thanks to science, the

nature of these storms is now well understood, and whole
fleets are no longer destroyed by them, as in 1782, when His
Majesty's ships *Ramilies* and *Centaur* of 74 guns each, the
Pallas frigate, five French men-of-war prizes to Rodney, and a
great number of merchantmen, and 3,000 sailors all went down
together in a cyclone.   Perpetually were we wearing or tacking
ship to dodge the centre of the cyclone, and men were always
standing by the haliards, ready to let the sails go in case of
sudden shifts.   The weather got worse until about the 25th of
April, when we were beating against a regular Cape Horn gale
of the severest kind ; the seas rolled over us, right over the
deck houses and the boats on their top, threatening to beat
them in, and sending the spray over the foreyard, while the
ship plunged bows under, almost standing on her head, and
rolled until she scooped up tons of water with her lee-gunnel ;
every moment we expected the masts to go over the side.   As
the sea struck her, the ship would quiver from end to end,
while her stern would bang into the hollow of the seas, as she
" scended" with a crash and thump that was awful to hear.
Sail was reduced to a small foresail, to close-reefed fore and
mizzentopsails, and double-reefed maintopsail, which eased her
a good deal, and she lay quieter ; still, to move about was
dangerous.   Both my friend and the second mate got heavy
falls, one being knocked senseless, and the other having his eye
laid open.   In my ignorance I now thought I had seen the
worst the weather could do, but it was not so.   After a slight
improvement, it blew a perfect hurricane (May 3) ; the jib and
foresail blew to bits, and the men on the jibboom were almost
washed away by the ship plunging under water as they were
stowing the tattered canvas.   "For the safety of all," as he
entered it in the log, the captain now determined to bring the
ship to, which was done under close-reefed fore and maintop-
sails and three small storm staysails.   I don't think anyone on
board the ship slept much that night, or expected to get
through it without severe loss of spars and masts.   From the
poop, where the officers and ourselves were clinging to ropes
under the shelter of a small tarpaulin, put up to break the
seas that leaped on board, the scene was sublime but awful.
In the midst of it, a seaman died most suddenly of heart
disease.   We were obliged to leave his body where he died,
among the other men ; there was nowhere to move it to ; to
have opened a hatch would have been destruction ; to have

placed the body in a boat (the usual deadhouse on board ship)
would have been to have had it instantly washed overboard.
With the morning the storm somewhat lulled. At noon the
following day we buried the dead seaman. He was lapped up
in canvas with 150lbs. of coals at his feet, and then, while
the ship's bells tolled dismally, borne aft to the lee-gangway
by four of his mates on a rude bier under cover of the English
Jack. The captain read the service; at a signal the bier was
tilted up, and the canvas package slid into the sea, took a
round turn, and disappeared. A burial at sea is always an
impressive ceremony; this was peculiarly so : the suddenness
of the man's death, the still raging storm which drowned,
even to those close by, the words of the service, and the
seamen all standing round in working dress ready for any
emergency. The man's bedding and blankets were afterwards
thrown overboard, and his effects catalogued. Among them
was found a certificate as a ship's officer, thus showing he had
once been better than a mere Jack before the mast.

From this time the weather mended ; the good ship stood
well the banging she got, but a wooden hull would have been
awfully strained and all hands would have had probably to go
to the pumps. Our cargo had however shifted, and we had
for the rest of the voyage a decided list to port. Of damage
done we had plenty; the studdingsail-booms were smashed
very early and blown through the foretopsail. The jib, foresail, mainsail, and foretop-gallantsail were split to pieces, and
a royal blown out of the bolt ropes ; the maintop-gallant sheet,
a stout iron chain, had snapped like wax, and the great iron
cleat, that holds down the main tack, had been torn up. The
rigging did its work gallantly, but was so strained and stretched
that, as soon as a calm came, all hands were set to renew it, as
rendered untrustworthy. Some of the bull-eyes in the forecastle were stove in by the sea, and a staysail that got loose
knocked the standard compass to smithereens. The worst
thing done was that the stout iron slings, supporting the mainyard, were found to be cracked through ; preventers were of
course put up, but for the rest of the voyage the condition of
the mainyard was one of anxiety.

After these troubles, we had the usual weather in the
Pacific : light winds, tropical heat, and an occasional squall, one
of which split the foretop-gallantsail in two, and another split
a jib. About the equator we had violent bashes of rain, and we

had a most tantalizing calm on leaving the N.E. trade winds. This calm was the end of those trades, which brought us well up from the line to the latitude of our port, but would not let us get within 1,000 or 800 miles of land. The calm was followed by a breeze, which took us along gaily, but, increasing to a gale, and carrying away canvas, compelled us to heave-to during eighteen hours, with heavy seas breaking over us, as we dare not run in with a fast increasing gale behind us, sending us along, under almost bare poles, at eleven knots an hour. We, on this occasion, lost our foresail, spanker, and a topsail, and the ship's tom-cat, leaving his tabbies disconsolate widows.

A Californian fog succeeded this, and we managed under its cover to pass the Farallone Islands without ever seeing them, the lights on them, or the pilot boats which were looking out for us. A friendly schooner gave us our position, we got a pilot, and passing through the Golden Gate, much disappointed that the weather was not clearer, dropped anchor off North Point, 'Frisco. It was hardly down when some forty or fifty crimps boarded the ship with a view of getting our men to desert. Their insolence was awful; they would hardly permit the ship's duty to be done, and the 'Frisco police warned us that any interference with them would probably be met by the production of six-shooters. I am glad to say that not a single man deserted from the *Francis Thorpe ;* but other English ships lost a large number.

Our voyage thus lasted from April 5th to July 2nd, or eighty-nine days, a far longer time than we had anticipated, but other vessels sailing at the same time did no better, one, the *British Consul,* being ninety-seven days, having shifted her cargo, and having had to run before the gale for twenty hours with her lee-rail under water, and her crew in mutiny. The *Melpomene* had, by stress of the weather she met with, been compelled to give up, after some days' trial, the passage round the south of New Zealand, and come up by the islands ; while the *Zealandia* had had her poop washed away, and with it the captain, steward, and a passenger.

We had, during the voyage, one day (28th May) of great excitement. About 6 a.m. I was aroused by an unusual noise, rushed out, and found everyone pouring upon deck. The captain himself was at the helm ; some men were backing the main and crossjackyards as hard as they could, some hauling down the studdingsails, while others were literally throwing the dingy overboard, and leaping in, oar in hand. The third mate was swimming some thirty yards astern, trying to catch one of the life buoys which had been thrown to him. The captain sent me to hold on to the wheel, while he went forward to let some ropes go, and sent the sailmaker aloft to keep an eye on the mate, who was seen to get hold of one of the buoys. The water being smooth, and he swimming well, there was little danger to be apprehended except from sharks. He was soon picked up, but not before he was three-quarters of a mile astern; both buoys were also recovered. It appeared that while setting the awning a rope had broke, and let the unlucky mate overboard, in shirt and breeches only, so that his swimming was little impeded. The whole thing gave me a very good impression of the captain's readiness in an emergency; he seemed to act without any hesitation, and under his management all seemed to know what to do, and to do it without confusion.

That the danger from sharks was not imaginary was soon proved : three or four hours later some of us spied a zebra-striped fish swimming astern, and in the afternoon this fish—a pilot fish—was again seen swimming alongside of a powerful shark, whose pilot he was. The water being beautifully clear, we could see the brute's movements well, as he swam rapidly about the stern, evidently hungry and in search of something, attracted no doubt by the smell of a sheep that had just been killed. A line and hook, baited with pork, was at once put out, and Mr. Shark contrived to carry off the bait; he was then tried with a fowl, to which he would have nothing to say ; so a fresh trial was made of pork and a bit of fresh sheep skin. After smelling it, touching it with his nose, biting at the rope, and being once or twice partially hooked, he gorged the whole thing, and was fast. A bowline was slipped over him, and by aid of a block he was run up to the rail, where a rifle ball through his brain put a *quietus* to his kicks. He was then hoisted on board, dragged to the main-deck, where his formidable tail, some two feet in expanse, was chopped off with an axe, and a handspike rammed down his jaws, thus incapacitating him for mischief. Immediately every Jack in the ship appeared, with watering teeth and open knife ; the shark was at once cut up, and, long ere his heart ceased to beat, bits of him were in the frying-pan. He was an average-sized ocean shark, seven or eight feet long, of the shovel-nosed tribe, immense flat head, with mouth big enough to take in a man's thigh, and armed with five or more rows of razor-edged teeth; he would speedily have pulled the third mate down had he caught him. His heart was very small, and continued to beat for a considerable time after it was taken from the body. The seamen said it would beat until sunset; but I did not verify this, as the cats stole the heart. The liver was very large, and contained a deal of valuable oil; it went overboard, as our black Bermudian cook objected to it being cooked in his pans, by way of extracting the oil. The flesh looked well, white and firm like cod, and the Jacks devoured it all with relish, but it was, *experto crede*, dry and rank; however, I would readily live on shark rather than starve. In the water the brute swam both swiftly and strongly, evidently a very powerful fish. One curious thing about a shark's skull was pointed out to me; it exactly resembles the figure of a woman from the neck down to the knees. For long after the capture the whole ship was redolent of shark, which is a somewhat stinking fish; relics of him, fins, tail, jaws, and backbone, were everywhere hanging to dry. His crop was entirely empty, which accounted for his eagerness. We saw other sharks, but none so well as this, nor did we catch any more. Two remora, or sucking fish, were clinging to the brute, which, by the way, was declared by the *cognoscenti* to be a female.

Dolphins we saw quantities of, one day nearly thirty at once, most brilliantly and fantastically coloured fish, with olive backs, green sides, blue fins, and yellow tails. Though they looked and bit at our baits, we could not capture any; four or five were, however, shot by my friend, with a pea-rifle, as they came to the surface. They are about $2\frac{1}{2}$ to 3 feet long. A few bonitas were caught from the bow, fish like very large mullet, and the determined foe of the flying fish, whole shoals of which we often saw flying away from a shoal of bonitas. These bonitas are very good eating. A large flying fish, the size of a herring, flew on board one day, but was stolen by the cats out of a bucket, in which it had been placed for safety and anatomical investigation. In the tropical latitudes, where we saw these fish, we also saw great ribbon-shaped streaks of whales' food, a substance much resembling coffee-grounds. We also saw, somewhere in these latitudes, a large waterspout in the distance. At an earlier period of the voyage we saw five at once.

Our great captures consisted of albatrosses, of which, in the early part of the voyage, we saw numbers, and also of molly-hawks. The albatross is a magnificent bird, measuring over outspread wings from 9 feet to 14 feet, or even 17 feet. As he floats in the air he looks majestic, with his great outspread wings, keen eye, and hungry beak. His wings are remarkable for having one more joint in them than those of any other bird. We fished for these with a line and hook over the stern, baited with pork, and caught three or four. When let loose on deck their first operation is to be beastly sick, and then they waddle about like an enormous goose, unable to rise. We killed them by choking and hanging, and dissected them for their feet and bones to make tobacco pouches and pipes of—an operation of great interest to the six ship cats. One we skinned *in toto*— a long and dirty, and in the event useless job : the rats first got at the skin and damaged it, and then it got hove overboard in the bad weather. We hooked several more albatrosses, but the heavy sea that was running broke our line and hooks, as we pulled the beasts in. One very large fellow escaped in a curious manner. He was fairly hooked, and was being drawn in ; as he got on the top of a wave he spread his wings and rose ; the wind took him (it was blowing very hard) and lifted him into the ship, where he struck the spankerboom, broke the hook, and got off.

The most beautiful birds we saw were the bo'suns, white birds with long pointed tails like marling spikes, hence the name. They fly very high, shrieking wildly as they fly, rarely touch the water, and are not to be caught. A booby one day visited us, and vindicated his right to a better title. We were fishing bonita from the jibboom with an artificial flying fish. Mr. Booby made several soars at this, but seemed to doubt it, as he always sheered off. Finally he flew down to it, and then flew up the line to where it was attached to the jibboom ; there he set up an awful yell of derision, a birdish " Not for Joseph Booby," and vanished ; we saw him no more. Some unlucky land birds followed us far out at sea, driven off shore by the heavy gales. They seemed weary, and anxious to rest on the ship, but afraid ; they doubtless perished from fatigue as countless land birds do at sea. A thousand miles from land we fancied we saw a swallow ; possibly it was only a Mother Carey's chicken, of which we saw lots.

Nearing the Californian coast the ship was followed by

numbers of stinkpots, a nasty smelling species of sea-fowl, which afforded great sport in the fishing and shooting line to my brother passengers. These fellows would fight vigorously for the bait, and sometimes we would have six captives on deck at once, big fellows, some eight feet across the wings. Their first proceeding on being caught was to try and bite, and then they spewed most nastily : this done they proceeded to show fight, champing their bills and running at the sailors ; one fellow attacked the steward and caused a grand spill of pea soup *en route* to the dinner table, while another clutched the ship's tom-cat by the small of the back, to that dignified quadruped's intense affright and disgust. We generally marked the stinkpots, and heaved them overboard, but latterly we gave them for grub to the ship's pigs, nasty brutes, who swallowed half-alive rats, sharks' and goats' inwards, and stinkpots with great relish. Several stinkpots were shot from the poop, and a dead or wounded bird was at once stript of his feathers and swallowed by his comrades.

Close to the American coast we fell in with many whales and whale-like beasts, such as black fish and grampus ; one whale was about 80 feet long, and came close up to the ship. The same day we had a very pretty visitor in the shape of a young seal some 4 feet long. This pretty creature swam round the ship with great grace and agility, every now and then pausing to raise its head out of water and take a curious look at us ; in this position it looked singularly like what one would imagine a mermaid to be. It fell a victim to its curiosity ; my bloodthirsty fellow-passenger shot it through the head, killing it instantly, and effusing the sea with its blood ; the stinkpots were down on the carcass in a moment, and we saw it drift astern with a dozen of these beasts riving and tearing at it. I felt quite sorry for the poor animal, which had been frisking so merrily around us ; it suffered nothing, for death was instantaneous.

During the whole of this voyage we spoke but one vessel, the *Ferdinande* of Falmouth, a three-masted schooner, which passed us so close that the captains were able to dispense with signals and converse *viva voce*. She puzzled us amazingly : a new vessel of most beautiful lines, sailing like a witch, carrying no cargo, but having her decks crowded with men and officers, all superior in appearance to the ordinary run of merchant officers and men, and yet flying the merchant ensign. What

could she be ?   We settled she had been after some robbery
among the islands ; the mystery was later on curiously cleared
up.   Some weeks afterwards an Englishman accosted me in
the bar at my hotel at Niagara ; his face seemed familiar, and
at last I recognized him as the captain of the *Ferdinande*,
which, he explained, had been surveying for Lloyds.   He and
I travelled together to Kingston in Canada.   It is an odd thing
to see a man for the first time through an opera glass a
thousand miles from any land, and then recognize him again
four thousand miles from there ; aye, and find in him a friend
of friends of mine.

One word as to our good ship that weathered the storm.
The *Francis Thorpe* was an iron ship, nearly new, and a Liverpool ship, while the *Agamemnon* was a London, and thus we
had full opportunity of becoming acquainted with the little
technical differences in rig and equipment by which a seaman
easily tells a Liverpool or London ship at sight.   The rivalry between the two is intense and amusing.   The London liners profess
to be the successors of the old East Indiamen, and affect a man-
of-war style : they have midshipmen, who are addressed as
"young gentlemen," the boson has a whistle, and the officers are
of the modern school, talk of their hunting and shooting, and the
park, and sink the sea when on shore.   On the Liverpool ships
there are no middies ; they are apprentices, are addressed as
" boy," and do the same work, dirty enough often, as the
Jacks.   The boson has no whistle, and the officers are of the
good old school, do rough work themselves, regard a horse as
a dangerous animal, and shoot cockatoos in a strange port with
a ship's musket, and are always unmistakably seamen.   They
have too, probably, seen more than the officers of a London
liner, who sticks pretty well to his Indian, Colonial, or China
line, while the Liverpool man roams away from one foreign
port to another, as they can pick up freight.   Thus, while the
London liner returns direct from Melbourne, or possibly goes
up to China for tea, the Liverpool ship takes horses to Calcutta,
and home, thence, *viâ* New York, or she goes to San Francisco, Callao, Valparaiso, &c., with coal from New South
Wales, and home with what she can get.   The Liverpool men,
too, have generally been first in small ships, and so seen all
sorts of out-of-the-way places, while the Londoner enters young
into the service of Messrs. Green, or Money Wigram, and
sticks to them and their routine lines of traffic.

P.S.—APPENDED IS AN ACCOUNT OF THE HOMEWARD VOYAGE OF THE "FRANCIS THORPE" FROM SAN FRANCISCO.

2 India Buildings, Liverpool, W.,
December 23, 1872.

Dear Sir,—We left San Francisco on the 9th August, but were becalmed all that day just outside the Heads; we, however, made a fair start on the night of the 10th, and from there down to the Line had a very pleasant run of twenty-five days, crossing it on the 3rd September. We very soon began to get into very much colder weather, and into the region where the strong winds and boisterous seas prevail; we, however, made very good work, and had only to heave-to on one occasion, and then only for about six or seven hours. I can assure you the seas off the Horn were something to be remembered, rolling up astern, as though they would overwhelm you. The good ship, however, came out of them all right, although it was the reverse of comfortable to have the decks full of water for a whole fortnight. At the time she was "hove-to" the lee-rail positively was at times as much as three or four feet under water. We rounded the Horn on the 5th October, after a passage of fifty-seven days from 'Frisco, making the islands of Diego Rameres (about 20 miles southward of Cape Horn) at noon that day. It was really surprising to note the difference in the weather immediately we got under the lee of the Patagonian land. From a stormy disagreeable day it became as fine as a summer's day. From Cape Horn up to the Equator on this side, we had very light and baffling winds, but we managed to get into the Northern Hemisphere once more on the 7th November, thirty-three days from the Horn, and ninety days from San Francisco. We spoke a great number of vessels from about thirty south, up to the time we made the land; in fact there was hardly a day passed without us seeing one. One morning (November 21st), on going on deck, we saw a ship to windward of us, which had evidently been in trouble; we luffed-up as close as we could to her, and then saw that she had lost her three topmasts, apparently but a few hours before. We asked her if she required any assistance, but she did not. Strange to relate, the very same afternoon we saw another ship ahead of us which had lost her maintop-gallantmast. We had all, there is no doubt, been close together during the night when the accident happened, as it had been very squally, but we fortunately came out of it without a mishap. I must not forget to mention, however, that we lost our jibboom on the morning of the 21st October. It was Mr. N——'s watch on deck, and blowing pretty stiffly, vessel going about eleven knots. This, unfortunately, was not the only accident which happened on board. On last Tuesday week, the 10th December, we had a tremendous gale from N.N.W., and the ship was "hove-to," under lower maintopsail and mizzenstaysail. About a quarter-past seven in the morning the inner jib began to break adrift (it had been stowed the night before, but the gaskets had got loosened), and six men of the port watch, which was the watch on deck at the time, went out to restow it. They were hardly on the boom when she put it right under, and a heavy cross sea coming up at the time swept five of the men off, leaving only one, who had contrived to hold on by the jibstay, on the boom. Four of the men, Bruce, Osborn, Mc.Glashan, and a man named Butler who was shipped in San Francisco, were all swept far to windward of the ship, and as she was drifting away from them so rapidly defied all efforts to rescue them, and the gale was blowing with such violence that it was an impossibility to throw them a line or anything, as the wind blew it back on deck again. Poor fellows, they sank almost immediately, as they were so heavily clad, all of them having their sea boots on; but even if it had not been so, it would have been quite impossible to have put a boat out in such weather. Another of the men who was on the boom, Paul Williams, was washed to leeward of the ship, and was got safely on board again, not very much the worse for his being overboard. This accident threw quite a gloom over the whole ship, as previous to this everybody, particularly the men lost, had been in such good spirits at the prospect of being home so soon. We made the light on Cape Clear at three o'clock in the morning of Monday, 16th inst., 127 days from land to land; but we did not succeed in getting to Liverpool until Friday afternoon, as we lay becalmed close up to Holyhead for nearly two days, and there was no tug-boat to be got.

J. J. R.

Note.—The men lost were all fine, good sailors, and (except Butler) well known to me. Bruce was a great dandy, very smart and active, and a wonderful hand at climbing; Osborn, a black from the West Indies; and Mc.Glashan, of Aberdeen, were pals, and both good men; Paul Williams, the man saved, was a Norwegian.

R. S. F.

LETTER V.

THE FOURTH OF JULY AT SAN FRANCISCO.

9th July, 1872.

It is somewhat unlucky for a vessel to arrive from a long voyage at an American port just before the great national holiday. Not only is the 4th of July itself observed by strict abstinence from business, but the preparations beforehand absorb so much attention that all work is completely of secondary importance. Thus, arriving on the 2nd July at San Francisco, after an eighty-nine days' voyage from Australia, we found that though the revenue officers sealed our hatches up at once, they would not, to our great inconvenience, search or unseal for three days ; nay, so universal was the excitement, that we could not even get a " heathen Chinee" to wash our clothes.

As our American cousins were thus all agog over their 4th, our curiosity was aroused, and was further stimulated to a high pitch by the flaming programmes in the 'Frisco papers, and by a proclamation from the high constable of the city. In this he informed us that the discharging of fireworks and firearms in the public streets was forbidden by Act of Congress, and that no exception was made for the 4th of July. A deputation of two hundred and twenty-five boys thereupon presented a petition to the constable, in which they requested him not to interfere with what they considered their right. To this the constable in a grave document replied ; he reckoned up the number of inhabitants in the town, the proportion borne by two hundred and twenty-five boys to that number, the value of house property, and the fires caused by such proceedings, and concluded to enforce the law.

The great day itself was heralded by a salute from the forts in the harbour at the unseemly hour of 4 a.m., and as daylight appeared the ships in port dressed, and the whole town broke out into bunting. Everywhere the gaudy stars and stripes of the State flaunted the air ; every house in the town sported one or two American flags, and many several, some of the modest size of 18 inches square, while others were gigantic, trailing from the roofs of tall warehouses almost down to the ground. There must have been thousands of them. The monotony was a little broken here and there by the sight of various other national flags; but nowhere, save at the Consulate, where one solitary Jack was raised, and in the harbour, could the British colours be found.

Towards 10 o'clock the chief streets were crowded with well-dressed people ; indeed, we hardly saw a poorly-dressed person in the place, while the women are dressed in very good taste and style, though we did see costumes in the hotels that were rather gaudy for midday. The order kept, the want of crushing, and the apparent absence of any police authorities, were remarkable. The streets are, however, wide ; and the crowds less than London or Liverpool would turn out on such an occasion, while plenty of police are in attendance, but hardly by their dress to be distinguished from the people they control. Quantities of Chinese were present in the throng, and most magnificent specimens of pigtails, some four feet in length, might have been culled by the searcher after such curiosities were he adroit enough to steal them unobserved.

About an hour later the procession came past ; it consisted of seven divisions, each under a marshal, and the whole under a grand marshal, a doctor by profession, assisted by numerous *aides*, all of whom—marshals and *aides*—were extremely well mounted, and wore light-coloured and gold-fringed scarfs, and Der Freischutz hats, ornate with silver stars, while each marshal carried a baton of office. The grand marshal and staff led the procession, which was preceded by an advance guard of some fifty Zouaves, and their vivandiere, a flaxen-haired child of seven or so, under command of a colonel ; very small bodies are in America commanded by very high officers. I saw a general of brigade in command of a company of forty-eight men.

The first division was composed exclusively of military, under command of a brigadier-general, assisted by a large staff in the neat uniform of the American army, and consisted of three regiments of infantry and a battalion of cavalry (I use the American terms). The unit of military organization in 'Frisco appears to be the company ; each company dresses as it pleases, has a full regimental stand of colours, and parades from fifty to seventy men. A battalion formed of these companies has thus a motley and many-flagged appearance. The variety of uniforms was great. Every European uniform, bar the British, was imitated. Most of the companies in the first regiment had imitated in cut the uniform of the old French Guard of Waterloo,—the dress coat with swallow-tails to the middle of the calf, the huge worsted epaulets drooping over the chest, and the towering bear-skin. The first company were in scarlet coats of this cut, and their bear-skins were snowy white ; the second was in blue and red, with white bear-skins, and a third in the same, with dark bear-skins. Then followed a lot of Fenians, in green swallow-tails and white bear-skins ; and a company or two in the modern French uniform.

The second regiment was in main a Fusileer one, but was headed by a company of cadets in grey, while various varieties of German uniforms—spiked helmets and all—pleasingly diversified its appearance. Regiment No. 3 was Fenian to a man, six companies, viz., the Montgomery Guard, the Wolf Tone Guard, the Meagher Guard, Shield's Guard, Mc.Mahon Grenadiers, and Emmet Guard, each differently dressed, mostly in some variety of green, and each bearing an American ensign, and a magnificent green silk colour emblazoned with the Fenian symbol of the crownless harp. The cavalry consisted of three troops of fifty men, one in hussar, one in light dragoon, and a third in dark dragoon uniform. This finished the first division, but the other divisions were escorted by military companies, one of which was composed of coloured men and dressed in grey, while Zouave, Garibaldi, Swiss, Sardinian, and other uniforms were all on view. Each company marched and carried its arms as it pleased; some marched in fours, some in threes, some in fours with wide intervals between each man, and some in company column, so that a battalion was a very motley thing; while the words of command were given in English, French, German, and Italian. The distances between the fours varied, generally from four to eight feet. Spite of all this, finer material for an army, men and horses, never paraded ; I should say the men were in height and weight above the average line regiments of any European army, and the cavalry horses were 15 to 16 hands high, brutes of enormous bone and power.

The second division consisted of the local big wigs in barouches, and included the Mayor, the President of the day, the Orator of the day, the Chaplain of the day, the Poet of the day, the Reader of the Declaration of Independence, and the Reader of the poem. The third division consisted of Masons, Oddfellows, Knights of Pythias, Druids, Red Men, Sons and Daughters of Temperance, Independent Order of Good Templars, Temperance Legion, Irish-American Benevolent Society, Independent Order of White Men, St. Mary's Temperance and Benevolent Society, The Golden Circle of True Friends, and the Narragansett Tribe of Red Men, No. 42 ; but perhaps the feature of the division was a handsomely decorated truck drawn by six horses. It contained a printing press of the style of one hundred years ago, with a representative of Benjamin Franklin at the press. Copies of Franklin's first paper, of date 1734, were printed and freely distributed. The fourth and fifth divisions consisted entirely of Irishmen, all Fenians, ranged in various military and benevolent societies, and were of great strength, while their rich regalia, and magnificent green silk banners emblazoned with the crownless harp, made these divisions very attractive. To one of these divisions was attached the Ship of State, a boat on wheels, full of young ladies, who represented the different States and territories in the Union. The sixth division was a miscellaneous one, mainly school children, the girls all dressed in white and clustered into large cars, while the boys walked, each carrying small flags. Specimens of the original Californian miners of '49 followed, a very choice lot of well-armed, coatless roughs, with their swag and pannikins buckled round them, nor could a model trapper or two, with short pipe and buffalo robe, be considered prepossessing individuals for a small tea-party. A team of six horses drew a waggon on which were illustrations of mining scenery, and the Queen of the Miners, who seemed fainting. The seventh division consisted of firemen and their engines. First came one hundred and twenty-five exempt or veteran firemen, dressed in scarlet shirts and red caps, and preceded by banners, axemen, and by a sort of sergeant-major, who brandished eight feet of polished brass, in the shape of the hose nozzle : these men drew the first fire-engine ever made in 'Frisco ; then succeeded one hundred and thirty boys in the same uniform, drawing a veteran engine, which was built in New York in 1820, and imported to 'Frisco in 1849. The five 'Frisco fire commissioners in a barouche, nine magnificently polished and decorated steam fire-engines, drawn by four horses, and various hook and ladder and hose machines followed, escorted by two hundred and eighty-five firemen in scarlet uniforms and quaint brass and leather helmets. A juvenile fire company and the Borer Guard finished this division—to a European, perhaps, the most interesting of all. The Borer Guard consisted of some sixty clowns from the 'Frisco Cremorne, dressed in burlesque military uniforms of all styles, ages, and clans, and their commander rode the " world-famed woolly horse" (see bills of said Cremorne). The eighth and last division consisted of butchers and milkmen, all dressed in white smocks, and driving their professional vehicles, and very smart vehicles and good cattle they drove ; some sported four-in-hand. The butchers exhibited specimens of meat, and perhaps a live lamb or so, while the milkmen carried highly-polished milk cans. The numbers of both trades were astonishing. Promiscuous citizens followed, and the rear was concluded by a caravan full of bears and monkeys. The procession took an hour and thirty-two minutes to pass a given point. The wonder to me was that the Fenians and the Garibaldi Guard did not have a free fight, while three companies of Germans in spiked helmets were uncommonly near Zouaves on whose flag were the words Alsace and Lorraine. We did hear the "marshal-medico" had some difficulty in keeping them apart.

The procession proceeded to the theatre, where the American eagle got on the screech, and the Orator of the day orated pure bunkum and transcendentalism to the extent of seven feet of very small type. This " used-up old country" of ours was let alone, save that it was made responsible for all the ills of American slavery.

The rest of the day was spent in an exciting and joyous manner ; fireworks and bonfires abounded, and by 2-30 p.m. the city and wharfs were on fire in three different places, and at least 40,000 dollars' worth of property were by next morning destroyed in honour of the "glorious 4th of July."

SAN FRANCISCO.

Peace being restored to the town, the 4th of July excitement having died, and its fires having been doused, in company with my friend I proceeded to take stock of San Francisco at my leisure, and here are the results :—

The city of San Francisco, or 'Frisco, is situated on the north end of the southern peninsula, which, with a corresponding northern one, separates the waters of the great San Francisco Bay from those of the North Pacific Ocean. Between these peninsulas is the beautiful strait of the Golden Gate, one mile wide and three in length, connecting the bay with the ocean, and guarded along its length by heavy batteries and huge forts, and blocked at its inner end by the fortified island of Alcatraz. The Golden Gate was first discovered by Sir Francis Drake, who, however, does not appear to have sailed up it, but to have landed a little north of it, at a place now called Port Drake. "Before we went from hence," says the chronicler of his circumnavigation, " our general caused a post to be set up on shore, a monument of our being there ; as also of her Majesty's and successors' right and title to that kingdom, namely, a plate of brass, fast nailed to a great and firm post, whereon is engraven her grace's name, and the day and year of our arrival there, and of the free giving up of the province and kingdom, both by the king and people, into her Majesty's hands ; together with her highness's picture and arms in a piece of sixpence, current English money, showing itself by a hole made on purpose through the plate."

The English did not follow up their discoveries, and the Spaniards took the country, and retained it under the name of California so long as they held Mexico. From Mexico it was taken in 1846 by the American General Fremont, and an army of forty-two men. The Spaniards and Mexicans did little to colonize the country. In 1847 a few *ranches* (cattle farms) were scattered over it, and within 500 miles of 'Frisco Bay there were barely as many white men. In 1835, the first house, a wooden shanty, was built at Yerba Buena (good grazing) the site of the present city of 'Frisco. San Francisco now has 150,000 inhabitants, forty-six places of worship, and sixty newspapers, of which eight are dailies. It has been four times, viz., in 1849, '50, '51, and '52, completely destroyed by fire: prior to 1852, the only building in it that was not of wood, was a gambling house built of adobe, or baked mud, but it now can boast as fine stone and brick buildings, and as broad streets, as any city in the world. From the sea it presents a broken and picturesque appearance, owing to a portion being built on the lofty sandhills which surround it, and which afford sites for most beautiful villas, varying in size from large mansions to cottage homes, built mainly of wood, coloured and worked to imitate stone. The roads on these suburban hills are *paved* with planks, laid across the road, and secured by tenpenny nails. I saw a fellow hitting them in. Where these hills interfere with the extension of the town, the Californians cut them down, tumble them into the sea, and build on them there, thus gaining a double extension of eligible building lots. They stick at little: I saw a two-storied house being towed bodily up a steep hill to a new site, and I was pointed out a church as big as St. Cuthbert's, Carlisle, and told it was to be dragged to some two miles away from its then location.

The three most marvellous cities of modern times, the most remarkable for their recent birth, sudden rise, and present importance, are Melbourne, San Francisco, and Chicago. I have seen men, little older than myself, who recollect these famous cities before they were made (excuse the plagiarism from the celebrated poem on Major-General Wade); no one of them has any pretension to an antiquity older than 1835 or 1830 at furthest. Of the three, San Francisco is by far the most charming; though of Chicago, in its present ruined state, one can hardly judge with fairness; in every point San Francisco outstrips Melbourne,—in the elasticity and joyousness of its air; in the magnificence of its streets and public buildings; in the excellence of its shops (equal to any in London, Paris, or New York); in the apparent well-to-do-ness of its inhabitants; in the good looks and stylish dress of its women; and, in short, in every point whatever. Over the East of the United States it has this advantage, that with all and more than Yankee go-a-head-ness, it is not a Yankee city like Chicago, nor an Irish one like New York, nor a German one like Philadelphia, but cosmopolitan, probably more English and Scottish than anything else. It may become Chinese, for of all the mixed races,—American, English, Scottish, Irish, Mexican, Spanish, Portuguese, French, Italians, Germans, Scandinavians, Polynesians, Chilians, Australians, and many more that inhabit 'Frisco,—the Chinese are the most numerous, and the Germans the least; but at present no one race in particular is predominant, except, perhaps, the English and the Scottish. Among these varied elements are to be found (as generally in America) numbers of men who have risen from nothing into sudden and great affluence, and who have had but little educational advantages; to this I cannot help attributing the support that fortune-tellers and clairvoyants met with in 'Frisco. Their advertisements fill the papers, and their brass plates glitter at every corner. Much that is peculiar in American politics, social institutions, and even in dress can, I think, be traced to the great abundance in the United States of *novi homines* (as such are called by Cicero), and to the fact that all of learning and refinement that exists in the States is almost universally abstinent from public life. Those in England who agitate for the abolition of the House of Lords, and for the transfer of power to the masses, should well consider this point, and study America and Australia closely. It would be too long here to go into the matter beyond this; money will, should these agitators succeed, be king in England; and an uncommon hard and cruel king, too, for the poor man, as I hope sometime to show.

To return to San Francisco. The Chinese quarter there is a great sight. There are in California at least 100,000 Chinese, and more are coming. The "heathen Chinee" is an admirable man; the best cooks, washermen, nurses, domestic servants, gardeners, railway workmen, labourers, and artisans in California are Chinese. In their persons they are marvellously clean. They have a patience that is wonderful; a "Chinee" will wash daily, with a camel-hair brush, every cabbage leaf in his garden, rather than let insects touch them, and thus no one can compete with him as a market gardener. As nurse to a fractious child he is wonderful; as artisan he will imitate anything, though he cannot invent. He never drinks, and for that reason alone the Central Pacific Railway have 1,000 miles of line entirely maintained by Chinese platelayers and roadmen. Never once have these Chinese, it is said, failed to do their duty. John Chinaman's frugality is such that, combined with his patience, he can pick up a fortune where others starve, from the tailings of disused gold diggings for instance. Don't, however, imagine that all the Chinese in San Francisco are in these inferior positions. Far from it; there are wealthy Chinese merchants in 'Frisco, from firms whose names are good for 100,000 dollars down to Chow, Chow, & Co. (Limited), dealers in firewood, and Ah Sing & Co., laundrymen. Ah Sing washed for me, entertained me at his house with first-rate cigars, and accompanied me to a Chinese theatre. A whole quarter in 'Frisco is given up to the Chinese: there they dwell; there are their joss-houses and theatres, tawdry places; their provision shops where they purchase queer vegetables and messes, and slices of roast pig; their shaving-shops, and their music and gambling-houses, and their doctors; I saw " Dr. Hung-Hung" on a brass plate. Scribes too abound—venerable men in gold-rimmed specs. Here too may be seen the women, unaristocratic, with large feet, their hair gummed into most eccentric shapes, and ornate with roses. John Chinaman himself dresses uncommonly well, and a deal more sensibly than we do; broad blue trousers, boat-like shoes, and a loose tunic or blouse, of the finest blue cloth for a " swell," or of cotton for a labourer, form a costume both gentlemanly, becoming, and convenient; his pigtail is coiled round and round his head, on which he generally wears a soft English wide-a-awake. Bar the queer shoes, the costume is a first-rate one for soldier, sailor, sportsman, or lounger.

This enormous influx of Chinese into America promises to be one of the future great political questions of that country. What is to be done with the Chinaman? with all his virtues he has many vices; he is a fearful liar, and his morals are awful; he will always be an Oriental, never an American; yet soon we shall hear of American politicians bidding for the Chinese vote, and the Chinese will certainly sell it. Between the Irish and the Chinese the native American vote will be apt to be squashed. The Irish and Chinese much resemble one another, neither ever amalgamates with the American; all other emigrants go into the crucible, and shortly come out American. The Irish don't; " they make bad citizens" was what I heard of the Irish in San Francisco, in Chicago, and in New York. The Americans are sick of them, and in all probability will soon be as much plagued by an Irish question as we are.

The great export trade of San Francisco is wheat, and beautiful wheat it is, too; small grain, but hard and firm. This year, 1872, the wheat crop in California is better than ever was known. There is more wheat than ships can be got to carry away, and freights to Liverpool are this year nearly £4 : 10s. per ton, as against £2 last year. English farmers would open their eyes at the sight of a Californian wheat field. 12,000 acres is the average size; and I was told of one 32 miles long, by 8 miles broad, one unbroken tract of wheat. The soil is virgin; needs no manure; rain is the chief necessity, and labour. Three dollars per day and keep guaranteed for three months, were, during my visit, being offered. John Chinaman was of course to the fore, but bloodshed was expected, as the Irish were burning the wheat, rather than let the Chinese cut it. The grain, the ears only, is cut by machinery, and the straw left standing. It is afterwards burnt, and the ashes, washed in by the rains, are good manure. Wheat is not the only product of California. It is rich in fruit of every kind, and its vineyards produce annually nine to ten million gallons of wine, which is readily sold in New York and Chicago.

We made a stay of some ten days in San Francisco, and enjoyed it extremely, our enjoyment being much enhanced by the kindness of the people we met. I was introduced to the United States Chief Justice of California as an English barrister. He invited me to go with him and see him formally open term, and after that ceremony he took me round the city, and showed me the law library and other legal institutions.

LETTER VII.

ACROSS A CONTINENT.

July, 1872.

On the 11th of July we left the charming city of San Francisco. Prior to the opening of the trans-continental railway, New York and San Francisco could only communicate by the stormy sea passage round Cape Horn of over 100 days, by the route across the fever-stricken isthmus of Panama, or by a tedious and dangerous journey of many months, made by mule or bullock teams, across the great American desert and the Rocky Mountains. The opening of the line of rail along the 42nd parallel of latitude has brought San Francisco within seven days' journey of New York, and linked together the Eastern and Western States in a manner that will have important political and commercial results. With the road of the 42nd parallel the 'Friscans are by no means satisfied ; it terminates at Oakland, in their bay, but opposite to their city, and they mean to have a line of their own. Two more railways across are projected, by which 'Frisco hopes to benefit, namely, those known as the routes of the 37th and 32nd parallels. A more northerly line is to terminate at Puget's Sound, and the Canadians propose a more northerly one still. The route of the 42nd parallel being the only one open, we had but Hobson's choice for greater part of the way, that is for some 2,000 miles, as far as to Council Bluffs on the Missouri. Thence we chose a route that conducted us to New York *via* Niagara and Montreal. From San Francisco to New York the distance by rail is 3,215 miles; as we came we railed some 3,300 miles, and took steamboat for a few hundred more. It was a matter of no little anxiety to carefully plot out our route beforehand, and then to get at 'Frisco the right tickets, which were given us in a long string a yard in length, costing us each 153 dollars gold. Provided with these, we came ashore early one morning from the *Francis Thorpe*, embarked on the steamer *El Capitano*, crossed the bay, and entered the cars at Oakland. From Oakland to Ogden our route was over the Central Pacific Railway

or a distance of 882 miles. Thence the Union Pacific line
runs to Omaha, 1,032 miles. From Council Bluffs, which
stands *vis-a-vis* to Omaha on the banks of the Missouri, several
routes to Chicago were open to our choice, and from that great
railway centre the traveller can be booked to anywhere in the
world.

Before starting our long land voyage, let us just survey
the train and note how it differs from an English one. The
makers of the first English railway cars were hampered by the
stage coach traditions; they put a stage coach on a railway
waggon, and thought they had done enough; on the Newcastle
and Carlisle line they even retained the coach guards in scarlet
coats and gold-laced hats. Now, the Americans started free,
unhampered by traditions, and certainly have managed to
furnish travellers on American railways with conveniences
undreamt of in England. The Central Pacific train consists of
some twelve carriages, each 70 or 80 feet long, and supported
at either end on four, six, or eight-wheeled bogies. The engine
is of (to English eyes) a novel aspect; its chimney, shaped
like a huge inverted funnel, its monstrous lamps, its huge cow
catcher projecting in front, its prodigious bell, its cab with
cushioned seats for the driver and stoker, its tender piled high
with logs of wood, and its amazing ornateness and superfluity
of polished brass, would all astonish Crewe or Swindon
Junction. Attached to the engine is an air pump, worked by
the superfluous steam : this works atmospheric brakes attached
to every carriage : the engine driver has but to turn a tap,
and the atmospheric brakes are at once acting on every carriage,
on every pair of wheels in the train; no whistling to the guard;
the mere turn of a tap, and the heaviest train almost at once
comes to a stand. I hope that soon every line in England will
be forced to use this invention. Three great luggage cars
follow the engine; then come three or four first-class carriages.
Each has a passage down the middle, external platforms at each
end whereon to lounge and smoke, and each is provided with
washing apparatus, closet, stove, spittoons, and filters of iced
water. A second class or two, much similar, are also on the
train ; it is unusual in America to have more than one class,
but the West is less democratic than the East, and a second
class is allowed. But the thing is fluked even in the East :
throughout America to have but one class of railway cars prevails ; the railway company have but one charge, and one class

of accommodation.   Then in steps Mr. Pulman the great, with
his palace-sleeping cars, drawing-room cars, and restaurant cars,
for the use of which the traveller pays an extra fare, not to the
Company, but to Mr. Pulman.   Mr. Pulman's arrangement
with the Companies is curious.   He pays them nothing ; they
pull his cars for nothing, take full fare from the travellers who
use his cars, and *have not to provide rolling stock to carry
them.*   Eighty of these Pulman's cars, costing on an average
£3,000 a piece, arrive and leave Chicago daily, thus saving the
Companies an outlay of £240,000 on rolling stock, and not in
one jot lessening their profits.   Mr. Pulman is now one of the
richest men in the States.   Three of his palace-sleeping cars
were on our train, which had, in addition to its own conductor
and ticket-collector, a Pulman car conductor and ticket-collector.
Each of these cars was beautifully fitted up in black walnut,
with silver plate ornaments.   The usual passage down the middle
runs the full length from outside platform to outside platform,
passing through a rotunda (a *square* place) at each end of the
carriage.   In these so-called rotundas are closets, washing
apparatus, filters, cupboards for valuables, and other conveniences.   They are also available as smoking-rooms.   Right
and left of this passage the car is divided into numbered
sections.   A section is very comfortable accommodation for
two ; four can sit in it, so that two have plenty of ·room.
At night a bed is made up on the seats ; a shelf lowers
down from the roof, and thus two beds are made like
those in a steamboat, but much larger, each large enough
for two, though usually occupied by one only.   Clean sheets
and pillows are furnished nightly ; heavy curtains are hung
from the roof, and from the end of the car one seems to
look down a vista of very tall old-fashioned four-post beds
ranged close together.   One can undress *in toto*, and go to bed
most comfortably ; it is rather odd to see the ladies hang their
crinolines outside the curtains on pegs there provided, and
one gets stray glimpses of odd things in the way of nightcaps.
A candle lamp is in each bunk, so that one can read in bed.
Each car has a mulatto porter in a neat gray uniform, who
blacks one's boots, and can even provide hot water for grog.
The train stops three or four times a-day at " eating-stations"
for " square meals," and, during the breakfast one, the car is
swept and garnished, and the beds stowed away.   Some people
bring their own grub, and a table can be put up in each

section. An old widow lady occupied the section opposite mine; she was taking a trifling trip of 7,186 miles (Boston to 'Frisco and back) to see a married daughter, and was alone. She had her hamper and tea-pot, and the porter got her hot water, so that she was as comfortable as possible. I may add she had the most wonderful nightcap I ever saw or imagined, out of a pantomime. The drawing-room Pulman cars are for short distances, where sleeping accommodation is not wanted. The restaurant cars have a kitchen on board, and twenty-four people can dine at once in them. I saw one Pulman car which had a kitchen at one end, and living and sleeping accommodation at the other. A party of a dozen occupied it; they had chartered it for a month or so, and travelled about as they pleased, having it attached to the trains on various lines. The great charm of American travelling is this—and without it no one could travel unceasingly for days and nights—one can relieve the monotony of travel by wandering about the train from the baggage waggons to the rearmost platform; where in beautiful scenery, an "observation" or roofless car is added at the end for the benefit of admirers of the picturesque. This freedom, the change from car to platform, the conveniences for smoking, washing, and the like, make the long railway journeys in America most easy, even for delicate people. During the journey merchants wander up and down the passage with goods to sell—cigars, sweets, papers, novels, curios, and aught that travellers can be induced to buy. There are other conveniences in American travel which we want at home. On first showing one's ticket to the conductor, one is supplied with a check to wear in the hat front, and thus much bother is saved, no fumbling in a dozen pockets for a ticket, and no being roused from sleep. The baggage system is admirable: at starting you hand in your baggage, and get a brass check for each article; you can check it on for days in advance of yourself. On nearing a large town, the agent of an Express Company walks through the train, inquires your intended hotel, takes your checks, gives you others, and also a 'bus ticket; your baggage arrives at your hotel without more trouble; you give your checks to the bar clerk, and find your things in your bedroom.

Before finishing our account of an American train, the system of coupling should be mentioned. The cars have only one buffer at each end, a central one, not two as ours, and they couple in the middle by a hook and catch out of the buffer; to couple two cars all that is necessary is to run them one against another, and they couple without any further help, and they are uncoupled as easily. The system is said to quite prevent the telescoping of cars, so dangerous and fatal in case of accident, while men are never injured in the coupling of cars, for the simple reason that it is done without them.

Long ago we left the cars standing at Oakland: "All aboard" (the usual formula), was shouted, and off we set, the great bell on the locomotive clanging vilely as we passed through the streets of Oakland. The track is not railed off, and the only protection to passers-by in the streets is a notice, "when the bell rings look out for the cars." Railways in America are rarely fenced at the sides, and we often had to slow to let cattle cross. On the Kansas Pacific Railway they sometimes have to stop to let wild buffalos pass, for during certain seasons vast herds of these beasts cross the line in their annual migrations after pasture. The train left Oakland about 8 a.m., and carried us through a country rich in vineyards, in orchards, in corn-fields, and in pasturage, until about two in the afternoon we reached Sacramento, the capital, though not the chief town, of California, and distant from 'Frisco 136 miles, a distance in which we made no less than twenty-two stoppages. The stations are very thick on the trans-continental railways, and all the trains stop at all the stations; wherein an ordinary differs from an express I cannot tell, except that an express takes seven days and nights to run from San Francisco to New York, while an ordinary takes twenty-two. We ran through the chief street of Sacramento, tolling our noisy bell as we went; and from the glimpse we thus got of it, it would appear to be a very fine city. Immediately after leaving Sacramento we crossed the American river, and the marshes that border it, on a trestle bridge. These trestle bridges must astonish an English railway engineer; they are literally rows of wooden trestles, over which the train crawls, at some four miles an hour, making the rickety concern to creek and to crack in the most ominous manner; the carriages far overhang the trestles, and from the windows one appears to be riding on a sort of railway tight-rope. At intervals, however, the trestle-tops are prolonged beyond the carriages, and carry on their ends great casks of water, ready to douse the inevitable fire, which sooner or later consumes most things American. We

now began to leave the vineyards and orchards, and commenced the ascent of the snow-clad Sierra Nevada mountains.
The scenery became wilder, and woods abounded, of white
oak at first, changing as we mounted up to pine, spruce, and
cedar, while the undulating and rich country of our early
journey yielded to magnificent wooded canyons or valleys, and
gorges round, across, or up which our train sped its way. Of
these canyons the most magnificent were the Blue Canyon and
the Great American Canyon; in the latter the North Fork of
the American river is compressed between two walls, 2,000 feet
high, and nearly perpendicular. The canyon is about two
miles long, and so precipitous are its sides, which are washed
at foot by the torrent, that it has been found impossible to
ascend the gorge, even on foot, and yet the railway engineers
have managed to cut a track on the side of one of the containing walls of rock; the workmen were lowered in baskets,
and swung against the face of the cliff until they could cut
themselves a foothold. Grander than the grand American
canyon is the passage round Cape Horn, in doubling which the
train sweeps along on the brink of a precipice, which drops
2,500 feet to the American river, which looks in the gorge
below like a winding thread of silver. These two places (the
great American Canyon and Cape Horn) are said to be the
finest scenery in the Sierra Nevadas; to do them justice is
beyond my powers of description : sublime is the word that
best befits them. A faint idea may be obtained by taking
some of the gorges on the Gelt river in Cumberland, and
mentally magnifying them until the cliffs rise 2,500 feet.
The interminable woods we saw struck the mind much; though
possibly they were no vaster than those of Australia, yet
for beauty, variety, and picturesqueness, the mixed white
oaks, pines, spruces, and cedars, far excelled the monotonous
red and blue gum of the southern continent. Man is,
however, making sad ravages among these glorious woods,
particularly the railway man and the mining man, those
dreadful foes to the picturesque ; whole acres had been, by
such agencies, reduced to a show of mere stumps; in other
places fire had been at work, and here and there we saw the
thin blue smoke that told its ravages were by no means done.
Mining man had, too, in these canyons done much more than
destroy the trees ; gold was there ; *placer working* (surface
mining, only possible where is much gold, and requiring

little capital beyond a spade, a pick, and a long-tom or cradle); had honeycombed nature's face, while hydraulic mining had washed her features away. This hydraulic mining is a most destructive method ; for miles and miles large streams of water are conducted in artificial channels, technically called "ditches, telegraphs, and flumes," from the summit of the Sierra Nevadas, and then directed through iron nozzles against the gold fields to be worked. The force of this simple machinery is astounding ; whole hills are speedily washed away, and carried in a semi-liquid state into flumes, where the gold is collected by "riffles," which are, I believe, ripples or wooden bars placed across the bottom of the flumes to catch the gold falling by its gravity to the bottom.

We reached our highest point on the Sierra Nevadas, some 7,040 feet above the sea level, about 10 p.m. on the first day. In winter the snow lies here from 16 to 20 feet deep, and for 45 miles the line is carried under the shelter of snow sheds, built of enormous logs of timber, and with roofs, so shaped as to throw off passing avalanches. To protect these from fire a locomotive always stands at Summit Station with steam up, and with eight huge water tank cars, and a force pump attached. I should mention here that, when the night of our first day's journey came on, a party of excursionists from Boston asked us if we objected to a little singing; of course, we consented, and every night after that we had regular family prayers in the car; some of the hymns that were sung were rather curious in both tune and sentiment to our English ideas.

Soon after leaving Summit we passed from the State of California into that of Nevada. All night long the train flew onwards down the mountains, and in the morning we stopped for a "square meal" at a place called Humbolt. These "square meals," with three of which we were daily indulged, were all alike ; tables spread with a bountiful supply of everything eatable, and in the drinkable line with tea, coffee, iced milk, and water, nothing stronger to be had in the far West at railway stations. The waiters were Chinese, dressed in the whitest of white linen ; as we moved eastward they gave way to elegant negroes, or else to "Yankee gals" in homespun dress. Our second day's journey was mainly over desert—first the 40-mile desert, and then the great American desert,—dreary and waterless plains, thickly covered with sage plant, alternating with glittering beds of dirty white alkali and gray lava ; many and many an emigrant has perished on these alkali deserts for want of water. They form the central area of the State of Nevada, and are destitute alike of wood, water, and grass. Our track was within a few miles of the beautiful lakes Tahoe and Donner, the latter famous for a horrible tragedy which took place on its banks : a snowed-up emigrant party, and the discovery by the rescuers of one solitary survivor maniacally gnawing the roasted arm of a companion ; that wretched man lived, and still lives, shunned by all, and suspected of crimes worse than cannibalism. We stopped during the day at a great number of stations, mostly small places, but local centres of lumber or mining districts, or else contiguous to U.S. forts, with which the country is dotted for the benefit of the Indians. At some of these stations great heavy stage coaches, drawn by four, six, or eight horses, were in waiting to take passengers long journeys to outlandish mining places ; while at others an army ambulance, drawn by wicked-looking mules, would attend the convenience of some military "swell." The most important station during this day's journey was perhaps Truckee, a wooden town of 2,000 inhabitants, all engaged in the lumber trade. At Winnemucca and other places we saw quantities of Red Indians, miserable beings of the Ute or digger tribe, a degraded and treacherous race, who live on grasshoppers, and the broken remnants from the refreshment stations, which are given them in pails. Both men and women wore the cast-off garments of civilization, with a few fancy adornments of their own, such as a feather or two stuck in a white felt hat ; the women attend each train, and beg persistently for victuals or coppers. Each squaw has her face painted red or yellow, and carries a " pappoose" on her back. A pappoose is an Indian baby, who is strapped on a board, 3 to 4 feet in length : leather, rags, and skins of animals are nailed to it in such a way that it resembles a large ugly slipper. Into this slipper-like apparatus is inserted the baby with a packing of rags and moss, and strings are folded round and round the slipper and its inmate, from the chin to the feet ; the hands are even tied down, and of the living mummy you see nothing but the head. This head is protected from the sun by a little roof of wickerwork, to which are fastened rags of various colours, some feathers, and a few beads and buttons, in the mother's natural anxiety to do something " tasteful" for her offspring. The entire apparatus is attached to the maternal head by a leather strap across her brow.

This day's line of travel ran near the old emigrant road, and we were pointed out various places on it famous for encounters with the Indians. We also passed through a magnificent canyon or gorge, known as the Palisades or Twelve-Mile Canyon. Bare, bleak, and broken cliffs towered on either side, while a little below us the Humbolt river rolled in a continuous frenzy. The morning of our third day's journey saw us at Ogden, situate in the Mormon territory of Utah, distant 882 miles from San Francisco, and the terminus of the Central Pacific Railroad. Instead of pursuing our journey eastward by the Union Pacific, we here deviated southwards some 40 miles by the Utah Central Railway to visit Salt Lake City, where we arrived at about 2 p.m., having travelled continuously by rail from 7 a.m. on Thursday to 2 p.m. on Saturday.

LETTER VIII.

AMONG THE MORMONS.

July, 1872.

"Far have I travelled and muckle have I seen," as the old song says, but a more lovely spot and a fairer scene than that occupied by the Salt Lake City " saw I never ne'en." 'Tis the happy valley of Rasselas, not existing in mere imagination, but reduced to sober fact. The snow-clad range of the Wahsatch Mountains enclose a vast, fertile, and lovely plain, and in an angle of these mountains the commanding genius of Brigham Young, a man with the genius and daring of a Napoleon, has fixed the capital city of his extraordinary religion. As one winds along the shores of the Salt Lake in the cars, one cannot but be struck with the beauty of the country, its fertility, and the marked prosperity of its inhabitants. Nearer the city lovely villas abound, while on entering it one everywhere beholds broad avenues of trees with running streams on either side, and comfortable detached houses standing, even the humblest of them, in their own gardens. Ascend to the North Bench—a hill overlooking the city—and you can scarcely see it, so embowered in green foliage is it ; while the white-topped and green-sloped Wahsatch hills give a background to as lovely a view as this earth can boast. We took up our quarters at the Townsend Hotel, a very large hotel, kept by a Mormon. *On dit* (but I don't quite credit it) that all the chambermaids in the house were his wives, and that all the waiters were his sons, and that he thus got the service of the hotel done for nothing. Spite of our landlord's religious principles and practices, the guests in his hotel discussed Mormonism with great freedom of tongue, while the hotel clerk stood up for it most vehemently. A stay of a few days in Salt Lake City convinced us, spite of the clerk's eloquence, that Mormonism (particularly polygamy) is a decaying institution, and presently our readers shall be shown a few of the reasons which led us to that conclusion.

Our first proceeding was to examine the city, which is of

an L shape, situate under the snow-clad peaks of the Wahsatch range, distant in reality some twelve miles, but seeming, from the clearness of the atmosphere, to overhang the buildings. All the streets are laid out of a width of 132 feet, and have streams of water flowing down either side, keeping the " shade trees," which line the streets, in lovely green foliage during the summer heats. Except in East Temple Street (the business quarter) each house is detached, stands in its own garden or orchard : the immense number of these, and of " shade trees," give the city the air of being a huge collection of villas and suburban cottages, all buried in a mass of luxuriant foliage, and thus creating that peculiar beauty which distinguishes Salt Lake City from all other cities. The houses are mostly built of stone and adobes (sun-dried bricks), and have an Italian look about them. In the business quarter space is now valuable, and the ground is getting closely built over. The shops and stores kept by Mormons exhibit a sign called by the Gentiles (as the Mormons designate all who are not of their body) the Bull's Eye, being a picture of a gigantic eye with " Holiness to the Lord " written over it, and Z.C.M.I. underneath, meaning Zion's Co-operative Mercantile Institution. Three or four years ago the Mormons were powerful enough to prohibit people from dealing at shops which did not display the " bull's eye" ; now the shops that show the bull's eye are in the minority. One huge dry goods store we inspected—that of Messrs. Walker—a magnificent building, fit to be compared with the similar establishment of Messrs. Banks Brothers & Bell, in Melbourne : we can best give our readers an idea of what Messrs. Walker deal in, by saying that they deal in all the vast variety of articles which Messrs. Copestake, Moore, Crompton, & Co., of Bow Church Yard do, and also in wines, spirits, preserved meats, pickles, picks, shovels, wheel-barrows, ore-sacks, and long-toms, and that they also keep a bank, at which we had to change our lovely gold dollars current in California for the dirty greenbacks current in the rest of the United States. Messrs. Walker, and one or two enterprising milliners, who have settled in Salt Lake City since the railroad was made, have dealt polygamy a deadly blow ; Messrs. Walker and the milliners have introduced the latest European fashions to the Mormons, and no Mormon can stand it. In early days Mormons wore coats and gowns of homespun " butternut," and it cost little to dress out several wives, but with the rail has come an influx of

Gentiles, land speculators, and miners, with fashionably-dressed wives, and to their level the Mormon ladies now insist on being dressed. No purse, however long, can dress out nine-and-twenty wives in Dolly Vardens, or even the moderate number of six in silks or satins. This revolution in dress has dealt Mormonism and polygamy a fatal blow ; like his Christian brother, a Mormon now finds one wife a quite expensive enough luxury, while a Mormon girl sees she will be better dressed as the one wife of a Gentile than the one-sixth part of the wife of a Mormon. Thus it is odd, but true, that a *chapeau à la Dolly Varden*, a sweet thing in *fichus*, or a *novelty in paniers*, may be to Mormonism as efficacious a missionary as one in a black coat and white choker, duly accredited by a pious society. In the business quarter we saw also the offices of several papers ; the official Mormon organ is the *Deseret News*, edited by George Q. Cannon, an out-and-out Mormon, with six wives. Up to this time the Mormons have never ventured to send to Congress a practical polygamist, but for the ensuing election [*i. e.* 1872], they are running George Q. on that platform expressly. The *Mormon Herald* and one or two other papers are anti-Mormon, and pitch into Brigham Young and George Q. Cannon in most unmeasured language. This is another sign of the times. Three or four years ago the editor of any paper, bold enough to attempt to write down Mormonism, would have got *(on dit)* a *Danite pill*, *i. e.*, been shot by the secret police of Brigham.

The most remarkable building in Salt Lake City is the Temple, only it is not built yet ; it is to be 186½ feet long, by 99 feet broad, and 100 feet high, with six towers 200 feet high. It has been many years in building, and is about three feet above the ground, and Gentile scoffers say it will never be any higher in the present state of Mormonism, until some Yankee speculator completes it as a dry goods store. The next building in the city, both in site and remarkability, is the Tabernacle, the most conspicuous thing in Salt Lake City. The Tabernacle is a vast oval-shaped building 250 feet long by 150 feet broad ; 46 great pillars stand round it, and support an egg-shaped roof, which rises in one unbroken arch. The building will seat 8,000 people, and has at one end an elevated platform, with three rows of seats and three pulpits in their centre, one above the other, for the bishops, high priests, and seventies ; behind this platform is the largest organ ever built in the States. We attended the service in the Tabernacle on

Sunday, and were amazed to find it almost empty, barely 400 persons present, and of those full 100 were strangers from the hotels ; as a rule, the other 300 were persons of an appearance intensely stupid. The fact is, all those Mormons who are not stupid, or in office, have apostatized. They got all the advantages they could at first out of the Mormon institution, such as help at start in life, and the like, but now that the United States law prevails in Utah, and United States troops are at hand, they apostatize to avoid paying tithes to the Bishop. During our stay a Mormon Bishop cited 120 Mormons before him for non-payment of tithes ; some twenty obeyed the citation, and told him they would not pay ; the others took no notice of him. Four or five years ago all would have paid, or Brigham would have known why. In the service at the Tabernacle we heard three preachers, some prayers, and some hymns. Two of the preachers were very common-place, and of these one, a dapper little German, had been on a missionary tour to Switzerland ; the third man was an out-and-out fanatic, a man who thoroughly believed all he said, and would probably stick at no atrocity in the interests of his religion. All three laid it down as a dogma, that there was no chance of salvation outside of the Mormon Church ; but that dogma did not strike me as novel, having heard it before from High Churchman, from Low Churchman, and from Mahomedan. Spite of the dogma and the fanatic, the impression the service and the congregation gave us was, that there was in the capital of Mormonism little or no enthusiasm in favour of Mormonism, and it is a religion that cannot live without enthusiasm in its favour. This view was corroborated by a talk we had with an old Mormon, a native of Croydon, and one of the survivors of the march from Nauvoo in 1848. " He never went to Tabernacle, nor paid tithes, few did; yet he called himself a Mormon, but had never been a polygamist. Mormonism had done well for him, his land lots had come in valuable for building ; had sold the Episcopal Bishop a site for a Church and house, and also the Roman Catholic." This again is another instance of the decadence of Mormonism. Formerly Mormonism brooked no rival in its territory of Utah ; now it has to allow religious equality ; and Episcopalians, Roman Catholics, and others have all built churches and schools within the last three years. Our friend also raised a point which will astonish many, and to which I may recur : he contrasted the administration of law in England

and in America. In England, he said, "the law is administered
equally to rich and poor ; in America the rich are above it." I
found respectable American newspapers taking this view, and
the thing can be fairly demonstrated, did space permit. The
question has been raised by the Stokes trial in New York, and
by Mr. Fisk's criminal career. Of other public buildings in
Salt Lake City, the chief are the Theatre (Brigham's private
property), the City Hall, and the Lion and White Houses,
where reside Brigham and his numerous wives.

The territory of Utah (pronounced U*taw*) contains about
65,000 square miles. It was formely a portion, nominally,
of Mexico, but in reality was a no-man's land, situate
between the Rocky Mountains and the Sierra Nevada range.
In 1846 the Mormons were by persecution forced to move
from Nauvoo, and Brigham Young, displaying a prescience
and statesmanship of the highest order, led them a weary
journey into this secluded spot. Here the Mormons under
Brigham's wise rule flourished exceedingly; the substantial
social advantages that Brigham could give emigrants, the
excellent organization he formed for transporting them from
all parts of Europe, and the ready hospitality with which
they were received, combined with a religious system emi-
nently calculated to work on the poor and on the illiterate,
ensured him plenty of comers from the labouring population of
Europe, drawn principally from the ill-educated States. Divided
by a terrible journey of months from all civilization, Mormonism thus flourished, and Brigham's decrees were enforced
by the "Danites," or secret Mormon police. So well aware was
Brigham, that Mormonism could flourish only in seclusion, that
he took every pains to preserve that seclusion. Gentile emigrants were, it is said, robbed and murdered by Mormons
disguised as Red Indians ; Gentile traders were driven away,
and *mining was prohibited on pain of death.* Brigham knew
that, were the vast mineral riches of Utah known, nothing could
hinder the whole world from pouring in. He did more than
this ; to preserve his necessary seclusion he actually, in 1857,
defied the United States troops, and by a bold night attack,
led by Orson Pratt and Fowler Wells, destroyed their supplies,
and left them to starve in the desert ; out of a convoy of 230
United States troops, all but eight perished of hunger and
starvation, and a force including three infantry regiments, of one
cavalry, and four batteries of artillery, was reduced to eating

the cavalry and artillery horses. But when Brigham saw that resistance was impossible, and that seclusion could be no more, he (and this shows his statesman-like genius) adopted an opposite policy ; he let the United States troops march in unopposed ; he contracted to make 150 miles of the Union Pacific Railway, and several hundred miles of telegraph ; he became chairman of, and chief shareholder in, and contractor for, the Utah Central Railway, and so realized an enormous fortune. He is also said to have speculated heavily and successfully in mines, for the miners have entered Utah ; Brigham can no more keep them out than Mrs. Partington could the Atlantic. With United States troops in garrison at Fort Douglas, two miles from Salt Lake City, with European fashions introduced there, with miners and mine proprietors, and fashionable tourists swarming over the place, Brigham's power is on the wane, and Mormonism is doomed. Still he is yet a powerful potentate : Utah has some 80,000 inhabitants, of whom the majority are Mormons (just as the majority in these Isles are Christian), probably because in Utah Mormonism is the respectable religion ; in every town in Utah, except Corinne, the Mormons have the political and municipal power ; this, however, will not last long ; polygamy is doomed, for one half of the Mormons are against it ; it will go when Brigham dies, and he cannot live much longer, as he is 75. The U.S. Government have just made an attempt to put polygamy down by trying Brigham for bigamy, or rather for polygamy : he was too much for the lawyers : he was acquitted, for he *never had been married to any wife at all by any ceremony recognized by any civilized nation ; he was merely living in promiscuous and extensive concubinage, and that is not punishable by the laws of the United States.* This shows the man's great genius ; he and Prince Bismarck are probably by far the greatest geniuses of this age ; with a better education, under better luck, and with more hypocrisy to conceal his salaciousness, he would have made a Cromwell or a Pitt. Another point in which Brigham has shown his wisdom is this : female suffrage prevails in Utah ; a Mormon with six wives has much more political power than a Gentile with one ; all Mormon women, for very shame, support the *statu quo,* or Brigham ; they won't vote for changes, which would make them out to be w——s.

The decadence of Mormonism and of polygamy is further powerfully proved by the following facts, which came under our notice :—one that the sons of Joe Smith, the first Mormon prophet, were, during our visit, publicly preaching in Salt Lake City against polygamy, and publicly accusing Brigham of having defrauded them of their father's property ; the other that a somewhat racy book was being publicly sold under the title of " An Exposé of Polygamy in Utah," by a Mrs. T. B. H. Stenhouse,* formerly a polygamic wife.   This book, of which I bought a copy, deals severely with the whole system, and with Brigham himself.   Polygamy will not survive Brigham's death, and then Mormonism will sink to the level of an ordinary dissenting sect,—powerful indeed, and long likely to be powerful, from its excellent organization and its wealth, but divested of most of its earlier tenets and dogmas.   Troops of emigrants still arrive to join the society, composed of ignorant peasantry, mostly from Northern Europe ; the substantial worldly advantages (now indeed lessening) that are promised them, and that they realize account for this, while polygamy is generally not disclosed to them until they arrive in Utah.

Mormon or not Mormon, there is a grand future before Utah ; its mineral wealth is enormous, and the inhabitants are anxious to get English capital invested in its working.   To the regret of the more honest and wiser of them, the beginning has been discouraging, and the first English capitalists have been heavily swindled.   In one case, that of the now famous Emma mine, the scoundrels who sold it to the English company immediately started a new mine to poach on the ore they had sold.   The English company appealed to law, and in a most able and dignified judgment, which I heard, the United States Chief Circuit Judge, Mc.Kean, decided in favour of the English.   The arguments on either side were *per se* of the driest description, but the counsel enlivened the proceedings by flowers of rhetoric. The counsel for the poachers indulged in a tremendous harangue against English capital, from which he digressed into a hot attack on English lords and ladies, and the English aristocracy and their morals.   Colonel (I forget his name), the counsel for the English company, replied, and I quote from Utah papers :— " He set to work in a cool, deliberate, and gory manner, as if he meant to have cold lawyer for his breakfast ;   brandished the

* Reviewed in the *Pall Mall Gazette* since this letter was first in print.

tomahawk of his eloquence, raised his opponent's hair, and held up the bleeding scalp to derision," &c., &c. "He concluded a magnificent peroration by calling his learned friend a *slimy smut-mill of abuse.*"

My fellow-traveller visited this famous mine, which is situate in the Little Cottonwood Canyon in the Wahsatch hills. He came back fully convinced of the wealth of the Emma, and wrote an account of it which has appeared in the *Glasgow Evening Mail,* and which is reproduced at the end of this letter. Life is held cheap in these mining districts; but he only saw one man stabbed, whereon he fled, as a free fight seemed imminent. I myself heard pistol shots one night, and a cry of "another man shot," whereon I carefully stayed in bed. I noticed also, while under the hands of the chief Utah dentist, that he had a loaded and capped revolver lying handy among his tooth-drawing and stuffing implements. (By the way, American dentists say they beat English out and out, but this one could beat the world. I never heard a man brag so of his own proficiency, and he made one pay proportionately,—15 gold dollars for stuffing a tooth.) I also saw during my stay the Sheriff of Utah trying vainly to raise a *posse comitatús.* Some twenty miners had annexed a mine without right, whereon the Sheriff gave them a call with a writ of ejectment in his tail pocket. The miners drew a bead on him with their rifles, and swore they would fire if he put hand to pocket. As the Sheriff believed the miners— indeed their captain was known to have shot two men already—- he came back for assistance, which he could not get, and finally had to call in the United States troops from Fort Douglas, with what result I did not hear.

While at Salt Lake City we attended an open-air meeting in favour of Horace Greeley's candidature for the Presidency of the States, and at it the whole Mormon party ticket for Utah was declared, George Q. Cannon being the selection for Congress man. Utah is not one of the United States; it is only a territory, possessing inferior political privileges to a State, which it is anxious to become. Thus far the political party in power in America has declined to admit Utah as a State until it abolishes polygamy: the Mormons were therefore hot in Greeley's favour, because they expected he would concede to them what Grant will not: Greeley, it was said, would wink at polygamy if he could get the Mormon influence, and would,

when elected, declare Utah a State, and give it State rights and
privileges. Should this be done, Utah would elect its own
governor, and no doubt would elect Brigham Young, a scandal
which respectable Americans wish to avoid. At present the
governor is nominated by the President of the U.S., as also
are the Utah judges. Up to this time the Mormons have
wisely returned to Congress a representative, who, though a
Mormon, was not a practical polygamist. He has now declined
to come forward again ; the Gentiles, conscious of their growing
power, have determined to run an anti-Mormon, whereon the
Mormons have hoisted the no-surrender flag, and started
George Q. Cannon of six wives.   We heard George Q.'s speech ;
he advocated free everything—" free press, free religion"—
which are very novel cries in the mouth of an out-and-out
Mormon.   There was plenty of noise, but no fighting, at the
election meeting ; two brass bands and two cannons played at
intervals to enliven the proceedings.   On one occasion one of
these cannons was badly loaded ; the cartridge blew out
unburnt, and knocked heels over head an unfortunate cow that
was quietly walking up street to be milked.

I have mentioned what I paid for tooth-stopping. Everything else is equally dear in America ; an American dollar
(worth from 3s. 4d. to 4s. of our money) will buy no more in
America than will a shilling in England.   A cigar that I can
get in England for threepence is in America a quarter of a
dollar ; a bottle of brandy is four dollars, wine is ruinous, and
a common round felt hat is six dollars ; a box of matches, such
as in England costs a halfpenny, is in America five cents, or
fivepence ! Heavy taxation has something to do with this, but
their decimal coinage has also something ; the unit, a dollar, is
too high in value.   In France the unit is a franc, in England a
shilling, and in America a dollar, and the price of many articles
is fixed merely by the unit.   If ever decimalists get their way
in England, and make a florin the unit, prices will go up.

Our stay at Salt Lake City was the best part of a week, and
then we started for Chicago, a railway journey of 1,605 miles,
which we did in one stage.

N.B.—This letter was in print in October, 1872, prior to Brigham's
resignation, and prior to the appearance in the *Times* of some remarks
on Mormonism similar to those above, and also prior to the death of
Mr. Greeley.

APPENDIX TO LETTER VIII.—ACCOUNT OF EMMA MINE BEFORE REFERRED TO.

Townsend House, Salt Lake City,
Utah, 16th July, 1872.

My dear H——,

Since arriving here I have sent you off several papers with notices of the trial of the Emma Mine *v*. Illinois Tunnel. It was only yesterday, while at the mine, that I got really to know what the quarrel was about, and I think you may take it thus :—The "Emma" was the first mine in the Canyon of Little Cottonwood, and, after being pretty well developed, was sold to an English company "bag and baggage." The people who sold it, being up to a wrinkle or two as to the nature of the vein of ore and its direction, "prospected" the Emma Hill about 2,000 feet down the canyon, and put in a large tunnel (the Illinois Tunnel), but found nothing till they came to the Emma vein. By this time they had overreached their claim* in getting at this lode, but so had the Emma also in following it up. However, it seems that the disputed part, being on neutral ground, the Emma, by some right in their original claim, have the privilege of following that up, which the Illinois Tunnel disputed, and hence this lawsuit, which involves almost certain ruin on the one hand, and immense prosperity on the other to whichever party wins. I have done everything in my power to get information on the subject, and consider I have been very successful. No one here seems to have any sympathy with the Illinois Tunnel, for they are said to have sold the Emma with the intention of getting at the lode in an opposite direction. I purposely have waited a day or two longer than I intended, to hear the decision in the case. We attended the Court-houses at 11 this morning, but the case was held over till 7 p.m. ; so, though we had intended starting this afternoon, we shall stay till tomorrow so as to hear it. From all I can make out the Emma seems very likely to get the judgment in their favour. Though

---

* A claim, in mining language, is the plot of ground claimed by a miner or company of miners and granted by the U.S. Government under the Acts of Congress regulating mining.

the Emma is only 17 miles in a straight line from this, it takes 40 of travelling to get to it, and I cannot do better than give you a short description of my journey thither. I was informed at the hotel that you couldn't go and come in one day, except by hiring both carriage and horses, which would have cost £6, *i. e.* $30 ; it would have been the best way to do, but I could not afford the funds just then. So, with the expectation of remaining over the night in the canyon, I started at 5-45 and got the train to Sandy, 22 miles south of Salt Lake City, where a stage, drawn by six Mexican horses, was in waiting to take us something like nine miles up the canyon. The Emma is situated on the Wahsatch Mountains, some peaks of which are 15,000 feet high, perpetually covered with snow. The scenery at the mouth of the canyon was very fine, and the horses pulled us quickly to our first halting place, though it was just the slightest thing rough. On getting out here I found out that by hiring a mustang (a Mexican horse) and pushing on, I could have two hours or so at the Emma, and either ride back or take the stage. Though costing a few of the almighty dollars, I mounted my mustang, leaving my bag and stick with the groom. Then I faced nine miles of the wildest country I ever saw, and all up hill, but you have no idea how the brute tore along. Before half an hour the snow was lying at my feet in every gully I passed, though the sun was very strong. I got my coat off, and strapped it to the saddle-back, and went at it. All down the canyon was a foaming torrent, made chiefly by the melting snow, and the bridges across it were simply two trees ; but trusting to my mustang, and shutting my eyes generally, got over all safe. I cannot say I ever in all my life saw such magnificent scenery. The mountains, 7,000 to 8,000 feet high above you, with all their crevices filled with snow, the melting of which made the most magnificent waterfalls one could imagine ; all over the sides of the mountains· dense forests of pines showing out through the snow—really it was enchanting. At times I was completely obscured from all observation by the hanging rocks over my head ; then, again striking a part of the road through a semi-burned clump of pines, I arrived at Alta City, right above which is the Emma. My first ten minutes were spent in a saloon getting a snack, and listening to some miners quarrelling over a game of cards. However, one of them producing a revolver, and another a bowie-knife, I bethought myself it was time to quit. After a good hard pull, and ascending some 1,200 or 1,500 feet, I reached the Emma, which is 8,700 feet above the level of the sea—the highest I ever was in my life. Right round about me there was nothing but snow, yet I am sure the thermometer could not have been less than 75 or 80 degrees. There is not much outward show about Emma : and it being dinner-hour, I walked about the place for a bit. They had a good suite of offices and dining-room, or somewhat of that kind, for the men, not by any means gaudy, but everything indicating a first-class business look. About ten mule-teams were waiting to be loaded with the ore at this time, and it was all weighed and checked by a clerk before being put into the team. I luckily got into conversation with the manager, enlisting his sympathy by saying I had seen big mines in Australia, and wanted to see the same here. He gave me a good deal of information, being a plain, steady-going chap. He said that they had been a little troubled by the melted snow getting in this year, but the winter had been unusually severe, and being rather put out anent this dispute with the Illinois Tunnel, they had been certainly, he said, working to great disadvantage.' However, he said that once these "d——d thieves" were settled, he'd have the whole thing in full swing and be loading, as of old, 150 mule teams per day. He never had any doubt as to how the claim would be settled, for he felt certain the Emma was right. He gave me a fine lump of the ore in a present, and I shall have the pleasure of letting you see it when I come home. The stage starting at two o'clock I had to hurry off and join it at Alta. Well, little I thought what was in store for me. You must remember that American stages are not by any means like an omnibus, but are three-seated buggies, covered in on top by an arched roof, open all along the sides, and hung on leather springs. Off we started down the same road I had ridden up in the morning. We had two lady passengers and one gentleman besides myself. I could have had the horse-back again to where I got it, but I felt so used up I thought I'd be easier in the stage—poor deluded being that I was. Then H. can you imagine such a conveyance as I've described, drawn by six horses, being dragged over—can I call it a road? No, by jingo, it's only a conglomeration of boulders, dust, ditches, &c. If you have ever seen the stones, lime, lumber, &c., laid down to begin building a house with, then you can form some faint idea of the road down Little Cotton canyon. At one time I was bumped smash against the other gent, then banged forward into one of the girls' laps, then back again to my own seat, only to be tossed up to the ceiling of the coach, bashing my sportive white tile over my eyes. Oh, it was killing. Then the dust got so great that you couldn't see three yards at times from the coach's side — that's a fact. One of the girls got sick with the jolting, and I had to hold her head. Then our way got blocked up by a slip of stones together forming the boundary of the road ; and our trestle-trees broke, so we had to lift the coach over a granite boulder about 3 feet high. But the worst journey comes to an end, and ours did so when we stopped at the side of the way to change horses. We had to drive like mad to catch the train at Sandy Station, getting in just as the cars came up. We took three hours to drive the first nine miles, and only one and a quarter to drive the next nine. I arrived at Salt Lake City at 7-45, most thoroughly done up, but more pleased with my day's work than almost any since I've left home.

Yours,

T. S.

LETTER IX.

ACROSS A CONTINENT.

(Continued.)

July, 1872.

Much to the disgust of my slumber-loving companion, we had to leave Salt Lake City at about 5 a.m., and retrace our route on the Utah Central Railway to Ogden, the joint terminus of the Central Pacific, Union Pacific, and Utah Central Railways. At Ogden we got breakfast, for our Mormon landlord at Salt Lake barbarously declined at that early hour to furnish us with any refreshment at all. After this important ceremony we embarked on the Union Pacific train, which much resembled that of the Central Pacific, described before, save that the locomotive's smokestack was in form a cylinder with a cheese a-top, instead of being an inverted funnel. Among the company on board the cars we found the Japanese legation, *en route* to England ; they numbered some thirty or forty, mainly lads, coming to Europe to study, dressed in European clothes, and speaking English remarkably well. They were a pleasant intelligent lot, keen after knowledge, and provided with note books in which they entered the names and descriptions of all that came new to them ; and bothered the Americans much by asking the name of "the chief noblemen" of every town we came to. We left Ogden at 8 a.m. ; soon after we left the town took fire, and by 3 p.m. a telegram overtook us to say that the whole town was in ashes ; it contained some 4,000 inhabitants, was built of wood, and the cooking of our breakfast was said to have fired the railway station, and so the town ; that, however, is a matter between the inhabitants of Ogden and the insurance companies. Shortly after starting, our road took us through the sublime scenery of the Devil's Gate, and of the Weber and Echo canyons, magnificent gorges in the Wahsatch hills, flanked by bold and precipitous cliffs from 300 to 800 feet high, and broken up into every variety of fantastic outline—pyramids and pinnacles, spires and towers, donjons and keeps, fortresses and cathedrals. So narrow are these canyons, the passes through the Wahsatch

range into the happy Mormon land, that the forces of Brigham
Young, in 1857, prepared to defend them against the U.S.
troops by balancing rocks and boulders on the edge of the
precipices, ready to be rolled on the invaders' heads.   For this
stage of the journey an "observation car" was attached to the
train, and our mulatto porter pointed out to us the curiosities—
the Pulpit Rock, the Finger Rock, the Devil's Slide, the
Thousand-Mile Tree (1,000 miles from Omaha), and such
freaks of nature as have acquired a name.   The track wound
in and out of the rocks in the most intricate manner ; in 26
miles it crossed the Echo creek or river no less than thirty-one
times ; occasionally it burrowed by a tunnel through the rock,
but generally it was niched-in between the Echo or Weber
creeks and the rocks at the foot of which they ran.   In Echo
canyon the grasshoppers were so thick as actually to impede
the train, and the cowcatcher was provided with bunches of
spruce to sweep these insects off the rails.   So numerous here
are the grasshoppers at certain seasons that the bodies of those
crushed by the engines actually grease the rails to the extent
of stopping the trains going up the Echo inclines.   My readers
will not believe me, but what I am writing is a well-authenti-
cated fact.   Whole tribes of Indians live, and live well, on
these insects, which they collect and dry for the non-grasshopper
season.

    After going through these canyons, the railway ran con-
tiguous to the old Emigrant Road, or California trail, and we
began to enter a country famous, or perhaps infamous, in
western history.   Prior to the formation of the railway, the
traffic across the country was conducted by waggon trains.   It
is estimated that nearly 9,000 waggons, 15,000 mules, 60,000
cattle, and 12,000 men were employed in this work.   As the
Union Pacific Railway was opened in sections westwards, a new
town sprung up at the temporary terminus, flourished as the
centre of the waggon business, and, as the railway was prolonged, died away.   We passed many such ruined cities, but
then, a western city grows like a fungus, and decays as fast.
In its glory a western city much resembles Epsom Downs
at the Derby ; the buildings are all wood and canvas, and,
except an hotel or two, are of but one storey ; drinking and
dancing saloons abound ; *corrals* for mules and horses answer
to the saddling and weighing paddocks and the betting ring :
the crowds and the betting men alone are wanting.   Green

ACROSS A CONTINENT. 77

River City, once a place of 2,000 inhabitants, but now utterly deserted, was the first of these ex-centres of freighting traffic that we came across : it is in the territory of Wyoming, a few miles from the border of Utah, and in its day enjoyed a very evil reputation.   After passing a lot of mining towns, we came to the great Red Desert, which (according to the guide book) an agile jack rabbit once tried to cross, but died of hunger and thirst before he accomplished his journey.   Nothing can live on this desert, some 40 miles across, and the lakes that abound on it are impregnated with alkali.   A few miles further on we arrived at Creston, a point in the Rocky Mountains, 7,030 feet above the sea, and on the " Continental divide," or backbone of America, though lower in altitude than a place we afterwards came to.   The morning of our second day we found ourselves crossing Laramie Plains or Park.   In Wyoming and Colorado there exist at very elevated altitudes great " parks," or immense bodies of table-land, enclosed by the peaks and ridges of the surrounding mountains, sheltered by them from the cold winds, and provided by them with never-failing streams which issue from above the line of perpetual snow.   Thousands of buffalo, elk, antelope, and deer, once found, and still find, food on these plains, which are probably the finest grazing lands in the world ; while along the banks of the streams are most beautiful meadows producing abundance of hay, and capable of growing to advantage, wheat, barley or rye.   The surrounding hills afford any amount of lumber, and the water-power necessary for mills.   Of these parks, Laramie Plains are a beautiful example ; their extent I could not ascertain, but we crossed them for about 60 miles.   Far, far away we could see the snow-clad peaks of the Rocky Mountains, some far distant in the very south of Colorado, 150 miles away, while around us spread this lovely park, rich in grass, and perfectly enamelled with red, yellow, blue, and white flowers.   I could not help thinking what grand galloping ground for racers could be selected on Laramie Plains.   Now that the railway has opened them up, I have little doubt but that emigrants in swarms will soon settle there, and we may yet hear of a Laramie Derby or the Rocky Mountains Gold Cup being run for.   As we ascended from Laramie Plains we came upon snow fences, and various dodges tried, and mainly tried unsuccessfully, to prevent the snow from drifting, which it does here deeply.   Here too we first saw the prairie dog, an animal which is said to include in his

domestic circle, or burrow, an owl and a rattlesnake ; the owls
and the rattlesnakes we did not see, but we saw lots of prairie
dogs (a sort of cross between a guinea-pig and a rabbit and a
rat) sitting about their warrens, yelping at the train, and rub-
bing their faces with their fore-paws. Presently we crossed
Dale Creek Bridge, a wooden trestle bridge, 650 feet long by
120 feet ; the guide book says it presents " a light,.airy, and
graceful appearance"; so it does, but one confoundedly suggestive of sudden death by collapse of bridge, train, and all. The
bridge was unfloored, and unrailed at the sides, and the cars
projected over its edge, and its top was a curve of considerable
quickness for our lengthy cars to traverse.   In the creek over
which it passed was a cattle ranch or farm, for even here, 7,000
feet above sea-level, cattle graze all the year round, and the
wild flowers were wonderful in their loveliness. Some scoundrel
has here defaced the world by painting on every bluff, in letters
some feet long, " Try Drake's Plantation Bitters," while on
others was the odd announcement " X.S., 1860, 10," said to
be a prophecy that in ten years from 1860, the place would be
an " excellent spec.," but it was beyond my comprehension.
More snow fences and snow sheds, and then we arrived at
Sherman, the highest point on.the line, and the highest railway station in the world, 8,242 feet above sea-level, and
" named for General Sherman, the tallest general in the U.S.
army." Here we saw our last of the sage brush, a plant that has
but one good quality—it is a specific for ague. Here too small
cactuses, in pots, were offered for sale, and plenty of beautiful
moss agates, which are very common in the Rocky Mountains.
There is magnificent shooting and fishing to be had at Sherman,
but there is one objection to the enjoyment of the same—the
sportsman has probably to run for dear life from the Red
Indians, who swarm along the railway.   During its construction the workmen had to work armed, and strong garrisons
now are kept in forts right and left of the line. We heard of
one angler who was casting his fly with great success, when a
yell started him, and he bolted to Sherman for dear life, where
he arrived full of arrows as ever was pincushion of pins, but
happy to have his hair still on his head.
    From Sherman we spun down very rapidly to the magic
City of the Plains, or Cheyenne, the largest town between Ogden
and Omaha. The extensive views we had during our descent
can only be compared to those one has at sea, substituting

rolling grassy slopes for rolling green waves. Cheyenne, in 1867, had but one house; shortly after that it had 6,000 inhabitants, and was rich in gambling hells and dance houses; it is now an orderly and well-governed town—thanks to a vigilance committee, who swung a lot of rowdies to the end of ropes from convenient elevations. Its population diminished when the railway was opened west of it, and its freighting trade so done away with. Now it is the Junction of the Union Pacific Railway, with a line that goes southward through Kansas. Cheyenne is a thorough western city, exactly like (as I have before said) to Epsom Downs, ready for the Derby; its concomitants are un-Derby-like, such as its rough-bearded miners, its *greasers*, or half-breds in Mexican sombreros (huge flapping hats), its Indians, its mustangs, its mules, and its huge tilted waggons, ready to start for the wildest journeys. From Cheyenne we descended through magnificent grazing country to a hut, which was, in the old freighting days, the populous town of Julesberg, famed as " the wickedest town in the west," where a man was said to be murdered daily. The wickedness and lawlessness of these ephemeral towns that sprang up at the temporary termini of the railway was beyond conception. Gamblers, rowdies, and scallawags, accursed these places by their presence, and throve on the hard-working but rough teamsters and railway men. To die in a bed was the exception. One of these towns boasts a cemetery in which the only buried person that died a natural death is a prostitute who poisoned herself: the rope or the bullet did for all others. This evil at last cured itself: Judge Lynch was called in, or the quiet inhabitants got Henry rifles (as at Bear Lake City) and file-fired on the gamblers, roughs, and scallawags, for fifteen minutes; the trestle-bridges on the line were found to make excellent gallowses, and we passed over one which was notorious for the aid it had given civilization: some twenty-four gentlemen having been hung up to it at once. Julesberg commemorates the name of an unfortunate half-caste, one Jules Berg, who had a difficulty, or shooting match, with one Jack Slade, a scoundrel who was said to have committed 13 murders. Jack's friends decoyed Jules into a ranch, tied him to a post, and sent for Jack. Jack on arrival took twenty-three pistol shots at the wretched man, retiring to the house for a drink after each shot, cursing horribly, as only western men can curse. He killed his victim at the 23rd shot, cut off his ears, and pocketed them;

for long he used to exhibit his horrible trophies in the drinking
saloons at Denver, until at last retribution overtook him, and
he was interviewed by Judge Lynch, and died in his shoes at
the end of a rope.　Julesberg station is but a few yards outside
of the boundary of Colorado; several American ladies would
try to run across the line, and there was a very pretty race back
at the word "All aboard."

The last portion of our journey to Omaha was very monotonous, being over the prairies of the River Platte, a stream
nigh a mile broad, and less than six inches deep, with a
quicksand bottom, a most terrible puzzler in the old days to
the waggon trains.　The prairies themselves consist of leagues
upon leagues of undulating meadow land, sometimes, and
generally on the Platte, as level as a bowling green, and sometimes broken up by considerable ridges or valleys : nearly
always, to the eye, as boundless as the sea.　Hostile Indians,
irate at the intrusion of white men on their hunting ground,
used to make the passage of the Platte prairies dangerous ; by
force, _i. e._, U.S. garrisons, and by kindness, _i. e._, blankets and
prog, they are now kept tolerably quiet.　We saw a tribe of
500 Pawnees crossing these prairies on their annual buffalo
hunt.　They were very different specimens of humanity to the
miserable Utes we saw in California ; they were fine, tall men,
all mounted on mustangs, or thorough-bred looking, wiry
ponies, and in their gay red blankets much resembled a
regiment of yeomanry gathering on parade.　A close view
somewhat destroyed the illusion, for to feathers and mocassins
and the due war paint some had added an old wide-a-wake, an
umbrella, or a poke bonnet, according to sex ; but they had
tomahawks (made in Birmingham), aye, and revolvers, and
spears, and guns, and _scalps_ of human hair hanging to their
mocassins.　We were not lucky enough to see any buffalo,
though they are common enough ; on the Kansas Pacific
Railway, a little south of us, the trains are sometimes stopped
by enormous herds of them crossing the line, and a friend of
mine shot several outside Kansas city with a revolver.　At
some of the outlying United States garrisons it is a standing
order that the soldiers are not to shoot buffalo _on the parade
ground_.

Crossing these ocean-like prairies, we saw a tremendous
thunder storm, exactly like a storm at sea ; great fireballs
rolling round the horizon.　Near Omaha we saw magnificent

fire flies, and in a pool by the line spied snapping-turtle swimming about.

At Omaha the Union Pacific Railway ended ; we changed cars, crossed the "mighty" but muddy Missouri, on a most skeleton iron bridge of great height, to Council Bluffs, and there took the Missouri, Burlington, and Chicago Railway to the latter place. We dined in a restaurant car, slept in the train, crossed the Mississippi river at daybreak, and arrived at Chicago at six on Saturday, having left Salt Lake City early on Wednesday morning and railed continually the whole time. The country after leaving Council Bluffs was very different to any we had seen,—more cultivated, more woods, rather copses and thick underwood than forests, more towns, and more inhabitants. And such inhabitants : they swarmed at every station to stare at the Japanese, sunburnt lads in vast straw hats and flannel shirts, yet without the wild aspect of the West, and sunburnt lasses in homespun finery.

Of all places in the world that ever I have seen, Heaven forfend that I should ever again see or hear Chicago. It is the noisiest place in the world ; beats out-and-out that Deanery at Carlisle of which Dr. Close complains so much. The town is an enormous railway centre, a regular Clapham junction ; the lines run through the streets everywhere ; the locomotives don't whistle, Dr. Dean, but each has a big brass bell a foot high, which the stoker tolls industriously as the machine moves. There must be in Chicago some hundreds of these great bells clanging perpetually, day and night. Chicago is also permeated with canals, on which ply numbers of tug boats, and these whistle more than all the Caledonian loco-motives put together. Why a town of any pretensions to civilization stands such diabolical noises I can't say ; there is in America little real liberty ; if a big company or two choose to make life a burden, Americans submit in the most slavish manner. Our hotel, too, was not a happy selection : it had *hoppers* and *crawlers*, and the brass ticket system was carried to a most abominable extreme—not a meal, not even a bath could be got without first applying to an official for a brass cheque. The hotel was very full : why the people were there I can't say, but most of them did nothing else than sit and look out of the hall windows with their feet and noses on a level. Chicago now resembles one vast builder's yard : there are acres of ruins, out of which are rising enormous buildings

G

of the modern ornate warehouse style of architecture. Here one comes on a bran-new copy of an Italian palace (a dry-goods store), or of a Greek temple (a grain warehouse), standing on the edge of a black and charred gulf, hideous with unromantic ruins. Chicago has unbounded credit in the money market, and to that is to be attributed the pace at which she is being rebuilt; cynics notice that the theatres rise much faster than the churches. The freaks of the fire have been in places very singular; one once gigantic hotel is utterly annihilated, except a very lofty and slender arch: the Townhall, a new and noble building, weathered the storm, but the whole of the stone has scaled from the heat, giving the edifice a most foully diseased appearance. A sewing-machine shop exhibited a curiously fried sewing machine or two in its window, and we saw many other relics of the fire for sale; the entire contents of a pantry had been fused together, including a dinner and breakfast service, some tumblers, and some tin tacks; this trifling relic, over 6 feet long, was offered cheap, at a dollar; in another place I saw a quantity of chimney ornaments and a pistol fused into one.

We stayed at Chicago over a Sunday, and gladly left it on Monday morning, convinced that however good a place for money-making it may be, it must be an awfully disagreeable place, one that would, to live in, soon make one lunatic. Our route was by the Michigan Central and Grand Trunk Railways, the latter, the Grand Trunk of Canada, being the worst railway in the world. From Chicago a vast number of railways run to the chief eastern cities of the United States; each of these railways touts for custom by issuing pamphlets and maps; a comparison of these maps reveals some odd geographical discrepancies; each railway on its own map (utilizing Euclid's famous axiom) draws a broad straight line from terminus to terminus that represents its own line, while faint, devious, and meandering curves represent its rivals.

I don't recollect much of the journey on the Michigan Central and Grand Trunk; I think I slept all day to make up for that sleep of which I had been deprived by the locomotives and steamtugs, the hoppers and crawlers of Chicago. Towards evening I awoke, and weakly gave a stout female party some information as to her route; then I slumbered once more. Presently I awoke: there stood over me the stout female party and a young woman from Boston. "Stranger," said the stout one, " me and this young woman from Boston are going your way; we'll cling to you, and you can help us." They did cling to me, and I did help them whether I liked or no. I had to put them on a steamboat (assisted by my friend, who took the young woman from Boston); pass their luggage and my own through the Canadian customs; and secure them places in a sleeping car. They selected places opposite to mine, that I might not escape in the dark; the stout woman got up early in the morning, to further prevent my escape, and sat and watched me wash in the rotunda. I had to arm her up and down Toronto from 5 a.m. to 7 a.m., while waiting for the steamer to Niagara. She was more fussy over her box than the oldest and wealthiest godmother that ever mortal man conceived, and I had to lug her and her box to Niagara, where we parted. She wished me to go and stay with her at her son-in-law's: I didn't go, but I felt for him.

ACROSS A CONTINENT.

(Continued.)

August, 1872.

I was last heard of by my readers arriving at Niagara in company with a stout old lady. We crossed Lake Ontario from Toronto in a steamboat, went up the Niagara River between the Forts Niagara (American) and Massasauga or Missisauga (Canadian), which lie so close that on stilly nights the sentry's "All well" can be heard from one to the other. We landed at Lewiston, on the American side, ran up to Niagara by a short railway on the high ridge overlooking the Niagara River, and then, dropping the stout party, crossed in a 'bus to the Canadian side, to the Clifton Hotel, a place so grand as to keep a custom-house officer (a decayed-looking one, but still a full-blown official) of their own, permanently on duty on the hotel steps, thus saving a stoppage to examine luggage at the frontier, *i. e.*, the suspension bridge.

Two points struck me on arrival at Niagara with great gratification : I had heard much of the *roar of the falling waters*, and of the *masses of spray that rose from them :* in neither was I disappointed : I heard the roar miles away, and the wind being in a particular quarter, I was perfectly drenched and chilled to the bone by the spray at my hotel door, more than a mile from the falls. In the falls I was for a moment disappointed, but that soon passed away : most people are a little disappointed at first. The waters fall into a gorge, and thus one's first view is from above : one cannot estimate the height, which is dwarfed by the breadth of the falls. It has been suggested that a visitor should be blindfolded, and never unbind his eyes till in the ferry-boat below the Great or Canadian Fall. There are two falls at Niagara ; the Great Canadian, or Horse Shoe Fall, is 1,900 feet across, with a drop of 158 feet, and stretches from Canadian to American territory. The Smaller, or American Fall, is 900 feet across, with a drop of 164 feet, and is wholly on American soil :

it is formed by a branch of the river, which, deviating from the main body, curves round, so as to fall in at right angles almost to the great fall. I ought to describe Niagara : I can't. Some prosaical fellows have calculated the number of cubic feet of water that goes over the Horse Shoe Fall per minute. I don't care to know that. A man who could look into the exquisite green of the tumbling-over water, into the foam boiling up and drifting away in snow clouds, or into the many unexpectedly-placed rainbows or spraybows that give such charms to the falls, and who could calculate, must be an educated pig, and nothing more ; the ever-ceaseless roll-over of water looks like eternity, and the ever-seething cauldrons of foam look like the entrance to Gehenna itself.

Man has at Niagara done his best to vulgarize nature, but has hardly succeeded. Gigantic hotels, where life goes on as at Scarborough or Harrogate, tower to heaven on both the Canadian and American sides. Touts for museums dog one's steps, and invite one to inspect grizzly bears, bird skins, fans, and Indian work ; while hack-carriages race after any sight-seer on foot. Worst of all, photographers rush out at every corner, almost imploring one to be photographed with the immortal falls as a background. Every convenience is supplied for sight-seeing at a charge of one or two dollars ; bridges and carriage-roads conduct to the islands between the falls, and to the tower which projects over the Great Fall ; hoists and perpendicular railways facilitate the descent to and ascent from the bottom of the falls ; guides and dresses are ready for all foolish enough to go behind the falling waters, a damp and chilling expedition, curious, but little else. It was really a comfort to get away from these mean contrivances, from the perpetual pic-nic and sight-seeing parties, and to find a secluded place from which to gaze at the rushing waters : one might really gaze for ever, and never be satiated, so sublime, so majestic, so unceasingly powerful is the never-ending tumbling of the waters.

The hotel on the Canadian side is the best, as it possesses a full view of the falls ; the American side is the sight-seeing side ; there you can, for a dollar, be free of the islands between the falls, connected with one another and the American land by numerous bridges ; there you can wander about the drives and paths, gaze from the tower down the Great Fall, take refreshment at the pagoda, or even, for a consideration, have a rod and line

and fish ; there too, on the American side, you can drive to the
Whirlpool Rapids and the Whirlpool, paying to see each a dollar
or half a dollar.   On the Canadian or English side all is free ;
it must strike an English Radical as odd, that when he visits
Niagara he cannot see it from the American side without dis-
bursing several dollars, while on the English side, under English
land laws, he pays nothing.   Beyond the falls and the river
there is little else to see at Niagara.   I drove to the battle field
of Lundy Lane, where an enterprising speculator induced me
to climb a tower for the view.   " The veteran on the summit
will point out the objects of interest."   The veteran on the
summit turned out to be a very old, decayed man, a sort of
badly preserved street preacher to look at, who had fought
against the British in 1812.   The fight was rather an odd one
as he described it ; it was fought mainly by moonlight with
the bayonet.   According to the rules of war the Yankees won ;
they outflanked the British, took their guns, and drove them
off the field.   The anomalous British declined to obey the rules
of war, and when the sun rose they were found in their original
position, in repossession of their guns, and with a fine stomach
for fresh fighting, which Yank had not.

In the bar at Niagara I recognized a gentleman whom I had
only seen once before, on the deck of a passing ship, a thousand
miles from land.   My travelling companion left Niagara the
day before I did, intending to meet me at Kingston ; and here
commenced a series of travelling misfortunes which lasted until
we reached Montreal.   My new friend agreed to go with me,
but we were hurried into different 'buses, sent different routes,
and only met by accident again at Toronto.   I retraced my
steps, by rail to Lewiston, and by boat to Toronto, where I found
the boat and rail did not connect, and nothing to be heard of
either of my friends : one had all my baggage, but I had all
his money.   At Toronto I had perforce to stay all night.
Next morning I found my 1000-miles-from-land friend, who
had equally missed the train, and had fared worse than I, for
he had got to an hotel full of jubilant Orangemen, and had no
sleep, his bed a mattress in a coffee-room, 'mid thirty more.
We had a long and weary day's journey to Kingston, where we
parted—weary, for the cars and everything on the Grand Trunk
Railway are so bad.   We travelled mainly along the shores of Lake
Ontario, through Canadian woods and clearings : the woods are
thick in this part, but of trees of no great size ; it must be a

heart-breaking job to clear a Canadian wood for pasture; so thick are the trees, that a new clearing, with the stumps undrawn, looks like an inverted harrow or an old hair-brush. There is little or no game in these woods. The lumber trade is carried on here to a great extent; we crossed one river, the Mara (if I rightly recollect the name), as big as the Eden at Carlisle or the Severn at Shrewsbury, completely concealed by floating deals; at several places we passed whole acres covered with stacks of cordwood for consumption in the locomotives. We saw too many quaint Canadian villages with queer ugly churches, which had roofs and spires of glittering zinc or tin. I was precious glad to arrive at Kingston; there I left my 1000-miles-from-land friend, and proceeded to search for my other lost friend who had been with me all along from England: the luggage I soon found, but he did not turn up until late. Meanwhile, I wandered about Kingston, which is a pretty place on Lake Ontario, with large fortifications, now denuded of troops: during the day I was highly amused by the number of different characters I involuntarily was taken for: first an old soldier insisted he had served under me; as he did not ask for coin or beer, I dare say he thought so; but I never had the honour of commanding him or any other soldier. Next a telegram was handed to me, bearing my name, but no initials; I tore it open, and found it related to monkeys, and that the agent of the Transatlantic Wombwell bore my name; thirdly, while presiding over our huge joint pile of baggage, I was taken for a bagman, and offered a room to show my samples in. The fact of our having between us four leather portmanteaus always looked odd to American or Canadian eyes; they always use enormous trunks made of painted wood, hooped, bound, cornered, and garnished with iron and brass, and often mounted on small wheels for convenience of moving. The size and number of these an American travels with is amazing; he has either a small hand valise, or else he has four or five of these "Saratoga trunks," standing two and a half to three feet high. We left Kingston early on a Saturday morning, and shall always retain a kindly recollection of the hospitality we received at the hands of some friends, and an unkind one of the inhospitality of the inn. The inn was bad, and was full: I slept in an empty house apart from help, was ill, could get no hot water; they would not light a fire after dinner on any account to boil

some ; finally, they turned six or eight of us out for the steamboat at four in the morning without even a cup of coffee ; the
landlord said he could not have his house disturbed at that
hour by cooking and bother ; I suppose during the travelling
season at least six or eight people left his house daily at that
hour ; he was called captain. On board the steamboat there
were 300 passengers, and seats for 150 ; the scramble for
grub was awful ; people seized seats at table at 5 a.m. and sat
on them not daring to move until 8 a.m. People like ourselves,
who were not up to this move, starved for an hour or two more,
until a second and third breakfast, which had to be supplied.
One of these breakfasts was enlivened by a scene : a traveller
said his eggs were stale, whereon a steward promptly called
him a liar, and a row ensued ; the captain and two stewards
set upon the man who objected to stale eggs, and he emerged
from the *fracas* with a considerably cut face ; it was a most
disgraceful affair. Meanwhile we were running through the
famous Thousand Isles of the St. Lawrence, so called because
there are 1800 of them, between which the channel winds in
the most intricate manner. They are famous for their beauty,
but disappointed us ; they sadly want background ; the banks
of the river are quite flat, and thus the scenery appears tame.
These islands are favourite resorts for pic-nics and fishing parties, who camp out on them ; and we passed several pleasure
encampments, at one of which General Grant was staying.
When clear of the Thousand Isles, the scenery grew decidedly
tame, but we had the pleasure of shooting several rapids,
including the famous Long Sault Rapids, some miles long. I
will here quote a little guide book. " The rapids of the Long
Sault rush along at the rate of something like twenty miles an
hour. When the vessel enters within their influence, the steam
is shut off, and she is carried onward by the force of the stream
alone. The surging waters present all the angry appearance of
the ocean in a storm ; the noble boat strains and labours ; but,
unlike the ordinary pitching and tossing at sea, this going down
hill by water produces a highly novel sensation, and is, in fact,
a service of some danger, the imminence of which is enhanced
to the imagination by the tremendous roar of the headlong
boiling current. Great nerve and force and precision are here
required in piloting, so as to keep the vessel's head straight
with the course of the rapid ; for if she diverged in the least,
presenting her side to the current, or ' broached to,' as the

nautical phrase is, she would instantly be capsized and sub-
merged." The reality is not quite up to the guide book, but
accidents do happen, and we saw a fine steamboat a wreck in
one rapid we shot down. The scoundrelly steamboat company
turned us all on shore at a place called Prescott, and kept us
there some four hours without refreshment, and then sent us on
in a slow and inferior boat, on which there was the same fight
for meals. At dark they stopped at St. Ann's, made us change
to another inferior boat, and stopped for the night. The ladies
got cabins in one or other boat, and the gentlemen slept on the
floor. I was lucky, for when all the ship's planks were full I
interviewed a steward, and for a consideration got his bed; I
also interviewed a cook boy, and got a pint basin of hot water,
which I took to the bar, and modified with O. D. V., to the
disgust and envy of the other passengers, for the officials refused
hot water, and that pint cost me two shillings. At 3 a.m. they
roused us all up, and declined to give us breakfast on board the
boat, because nine o'clock was the breakfast hour, prior to which
time they turned us on shore, ten miles from Montreal, thus
doing us out of the shooting the Lachine Rapid, the great lion
of the trip, and out of breakfast. We were taken to Montreal
in omnibuses, one of which was upset, and we who were not
upset arrived there at 10 a.m. on Sunday morning, instead of
the company's advertised time, Saturday, 6 p.m. How the
ladies managed I don't know, but they were all roused up at
3 a.m., and had nothing to eat or drink until after 10 a.m. An
indignation meeting was held on the steamboat before leaving,
an American judge in the chair; a committee was appointed,
ferocious speeches made, and resolutions passed, one of which
I moved in a much applauded speech, viz., that a deputation
should wait on the captain and ask him to give us something
to eat; the brute flatly refused. I was never so eloquent in my
life before; but *facit indignatio versum*, or hunger makes one
speak. Finally, a series of very strong resolutions were penned,
and signed by some fifty of us, on behalf of 300 starved and
ill-treated passengers, and sent to the chief American and
Canadian papers : I hope seriously that their publication may
by now have ruined the company. I believe the captain got
his dismissal for the egg *fracas*.

Montreal is a quaint French-Canadian town, with a very fine
Roman Catholic Cathedral, and a very wonderful tubular railway bridge, a mile and a quarter long, over the St. Lawrence.

Quaintest of all the quaint things we saw there are the carriages, the like of which I have never seen out of Turkey; high-hung vehicles on C-springs, gaudy with gold, silver, and brass, with large glass windows, and with landscapes painted on the panels, which were generally of a claret colour; the lamps were wonderful, each some two feet of polished metal and glass. It is curious to find precisely similar carriages in Constantinople and in Montreal. One other thing have I noticed to go nigh round the world, and that is the Eastern saddle; the Moors took it to Spain, and the Spaniards to Mexico, and it is now prevalent all over America, both North and South. I may mention that at Montreal I saw the greediest man in the world, a Yankee. At the *table d'hôte* we dined at tables for sixteen; this Yankee seized the salad for the whole sixteen, held it at his side, and swallowed it all, utterly heedless of the waiter's complaints. I took care he should overhear a hope "that he would not eat himself ill," but he only glared viciously.

ACROSS A CONTINENT.

(Concluded.)

August, 1872.

I left Montreal early on a Tuesday morning, *solus*, for at that place I parted from the companion who had travelled with me from England, and who remained to visit some Canadian friends. A short railway journey brought me to the head of Lake Champlain, and again into American territory. Lake Champlain, and its neighbour, Lake George, in olden days formed the readiest passage from Canada to the State of New York : thus it happens that there is hardly a bay or a promontory that has not been the scene of some famous fight between French and Indians, between English and French, or finally between English and Americans. The whole scenery is redolent of famous memories—the memories of Munro, of Montcalm, of Abercrombie, of Amherst, of Putnam, of Rogers the Ranger, and of many a long score of those invested with historic renown, and whose deeds read like those of the heroes of romance. Nor is the interest of fictitious romance lacking, for on these lakes Cooper laid the scenes of his best novels. Time has changed all this ; Ticonderoga Fort is now a grass-grown ruin ; Crown Point Fort is no more, and Fort William Henry exists only as a fashionable hotel ; the transport *bateaux* and armed sloops of Munro and Montcalm may still occasionally be seen, but they are sunk fathoms deep in the clear lake waters, and the only invaders are countless herds of American and Canadian tourists, armed with portentous guide books, and laden with the most marvellous and mightiest of Saratoga trunks.

In common with many a score of tourists, I embarked on the *Adirondack* steamer, and then first learnt what American steamboat travelling is like. Larger boats than the *Adirondack* I had, perhaps, seen in San Francisco Bay—a more sumptuous one never. She was of vast height : in the hull just above the water level, was a fine dining saloon ; on the deck above that were ladies' saloons, engine rooms, barber's shop, drinking bar, and luggage rooms, all of lofty size and proportions : above that again came a magnificent saloon extending the whole length of the vessel, with sleeping cabins all round, and with open-air lounging decks fore and aft : above all this, " a Pelion on Ossa piled," towered the pilot house, and a portion of the great walking beam engine. The whole construction was as fine and gay as paint, mirrors, pianos, sofas, armchairs, marble tables, carpets, and the upholster's art could make it; the engines were polished and brass-worked to the nines, and the very axes that hung with the lifebuoys were gilded. Meals too were well and comfortably served, without a scramble, or the necessity of sitting down to table an hour or two beforehand. The Americans are justly proud of their boats, and many an American who had heard my hunger-eloquent oration on the Canadian boat, called my attention to the contrast. " Yes, sir, this is steamboat travelling." These huge, top-heavy, but luxurious boats are, however, only safe in inland waters, such waters as England does not possess ; and, therefore, we at home must yield to America the palm in this mode of travelling.

Lake Champlain is about 150 miles long, and lies between the wild and yet unexplored Adirondack mountains on one hand, and the well-cultivated and well-wooded farms of Vermont on the other. The scenery is most lovely, especially at the north end, where the breadth is some thirteen miles, and the water clear as crystal, and set with charming and picturesque islands. With a strange perversity, man has selected the most lovely spots—Ticonderoga, Crown Point, Valcour Isle, and Plattsburgh—as the scenes of some of the bloodiest actions ever fought or done ; the latter two places being the scenes of severe naval actions between the English and American fresh-water fleets ; Crown Point being replete with thrilling interest, as once the rallying-point of the red savages who devastated the farms of New England ; while the ground round Ticonderoga is perfectly soaked with the truest and best of British and French blood. Little but a few mounds and crumbling walls now remain of the once-famous fort, but a traveller told me that twenty-five years ago he had there picked up English regimental buttons, flints, and bits of firelocks. At Ticonderoga most tourists leave Lake Champlain for Lake George, a *portage* or land journey of eight miles, every inch of which is of blood-stained memory. I continued my route down Lake Champlain. Although so near the most civilized part of the States, the

Adirondacks are but little explored; their extensive forests and hills shelter no end of game, both large and small, and many adventurous spirits spend their annual holiday in wild life in the Adirondacks. A Mr. Murray, a clergyman in New York, wrote a most charming book, giving an account of his holidays in the Adirondacks. The book took: every one was bit, and all the belles from Saratoga set off with their boxes, thinking it would be but a pic-nic. People so unfit to camp out were of course sold; they denounced Mr. Murray and his book in all the New York papers, but were themselves laughed at and christened "Murray fools." On the Vermont side of the lake the scenery is less wild, but still lovely : here are some of the finest farms in the States, while vast maple woods ornament the scenery, and bring profit to the farmer's pocket, for they provide him with a periodical harvest of maple sugar. , We touched at Burlington, in Vermont, a great centre of the lumber trade ; a pretty place, where, if one was very young and innocent, and had never "heard the chimes at midnight," one might fancy one would like to live " far from the busy hum of men," except lumbermen, who, however, hum most horribly in the cursing and swearing line.

The churches in Vermont are the ugliest erections I ever saw ; little square boxes, erected long ago, with cotton-factory windows, a low, squat, square tower, with thereon a shiny tin or zinc extinguisher, and shiny tin or zinc roofs. Towards the southern end Lake Champlain grows very narrow, and the steamer glides along within a few feet of overhanging cliffs, which lie on the east side; while on the west are the so-called " Drowned Lands," consisting of swamp and marsh. The boat stopped at Whitehall ; thence the rail, or, as an American would say, the cars, carried me through fashionable and extravagant Saratoga, the most dissipated and money-spending watering-place in the States, to Albany, where I found my hotel was called " The Stanwix Hall."

Why Stanwix Hall ? I cried, and was told it occupied the site of an old building of that name pulled down long ago. Then who was Stanwix ? None could tell but I who asked. General John Stanwix, M.P. for Carlisle from 1746 to 1760, and for Appleby from 1760 to 1766, served from 1754 to 1759 in America as colonel of the first battalion of Royal Americans, and there lost his son, a captain in that regiment. This hotel at Albany occupies probably the site of the general's house, while he lay in winter quarters in Albany City. A fort in the Mohawk country, not far from Albany, also once bore his name, but became famous in the Revolutionary war as Fort Schuyler. Stanwix Hall, in Albany City, State of New York, was certainly an odd and unexpected reminiscence of home and the village of that name near Carlisle to come across.

From Albany I journeyed next day in the *Chauncey Vibbart* down the Hudson River to New York. The *Chauncey Vibbart* was one of the line of boats owned by the notorious Jem Fisk, and was bigger, finer, and gayer, than the *Adirondack*, a perfect floating palace, and on board they gave me the very best dinner, the best cooked and best served, that I tasted in the States. The Hudson River is said to resemble the Rhine: it does not, except that there are steamboats (of a very dissimilar kind) on both. .The scenery, though un-Rhine like, is fine, but I saw it on a pouring wet day, which much marred its appearance. The company was amusing: we had a solemn and queerly-clad party of Shakers, who contrasted oddly with the merry pic-nic parties on board: disappointed by the rain of their trip on shore, these parties sung, romped, played round games, and laughed on board the boat without restraint. I noticed that to none of these pic-nic parties, and there were several, was the incumbrance of a *chaperone* attached, or if one was present, she was remarkable for her youth.

We arrived at New York late in the evening, and I took myself to the Fifth Avenue Hotel. I expected to see wonders in New York; I hardly expected to see a railway train running in the air, but I did. A single row of stout piles carried cross girders, the ends of which were connected by longitudinal beams; on this fragile erection was running a passenger car and a small locomotive at the level of the first-floor windows. Tramways run everywhere in New York; not a street or avenue but what is traversed by one, and rendered almost fatal to the springs of private vehicles. By these trams, and by omnibuses, locomotion in New York is cheaper than anywhere else in the world, provided you stick to the trams and the 'buses; once off them it is ruin. It cost me twelve shillings for an hour's drive with luggage in a cab, and that was the correct fare. New York is laid out in a series of parallel avenues, numbered from one to eight or more; these are crossed at right angles by parallel streets, numbered from one to nearly forty, and the famous Broadway runs obliquely through the whole lot. I was not much charmed with New York, except with the beautiful Central Park, which seems to combine in itself the excellencies and charms of the best London and Parisian parks. Everything in New York is on a vast scale; I was Number 256 in my hotel, and ascended to my room in a perpendicular railway. The bars, the reading and feeding rooms in the hotel were vast, magnificent, but they lacked comfort and quiet. Then, too, in these big hotels one must go by rule ; meals between certain hours, and then only. It simplifies bookkeeping : they charge by the day, and fraction of a day. When you go away, you ask the hotel clerk "what's to pay;" and he turns up a ledger, notes hour of your arrival and departure, so many days and such a fraction, so many dollars ; no bill, that is all. The Americans don't, as a rule, drink at meals, but have drinks at the hotel bar, and pay on the nail. I have mentioned before that New York is badly, atrociously paved ; it is also ill lighted at night. With all the ingenuity of Americans, they somehow fail in many things ; they invented and started street trams ; every town in the States has them, and yet they do not run so smooth as ours, and most certainly they seriously impede and endanger by their high rails all private traffic in a way that would not be allowed in England. It is thus with many things Americans have invented ; we have improved their inventions. The buildings in New York are fine, but uninteresting : Mr. A. T. Stewart's drygoods store in Broadway, of white stone, is an enormous pile, while his private house, of white marble, in Fifth Avenue, is one of the sights of the place.

I left New York in a White Star steamer, *The Republic*, one of the finest ocean boats afloat, replete with comfort and luxury ; electric bells and water laid on in every cabin ; fresh fish for dinner the whole voyage, and occasionally real turtle soup. My main objection to the boat was, that so crowded were her decks with cabins, and houses, and smoking rooms, that one had not that fine, clear sweep of unincumbered deck which much sets off a vessel's appearance. The voyage was monotonously slow; the only excitement was the appearance of a raft with three men on it, but closer view showed the supposed shipwrecked mariners to be gulls. We arrived at Liverpool on the 13th August, and I was soon home, having travelled nigh 40,000 miles since I left it.

NOTES ON THE UNITED STATES.

There is a tone about everything Americans say and do essentially different from that prevalent in England, but a tone with which penny papers are gradually familiarizing England. This tone is of a feverish and excited kind, prone to attach great importance to little things (such as Sergeant Bates and his comical tour); prone to bluster, to exaggeration, and to spread-eagleism, and unrestrained in America by certain influences which have in England, as yet, great weight, and to which I shall presently allude. Charles Dickens in 1868 well writes of America:—"I see great changes for the better socially; politically, none; England governed by the Marylebone vestry and the penny papers, and England as she would be after years of such governing, that is what I make of that." Except the first sentence, Dickens never penned truer words: we can see it in the attorney-like spirit in which the Alabama claims were urged, and in the corruption prevalent among American state officials, not unlike the scandal a short time ago afloat about certain London vestries. That in 1868 Dickens saw "changes socially for the better" is astounding: perhaps a few words on America, socially and politically, and on the restraining influences alluded to before, may interest some.

And first of the restraining influences: Mr. Buckle in his History of Civilization says that nowhere in the world is there so much learning and refinement locked up and rendered useless as in America. This is so: the men of learning and refinement stand apart from public business, and thus it gets into the hands of an order of men who are at once unscrupulous and ambitious, keen in the race after wealth and power. The possessors of wealth and power thus become the idols of American society, and can do no wrong; are in fact utterly above the law. Now, in England, mere wealth cannot confer the distinction it does in America; mere wealth in England is dimmed by such things as the prestige of a long line of ancestors, of great landed estates, or of a title. As a rule, the enjoyment of any one of these advantages binds its possessor down to a certain decency of conduct and decorum of manners ; as in England those who are accumulating wealth aim at being incorporated into, and associating with, the class or classes possessing such prestige, the *novi homines* imitate (perhaps insensibly to themselves) the decency and decorum we have just alluded to. Thus it happens that the class of men who run rampant in New York are almost impossible in London ; and in this way our House of Lords, our titled and untitled aristocracy and squirearchy, keep us from social and political evils which flourish in America, with its herds of *novi homines*, unrestrained by the example of a refined class, with which they hope to be ultimately, they or their sons, incorporated. Our English habit of accumulating for our posterity, too, has a similar tendency : a wealthy *noveau riche* in England contemplates founding a family ; with that view he sends his lads to Eton and Christ Church, and the lads cannot fail to acquire some polish, some " *emollitment*" of their "*mores*" rendering them less " *feros* ;" but the Yankee accumulates for himself, and spends freely ; his lads must do as their father did, fight for themselves ; thus at sixteen or so, they start in trade with but little education beyond a commercial one. Besides the want of refinement (and by refinement we don't mean mere superficial polish, but more—kindliness and courtesy to all) springing from this cause, there is another curious result —a universal credulity, arising, I believe, from want of sound and logical education, which, combined with the American excitable temperament, makes America the happy hunting-ground not only of spiritualists, but of patent-medicine sellers, conjurors, astrologers, and fortune-tellers. Everywhere are these people's brass plates to be seen, in every newspaper their advertisements are prominent, and everything about them indicates that they drive a flourishing trade, not alone among the poor and most ignorant, but among the wealthy and better classes. This want of education and this excitable temperament leads to another trait in the American character, a love of sensational show, and an overwhelming idea of their own grandeur, which Dickens well hits off in the following passage : " They seem to take it ill that I don't stagger on to the platform overpowered by the spectacle before me and the national greatness. They are all so accustomed to do things with a flourish of trumpets, that the notion of my coming in to read without somebody first flying in and delivering an oration about me, and flying down again and leading me in, seems unaccountable." This want of refinement and of education is, too, a probable cause of the irreverence with which the Americans treat and speak of religious matters : American anecdotes in plenty, where the point arises from a Biblical joke, will occur to my readers; but I was astounded one Monday morning to find a Chicago paper reporting the Sunday sermons in this style—" Dr. —— down on the old devil again. His reverence preached from such-and-such a text, and so on."

If my readers have followed me thus far, they will see that I have ventured to attribute the overweening power of mere wealth in America, the vestry-like statesmanship, the want of higher refinement, the credulity, and the love of sensationalism to the want of a general high standard of education, and to the want of a general high standard of decency of conduct·and of decorum of manners. It is my belief that in England our institutions, our House of Lords, our titled and untitled aristocracy, the *prestige* we accord to a long line of ancestry, do conduce to such education, and to such decency of conduct, and to such decorum of manners in the higher classes, and also in those who wish to rise into such higher classes. I believe that thus great benefit extends throughout the whole nation, extending down to the humblest artisan or labourer in it. Some people may deny that these things do a nation any good, but I will try and prove from American instances that their absence does harm. Let us have a look, then, at some of the social peculiarities of New York. We in England are not famed for our hospitality or attention to foreign potentates and swells, but still the people who represent to them " our prominent" citizens are not such as we need be ashamed of. Now, in New York one of the most forward in welcoming and entertaining the Russian Grand Duke Alexis was the notorious James Fisk, a man who stepped almost from out a police court, where he had been on a squabble with his mistress, to the Duke's side. The whole career of Jim Fisk is one that well merits perusal by the student of American manners. He rose from being a pedlar to being a millionaire, and the manner of his rise is well set out in an amusing little book, entitled " The Life of James Fisk, jun., by Marshall P. Stafford," and published by Polhemus and Pearson, of New York. Space serves us not to give his history. He was the very Napoleon of swindlers, and he rose to great wealth by a long series of successful swindles : once in the possession of wealth, he employed that wealth in some of the most gigantic and daring swindles ever done. In conjunction with Vanderbilt, Drew, and Jay Gould, he carried through the great Erie Railway ring, and the great gold ring, ruining many others to enrich himself and his colleagues. To carry out his schemes he openly defied the law, for his wealth enabled him to bribe and control the very judges, so much so as to be able to send to prison his private enemies on perfectly groundless charges. While he was doing all this, what was the attitude of New York to him? He was the most popular man in New York ; his wealth made him powerful, and his extravagance and dash made him popular ; by maintaining in sumptuous style an Opera House, by driving four-in-hand, and by magnificent entertainments at which *judges* and *statesmen* sat down with Fisk's mistresses, he pandered to the American taste for display and sensationalism. He became notorious for open and flagrant immorality, and yet New York society did not turn away from him ; on the contrary, they made him colonel of a militia regiment that had earned a gallant reputation in the war ; they put him to the front to receive illustrious strangers, and he was even seen on occasions in familiar converse with the President. Such prominence can wealth in New York confer on a flagrant scoundrel ! At last he was shot (a squabble about a courtesan). Well might I be told in Utah " that in America there was no law for the rich, they were above it," and at that time (in July 1872) certain American papers were drawing bitter contrasts between America and England, for in the latter country the law, they said, knew no difference between rich and poor. Fisk is no solitary instance of the unrestrained power wealth gives in America : read this from the *Times* of the day I write on (December 6, 1872): " The last journals from New York contain accounts of the discovery of heavy defalcations on the part of Mr. Sweetzer, the manager of the Atlantic and Great Western Railway, and add that 75,000 dollars had been obtained from him, together with his immediate resignation. The *New York Times* states : ' Mr. Sweetzer is reported to have said that he was not the real culprit, but that others were implicated more deeply than himself. From no statement, however, does it appear that he was not guilty of a deliberate conspiracy to swindle the stockholders of the road, and enrich himself at their expense.' Mr. Sweetzer held a former position on the line under Mr. Jay Gould, and it seems to be believed at New York that, although previously in good repute, he has been, like scores of others, corrupted, not only by the bribes held out, but *by the influence of the social sanction* accorded to the leader of the Erie ring (Jay Gould), and which has this week been shown to exist in undiminished potency, when two among the leading men of the city have come forward to relieve him, when under a criminal charge, with bail to the extent of a million dollars." That is just the point: wealth in America may do what it pleases, break all laws both of God and man in the most open manner, and *social sanction* will be accorded it.

As for Fisk, so great indeed was the power and position he had acquired, that his biographer writes, " The news of his assassination produced a sensation second only to that of President Lincoln, throughout his own land and in Europe. It had a marked effect upon the London Stock Exchange." In another place he writes apologetically of Fisk : " Was he not a legitimate outgrowth of the prevailing morality of New York ? The legal tactics that scandalized the country in his name were not his work, but those of men of the *most eminent professional and social standing, hired for the purpose.* The judicial fiats that robbed many men of their rights and dues were not issued by him, but by *judges whom he found* on the bench of the Supreme Court. If infamous bills passed the Legislature for his special behoof, they passed by the votes of the people's chosen, and were signed by the governors of the State."

When wealth, and wealth alone and unrestrained, is sole monarch, bad times are at hand for those who are poor. That is where the shoe will soon pinch in America. Our old feudal traditions and institutions do still carry with them some idea that protection and kindness is due to those below one; wealth looks on them as mere machines for work.

A point which cannot fail to strike the Englishman in America is the multitude of cheap papers that flourish there, and their difference from the English ones. The American papers are from size and type very unpleasant to read, and I do not believe the average American ever reads one through, or even reads a lengthy article. To get the information into his mind, the following plan is adopted: an article, is split up into paragraphs of six or eight lines, and each paragraph has a heading in capital letters, generally as sensational and attractive as possible, like the posters of an English penny daily. By glancing down these headings, one may get a superficial idea of what the article is about. I believe that a vast number of Americans imbibe their political ideas solely from the sensational headings, which certainly make a news-paper article repulsive to read. The style in which events are reported is curious. When at Chicago I saw my name an-nounced in visitor lists in the papers thus, " General Jones, Judge Dodge, Messrs. Bones, Snooks, &c., are taking their tucker at the Sherman ; the Hon. Senator Doolittle, Messrs. Robinson, Roving Cumbrian, &c., are crowding down the elegant fare provided by the hosts of the Bridge House ; Messrs. Balls, &c., are victualling at the Triermain." This is the latest way of giving a list of the visitors to the leading hotels, and I noticed it at more than at one large town. Another astonishing thing is the minute particulars into which American papers go about individuals. One paper gave a life of Horace Greeley, and commenced with his birth, stating that he was black in the face when that event happened. When he became a candidate for the Presidency, reporters swarmed down to his place at Chapaqua, and gave the most minute particulars of his domestic arrangements, including an account of his daughter, her dress, personal appearance, method of doing her hair, and supposed favoured adorer. The Illustrateds even gave a picture of him at dinner, and mentioned his favourite diet. The Americans have a curious taste for this garbage; an English literary gentleman has just been lecturing in America on Dickens, and his American audience are disappointed because he would not go into the differences between Dickens and his wife. This Paul Pry-ishness easily degenerates into low abuse. In the heat of the Presidential election nothing was too bad to be printed of an opponent; Mr. Gratz Brown (candidate for the Vice-Presidency) was ill ; forthwith the Grant papers an-nounced that he had had a big drink, was drunk for a week. The Greeley papers on the other hand appeared with portraits of Grant and his friends in a beastly state of intoxication. No wonder, that in America men of education and refinement shrink from public business, and from the abuse showered on them and every relation male and female they may have, and from the manner in which their most private doings are pulled into print.

From all that has been said, our readers will not be

surprised to hear of corruption in the Government, and in the
recent Presidential election the main point relied on against
General Grant was the corruption of the Civil Services of the
United States, a thing perhaps little to be wondered at when it
is considered that 60,000 officials change their places with
every new President; thus an official knows that he has but
some four years of sunshine in which to make his hay, and
also that no zeal or ability in his office will secure him a re-
appointment from the next President, who must reward his
own partizans.   Now, although General Grant was by no
means the originator of this system, yet he had put some of
his family in Government places, and had consorted with shady
characters: thus he had become, justly or unjustly, to be regarded as typifying the corruption prevalent in the Civil
Services, and had the Cincinnati Convention nominated Charles
Francis Adams, and not Horace Greeley as his opponent, the
General would have in all probability on that ground alone
been defeated.   This fungus of corruption flourishes most in
out-of-the-way places: thus the salaries of the agents appointed to manage the Indians are very small, but the agents
speedily accumulate immense fortunes by wholesale plunder of
those whom they should protect, and who revenge themselves
by rates and forays, whose suppression costs the United States
a large amount annually.   To take another instance, the post
of the United States Consul-General in Egypt has long been
considered a mere post for plunder, and has been filled by some
very discreditable men; one who recently held it could never
go into society without getting drunk, while the last occupant
was a notorious San Francisco scalliwag, a man universally cut,
but as the nephew of a notorious politician he was appointed
by General Grant to this important post.   Not only did he
plunder, speculate, and sell for hard cash or good wheat every
post in his gift, but he disgraced his country still more; he
went in grand procession, *preceded by his cavasses and by the
American flag*, to the lowest purlieus of Luxor, to see an
exhibition of women dancing naked.   I know this to be a
fact; I heard it frequently commented on by the natives, and
it has been stated in the columns of the *Nation*, the most respectable of all American newspapers.   If the natives of Egypt
think oddly of the Americans, what must the Japanese do?
They applied to the American Government for four or five
Americans as instructors of agriculture, engineering, &c., and

offered £2,000 a-year pay. The authorities at Washington nominated five politicians, who were utterly wanting in the necessary knowledge, and two of whom were confirmed drunkards. These precious nominees went to Japan some time ago, and still draw their pay ; but the Japanese, having discovered their worthlessness, have suspended them from all work or authority. Out of this mass of corruption has sprung a peculiar class—that of " politicians." A traveller on board the s.s. *Republic* described himself as a " politician" by profession. What is that? I asked of an American. " Why when you want to bribe a member of the legislature, or work a job, or do a dirty thing, you employ this fellow." A similar institution was said to be growing up in Victoria when I was in the colony, but public opinion there was likely to squash it in its inception, and bills for that purpose were talked of.

Thus far Americans have in this paper been dealt hardly with : the writer would say that both in the States, in Europe, and in the East he has met with Americans of the greatest refinement and culture, and from many of them he has met with great kindness. There is no more genial or nicer companion than a well-educated American, but then such abstain from public business, and thus to many Englishmen the worst side of the American character alone is visible, that of the rowdy, noisy, pushing, bar-hunting politician and speculator. For the sake of both England and America it is much to be regretted that such is the case.

I cannot help thinking that many English Radicals would derive much benefit from a tour through the United States of America, and that probably they would return home with a much greater admiration for the institutions of their own country than they had when they first left England. Indeed, I have seen in more than one instance an almost total cure effected, and Philo-American Radicals return home from a visit to New York good High Church and State Tories. In the first place a Radical would soon learn that there is no analogy between England and America in respect of land. Land is so plentiful in America that it is a mere drug, and American institutions do not cultivate that sentiment for the land, or rather for particular lands, which makes a Briton cling so to the estate his fathers owned or cultivated. On the contrary, an American farmer will move off west when his farm is overworked, rather than manure it, and will take up a new location, virgin soil, which will grow wheat without any manuring or expense.   On the line of the Trans-Continental Railway lie thousands of acres of prairie land, yet untouched, but ready to grow wheat or graze cattle to perfection; no timber to be cleared, or stones to be grubbed up.   Homesteads here are to be had for ten years' purchase, and the purchase money can be left on mortgage on easy terms.   Between America, with her millions of acres of rich, unoccupied lands, and England, with her utter lack of such, there can be no fair analogy; the clamourers for alterations in the English law know not what they want: *more land* is what they want; more facilities for its sale and purchase would only send the existing amount of land into the hands of great proprietors.   Again, the opponents of the English laws of entail and primogeniture (to use illogical terms) refer to America as a bright example.   Now Americans and Englishmen differ essentially in this.   An Englishman makes wealth and retains it for his family, to found or keep up a family; an American does no such thing, nor does the possession of land in America give high social position; to keep a big hotel does, but not to have large acres.   This difference is ingrained in the characters of the two nations; therefore the Englishman needs and will long retain his so-called laws of entail and of primogeniture, while the American would regard them as an incumbrance : in their place *each State has its own way* of dealing with a man's real property, that is, there are some thirty different ways in the United States in which a man's reality goes on his death intestate, according to the *locus in quo* of the property.   Again, the opponents of the English system of conveyancing often point out the superiority of a system of registration of titles.   Now in Illinois State titles are registered : the register was burnt in the Chicago fire, and the whole of the titles to landed estates in Illinois are lost.   Large sums are being offered by the Government for the purchase of solicitors' notes and drafts, from which to patch up a register : the solicitors have combined, and demand still larger sums. This, of course, is a mere accident; but I consulted an eminent Chicago practitioner about the sale of real estate; he told me they always, despite the register, required a full abstract of title back to the original Government grants, which in Chicago is forty years, and went through the whole routine, as in England; that the titles were invariably incumbered and intricate, not so much with marriage and other settlements, as they would be in England, but much more with mortgages and by being used as securities.   In New York and the older-settled States, much larger and more expensive abstracts of titles were required on a purchase.   I would a few land-law hating and ignorant Radicals could be sent out to the States to study there the American land laws, after being first put through a course of study in the English land laws, for such agitators are generally profoundly ignorant of both.   The anti-game law agitators would find in America that stringent game-protection laws are being passed, enforced by very severe penalties.

Printed at the Offices of C. Thurnam & Sons, Carlisle.